Also by Crystal Collier

Maiden of Time Trilogy:
Moonless

Short Stories:
Through the Portal (Heroes of Phenomena)

Book 2 in the

Maiden of Time
Trilogy

By Crystal Collier

Published by RAYBOURNE PUBLISHING
Copyright © 2014 by Crystal Collier
Cover Design by J. Matthew Collier

Summary: When Alexia's wedding is destroyed by the Soulless—who then steal the only protection her people have—she's forced to unleash her true power and risk losing everything. [1. Fiction. 2. Historical-paranormal. 3. Soulless. 4. Wraiths. 5. Supernatural Creatures. 6. Historical Fantasy. 7. Time Travel. 8. Maiden of Time. 9. Passionate and Soulless.]

ISBN: 978-1-62983-003-2

For Quin,

best brainstorming budding,
and incredible son.

From the night's darkness the lost ones are cryin'
Seeking to claim for their own, the new queen
War rises up, the forces now vyin'
To possess or deny her long-lost vict'ry.

—Author Unknown

Dearest Sarah,

I have not dreamt in over a month, not nightmares of people's deaths, not hints of things to come. Nothing but silence since the night I lost you.

My purpose in writing this letter is not to reach you, as I know I never shall. I wish to believe the last two years were but my imagination, that you are a week's journey away in Liverpool with your disgustingly rich, and elderly husband, that I am writing you the same way I have for five years since you were married and taken away from me.

It is easier to believe. Easier than the truth.

That the Earl, your husband, is dead. That you...

My dearest aunt, bosom sister, I have always been ignorant to the sacrifices of those about me, but I am no more. I have chosen to see. I have chosen the life of the Passionate. Lest you should fear for me, I am in good hands. The best. My own treasured Kiren has asked for my hand in marriage. Father is against the match, but what can he do to stop us? Kiren is powerful. He commands the Passionate: a host of gifted persons who can rob men of their memories, travel the globe in but an instant, or heal the deadliest of wounds.

And yet, we are not without our enemies, of which I hope, my most cherished heart, you are not one. Though it grieves me, I recognize that you and I can never exist as we once did. John has taken you from me and laid the curse of the Soulless upon you. Kiren says the Soulless are empty, always hungry for the Passionate. Are you starving, my aunt? Do you hunt with your kind on the moonless night? These and a hundred other questions plague me as I sit, recovering. Always recovering.

"Do not use your gifts." "Do not slow time." "Do not undo the healing you have accomplished." I hear these so often it is a wonder I do not write them in my sleep. While I could not save you, dear Sarah, I did find the strength to stop the Soulless from harming the man I love.

But at what price? I have lost a dear friend, Miles, because he welcomed those creatures into his mind to save me, and now they hunt him for the secrets he keeps. He has gone to the Americas, and I miss our quiet conversations, though I cannot possibly know how much greater Kiren's heart grieves. He and Miles have rarely been apart. He does not think I see it, but he often becomes silent, his gaze lifted to the distance as though he can see across the ocean that separates them.

Enough of heartache. I am to be married! I shall marry the man I love, not some miscreant who saw fit to blackmail Father into an arrangement. (I am told that Roger Whitaker has quite forgotten me since my supposed demise winter last. The brigand. He is seeking a bride for himself in London, though for her sake, I pray she has the fortitude to withstand his vile advances. Heaven knows how I would have fared without my gifts!)

Other news—I hear that Abigail Vanwick has secured a healthy dowry from her great aunt and hopes to marry well in the future. And Rupert... Our very own Rupert has gone to the New World as a lieutenant. I hope when he thinks of me, he does so with kindness and not as a man shunned by the object of his heart. I regret I never was able to say goodbye or *explain why our lifetime of friendship ended so abruptly. He deserves better. I trust he will find it in his adventures.*

I miss you, dearest Sarah, every day. You are a lifetime away, but you reside here too, in my heart, so close I can feel the steady stroke of your brush through my hair, the glow of your approving smile, or the whisper of your promises that soon this nightmare will end and we shall find ourselves in the nursery, hiding from the maids and giggling over our cherished secrets.

My dearest aunt, until that day, all my love,

Alexia Dumont

PROLOGUE

Darkness rustled about Amos, a horde of hungry bodies eagerly awaiting the fall of night while hidden from the sun's angry rays. Raspy voices whispered in the gloom from the throats of those who had begun to decay after centuries of starvation and immortality.

The moonless night was moments away.

The swarm pressed forward and Amos lifted a hand, staying them in the cave's mouth.

Tonight it would begin. Tonight the players would fall into place like pawns on an elaborate chessboard. Very soon he and his comrades in suffering would have justice, and then the sweet revenge they deserved.

It all began tonight.

One

Predators and Prey

Alexia's eyes snapped open, heart thundering.

Well, she wasn't dead. Yet.

Alexia uncurled stiff fingers from around her blanket and pressed further into her pillow. Caught somewhere between annoyed and relieved, she settled on grateful—that she'd recovered enough to dream again, even if her nightmares always came true. She could still feel phantom fingers at the back of her skull, crushing her face into the pillow until she ceased to breathe.

She shuddered.

Lace curtains scattered shadow creatures across the wood floor, twisting them in a late summer breeze from the unlatched balcony door. Specters clawed at the pastel walls, up a bureau, and over a wardrobe of fashionable clothes for 1770. Costumes. Façades. Pretensions.

She sat up in the bed she'd used all eighteen years of her life. Father slumbered at the other end of the too-empty estate, too far away to call for help.

Father, whom she had never expected to see again.

Father who had begged her to abandon her true heritage.

In this very bed, Alexia had witnessed death after death through her night terrors. She had hoped the dreams would cease for good now that she'd discovered the true extent of her gift, the ability to slow or freeze time. But wishing was futile.

And now—according to the dream—*she* was going to die.

But not if she could stop it.

She searched for a weapon, her fingers scraping over a hairbrush and unlit candle on the dressing table beside her bed. What she wouldn't give for a dagger!

Ghostly light from the open balcony drew her gaze to the mirror and her evergreen eyes. She shivered. The reflection she recalled was that of a rat-child—thin, sickly, sallow, revolting by all standards, and befitting a horror story. Instead, flawless skin and ebony curls gleamed in the glass.

It was a part of being Passionate: coming of age and maturing into an unnatural beauty. According to Kiren, their lack of beauty in childhood was a defense mechanism, a protection from humans who might otherwise take advantage of their young. It was during the moonless cycle following their sixteenth birthday that their gifts bloomed into existence along with an exquisiteness no mortal could resist. That change had taken place two years ago, heralded by the nightmares which warned Alexia of future deaths.

Beauty had brought only misery. She bit back the memory of Roger Whitaker's hands on her, the crash of her skull against the wall as he attempted to take what she wouldn't willingly give. And when he failed, the forced betrothal that followed…

She shook the memory away. Roger's attack proved that she'd never be able to live among the gentry as a Baron's daughter, not with a Passionate heritage. Instead, she had to survive a secret war long enough to marry Kiren, the leader of the Passionate, whom she'd chosen for herself.

Starting with finding a weapon.

Father's pistols were housed only a few rooms over, but she knew from the nightmare she'd never make it that far.

Ethereal light glinted across the brass door handle—metal because it deflected the Passionate and burned their bare flesh. But not hers. That was what came of being a half-human.

The door handle twisted.

Her heart leapt. It could be Kiren, finally come after three days of absence. Since Father couldn't accept her choice of suitor, Kiren might merely be sneaking in to avoid conflict, but then why would he use the door? Why not simply come through the balcony as he had so often done in the past?

Because it wasn't Kiren.

Her heart seized at a possibility she didn't want to consider: that it might be Sarah, her missing aunt, best friend, and near sister.

She forced her heart to slow, her mind to work. Surely it was a servant coming before dawn to clean the chamber pot or deliver fresh water.

Except servants didn't move as silently as death.

The door flew open and a shadow reared out of the blackness. Alexia rolled away, determined to escape the murderer of her nightmare.

Blankets snared her legs. The mattress dipped behind her under new weight. Material yanked tight against her neck. She gasped. Fingers knotted in her hair and wrenched her backward.

Alexia shrieked as her face slammed into a pillow. She thrashed, and the pressure on the back of her head doubled. She tore at her captor's small hands, digging her nails in.

"I warned you!" High soprano cut through the pulse in her ears. "Die!"

Alexia gasped, desperate for air. Instead, she sucked in cushion and cloth. Darkness crept over the corners of consciousness—the inky silence of the nether realm.

She was not ready to die—not when she had the power to escape.

The power to stop time.

She yanked the seconds to a halt, and an ache crawled up the back of her head like the burn of a hundred ant bites. The cushion beneath her cheek stiffened, solidifying into stone. Her attacker's panting slowed to a low-pitched hiss. Then there was silence—the silence of stopped time.

Alexia turned her head and gasped, scraping her cheek on cotton-granite.

Air! It tasted like an old crypt and hung immobile, but she inhaled with force. Her head cleared enough to register the ripple of pain crushing through her skull.

She slid out from under the child's grasp, her hair catching on immobile fingers. Sucking in a second breath, she whimpered at the lava eating into her brain. Kiren had warned her not to use her gift. She was not recovered enough. Not yet.

Alexia released the flow of seconds and her assailant smacked against the headboard, cursing as Alexia tumbled to the floor, holding her head. Pounding dragged her down. Her brain blazed like a flaming knife had skimmed off a fresh layer of skin. Four weeks of healing, four weeks of avoiding all thought, four weeks of dreamless sleep, gone in an instant!

She focused on breathing. *In, ignore the pain. Out, let it go.* Her knees shuddered as she lifted her forehead from the floorboards, her brain throbbing.

Golden ringlets dripped down the child's shoulders, and large, brown eyes glared above vibrant red lips in a portrait-perfect countenance of thirteen. A porcelain doll. The girl coiled on the edge of the bed, swathed in raven-brocade, poised like a snake to strike. Two years they'd known one another, and Bellezza hadn't aged a day.

"How do you do that?" Bellezza's perfect mixture of soprano and terror slapped Alexia's ears.

The child leapt.

Alexia jumped, a headache hammering through her temples.

The malevolent girl landed next to her, eyes a hand's width away, consuming her in their earthy dark swells like midnight quicksand. Her cruel mouth twisted in menace.

The last time they had come face to face, Alexia had been in a race to save Aunt Sarah, whom Bellezza had thrown to the Soulless.

Every muscle tensed and Alexia's vision bled out to red. She had never hated anyone so much as this girl! She balled her fists and swung at the selfish imp.

Bellezza leapt back.

Alexia's knuckles grazed the girl's cheek, barely missing her. Nightmare pain shot down her neck. Her body was not ready to halt time, not ready to move, and she'd pushed it too far. Pain swallowed the world. She was falling, falling into blackness.

Her brow thumped on something solid and she grunted.

"Dear me, did you hurt yourself?" Bellezza giggled.

Alexia pressed her palms to the uneven timbers, trembling. "Stay away from me." Every word fired knives at the back of her eyes.

Where was Kiren? Why would he allow this heartless, vile creature to come so close—the one who had almost killed her before? The one who had robbed her of Sarah?

Bellezza batted her eyelashes. "Why would I do that when you are so fun to taunt?"

Alexia pushed herself up. Bellezza could have easily ended her in the last minute, so why hadn't she? Surely she'd come to do more than deride her, but Alexia didn't want to play this game. "Go away, Bellezza."

The girl's sneer broadened, morphing her face from a porcelain doll to a bloodthirsty savage. "Is that it?" Near-black eyes exacted hers from the shadows. "He kept you because you are talented?" Her lips pulled back in a vicious smile. "How precious. How do you like being one of his *pets*? Tell me, is it"—she looked Alexia up and down—"rewarding?"

"Go back to your prison."

The child's grin widened. "Oh, but Alexia, I left that place months ago. I have been here, watching over your precious daddy and half-wit aunt."

Alexia bit down against the pain in her head, her knuckles aching for how tightly they strained. Sarah had been everything to her, her only true confidant and bosom friend.

The girl sniffed. "Anyone cork-brained enough to *marry* one of the Soulless deserves their misery."

Alexia swallowed the verbal slap. Bellezza was right. Sarah had known John was one of the Soulless who could walk in daylight, known her fate would ultimately end in becoming one of those empty creatures. John had seemed so above the Soulless, so rational and normal. But it had been an illusion. She chose him. Sarah chose *John* over a life with the Passionate, and Alexia had only herself to blame.

"What do you want, Bellezza?"

"I want you dead!"

"Then why have you not done it?" The child had a much easier way of ending a life than smothering or talking Alexia to death. She shivered at the memory of toppling blindly down flights of stairs to the sound of Bellezza's shriek.

The girl sighed and frumpled into a seat next to her. "Because I like you."

Alexia blinked at her.

Bellezza's mouth tightened. "I told you, he is mine!"

"And I believed you."

Her eyes darkened. "Why do you have to be so likeable? I cannot even hate you for marrying him."

Alexia started. "We are not married."

"You will be soon."

Soon? Alexia straightened up. What did Bellezza know? Had she come to preempt the wedding? Was that why Kiren had been absent for three days—preparing for their union?

A throat cleared from the door way.

They both turned. Starlight glistened across the worn leather of his boots, and the gray of his suit coat, unbuttoned to reveal tan trousers, a matching long waistcoat, and the hint of a white shirt. Ginger waves fell about his brow, shading the jagged white scar which barbed from his right cheek to his chin. His skin held a luminescence that filled Alexia with awe, and his eyes, which left clear coastal reefs at nightfall in envy, crashed soberly over Bellezza.

Two

Escape

"What have we here?" Kiren crossed his arms, trapping the deadly child with his stare. He locked each foot to the floor, projecting a calm facade, although his muscles screamed to close the distance and thrust her away from his future wife. At Bellezza's slightest move, he would pounce.

Bellezza's scowl deepened. She muttered, *"Coward,"* a word she didn't expect him to hear. Black skirts rustled as her nutmeg scent wafted at him. "I came to congratulate you."

"Do not lie to me, Bellezza." Her choice of dress alone communicated otherwise. He dove into her eyes, reading the truth in her thoughts. Wishful images surfaced: her fingers curled about Alexia's neck, squeezing until the dark-haired girl stared back with glassy eyes.

A wicked grin tickled across the child's face.

He approached slowly, holding himself in check. Bellezza wanted him to see those things, wanted *him* to suffer. Not Alexia. Reacting would only reward and incite her.

He delved deeper into her chocolate eyes. The fury smoldering behind her glare was meant for men, or a man—one she couldn't reach, one she feared above all.

"Stop reading me!" Bellezza's fingers flexed like claws, her brows low, body poised to spring on Alexia like a ravening lioness.

He inhaled, the weight around his neck lifting with his chest. The pendant might be able to stop her if she decided to attack, but he didn't want to hurt her.

So much hate. So much pain. He ached for the child, for all she'd suffered. Had she ever known love?

And at the same time, he wanted nothing more than to toss her tiny carcass out the window for even contemplating harming Alexia.

Corralling the instinct, he extended a hand. The best he could do was show her a different world, one where she didn't have to fear, one where she could thrive in her gifts and become a civilized being.

He glanced at the balcony, out into the moonless night. How much time did he have?

Kiren cleared his throat. "I see your irons can no longer hold you."

The skin about her wrists was healed, no longer charred black from the manacles she'd carried for decades. She wore a choker with a ruby stone, likely to cover the healing flesh.

He'd never witnessed it before—one of the Passionate so powerful they could conquer the dead weight of iron shackles. She was strong, so much stronger than she knew. If only he could help her use that strength for worthy purposes.

He smiled. "Good for you."

Bellezza's lip pulled up in a snarl, but the question hung in her eyes: *Does he really mean that?*

He nodded, holding her glare.

Her shoulders relaxed inward, limbs trembling as she blinked repeatedly. Her head tilted. *You really meant to free me? To grant my wish? To make me strong enough that no one will chain me again?*

Once more he nodded, adding a grin she couldn't misinterpret. "You are exceptional, Bellezza."

Her eyes widened. Hope sprouted behind them, a tentative plant pressing through desert soil that had oppressed its growth for too long—but he couldn't read the direction it tilted.

He asked, "What do you want now?"

Her hands writhed over one another before falling to her sides, determination in the set of her shoulders. "Sanctuary."

"Sanctuary?" He scrutinized her. After inciting a war with the Soulless and slaying dozens of noblemen in the most brutal manner, she couldn't possibly mean to align herself under his command. Then again, perhaps she hoped an allegiance would spare her.

The answer hovered in her eyes: A man stood before her at the doorway of a thatched-roof house, grinning greedily as golden coins fell into his palm from the stranger outside. *She'll be perfect for breeding.* ...Hours later the man chased after her, a red-hot firebrand in his gloved hand, his screams echoing after her as she misted into the trees: *You belong to me. You are mine, mia bella!*

Her eyes widened, then tightened. *I want to destroy them. You can give me that?* "Sanctuary."

He neared a step. Never could he condone the cold blooded murder she desired, but since she'd launched this war between Passionate and Soulless, they would either have to reconcile the different agendas among the Passionate, or succumb to their enemies. He had been working toward that union a long time. She'd destroyed all hopes of bringing it about peacefully, and all that remained was war. If she wanted to be a soldier, indeed she would prove an invaluable ally—but only if she could take orders.

"Sanctuary." He nodded slowly. "You know the rules." Rules she had learned and flouted when she abandoned her prison and started the war. "One more offense and you will be tossed into the deepest prison."

Bellezza's brow twitched. She bit back a snarl and curtsied. "Hail, o mighty king."

He shook his head. "I will meet you outside."

She growled, stormed forward, and brushed past him with a snort. He listened as her near-silent footsteps distanced, gradually fading to nothing.

Kiren turned to his beloved. She blinked up at him from the floor, starlight streaking her raven curls and illuminating the pale cotton of her nightgown. His own angel.

Her gaze traveled up his body to meet his.

Kiren's breath caught.

The thriving green of her stare carried him to the heart of a youthful jungle, entwining his limbs with thick vines, trapping him in the heart of need. Her pink lips pressed together, and he wanted nothing but to possess them.

Alexia pushed off the floor, slipped on the hem of her nightgown, and flailed forward.

He caught her, startled by how sheer the fabric was between his fingers and her warm skin. He set her on her feet, curling an arm about her back, unwilling to let her go and lose the sudden electricity tingling through him. She set him on fire, every nerve, every heartbeat. He inhaled her ambrosia scent and trailed his fingers down her blushing cheek, aching to satisfy this craving for her, to kiss away all sense and reason, to tear down the few barriers that stood between their complete union.

She met his gaze.

"Hello," he whispered and kissed her cheek, tasting the amber-pomegranate of her skin. Only a month ago he thought he'd lost her, again, and during these three days apart, every second had been torture.

She threw her arms around his neck and pulled him down to her.

"Slow down, love." Curling his fingers around her waist, he pushed her away. She held tighter, and he smirked.

Alexia lifted her stubborn chin. "Where have you been? Why have you not sent word?"

He froze, unwilling to lie to her yet afraid to overwhelm her with rumors of a rising threat, one he'd been unable to verify. She still knew so little of their world.

Her fingers squeezed at the back of his neck, head tilting. "What has happened?"

He glanced away, certain she could see the answer in his eyes: *Trouble*. Pulling her hand from around his neck, he kissed her fingers. "I do not like being away from you."

Her brows pleated. "I do not like you being away from me either." Her grip over his shoulder tightened, dragging his attention back to her pale lips and begging eyes. She pushed up on the balls of her feet, stretching for his touch.

Kiren leaned down, aimed toward her waiting lips, unable to resist a moment longer. But if he lingered too long... He caught both her arms firmly, halting her where her ragged breath teased his aching mouth. "We need to go."

"No." She shook her head and winced.

"You are hurt."

"Not as badly as you will be if you continue to deny me."

He chuckled. "One kiss." Lifting her jaw, he guided her to him and captured her mouth, savoring the warmth, the calm glow that accompanied her touch—like a welcoming fire after weeks of blinding white blizzard.

Kiren pulled back. She threw her arms around his neck with force, dragging him down to her. He toppled forward.

She giggled against his lips. He chuckled with her, holding her safely against him as he slammed into the mattress with one hand. He lowered her safely to the surface. Her passion cut through him like a torch to snow, melting away all resistance. His entire body heated, charged. Primal need surged through his veins. He gripped the sides of the bed, fighting to hold himself in check.

She grabbed his waistcoat and yanked him toward her. Barriers tumbled, like a crumbling wall. White burst behind his eyes, the space opening up between them, their shared mental space, the place of merging and her recent dream...

A dark form huddled on the other side of her locked door. The knob turned.
Alexia pushed up in her bed, heart pounding.
The door flew open. A black shape leapt through the shadows. She twisted to escape.
Fingers crushed down on the back of her skull. She couldn't breathe!

He pulled back, his breath ragged, fists clenched. He reminded himself it was only the memory of her nightmare, that she'd survived and he had no cause to charge after Bellezza and make her suffer.

Alexia's chin tilted up after him, eyes falling open but lost in a wash of desire.

She gasped, hands exploring the mattress below her, furrowed brows straightening as her mouth dropped open. Shock and embarrassment filled her stare. Heat radiated off her cheeks, eyelids lowering demurely as she swallowed.

Kiren followed the movement of her lashes as they pointed him back to her vulnerable lips. Two voices screamed in his head: one that remembered danger lurked on the horizon, and the louder one that growled to be appeased.

He lifted himself a couple inches. "You should not place yourself completely at my mercy."

She caught the collar of his waistcoat, her pupils dark and wide. "But mercy is your strongest virtue."

Did she have any idea how difficult she was making this for him? He groaned and pressed a kiss to the side of her neck. "This is not the kind of mercy heaven would smile upon."

She swallowed and he traced the movement with a finger.

"You have been dreaming again," he said.

"And you are prying."

He opened his mouth and closed it. It was true. She had asked him not to intercept her thoughts, but he couldn't stop it from happening when so intimately connected. He put a little more space between them.

Alexia looked away. "You promised you would not—"

"Sorry." But he wasn't. If she was withholding vital information, he must know. "You did not think it important to tell me you are dreaming again?"

"Only one dream." *Twice.* She scowled. *And how am I supposed to tell you anything when you are dazzling me?*

He smirked, one eyebrow peaking. "I dazzle you?"

She pushed against his chest and rolled out from under him. Kiren moved an arm and let her go, although it took all his self-control. She moaned and sat up, holding her head.

He sat next to her. "Love?"

She lifted a hand.

Scooting closer, he massaged the back of her neck. Only a month ago the Soulless had ambushed them in this estate—after he'd been shot by John while attempting to rescue Sarah. Alexia had fought the Soulless off, using her gift to slow time, until it nearly killed her. He had yet to forgive himself for being so vulnerable, for allowing her to save him at such a high cost. She would recover, eventually, if she would just stop using her gift.

He closed his eyes and probed. Her tender cerebellum pulsed, swelling as it had right after the incident. Kiren groaned, wishing he could heal it completely. He never wanted her to suffer, to experience the pain he was directly responsible for bringing into her life. The best he could do was soothe her physical aches.

Cells throbbed under his touch, ripe for his command. He summoned blood flow through the region and a release of endorphins while reshaping damaged cells. Strength seeped through his fingers, fueling her remedy.

"Should I wonder what else you have been dreaming?" He kept his tone light, but the question weighed on them both.

"Why?" She looked up. "What are you afraid I have seen?"

He smiled sadly, wishing he could tell her everything; that he didn't have to withhold some secrets for now. He brushed her cheek and she winced. Redness he'd mistaken for a blush spotted her cheekbone. He flattened his palm across it and ordered the cells to replicate, relinquishing another dose of energy.

He nudged her chin up. "I will not leave your side again."

She grinned, her emerald stare narrowing around dark pupils. "Is that a promise?"

Do not look at me that way, Alexia. His own need for her was difficult enough to stave, but to combat hers as well?

He inhaled a calming breath. She shifted and light twinkled off the chain around her neck. He touched the golden ring it bore, a coral diamond center with five teardrop petals, his vow to her. Her father, Charles, didn't approve of them. He believed the Passionate to be cursed, destined for tragedy, but he had agreed on this one point: Kiren protect her as no other.

Kiren traced the chain and she trembled beneath his touch. He grinned, loving her reaction. Unclasping the necklace, he teased the glittering snake until it surrendered her ring and slipped it onto her finger.

Alexia grasped his hands. "What if Father sees?"

"I intend that he shall."

She seized his shoulders, seeking his eyes. "You convinced him?"

Kiren bit down, keeping the grin plastered on his face.

"This is wonderful!"

Oh, that it could be as wonderful as she believed. He wished he could share in her rejoicing, but he would not taint her happiness with the truth. Not yet.

He released her, gaze bouncing down her thinly veiled form. He quickly averted his attention. "Please, dearest, you must put something on. We need to leave."

She reddened and hugged herself. Kiren rose and escaped to the hall.

Three

Breeders

Two quiet shadows raced toward the manor house, cutting through the woods and dodging branches. Elizabeth glanced at her companion, snorting at his wild hair and too-short legs as he stumbled and nearly tripped on a protruding root. They could make this journey so much faster on horseback, but the dwarf was far too jittery around animals, plus he might crush the creature on accident with those massive, too-strong hands.

She grinned wickedly into the night, brushing the leaves away from her famous auburn locks. He was just the kind of ally she needed on this mission: to capture and return the young woman who could alter time before the leader of the Kingdom faction stood between them.

She hoped the leader had returned. She'd never had a reason to attack him, but she'd always wondered if he would fall under her power.

Red Pain they called her. She loved the title. Let anyone challenge her and she would launch an attack on their minds that could cripple an elephant.

She glanced up at the moonless sky, hoping the Soulless had not arrived before them.

Four

Choosing

Despite Kiren's mending, every movement set off a twinge of pain as Alexia tucked into a corset, stomacher, and fastened her petticoats. She silently wished she had a domestic to assist her, as the process would go much smoother, but she'd been playing the role of a servant since returning to Father's home.

No one knew her secret. Father (a prominent country baron) maintained that his daughter had "fallen prey to wolves" last winter when she'd disappeared. He had dressed her as a domestic, allowing people to believe her presence a boon of charity, nothing more.

And she never should have had that much.

Alexia retrieved a single black hairpin from her bureau, examining it in the starlight before tucking it over her neckline, right over her heart.

Dana's gift.

She wasn't sure if its placement was correct.

Dana had been but a child when she and Father fell in love, but that love resulted in the death of Alexia's grandparents, the destruction Father's marriage, and his broken heart. Only Kiren, she, and Father knew he'd sired a child out of wedlock with his Passionate mistress who died in childbirth. Alexia had been raised by Rosalind, Father's now-dead wife—a woman who'd selflessly claimed the babe for her own. The sorrow eventually killed her surrogate mother.

Alexia missed the quiet woman with her perfect poise, flaxen tresses, and admonishing looks. She never said a word, merely led and expected to be followed. Rosalind should have sent Alexia to be with her kind instead of sacrificing her own heart day in and day out. At least then Father would have avoided that terrible raid on his home...

She hugged herself against a tremor, unwilling to remember.

It was good that one of her Passionate friends possessed the power to alter people's memories, to erase the midnight wraiths that still flitted through her conscience. Edward took away the servants' terror. Not hers. Not Father's. They remembered everything, and Father blamed Kiren.

She sighed and pulled on her baby-blue overdress.

Well, she blamed Father for arranging her marriage to a rapist, the bargain that drove her away in the first place. At least *the miscreant* still believed her dead.

Alexia laced her shoes quickly, and exited to the hall, her vision adjusting to the dark, portrait-filled walls. Her favorite painting waited just across from her, two young ladies with dark hair reclining against a forested backdrop, she and Sarah as children.

Sarah who was lost to her.

"Kiren?"

He shifted to her right, propped against a doorframe. His eyes glittered, even in the dark.

"A thousand years could sweep this earth clean and I would never meet a sight as breathtaking," he whispered.

She blushed. "Is that how long you have been alive?"

His jaw clenched.

She understood their kind could live indefinitely if their blood was not deluded by humanity—which meant she had no idea how long she'd live. Or him. How many times had she asked him about his age, and he avoided giving her an answer? She would discover one day, when he finally allowed her in *entirely*. It was just one of the truths she intended to pry loose from his mind once they were married. Before, if possible.

Alexia took his outstretched hand. His fingers laced through hers, skin on skin—terribly inappropriate, at least within society. She had no idea what the Passionate labeled appropriate, but this overwhelming bond—being destined or damned—rendered their kind inseparable. His death would mean hers, as hers would result in his. Since he led the world of the secret Passionate, it made both their lives more complicated—especially when considering the vast army of enemies conspiring against him. Her love for him was simple. His came at a great cost.

"Now why this hasty escape?" she demanded, each step shooting a midnight spark at the back of her skull. She wanted to stop him and take an easier pace, but the tension in his fingers seeped into her skin. "And why have you been away?"

He grimaced.

"The Soulless are coming again," she guessed as they reached the servants' stairs. She'd been watching the skies. Tonight marked an empty moon, the night the Soulless emerged to feast. From what John had told her, the Soulless were once Passionate, before they'd given their very essence over to a madman and been damned to a state of perpetual starvation. Since that time they'd been rotting, seeking what was lost, only satisfied when they fed on the remaining Passionate. Those taken by the Soulless became like them: hungry, eternal, decaying in their own bodies and taking on a wraith-like state under the new moon.

A nervous laugh escaped Kiren—so new a sound she paused to take it in.

He pulled her after him down the steps. "Them coming, yes, that would be troublesome, but not fatal."

"Fatal?" A cool breeze curled across her arm. The servants' door to the yard stood open, a gaping maw to the outside world and shadowed walkway.

Kiren cleared his throat. "Alexia, there are..." His head flew up, fingers tightening over hers, ear tilted. "We must go, now." He grabbed her arms and slipped them around his neck, lifting her off her feet.

She gasped, unable to restrain her grin at the unexpected brush of his breath across her lips. "What is it? What did you hear?"

His head shook.

"Can you *hear* thoughts now?" The idea made her cringe.

He chuckled. "I can only read what is in a person's thoughts, and only when staring into their eyes. You know that. However, my ears are slightly more keen than most."

"From practice or inheritance?"

He grinned. "Yes."

"Is it common for Passionate to possess more than one ability?"

"Strengths. We call them strengths, and yes."

They stepped outside. Alexia clung to him, resting a head on his shoulder, eyes closed to block out the flashes of pain. Insects hummed in the late summer evening, the air thick with expected rain.

"Who is coming?" she grated through her teeth.

A groan rumbled in his chest. "There is a general air of panic when a being as powerful as yourself emerges."

She blinked up at him. "But I am not powerful—"

"You will be." The confidence behind his words flattened her argument like a press to fresh laundry.

Trimmed grass extended about them, halted at a black line of trees clustered ahead. Alexia did not relish entering them, recalling how she had stumbled across one of the Soulless within a similar set of woods—a creature Kiren had destroyed to save her.

He flashed a jerky glance either direction and broke into a jog.

"How could anyone know about me?" She clung to him, focusing on the curve of his chin and the white scar he had yet to explain.

"Word travels quickly." His lips pressed in a tight line, lengthening the jagged blemish across his cheek. "And not all Passionate are anxious for you to be mine. Some even prefer your death to the shift in power."

She squeezed his shoulder, searching for his gaze. "You speak as though you do not lead them."

He heaved a breath, lashes brushing his cheeks. "There are factions among the Passionate seeking power."

"But you are their leader—!"

"I protect them," he said between breaths. "I keep the unruly in order. Some do not share my ideals of how that is best accomplished."

15

"Like whom?"

His brow wrinkled, starlight catching his pupils. "The strongest group is the Breeders."

Her blood ran chill.

"They believe this world should belong to us, and us alone."

She grasped the cottony material along his neck. "But if not for humanity, I would not exist."

Kiren's cheek dimpled. "You understand my position then."

"I am not certain I will ever fully understand your position."

His grin faded. He slowed to a trot, then a walk, not meeting her gaze.

She hadn't meant to hurt him, but it was true. She loved him, but she worried that there were reasons she didn't and couldn't deserve him. Why had he chosen her?

Kiren cleared his throat. "Breeders seek to spawn the most powerful Passionate by breeding unique bloodlines—children strong enough to overthrow the world. I have hopes that they will one day be persuaded to reason, along with the other factions, and unite with us."

She nodded. "These other factions..."

"The Southerners and Ritualists are very weak, as are the Fishers and Old Believers. Only the Breeders pose a threat."

"And what do they call us?"

His arms around her stiffened, gaze darting away. "Kingdom."

Bellezza's earlier hail suddenly made sense. Alexia narrowed her stare, a look he didn't return. "They accuse you of setting yourself up as a king?"

He placed her back on her feet. Unkempt grass tickled at her ankles as his bottomless eyes swallowed her into their marine depths, promising an eternal Atlantis. "The important thing for you to know is that they are no friends of yours."

"And why is that?"

He tugged at the necklace that disappeared below the cut of his shirt. "Because they are in a race to either claim or destroy you."

She braced herself with a hand on his chest. "Me? Because you and I are—"

He shook his head. "Because when someone with rare talents arises, everyone rushes to take them."

Had that been the reason he came for her at first? The reason he chose her? Alexia shied. "Including you?"

His head tilted, mouth puckering in disappointment.

He hadn't forced her into an allegiance. He had done the opposite, pushing her away from this perilous existence and keeping her strictly in the human world. Even so, the choice had been hers.

His arm rounded her back, shepherding her toward the jagged tree line. "Edward tracks the family lines and identifies our kind before maturity—usually at birth. All are offered the choice to join us."

She recalled his hidden estate deep in the woods and wondered how many other hidden sanctuaries occupied England. How different would her life have been if he'd swept her away when she was a child? Might she have become a mere servant like her mother at a country inn?

The corners of his mouth creased, face darkening. "Occasionally the Breeders reach one of us before me…"

"What do they do?" She touched his chin. "What would they do to me?"

His fingers bit into her side. "Any risk to you—!" He shuddered.

Any risk to her directly affected his beating heart—in theory. She felt silly for suggesting it, "But you have not even…"

His fierce eyes returned, a towering wave on perilous seas. "Have not what?" he asked, voice terse.

Her entire face burned. Why was it so hard to say? They were to be wed! A wishful tremor rattled through her and her ears flamed. "You have not touched me." Not intimately enough. John—the Soulless man who had married and destroyed her aunt—said an eternal bond formed through sexual relations.

Kiren stopped and took her shoulders, meeting her gaze. "I have not, which means someone else could."

Panic roared in her ears, her pulse quickening.

His voice quieted. "That is what they do, Alexia." The backs of his fingers grazed down her cheek. "They take the choice away."

She swallowed. Her lips moved in protest, but no sound argument lit her mind. Could there be a deeper hell than being forced into an eternal bond?

He stepped closer. "They combine the rarest talents and strive to create pure elementals, regardless of people's will. What do you think would happen if they caught you? Where would your loyalties lie?"

"With you," she whispered and looked down—though she couldn't know that. To be touched, to be eternally bound to another being… She gazed again into his stormy eyes.

"I hope so."

Alexia grabbed his coat lapels, pulling him closer. "Then, then we must end the possibility!"

He pushed her away, eyes a billowing sea of reprimand. "Alexia…"

She bowed her head, her cheeks burning. Shame spilled over her like a spring waterfall. How could she think such an idea, no less suggest it to the man who had only ever been the most considerate, upright gentleman?

Both his hands gripped at the back of his head, shoulders tense, elbows extended. His head shook, mouth working. He closed his eyes and exhaled a cleansing breath. "Our laws dictate that intimate relations outside of marriage are strictly forbidden. We are not like our human counterparts. We are forever." Frustration leaked out of every word, a furious passion she yearned to know, yet so clearly forbidden her.

She folded her arms, unable to meet his scrutiny for her inappropriate suggestion.

Kiren's arms dropped, his shoulders sagging. "The age-old tradition is enforced by our society as a whole. Those who break this rule are ostracized, banished, and occasionally put to death."

"What about the Breeders?"

"Mostly they operate in secret, but any who have been discovered are no longer part of our society."

She met his stare, startled. "But how could anyone know about the bond?"

He looped a finger through one of her loose curls. "It is reflected in their countenance."

John had said as much, that two people who were bonded shared a glow. He had also accused her of already being bonded with Kiren, so she hadn't known how much weight to give his declaration.

Kiren's voice quieted. "The Breeders are at war with us." An apologetic smile lifted his cheek. "They would like nothing more than a reason to remove me from power."

"Could they?" she whispered back.

His mouth tightened. He gave a single nod and clasped her hand, pulling her toward the trees. "If I gave them reason. They, like the Soulless, will not falter to use every advantage against me." He stroked her jaw, tenderness crinkling the corners of his eyes. "Our union will only place you in greater danger. Are you prepared for that?"

She huffed. "I survived Bellezza."

"So you have." He studied her a moment longer, then nodded, coming to a stop again. "Marry me today, Alexia?" The depths of his eyes blazed like the first azure touch of light in the morning sky. Darker flecks broke the color with aching need.

Tears stung at the backs of her eyes. "You know I will."

His chin lowered, quickened breaths rolling across her lips. Her eyes fluttered closed, mouth reaching for his.

"You are my equal," his lips grazed hers, "my better," they skimmed across hers again, "my heart."

She didn't believe his words, but it didn't stop her from sliding her hands into his hair and pulling his mouth to hers. He smiled against her lips before they parted. She pressed against his body, aching for greater contact as their minds connected. She stumbled across his cloud of worry—dark and billowing. He was afraid he'd lose her, but what could anyone do once she was his bond, forever?

Five

Into the Mist

The sky hung black like a vat of tar stretched thin. Like Alexia's nerves. Starlight dappled the moss under foot as they hurried between the thickening branches of Father's hunting grounds, haze curling between trunks as though a cloud had dropped to the earth for the purpose of concealing them. Late summer pollens soured the air, too sweet for even honey bees.

Alexia's heart echoed in her ears, but the warmth of Kiren's fingers filled her with assurance all would be well. His other hand gripped around his mysterious pendant, knuckles white.

She had seen him use the medallion twice before, always against the Soulless. She recalled the feel of heaven on her skin as the pendant enticed the suffering creatures free of their tortured bodies, a sensation she'd been desperate to keep.

A silhouette shifted against the vapor.

Alexia startled and Kiren squeezed her hand.

The person approached, frame bent with a hint of age, scraggly hair tucked in a tie. His dark eyes danced with youth that belied his physical presence while his hand tapped a rhythm on one leg, his bare feet silent.

"Lester." She looked questioningly to Kiren. If he'd brought the elder, he anticipated trouble. She quivered. Lester had always been kind to her, but a brutishness hid behind his mask, a savor for suffering she could never wash from memory. She'd been told he ran faster than any Passionate had ever run, making him one of Kiren's most trusted and reliable sources for information.

Kiren nodded at the elder.

Lester nodded back.

They moved past him into a small clearing. Bellezza's golden curls glistened in the starlight, her glare narrowing as they neared. Kiren's protective arm tightened around Alexia. She looked up into his face, questioning the wisdom of their display as he pressed straight ahead, features drawn in concentration.

A wheezing like a giant inhaling whooshed through the trees. Fog pulled toward them. It swirled into a hazy cyclone, and the specks condensed and solidified into a woman's profile, catching starlight as she thickened into a tangible body.

Silky white strands swirled loosely about her radiant, smooth face. Her mouth turned upward naturally in full lips, nose curved and petite, thin brows arching. The fine roses stitched along her neckline and sleeves were so realistic, Alexia expected catch a whiff of their perfume.

"Ethel!" Alexia threw her arms around the woman. Last winter when she'd lost her way in the fog, dear Ethel had found and nursed her back to health. Since that time she'd been a constant friend and guide, always ready with the words Alexia most needed. She felt more real than any mother Alexia had known.

"Have they successfully arrived?" Kiren questioned.

"They have, sir." Ethel half bowed, her hair blending into the pastel material of her dress. "The baron and his servants are safe."

"Father?" Alexia blinked. "You have moved Father?"

Lester stepped forward. "Yer Father be—"

A frigid gale blasted between them, a shriek on the wind. High soprano rent through Alexia's ears, launching its power down her neck and into her pumping heart. The muscle seized.

She gasped. Pain launched outward as though a fist squeezed about her vulnerable organ. Her knees slammed into the earth, ice sizzling through her veins, the freeze of death.

The scream bit off.

Alexia's knees shook as she lifted her head. Bellezza knelt atop Lester's prostrate body, melanic skirts veiling all but his bare, kicking feet, her arms flailing as she raked at his face with her nails.

"Bellezza!" Kiren's fists balled, his lips twisted with rage.

The girl jumped.

Kiren's glare bored into the vicious child. She snarled back.

In a blur of motion, Lester stood at the far end of the clearing. "You stay away from me, pigsty! Blasted banshee mongrel."

Bellezza glowered at Kiren. His head shook. She growled and rose, vacillating forward with each intake of breath, fury furling her nostrils.

Alexia pressed off the ground and tottered. Kiren caught her, and Bellezza's gaze shot to her, the rage melting out of her like butter against a heated skillet.

Alexia knew unlike anyone else why the girl had attacked Lester. She was justified. Months, Bellezza had occupied a lonely cell in a prison. The only light came when Lester brought her meals and taunted her with insults and threats. Purgatory she'd called it. Purgatory.

Bellezza roared and tumbled to her knees, clutching her head, eyes squeezed shut. A whimper escaped.

Alexia turned, searching for Bellezza's attacker as Kiren crunched to the child's side. Lester was gone. Ethel stood a couple steps away, scanning the woods, legs wide, elbows lifted as though seeking balance.

Bellezza cried out and dropped onto her side. Alexia reached for the girl as Kiren tilted her head back. Sweat glistened across Bellezza's upper lip.

"What is happening to her?" Alexia asked.

He turned wide eyes on her. "*Breeders*. Go, now!"

Fingers rounded her arm, the tender grip of her mother-figure. Ethel nodded.

Movement tore Alexia's gaze away. A short, barrel-chested man erupted from the trees behind Ethel, lifting a knotted club.

"Ethel!" Alexia screamed.

He swung.

Ethel shimmered.

The club sliced through mist as Alexia tumbled backwards.

Ethel reappeared on the other side of the clearing. The man lunged at her. She faded again, popping into existence near the tree line, an assured smirk on her face.

Ethel's grin dropped. One hand flew to her temple and her eyes rolled back. Like Bellezza.

Alexia reached to warn Kiren about a second attacker as the man leapt across the distance and grabbed Ethel's long hair. She yelped.

Alexia stood. Black sparkles fired through her vision. She cursed her injured brain and teetered back, catching herself on Kiren's shoulder.

Crack!

She blinked the darkness away. Ethel lay silent, her back bent around a tree, one leg flailed the wrong direction.

Alexia's fists balled, nails digging into the flesh. She turned on the dwarf, aching to wreak havoc on him. The enemy's gaze darted between Kiren and her. The attacker stepped forward, reaching for her with mammoth-sized fists.

Six

Blast

Alexia tensed, watching those giant fingers stretch toward her, panicking over what she could do without killing herself in overexertion, and by extension, Kiren.

The meaty hooks slipped across her loose curls.

Electricity crackled in the wind.

Decision made, she reached deep within to slow time. Her arm hairs stood straight, the air about her thickening as time stilled. Her brain wailed in protest. Liquid fire ate through her skull, every muscle seizing.

A burst of light launched from the sky, reaching with three pronged arms, veins of luminescence. Lightning. One stream zipped toward her.

She tripped backwards on her iron-like skirts and the world lurched into real time. Whiteness blinded her.

Crash!

Energy sizzled through the ground as she flailed backward, smacking into someone. Her ears rang, nerves thrumming.

Alexia rubbed her eyes. She blinked. The world was white, nothing but white.

She turned, fingers exploring. They brushed over a man's waist-coated chest, up to his collar as a heavy necklace dropped across her skin. The metal buzzed, vibrating into her bones.

He pulled her searching grasp away and a palm landed against her cheek. Heat surged through her skin. She gasped, shivered, and looked into Kiren's brilliant face. He searched her gaze a second before nodding.

She swallowed and nodded back. She could not be too grateful for his healing gift.

The dwarf who'd attacked lay silently on the ground, blackened earth starring out around his prone form.

Had the lightning struck him? Who had called the lightning—another of the Passionate?

Bellezza clambered onto her knees, holding her head. Kiren's arm rounded Alexia, dragging her toward the dark of the woods. The determined set of his jaw halted her questions.

He stopped over Ethel. She lay on her stomach, unmoving. He crouched down and touched both sides of her brow, focusing.

A shadow stepped from the trees, a woman with long, auburn hair and ghostly-pale skin. She smirked wickedly at Alexia before turning her attention to Kiren. She rubbed her temples.

Kiren shuddered. The woman glared at him. He grabbed his head with one hand, toppling onto an elbow.

Alexia stepped forward. The woman's face slackened, hands dropping.

Bellezza leapt between them, her hideous snarl turned to the attacker. "Only a coward fights from the shadows. I *hate* cowards." Her chin lifted toward Alexia. "Cover your ears!"

Alexia obeyed but the girl's shriek pierced through her fingers. Her heart clenched and ceased beating. Red lines zipped across her vision. She landed on her hip, begging for Bellezza to stop. The sting of pollen haunted her nose, like the sick perfume of soon-to-be decay.

Silence.

Her heart thudded again. Alexia's head snapped up.

The deadly child crouched, muscles tight, head turned—as if listening to something behind her. Their attacker was gone.

Alexia twisted.

Between trees, the estate sat on the shoulders of thick blackness. At least a hundred red eyes pierced through the darkness, a blanket of ragged pitch writhing across the yard.

The Soulless.

Seven

Hazy

Alexia couldn't breathe. Eternal misery sped toward her, and all she could think about was the fulfillment promised in their hungry eyes.

Bellezza cursed behind her. Fog billowed up around them, solid mist. The world, Alexia's friends, everything disappeared behind a wall of white. Fingers latched about her arm. She tried to jerk free, but the grip tightened, her captor lost in the haze. Her body lifted off the ground like a feather caught on the wind. She swung her legs, seeking a solid perch, and met only air.

A tempest screeched across her ears and whirled her skirts, whipping her hair free. Damp white particles crawled down her arms, raising the flesh—the probing touch of a self-aware element. They plumed about her like a great living cloud. She covered her mouth and nose, keeping them out.

Bellezza. It had to be. She'd whisked Alexia somewhere within the mist once before.

The airstream died down. Fog melted away. Darkness and the rustle of leaves trembled about her, vapor retreating into a ghostly silhouette. Her knees crushed into blanketing moss, full weight returning, but the solid hand of her near-murderess remained about her arm.

Bellezza released her.

Alexia twirled. Giant sable trees drooped over her, ancient branches dangling with lacy vines and closed blossoms. Two of them wrapped about one another at the center of the grove like a lovers embrace. Swaths of light littered the moss like tiny stars, the reverse of the heavens hidden behind the canopy.

Alexia scrambled to her feet, tilting with the unexpected weight in her aching head. She stumbled and steadied.

"Did the ride addle your brain?" Bellezza gave her a wicked wink.

Alexia shivered and leaned on a tree. She shoved the heels of her hands into her eyes. "Take me back." She stepped toward Bellezza. "We need to go back for *him*."

"Naïve infant." The girl rolled her eyes. "Who do you think sent us away?"

24

Of course he sent her away. She was too weak to battle the Soulless, and people were suffering and about to be taken by the enemy. Kiren didn't need her there to distract him.

Alexia deflated. "You should return and help him."

Bellezza snorted. "And risk his wrath for leaving you?" She tapped a finger to her chin. "Hm. That sounds like fun, now that you suggest it."

Alexia smiled, despite herself. "Why do you enjoy tormenting others?"

"Why do you enjoy breathing?"

She crossed her arms.

The girl huffed. "I like your ring." Her lip twitched, threatening to break into a scowl. "Although it would look better on me."

Alexia glanced down at her diamonds. They were the cause of so much turmoil. If she'd turned Kiren away, her existence would still be a secret. The Passionate would not be at war.

She eyed Bellezza. Or perhaps they would, but she wouldn't be around to cripple their leader and expose his weaknesses. Again she studied the diamonds and whispered, "I am not certain you would like its weight."

"Too true." Bellezza sat on a stump, skirt wide, arms clasped in her lap. "I will never be like you, Alexia, promised to a *good man*," she growled the words as if they hurt her to utter, "or happily settled in marriage."

"Clearly—as you are too busy sending the Passionate to their doom." She couldn't keep the bitterness from her tone.

"I am a tool of vengeance." The girl lifted her chin with dignity. "What I do is evil, but it must be done for the betterment of our kind."

Alexia's muscles stiffened. "Like destroying Sarah?"

Bellezza waved a hand. "She chose that path the moment she married one of the Soulless."

"And you had to bury her in it?" She was shaking, ready to launch herself at the girl the same way Bellezza had attacked Lester but moments ago.

Bellezza's lips twitched upward. "Ah, you do understand."

Losing control was exactly what the demon child wanted, a viable excuse to defend herself and possibly terminate Alexia in the process. She bit down on the sides of her tongue.

"That pain you are experiencing?" Bellezza trilled, "Magnify it a hundredfold. Allow it to simmer for a decade and you will recognize the gift I have given you."

"Rage?" Alexia couldn't believe she was rising to the bait. "A lack of control like the way you attacked Lester?"

The girl growled. "*Lester* deserves the ladle as badly as Galedrew ever did."

Alexia stiffened. She'd spent two years trying to forget the night Kiren stole Bellezza away to rot in that terrible prison for her crimes. Alexia could still see Baron Galedrew's blank eyes as he lay in the grand entry of his estate, blood seeping around the ladle thrust through his chest by a vicious child.

"I have always liked you, Alexia." Her nose wrinkled. "But as no one else seems capable, allow me to tell you the truth."

The last time Bellezza had said those words, she'd destroyed Alexia's world by revealing she was one of the Passionate. Part of her wanted to hear every word Bellezza would utter, all the secret truths Kiren withheld, while another part ached to stop the girl and keep what little innocence remained.

"Do you know what the baron did to me?" The girl's voice shook, but not with fury. A tear streaked down her porcelain skin.

Alexia shook her head, too shocked to speak, not wanting to know.

Bellezza's eyes squeezed, her mouth tightening at the corners. "He belonged to a *gentleman's club*, an elite group of acquirers."

"Acquirers?"

"Humans who seek and then imprison our kind." She pulled absently at the folds of her skirt, flattening them in random swirls. "I had just found my freedom when he discovered me."

"Your freedom from what?"

Bellezza's eyebrows lowered. "Iron shackles. He put me in iron shackles."

Alexia had never experience the burn that made pure blood run chill—because she was half human—but it had scarred others, charred their flesh permanently.

"And that was the least of his crimes," Bellezza hissed between her teeth. "Do you know why these gentlemen collect their prizes?"

Alexia shook her head.

"Because they can *bond* one of our kind to them and command their slave's loyalty forever."

She was going to be sick.

Bellezza smirked and studied the ground. "For years I rotted in his cellar, unable to escape my burning chains, unable to do anything but ache for him to violate me again."

Alexia opened her mouth to refute the story. She had known the baron and he'd always been a kind old man. He couldn't possibly...

"And yet after all that, *Mister Almighty* throws me in another prison!" Bellezza's shoulders trembled. "He promised it would be for my good. He said I was needed in the upcoming war, and look at us!" She leapt to her feet. "We sit in the woods playing at life, hiding from the world, cowering because he does not have the courage to seize our true potential!"

Alexia pressed into rough bark.

Bellezza raised a fist. "I will not be controlled by another spineless male." She threw her fist down. "He would rather delude himself into thinking everything is fine, paint his portraits, tend to his flowers, pretend at love." A scathing look passed over Alexia. "He allows those about him to suffer rather than taking a stand."

Alexia stepped forward. "And what would you have him do? Go to war with the Soulless *and* the humans?"

A single laugh escaped Bellezza. "Apparently he is incapable of either. Thus the reason he needs me."

Alexia's mouth flapped.

"A warning to you: he desires this war, but he is too noble to admit it."

"He wants peace."

"Is that what he told you, or what you believe?" Bellezza sneered. "You cannot climb inside his head. He does not let anyone in. Never has, never will. You *will* see."

Alexia shook her head, but an inner part of her was shriveling. Even while professing his love, Kiren withheld so much—truths about their kind, about his own origin, about his plans for their future.

"He is a coward!" Bellezza spat, leaning forward. "Like all men. Like the Passionate *fisherman*, a pathetic nothing, who *chanced* upon my mother in a vulnerable state."

Alexia half-listened, the quandary of Kiren's silence staying her tongue.

"And of course she died in childbirth—not that it matters." The girl shook. "She would have killed us both the instant she realized what a disappointment..." Her mouth froze, knuckles white and quivering, eyes burning. "He was a coward. The kind of coward who...who defiles his own flesh!" A new tear spilled over her wide cheeks.

Alexia wanted to back away, but she couldn't move under Bellezza's stare.

"Do you know why I am trapped like this"—she outlined her youthful figure—"forever? Has he explained that to you?"

Goosebumps sprouted over Alexia's flesh.

"Of course not," Bellezza said. "Nothing so vile should enter the ears of his precious *Alexia*."

Alexia forced her eyelids closed, unable to battle the mixture of pity and loathing swelling through her chest, unable to dim those odium-rich eyes, and desperate to escape this trance. Hairs stood up on her arms.

"When Passionate are *touched* prematurely—" The whisper originated within inches of her ear. "—they stop growing."

Alexia choked on the news. "Stop growing?"

Bellezza rolled her eyes. "We are preserved in our '*most desirable*' state, only precious little morsels like you don't get forced into daddy's bed at thirteen, do they?"

Alexia covered her mouth, shaking in horror.

"It is the highest crime to force another." Bellezza thumped away. "For once *taken*, you will always desire the one who did the taking." She snorted. "Unless that someone is dead."

Dead. Her father was dead. She'd killed her own father who had... Alexia's stomach clenched.

The girl straightened as though a great burden had been lifted. "And now you know." She twirled away on a single foot, skirts swirling like the wings of a freed raven. "Men are weak. They are driven by their lusts." She planted her other foot, facing Alexia, brows low, fabric curtaining around her like a folded flower. "I would save you from him if I could, but I know." She nodded. "Yes, I know what it is to *desire*, even when it means losing everything you love, even when it makes your skin crawl like it's covered in maggots, even when it means damning your future!"

"But if your partner is killed—"

Bellezza bobbed back onto her toes and spun, twirling her arms overhead. "Then you are set free!"

"No, if your partner is killed, you die."

"Not if you are the one who does the killing." Bellezza's lips lifted, pleating wickedly. "It is also our right under the law to break an eternal contract if it is not...by choice."

Alexia swallowed. "You killed...?"

"My father? Yes." She curtsied. "The baron? Yes." Again she dipped. "Several others?" Both hands came together in front of her, a picture of innocence, but darkness curled the corners of her mouth. "We are as powerful as we allow ourselves to become."

Alexia hugged herself. "I am so sorry, Bel—"

"Do not feel sorry for me!" A finger flew forward. "Don't you dare!" Her lips pulled back, teeth exposed. "Feel sorry for yourself, and when you look back twenty years from now and wonder if it was worth it, when you see the web of deception and propaganda, when you realize all you have sacrificed is for a lie—!" She huffed and backed away, nodding. "When that happens, you will understand why I came tonight. When that happens you too will break free. When that happens you will not pity *me*."

Eight

Furies of Hell

Shadows sped across the estate yard, an army of crimson eyes promising a fate worse than death.

Cold swept across Kiren's neck, the chill that witnessed Bellezza was gone. The Breeders had not been mistaken to seek Bellezza out. He questioned if he'd met any Passionate so powerful. *Rarely. Very rarely.*

His anxiety deflated, relieved Alexia would be safe. He straightened Ethel's broken leg. Perhaps a minute and the enemy would be upon him. Ethel must be whole before then. Power rippled through his fingertips and into the marrow of the mist maiden's bone. It sealed the gap, cells multiplying, blood carrying away the damaged tissue.

He leaned his shoulder against a tree, forcing his ribs to expand and pull in air. That cost more than he'd expected.

"Have you left your back open to me intentionally?" a woman's cadence drizzled with menace.

Kiren brushed a hand along Ethel's bruised spine. "Hello, Elizabeth." He thought she'd fled. She should have. It was insanity to remain here while the empty creatures neared, even if she'd learned to defend herself against them.

"Do you believe your gifts against the Soulless will save you?" Worry hid beneath her indignant words. Of course she was insulted he hadn't turned to face her—not that he needed to. He could envision her auburn locks just from hearing that sultry voice.

And he didn't have time to humor her.

He focused on Ethel's upper-most vertebrae where nerves frayed into discord. "I believe my gifts will save *you* from the Soulless." That was what she'd been asking after all, knowing their numbers were too great and she had no chance to flee. He glanced toward the threat closing off the horizon. Seconds remained. He poured energy into the severed nerves, quaking from the strain.

"Is it true what they say about Deiliey's return?"

The name hit him with the force of a hammer. He didn't have time for this conversation! "Deiliey is gone."

A hole deep within opened up. The vaguest hope and fear had been growing since the first rumors three days ago: a mere mention of his old nemesis. Deiliey was the only other person who'd dared to stand against the Soulless, a natural leader. Would that he had such an ally now, but with the war against the Soulless, this was the perfect time to usurp power among the factions.

A chill seeped into the clearing, the ice of the Soulless.

"Run, Elizabeth!" He forced more energy into the mist maiden. If she didn't recover, he was finished.

"We want Alexia."

"You cannot have her, as you well know."

Ethel gasped, hands fluttering into the air. Kiren caught the tree again, panting.

Ethel met his stare with wide eyes. "They are upon us."

He threw his shoulders back, hiding the quivering of his insides. "Are you well enough to move?"

Her mouth quirked. "Are you?"

He couldn't help a grin. Ethel didn't miss a thing. "Take Elizabeth and Pint"—he motioned to the still midget—"to safety. Quickly."

"It will be done, sir." She reached for Elizabeth.

The woman didn't move, her brow wrinkled. "Why are you doing this?"

Kiren shook his head. After all these years of protecting her, whether she asked or not, she still didn't understand.

Ethel exchanged a look with him. She had always approved of his tactics: winning his people over with compassion and love. It was why his enemies could gain no solid footing against him. Those who served under him shared his vision for a peaceful alliance.

The first of the Soulless slipped into the clearing.

"Go, you foolish woman," he commanded.

Elizabeth took Ethel's hand as the mist swirled into the air.

"I will still come after you!" Elizabeth growled between hazy whorls.

She wouldn't. She knew how utterly she depended on him for her own protection. The whiteness swallowed her and Kiren turned.

Wraiths poured into the glade, silent as midnight, ethereal cloaks obscuring all but their murderous crimson eyes as they circled him. Decay assaulted his nose. Their bodies should have been laid to rest long ago but were kept from their graves by this impossible curse.

His heart sped.

How many of these poor souls had he failed? He couldn't think about that now. It was time to release them from their suffering.

Before they finished him.

Kiren lifted his medallion. He sucked in and focused his energies through the pendant.

Blinding light bloomed from his fist and warmth radiated from the metal beneath his palm. Rays descended like pure sunshine, settling over the upturned heads of the now motionless creatures. Kiren lifted his face to the warmth. It was heaven, beckoning him to abandon his physical tabernacle and ascend. His body weighed him as though the earth wrapped its fists about his legs.

A wraith thumped to the ground. Its decaying corpse lay sprawled, rotted fingers outstretched beneath frayed cloth. Others reached for the light, one by one.

A tug pulled at Kiren's gut—the release of strength—the price of freeing the tortured soul.

Another fell.

Three more.

Kiren gasped for air. He clutched at his chest. An invisible hand had reached down his throat and seized his lungs. It tore upward, pulling him inside out. He dropped to his knees, unable to breathe past the pain.

Bodies pelted the ground about him.

Power suctioned out of him like sand through a sieve, flowing faster and faster. Only a few black pillars stood in his hazing periphery.

He tightened his grip around his medallion. He had to hold on. Just a little longer...

Blood stung his nose. Warm liquid dripped down his lips. The whiteness about him winked into black, glistening black.

Thunk.

Nine

Close

Kiren blinked into wakefulness. Night stars glittered against the cool metal of his pendant, lying in the moss next to his head. He sucked in a breath, startled by how thin he felt, like the life had been leeched out of him, leaving a narrow husk behind. He tried to lift his hand. It didn't move.

How much time had slipped by while he was unconscious?

His heart beat too slowly. Not enough oxygen flowed through him. Very soon his brain, then body, would cease functioning. He slumped into the earth, breathing and focusing on the life about him; the moss, the breeze, the call of a bat, slumbering insects beneath the soil.

Please, he asked.

The ground beneath him warmed. Minute swirls of energy seeped into his prostrate form, tingling through his skin.

Enough.

He closed his eyes and utter a silent prayer of thanks. The murmur of rustling material perked his ears. A bare foot whispered away from moss, and pressed down again, closer. So careful.

Hurried footsteps darted toward him. A hand landed across his brow, trembling, then at the pulse in his neck. "Master, you do too much."

He tried to smile for Ethel, but his cheek merely twitched.

Ten

Rights

Alexia was relieved when Ethel returned with Kiren, but the pallor of his skin set off the glacial fire of his eyes before they closed and would open no more. Alexia had only seen him this drained once, and it terrified her.

"There must have been fifty Soulless lying in that field," Ethel said. "It is a wonder he is breathing at all."

His head rested in Alexia's lap while she brushed hair away from his face. "How many has he subdued in the past?"

"Once as many as twenty, but not after draining himself with so much healing." Ethel rubbed her lower back. "Let us pray there is no lasting damage."

"Did he burn himself out *again*?"

Alexia's head jerked up.

Lamplight illuminated leaves, melting away the tree's shadows to reveal an aged fellow with bouncing gray locks, carrying a candle lantern and wearing a handsome dress suit stitched so finely it could only have been spun by Ethel's loving skill.

"Edward." Alexia blushed, recalling how Edward had approached her father on Kiren's behalf two years back, causing her to believe he petitioned for her hand.

He bowed in true gentlemanly fashion. "Nelly sent me to retrieve you before she worries us out of a winter storage. She must have eaten seven jars of pickles already."

A blur of motion gusted into the clearing, catching her skirts and whipping them. Alexia met youthful black eyes. Lester grinned toothily and gave a nod. Those eyes didn't look right against his aged skin and wind-tossed hair, but they never had.

"All accounted fer?" he asked.

Bellezza hissed.

"Why is the young Bellezza here?" Edward asked Lester quietly.

"She has decided to join our faction." Alexia turned on them, receiving startled stares from both men.

33

"And such excellent timing!" Edward straightened his coat and turned to Bellezza with a bow. "You possess the strength, do you not?" It wasn't a question. He catalogued all the Passionate and their unique gifts.

The girl's glare narrowed.

"How very fortuitous! The estate is not far if you would be so kind as to carry the Master."

Bellezza rolled her eyes. Shaking her head, she muttered, "What I get for siding with fools." She picked up Kiren, shifting him over her shoulder like he weighed no more than a shawl. Turning an expectant stare on Edward, she growled, "Well?"

"Right this way!" He led on.

"Sparrow." Lester helped her up and fell into step beside her, almost as though he were guarding her.

"You do not approve of Bellezza joining us," she guessed.

"There be some souls what are so tortured they ain't never goin' to straighten out." He nodded toward Bellezza, his gaze filled with compassion and earnestness Alexia yearned to embrace rather than shun. She and Lester had rarely spoken, but he did possess a kindness, a steadiness she had witnessed only in Kiren. "She is one never to be trusted."

"Is that why you treat her with such disdain?"

Lester wrinkles fell slack. "Had ye seen what she's done..."

Alexia toyed with her engagement ring. Kiren had confessed that Bellezza killed several noblemen, and she'd heard whispers of how it was accomplished—severed hands, impaling, hanging, drowning in brandy, fires...all slow jobs, torturing her victims beforehand.

"But you disliked her before that," Alexia reminded.

His head bowed. "Be careful 'bout her. Don't trust her."

She'd been told she trusted too easily, that she believed too readily in the good of others, and perhaps that was true, but she didn't want to live in a world where every relationship was shrouded in suspicion. It would kill her.

A half-grin puckered Lester's cheek. "S'pose that wedding ain't goin' to happen tonight. But it will happen."

She blinked up at him, baffled by his need to reassure her. Of course it was going to happen.

"Ye must guard him from the beasts what will steal yer happiness," he continued. "Ye can't be blinded to the dangers."

"I will be careful."

"Even if it means denyin' yer own kin?"

She glanced at Lester and bit her lip, that stab of sorrow resurfacing. He was definitely referring to Sarah.

Her aunt was dead to her. Dead. And not dead. As one of the Soulless, Sarah would endure eternally, chained to the man—no *beast*—who had claimed her sympathies and damned her to this reality. Insatiable hunger would drive her to feast on the remaining Passionate.

How would Alexia react if her aunt suddenly appeared? Embrace her as a friend? Run?

An ominous building emerged from between trees. Cobble echoed under foot as they rounded the pleading angel fountain, filled with glimmering water and mulch. Grand doors waited and they slid under their arc, mahogany seraphim in their surface foreboding.

Edward stepped in ahead, lighting the tapers to either side with his lamp and pressing the doors open.

Alexia was home. Not her father's house, but the place she'd truly come alive—the place she hoped to make her own, once married.

Glazed wooden floors reflected back the light, bringing out an inlaid pattern she suddenly recognized mimicked the forest floor. Stairs waited ahead, dark but welcoming, factions of light catching the stained glass at their apex.

The ground trembled. A glass chandelier above them jingled menacingly.

"Nelly?" Edward called casually.

Bellezza turned wide eyes to Alexia.

She gazed back, startled by the girl's reaction, wondering what it meant.

"Scared the livin' daylights out of me!" A squat woman emerged from the right hall. A kerchief was tucked about her round face, occasional corkscrews peeking from below. She hugged a dusty apron across her wide form, tiny black eyes dancing about the chamber. "It would do to give some warnin'."

Alexia clasped both hands in front of her. She'd missed Nelly's rampant chatter and motherly bullying—and her pastries. Definitely her pastries.

Nelly's face bloomed into a cheery melon. "Alexia! Bless my soul!" She circled, squinting, the scent of cloves and dough wafting up. "Look at this, you've thinned out!" She jabbed at her stomach. "You haven't been eating proper."

"You are not accustomed to seeing me in a stomacher." Alexia laughed.

"Stomacher, posh! I know starvation when I see it." The woman froze. All mirth—all life drained from her merry cheeks. She stepped past Alexia through the door. "The Master, he's not—"

"Overexerted." Edward placed a hand on her shoulder.

"Well, that's a fine way to spend your weddin' night."

Alexia's cheeks heated. "We are not—"

"Of course you're not." She waved a hand. "But you shoulda been."

Bellezza carried Kiren up the stairs into the west wing with Edward leading the way. Alexia followed with a candle.

Windows paneled the front wall of Kiren's chamber, covered in rich brocade drapes. In the corner sat a simple desk. Along the back wall a bureau and several dark-framed portraits hung, as well as wide curtains which revealed a narrow balcony beyond night-blackened panes. Directly center stood his bed—

four posters intricately carved with blossoms and leaves. Emerald hangings waited to be drawn about the mattress, and though it should smell like dust, a hint of Kiren's oaken musk hung in the air, quickening Alexia's pulse.

Edward rolled a meager mat at the foot of the bed.

A mat?

Alexia scowled at the bed.

Bellezza snorted. "He would." She deposited Kiren, heaved a laugh and strutted out into the hall.

"Edward, will he not rest more peacefully—?"

"No, my dear." He smiled an apologetic grin, joining her in the doorway. "He never sleeps there."

"Then why should he possess such a fine piece of furniture?"

Edward shrugged, pulling the barrier shut. "Should anyone come upon this house or should we be forced to allow entry, such furnishings would not seem out of the ordinary. However, if for so grand a building the Master's chamber housed only a rug?"

"I thought no one could find this house."

He smiled. "No human or Soulless. Still that leaves some wide category of individuals. Believe me, the Master has contingency plans should anyone else find their way here."

"Other Passionate?" She suggested, "From the Breeders?"

His smile faded. "I have first watch tonight. It is possible Ethel's twin will follow her through the mist, and while I think Sybil is quite noble, we do not want her or her Breeder friends taking us by surprise."

"Ethel has a twin?"

"They share a bond. One can join the other simply on a whim. Time and again they check in—occasionally in a friendly manner, but most often in a less than cordial way. You see, Sybil is precisely everything Ethel is not—fierce, unreasonable, jealous. She has chosen a different cause to support and it affords the two some pain."

Alexia crossed her arms. "And that is why Ethel resides at that shack in the woods? Lest her sister should come looking for her?"

Edward sighed. "It is very unwise for my dear, sweet wife to occupy the same space our Master hides so many of his secrets."

That one hit Alexia over the head like a bludgeon. They were married. It made sense. She could hardly imagine someone as good as Ethel engaging in immoral practices—especially after Kiren's revelation about their laws—and certainly the mist maiden and Edward had a physical relationship.

Which she didn't want to think about.

Alexia frowned. "You never told me you were married."

"You did not ask." He winked.

Bellezza stood cross-armed in the hall.

"Come, dear," he said to the child, "allow me to settle you in."

"I can show her where to stay," Alexia volunteered, certain she didn't want Bellezza near any of the men in her life after what she'd learned in the woods.

His brow rose. He glanced back and forth between them. "If that is what you would like. Goodnight to you both, then." He bowed and returned to the lower levels.

Alexia smiled at the girl, but Bellezza returned a calculating scowl. She likely had Alexia's motive figured out, but it mattered little.

"Right this way." Alexia aimed toward the guest chambers at the opposite end of the hall.

"You have no idea how deep you are in this dung pile." Bellezza scoffed, eyes traveling up and down the walls.

"And here I thought it was a rather fine house."

Bellezza huffed, leveling next to her. "Your life is going to be plenty miserable without my help. Sorry I tried to kill you."

"I do not mind."

"Honestly?" She sneered. "I would mind if I were you. I would mind a great deal. I would mind so much I might kill you for attempting to kill me!"

Alexia laughed awkwardly. "I am afraid killing people is not something I do."

"Yet." The child glanced up dolefully. Her frown deepened. "You will learn that anything worth living for is worth killing for."

Alexia stopped at the second guest chamber. What emotional scars severed Bellezza's ethics so severely in those impressionable childhood years that she couldn't imagine a peaceful living? How had she endured? "We have lived very different lives. I should like to know of yours, if you are willing."

Bellezza frowned, swiped Alexia's candle and moved into the darkness. The door slammed shut in her face.

Expected.

Eleven

Desire

Morning roused Alexia to a slightly less aching head, and the whisper of action on the floors below. She halted at the top of the stairs, examining the sculpted flowers across Kiren's closed door. Surely he should have awakened by now. She wrung her fingers. Perhaps his injuries were greater than could be sustained. Perhaps he was slowly slipping away into the next life because no one considered he might need medical treatment.

Or perhaps she simply ached to see him.

She tested the ivory knob and the door clicked open.

Kiren lay where they'd left him, unmoving except for the slow rise and fall of his chest. His pendant bulged beneath his coat.

No harm could come of examining it closer while he slept, could it? He might never know, and she was dying to understand its importance.

Alexia entered and pulled back the curtain, sending a stream of light across his comatose body. She neared slowly and glanced again at the open door. To close it, to isolate them...

Breathe.

She knelt. The cool buttons loosed easily beneath her fingers and his coat fell back. The charm had found its way between his vest and thin shirt. She touched the chain tentatively, sliding along its length, gliding toward the hidden treasure beneath his waistcoat...

Fingers seized hers.

She jumped.

Fierce blue eyes sought hers beneath lowered brows, the purest night sky littered by a sea of stars. She looked away.

"Are you undressing me?" he whispered.

"What?" Her cheeks flamed. She backed away.

Kiren rolled onto his elbow and pressed off the floor, stumbling. Alexia reached to steady him as he propped against one of the bed's four posters. He shook off the dizziness and pulled her close.

Her breath caught. The press of his hands on her back, the heat of his body so near hers, the aroma of his oaken musk... Her heart thumped like a rabbit's, and she couldn't help thinking: very soon he would be hers.

She couldn't meet his stare. "Kiren, I-I was not attempting to—"

A finger landed across her lips as he probed her gaze. His eyebrows tightened. He released her.

"Shall I assist you?" He slipped out of his coat.

She gasped. "Kiren!"

He chuckled, unbuttoning his waistcoat.

Alexia could not believe what he was doing and she couldn't look away. He wouldn't honestly undress before her and chance such overwhelming temptation, would he?

The waistcoat dropped to the floor, leaving a thin shirt to veil his chest. His pendant sat atop, a flattened pewter diamond with symbols etched across the surface like calligraphy-styled runes. A larger Z with a cross stroke and rounded tail engraved its center, encircled by a ring of smaller characters.

"So, which is it that has you?" His head tilted.

She staggered backward and landed on the bed, her headache thumping dully. Each of his arms propped by her sides, his alluring lips hovering within inches.

"The necklace or the man?"

She breathed in oak and a hint of pollen, aching to reach out and brush her fingers down the cotton which barely masked his solid form. She swallowed. "The-the man."

"I would swear you thought otherwise but a moment ago."

Alexia shook her head free of his clouding influence. "What is it?"

He grunted and plopped onto the bed next to her.

"Kiren?"

"It is all I have left of my family."

She slid a hand over his. Only once had he addressed this subject, and it ended as abruptly as it started.

"I do not speak of them." His eyes pierced her, pigment darkening. "And I choose not to do so for a wise purpose."

She turned toward him. "What happened to them?"

His brow crinkled. She reached up and smoothed a finger over the worry lines, dragging her touch down the white scar that ran from his eye to chin. "Is that how this happened?"

He pulled her hand away.

There were so many things about him she didn't know, but the pain in his twitching frown—that she understood too well. She would not deepen the wound in his heart. "Why do you sleep on the floor when you possess so fine a bed?"

He met her gaze and shrugged. "It is comfortable."

She giggled. "Comfortable?"

39

The corners of his mouth turned up. He brushed her cheek, and the smile faded. "I want to tell you everything."

She trapped his hand against her skin. "Then tell me."

His brows lowered. "As soon as you are mine."

"I am yours." Was he afraid of what she'd learn? Afraid she would no longer want or choose him?

"Our enemies, dearest. If you and I are prevented from..." He touched a finger to her lips and his head shook. "I am going to marry you. Today."

The aching need in his gaze immobilized her as he fixed on her mouth. She cupped his hand and his head tilted, breath brushing her lips. She closed her eyes, trembling from the sunshine his touch sent through her soul. They should be married already.

His lips teased across hers. She looped her arms about his neck, drawing him solidly to her. His lips captured hers like a rogue at sea, deprived of womanly company. They trailed down her neck and back up, sending bursts of need through her limbs. He slid her back onto the bed. She gasped.

He climbed over her. "Are you afraid of me, Alexia?"

"No."

Their bodies aligned, his hand pressed at her hip. "Not even the slightest?"

She swallowed, a tremor of need slithering through her veins. She was vulnerable under his weight, but this was Kiren. "You would not hurt me."

He frowned and sat back.

She pulled her skirt around and tucked her legs beneath her, sad for the loss of his closeness and determined to regain it. "And I would never hurt you."

He drew a knuckle over his scarred cheek. "How much we still have to learn about one another."

"And we shall." She leaned forward, catching his shirt and pulling him closer, too aware that she was nearly touching him skin on skin. "Right now I wish to learn more about how you taste."

His eyebrow peaked. She giggled and seized possession of his mouth once more. He tickled her sides and she squealed, trying to wriggle out of his grasp. Kiren pinned her flailing limbs against the mattress and leaned over her. The mirth in his grin trickled away. His breath cut across her chin, ragged, eyes an oceanic maelstrom of desire. Alexia surrendered to them, welcoming the press of his body against hers.

Blinding warmth burst through her frame, and she was no longer alone inside her head. Their minds danced about one another like two frolicking deer. Father's gardens emerged, swallowed by a little church on a hill, her reflection in the mirror, his home in Wilhamshire.

I want you to see me, the words echoed. *See me, Alexia.*

She stilled.

Glades and ancient buildings filtered by so hastily, she could not fully envision a single one, or recall if they'd been her habitation or his. The loneliness which had possessed him seized her heart, like a gaping blackness now banished by the rising sun of hope. That sun brightened the spires of a gleaming white building, seven diamond spears reaching for the sky, and within the translucent walls he knelt, head bowed, chained by manacles of shadow. The chains glistened, evolving from pitch to crystal, and then dissipating in sparkles. He lifted his freed wrists, hair falling back to reveal his pronounced nose. A tenuous gasp echoed through the tower. She reached to touch him, her fingers the essence of light warming his skin. She lifted his chin. His eyes were as clear as glass, drinking in the radiance, his mouth open in awe, in gratitude, in aching submission.

"Ahem." The sound was far away. It shook the glistening floor beneath her feet, and the vision evaporated as Kiren's mouth lifted from hers. He gazed into her eyes, his filled with wonder and vulnerability.

She brushed ginger hair back from his face, becoming aware of his body, pressed to hers, separated only by a few thin layers of cloth, the rigid lines of his pendant cutting through her gown.

"Sir?"

She gasped and scrambled back from him on the bed, his pendant swinging free. Her entire body was a torrid flame.

Kiren's eyes closed. His Adam's apple bobbed as he straightened up. "Yes, Edward?"

The memory keeper stood in the open doorframe, gaze averted toward the hall. "Lucian has arrived, sir."

Alexia pressed a fist to her mouth, ashamed both of being caught, and of being so very loose.

Kiren met her stare. His head tilted, concern in his oceanic swells. "Very good. Make preparations for departure."

Edward nodded and hurried away. Kiren scooted closer, a hand lifting hesitantly to her cheek. She couldn't meet his gaze. He cradled her to his chest, fingers stroking over her hair. He turned her face to his, but she focused on his shoulder. He placed his lips against hers, tenderly.

"Forgive me, love?" He brushed a wisp of hair from her eyelashes.

She pressed the backs of her hands against her flaming neck. "You wish me to see you?"

His cheek dimpled.

Alexia couldn't remember how to breathe.

"The man who will marry us awaits my company."

"Lucian?"

He nodded. "And your keepers are anxious to prepare you." He slipped off the bed and assisted her down. "In the course of but a couple hours, we may share this bed again as man and wife."

She blushed.

He lifted her chin. "Unless you have any objections to our union?"

She shook her head vigorously. He chuckled and his mouth touched hers again, this time interrupted by a grunting Nelly.

Twelve

Jitters

Alexia brushed a hand over silver lace, unable to stop her trembling. Ethel patiently gathered the shimmering material to fit it about her sleeves.

"It looks better on you than it did her." Nelly winked.

Alexia heaved a breath, constricted by the boning of the corset. The style was dated, but the richness of the gown's heritage filled her with gratitude. Ethel had explained it would have been Dana's, had her mother been married, but originally it had been Ethel's.

Alexia would have liked to wear Sarah's first wedding gown, but the dress was certainly gone after her aunt's disappearance. To the Soulless. The Soulless who may very well find her this evening.

"Is there a reason we do not wait to marry until after the moonless cycle?" Alexia asked.

"How very astute of you to notice." Ethel grinned.

"It's our way." Nelly dug through a satchel of sewing stuffs.

Ethel bit off the final thread. "The moonless night symbolizes new beginnings. We come of age on moonless nights, most our women give birth on moonless nights, and we marry on moonless nights."

Alexia scowled. "But the Soulless are out on moonless nights."

Ethel nodded. "It resounds with them as well."

"Enough depressin' prattle." Nelly finished with Alexia's hair and slipped a crimson ribbon about her neck. "Silver, for the purest life, red for power and prosperity."

Ethel tucked green buds into Alexia's sculpted curls. "Green for wisdom and new life."

Alexia clasped her hands before her to stop them from shaking. All her life she'd believed this day impossible—and now here she stood, dressed as a bride. So why did her knees rattle and every breath cause her pain? She was marrying the man she loved. Her days of loneliness and isolation were over.

The trembling increased. She had always been a solitary individual. The idea of sharing the space in her head...

She pressed her clammy hands to her cheeks. He would see her as no one ever had, not merely in the flesh, but the intimacy of her inner thoughts. They would be eternally bound, endlessly connected, unquestioningly one. Would he like what he found, or would he toss her aside as some silly wife once he'd had his way? Would her relationship end as badly as Father's?

Bellezza's warning remained. Alexia ached for the girl, for how much pain and suffering she'd endured, but some truth resonated through her words. There would never be another choice after today, unless she murdered the man she loved. All growing up she'd believed she would end up a spinster in Father's library, or perhaps a governess to Sarah's children.

Sarah.

Her heart seized. Her dear sister would not be there to witness her marriage, nor would Father. It was as if her old life truly were dead. Past Alexia had been slain the instant she froze time and became a powerful Passionate asset. But she couldn't believe that was the reason Kiren wanted her. Surely the others, but not him. And yet, she questioned if perhaps some small part of him was driven by that motive.

"There. All finished." Ethel stood back, beaming at her handiwork. "Shall we be off then?"

Lester appeared in the doorway, a sword-bearing scabbard in his grip. "Aye, she's perfect 'cept fer one thing." He offered the weapon.

She couldn't help her own blush. "Lester, I am going to my wedding, not to war."

"'Tis tradition in times of war to wear ones' weapon, even to the altar. Besides, no weddin' is complete without a gift or two."

"We have no need of gifts."

He placed the scabbard in her hands, belt dangling off the sheath. "But this one already belongs to ye."

Confused, she scanned the saber's casing, startled to find red ribbing around the hilt, its antique weight familiar in her grasp.

Her mirth dropped into a chasm. This was the very sword she'd wielded against the Soulless when they ambushed Kiren at her father's estate. It weighed heavier on her now than it had, a tool that deflected numerous creatures and took the life of one.

She scowled. But everyone insisted the Soulless couldn't be killed.

Lester's dark eyes found hers, the youthful cores filled with something ancient and ominous. He patted her hand over the hilt. "Keep 'er safe."

Why did it sound like he was addressing the sword?

Alexia swallowed, not excited about the anvil weight Ethel fastened about her hips, or about the silence of traveling by mist.

"Keep this up and you are going to shake to pieces." Nelly caught her elbow and nodded at Ethel. "Just do it then."

Father paced between trees, chest heaving. Alexia couldn't believe he was here. She waited for him to notice her and her two escorts. The peak of a shingled roof poked above the young willows, their destination.

"He has been here all night," Ethel whispered, "staying in the church rectory since his rescue."

Alexia turned to her mother-figure who had disappeared after delivering Kiren the previous evening. "Thank you for bringing him to safety. Is this where you weathered the night also?"

A smile spread across Ethel's face. "The master asked me to ensure his wellbeing."

She embraced the dear woman. "You have my eternal gratitude."

Father glanced up, his grimace dropping along with his mouth. He blinked at her and crossed his arms, inhaling a slow breath.

"Hello, Father."

He extended a hand.

She looped his arm and took up his side.

"You are quite breathtaking, child."

She blushed, her heart swelling in joy, in gratitude. Perhaps all was not right, but Father was here! Warmth lodged in the hearth of her soul. Tears pooled and she wanted to clap or sing or dance in thankfulness. She could marry Kiren now.

"I wish your mother could have been here." He patted her hand.

"As do I." Though she couldn't decide which one he meant. She would have liked both, Rosalind, who raised her, and her natural parent, Dana. Of course, Dana had probably watched all this in her dreams or from the absence of time.

"Will you excuse us?" He nodded to Ethel and Nelly. They turned and disappeared toward the building. His voice quieted. "You have seen so many things from which I hoped to shelter you, and you are much stronger than I thought."

She grinned and studied the soil under foot.

Father bit his lip, glaring straight ahead. "His ways are foreign to me, and I admit, they frighten me."

She patted his arm.

"I worry about you." He glanced at her.

"I will worry about you as well."

He pulled her around to face him, mulch twisting under her slippered soles. "Are you certain this is what you want?"

Was she certain? Could she even bring herself to consider life without Kiren? "He brings me great happiness."

He grunted impatiently. "But this is much more than a question of happiness—it is a question of family. Is this the man you would have father and raise your children?"

She blinked up at him. Children? She hadn't given the idea any thought, but that was the way: marriage, then family. Her parents had certainly followed it, but they had only one child, their marriage destroyed. She knew nothing of raising children. Did Kiren even desire a lineage—or would they too cause him stress and constant anxiety? She had heard nothing of Passionate offspring beyond Miles and her mother's sad story. Was progeny so rare among their kind for a reason?

But Kiren had raised Miles, and Miles had been so kind, so gentle, and so dear—despite his rare talent and the distance others kept.

Miles...

Her heart ached at his absence. If Kiren could cultivate one so challenged, surely he would prove a better parent than she could ever hope to be.

She nodded. "If I should be blessed with children, I should wish for no better partner."

Father gave her a tight smile.

Thirteen

Anticipation

Kiren paced in front of the little church, unable to focus on the script of his pocket Bible. He tucked the little red book into his coat.

Edward and Lester were inside the white building with the priest, informing Lucian of all the battles and changes that had occurred while he was away in the orient. Normally that would be Kiren's job, but at the moment he was finding it difficult to tether his thoughts.

Batting away a hanging tree branch, he closed his eyes.

Soon.

Soon Alexia would be his. Every second that stood between now and their union was torture. He ached to be for her what she'd been to him: stabilizing, constant, compassionate, hope—the promise of a brighter age. He could hardly imagine their world together, a place bursting with color where every thought, every touch, every interaction held meaning. Never again would he wander alone through the vales of his impossible decisions. Never again would she question her worth. They would share in everything, his wisdom and her selflessness guiding them both into a vibrant future.

He could want for nothing more.

He froze. But if she knew too much, would it change the future? Or the past?

Kiren pulled a hand through his hair. Time. It wasn't set. If his years had taught him anything, it was that life could change in an instant. Everything he treasured might be snatched away at any moment, and she might have already seen it happen.

Promise me you will keep our secret. The words echoed in his mind.

He bit down on the bitter oath, souring in his mouth like overcooked Brussels sprouts.

He couldn't risk it.

Some truths would have to be withheld, but could he do it? Could he fracture that piece of himself and tuck it down so deep she'd never find it? And more importantly, could she truly love him if he couldn't give her absolutely everything?

Feet crunched through the underbrush. He straightened up, tugging at his coat to smooth the impeccably starched wool, heart skipping a beat. This was it.

Ethel and Nelly emerged through the branches.

He scoured the woods beyond them. "Where is Alexia?"

"Speaking with her father."

His mouth was instantly dry. "Alone?" He didn't wait for an answer, speeding past them into the woods. Air caught in his throat, his breathing too shallow. If anything happened to her, right at this instant when the world was about to turn right, he would never forgive himself!

Charles's bass pulled him forward, the patter of Ethel and Nelly's feet assaulting him from behind.

"Sir, wait!" Nelly called.

Kiren skidded to a halt. His mouth dropped open.

Silver silk flowed down Alexia's thin frame and beveled over her hips where a sword hung—an appropriate addition. The crimson band about her neck drew him to her heartbeat, pumping within that perfect breast, rising and falling in short breaths.

Safe. She was safe.

But something was wrong.

He met her eyes. They pulled him into the emerald depths of her forest glade, shaded by the secrecy of hushed woods.

The two women stopped in his periphery as Alexia bit her lip, both hands twining before her. Apprehension twisted in her forced smile.

He hadn't imagined it. Something was wrong.

"Charles, Ethel, Nelly, will you afford us a moment of privacy?"

"Agh! No you don't!" Nelly set herself squarely between them, turning him about. He glanced back over his shoulder, and Alexia ducked around her father to meet his gaze. "You ain't to see yer bride yet!" She arched her neck the direction of the church.

Alexia slipped closer. His pulse quickened.

"Perhaps we might blindfold him if he is only to not see me," she said.

Kiren silently applauded her. She blushed and grinned bashfully back at him.

Nelly and Ethel exchanged glances. Ethel shrugged. Nelly muttered as she searched her apron pocket and came up with a leftover strip of silver fabric. "Bend down, you."

He dropped to one knee and the whisper of cloth brushed over his cheeks, blocking out the wooded boughs. He rose.

Alexia slid her silky fingers around his. The staccato of her pumping blood startled him, and he listened as the wedding goers paced ahead of them toward the church.

He tilted his head. "What is bothering you?"

47

She laid her other hand on his arm, and turned him after their escorts. "I have been thinking..."

He overlapped her hand with his own, loving the feel of her skin beneath his. "About?"

"Sarah."

He nodded, leaves from the previous season crunching beneath their feet.

"And Father. He did not simply let me go, did he? How have you convinced him to consent? He was so adamant against us."

Huffing, he closed his mouth.

Her fingers slipped between his. "Show me."

He groaned and squeezed, stopping. "You are certain you wish to witness this?"

"Completely."

"Do not be angry."

She shook as though she'd waggled her head. He opened his mind, recalling the memory and sharing it through their connection...

Kiren sat at the foot of the bed as Charles fumbled from beneath his blankets, his nightshirt twisting.

"I told you never to come back!" he growled.

Kiren glanced at the window. So little time...

Charles shoved into a sitting position. "Seven of my servants, seven dead and nearly my daughter as well—all because of you! God knows what else you have done to her—"

"Let us not speak of stealing young women's virtue," Kiren said. "I would not want you to feel...uncomfortable."

Charles's face reddened.

"Rather, let us discuss your safety, and hers."

The baron's flush deepened. "She would be plenty safe if you had stayed away from her."

Kiren moved to the window, pulling back the drapes to reveal a moonless evening. It was true. If only he'd had that much discipline. "She came to me," he reminded them both quietly.

"Why are you here?" the nobleman snapped, rising from bed.

"Have you looked at the sky tonight, Charles?"

Blood drained from the nobleman's face. He growled. "Stay tonight then, and be gone from our lives in the morning."

Kiren examined his fingernails. "Do you recall the debacle of Alexia's forced engagement?" An uncomfortable silence stretched. Both of them remembered the bank share owner who had threatened Charles's estate if he didn't promise her hand in marriage. "How long before you are placed in a similar circumstance?"

"I will not be blackmailed again."

Kiren huffed. "And you think that will protect her?"

Charles averted his gaze.

"Your world is not safe for her, and neither is mine."

"Then there is no safety." The nobleman glared.

"I know only of one place." He lifted Charles's dead wife's wedding band from the dressing table, recalling the selfless woman who had bourn its tremendous weight, the woman who had raised Alexia.

The baron stepped forward. "You cannot have her!"

Kiren faced the nobleman. "I could have sent someone to rob you of your memories and taken her away."

"You would not dare!"

"If it was the only way to guarantee her safety, I would!" He challenged the man with a glare. Charles's eyes widened. "Only I seem to recall a promise. You might remember it as well, something about not tampering with your mind?"

The baron's shoulders heaved.

"You have a choice to make." Kiren spun the ring in his fingers. "Give her willingly, or lose her—and not necessarily to me. Can you imagine which fate would be worse?"

The stubborn man's fists tightened.

Kiren bowed his head. "What is the one thing you desired most of your father?"

Charles blinked, jaw flapping. He closed his mouth and his brows lowered. Kiren read the answer in Charles's eyes, an answer he wasn't willing to utter: he had desired his father's acceptance of Dana.

The nobleman stared at the floor, his shoulders dropping. "This can only end in tragedy."

"Not so long as I possess breath." Kiren placed the ring in Charles's grasp. The baron groaned. "Will you grant your daughter and myself your blessing?"

Charles rubbed his forehead. "I expect to be present for the wedding."

Kiren grinned. "I shall see you shortly."

Fourteen

Secrets

Swaying branches and a leafy awning appeared suddenly, Alexia's skin tingling from Kiren's touch. The church's roof poked out of the canopy just ahead and she breathed in the reality: They were about to be married.

A tear streaked down her chin and her cheeks ached from the depth of her grin.

Kiren's fingers swept from her ear to lips, catching the moisture. "You are sad? Have you..." He cringed. "Have changed your mind?"

"Never." Let the earth fold in on itself, life could not be more wonderful.

"Tell me, love, are they watching us?"

Or perhaps it could. Their friends' voices carried between trees, but they were obscured by trunks and bushes. She stepped closer. "No."

He chuckled. "And what shall you do with me, as I am your own, blind captive?"

Alexia pushed up on her toes and their lips met. She ran her hands down his chest and pulled his arms around her waist. He groaned, fingers cinching the material about her center. She parted her lips and wriggled closer. He enwrapped her, the floodgates of restraint obliterated.

The realm they shared burst into light, and she skipped through it like a stone on water, diving deeper into him. Scenes whirled by her, some distinct and open, but some guarded by a smoky haze, as though cloaked in shadow.

Strange.

She pressed forward and parted a veil.

His mouth tore away from hers. He stumbled back a step, nearly losing his balance. She reached to steady him, but he regained his equilibrium. His lips pressed tight, both hands cupping his brow.

Kiren pulled his hands through his hair, catching on the blindfold. "Boundaries. We must establish boundaries for what is and is not acceptable."

She scowled. "Am I to understand that, as my husband, you will hold me at arms' length? What are you so afraid I will discover?"

His shoulders hunched inward. "I can teach you to shade your own thoughts."

Deflecting. Why was he always deflecting? Her fingers cut into her flesh. She whirled and started toward the church to find Ethel and return to the estate. Perhaps there would be no wedding after all.

"Alexia?" He stumbled after her, tearing the blinder off and throwing his arms around her. "Please, dearest." His eyes crinkled, the inner tides swirling with agonizing demons. She wanted to wash them away, to banish them to a moored island where they might never escape to torment the man she loved.

The muscles in his cheeks twitched, straining to pull the corners of his mouth upward. "Ask me anything and I will answer, but give me time to open my thoughts."

"Anything?"

He nodded.

She lay her palm flat against his chest, over the medallion. "Lightning. When I was almost..." She swallowed. "Who brought the lightning? Ethel was crippled, Lester was gone, and Bellezza hasn't the strength or I should have seen it before."

His grasp on her shoulders tightened uncomfortably. "I lost you once. I will never lose you again. You are my life, Alexia."

"*You* summoned lightning?"

He looked away.

She worked to slow her breathing. "What else can you do?"

"Nothing." He caught her chin. "My gifts are limited to healing and reading thoughts. The medallion, however, is a weapon and can be used to call upon the forces of nature. I have never told anyone that for fear they would try to wrestle it from me, nor have I used it in that fashion save twice."

"Sir?"

Alexia twirled.

Edward stood in the distance, twisting his coattail. "Bellezza has vanished, and..."

Kiren's back straightened, his grip falling away from her arms. "Tell me, Edward."

The memory keeper's eyes turned to Alexia, and he cleared his throat.

Kiren's forehead smoothed. "She will very soon be my wife and equal. Speak."

Edward scowled, continuing quietly. "Right before she disappeared, Lucian said the young lady debated turning you over to the Soulless."

Kiren's brow tweaked. "She is always pondering—"

"Not like this, sir."

He groaned. "Take Ethel and track her—after the wedding."

Edward scratched the back of his neck. "Perhaps it would be best if we rescheduled?"

51

"No." Kiren's fierce eyes radiated a heat that sent waves of awe and excitement racing through Alexia's veins.

Edward's jaw squared. "As you wish, sir." He spun and crunched away.

Bellezza would not be present. It shouldn't have hurt, but Alexia's heart pricked. She thought they had come to an understanding, that the girl would accept their union. Just one more absence to add to the number of people who should be here today.

"I cannot wait to be yours," she whispered. "But I do wish—" She stopped short. It was a cruel thought, and even crueler to state.

He tipped her chin toward him, brows scrunched low.

"Sarah." The single word barely escaped.

His nose flared.

"She would have been present." She choked on the rest of the statement. *If she hadn't been attacked by John, by the Soulless.* Alexia blinked back a tear. He'd tried so hard to save her aunt, and still she'd been lost.

His piercing eyes delved into her, like plunging a sword made of water through her being. "You have made so many sacrifices for me. You have made me what I am."

A chilly wind prickled over her arms. She glanced back over her shoulder as the breeze faded, unable to meet his stare. "*You* have made you what you are."

"Before meeting you, I was a selfish young man who cared only for the family and life he had lost."

Alexia laughed. "You? Selfish? That is impossible."

He brought her fingers to his lips, grinning. "Would you like to know a secret?"

She nodded anxiously.

He leaned in to her ear. "That morning on the roof, that was not the first time I kissed you."

"What?"

Kiren's cheek dimpled, pulling at his scar. "The night of your sixteenth birthday, you were entrenched in nightmares. It pained me to see you thus, and I..."

She gasped. "You did not!"

He smirked.

She covered her mouth, cheeks threatening to split for her smile. "How did I not wake?"

"You did." He waggled his eyebrows. "But I escaped before you discovered me." The mirth faded. "As you will recall, I had determined you should not know me, and feared it would be my only chance to experience your lips."

She jerked free of his grasp. "You rogue!"

"Guilty." He chuckled.

She crossed her arms. "How dare you sneak into young girls' rooms and force yourself upon them!"

"Only one." He touched her nose. "And I knew even then I should love her far deeper than I dared."

The confession melted through her bones. Twirling her arms around his neck, she pushed up onto her toes, and whispered, "That was not the only time we met, the evening when you stole a kiss?"

"Hardly. When you were seven, you injured your ankle in the woods. I carried you home. That memory was taken at your father's request."

"What else?"

"Every winter, when I came to heal your surrogate mother, I'd find you waiting in the hall—always the same place. Sometimes we would talk. Sometimes you would stare. Every time I found it nigh impossible to leave."

She squeezed closer and shivered for joy.

He asked, "Do you remember returning home after Sarah's wedding?"

Focusing, she tried to bring the memory back. "When I was eleven?"

Kiren nodded. "You were so distraught. That night I joined you in the nursery and read to you until the sun rose."

It was one of her strongest memories, but she'd never been able to identify the reader. She'd always assumed it was a servant who no longer worked under Father's employ.

He kissed her cheek. "Edward only took what was necessary."

"That memory is what spurred me into reading for comfort. The words were such a balm. You were such a balm." Alexia tickled a finger down his neck. "Tell me more," she whispered.

"When you were quite young, I often met you and Sarah in the woods. You called me *the woodsman*, and I thought it adorable. We would play games, and Miles usually joined us. It was the only true play he experienced." His smile faded.

"I knew Miles as well?" Alexia teased his collar.

His head tilted, pain clenched in the wrinkles about his eyes.

She slipped free from him, guilty and saddened for bringing Miles up and the part she played in his absence. In exchange for her, Miles had given the Soulless access to his mind, to his knowledge of Kiren's entire infrastructure—along with his gift, *his seeing through others' eyes*. He would forever be running from the Soulless, and all because of her.

She hated herself for coming between them. Miles had been like a son to him, a prodigy gone wrong, a danger and blessing all in one.

Alexia touched Kiren's arm.

He focused on her. "He is strong. He will be happy."

She nodded.

"Come now," Kiren twirled her about, a teasing smirk twisting his mouth upward. "I believe we have a wedding to commence."

Alexia trotted through the trees, fingers linked through his, returning his world-bursting grin. Was there anything so complete as simply being with him?

So long as she had this, had him, let wars and sorrows rage. Nothing could stay her joy.

Fifteen

Marriage

The single-room church waited, its white framing set off by the stone exterior. Father straightened up from the door frame as Kiren hurried up the steps past him, shaking hands briefly.

Alexia's heart gave a trill of sheer bliss at the exchange. She didn't think she could be happier as she skipped up the steps and took Father's arm. Inside, wall-length windows welcomed adequate light to brighten the faces of her friends and adopted family. They stood at the front of the building, gathered at the far end beyond the pews. Heads swiveled her direction and a hush fell.

Edward straightened up and tugged at his lapels as Lester winked. Ethel beamed and brought her hands together in a single clap while Nelly crossed her arms and nodded in approval.

They stepped back to reveal Kiren, ever so handsome in his fine suit. His natural luster put the others to shame, brightening the front of the room and sending waves of heat washing over her. Every cell pulsed with life, with excitement and a giddiness that threatened to explode from her like sunbeams refracted through glass.

Behind him, a priest in simple robes shifted.

She met gazes with Father at her side, his brow raised in question. She nodded and they moved forward.

Kiren's nose flared, his eyes as wide as the sea. She swam toward them, ready to be forever encompassed by his tender floods. His honey-oak musk carried over the closing distance, intoxicating her in the realization that very soon this breathtaking man would be hers, forever.

He offered a hand. She pulled away from Father, fixated on the wellspring of her eternal happiness, flesh brushing over flesh. He lifted her hand to his lips, gaze never leaving hers.

The priest uttered words, and she heard them in the distance, a hum of noise.

Listen, Kiren mouthed.

She attempted to sort through the drone, but his summer tides swallowed her awareness, bringing her down to the *thump-thump* of her own heart and the tingles traveling from their overlapping fingers.

This was it. The moment. Never again would she be alone. Never again would she worry and wonder if this day would come. Never again would she question if she was worthy of his love.

Perfect joy blossomed from her chest outward, a matchless white orchid brought forth by the man who had nurtured this hope into being. Happiness pulsed off her skin, saturating the air. The space charged with warmth, with a brilliance.

She gasped.

Luminescence permeated off her skin.

Radiance shone from Kiren's wrist and face as well. Did she imagine it, or could she actually feel his splendor mingling with her own, like particles of light kissing through their skin and becoming one?

It was happening: The bond. All her doubts, all her reservations were swept to the invisible corners of her mind as she offered herself up to him.

A chill seeped down her spine, the spell shattering.

She snapped to awareness. That wasn't right. Something wasn't right.

No, no, no!

Ice curled through the room, its serpentine tail flicking at the back of her neck and raising goose bumps along her arms.

The priest's words died off.

Kiren's fingers bit into hers, his jaw clenching.

Darkness dropped over them like a curtain had been drawn across the windows.

Sixteen

Barrage

Alexia jerked out of her trance.

The chill of the air could only mean one thing.

The Soulless. Silhouettes obstructed the window panes from outside, multiple beings whose eyes would glow crimson when the sun set.

Kiren jerked her behind him.

She reached for the greatest weapon in her possession, the power to freeze time—even if the ache at the back of her head warned against it. She gripped her sword's hilt.

Glass shattered inward. Kiren threw himself around her, blocking the deadly shards with his body. Feet reverberated behind her. She peeped under his arm as hooded bodies flooded into the small space.

Whiteness cascaded around them, a tunnel of cloud. The chapel faded completely, replaced by transporting fog, the hollow silence echoing in her ears.

Kiren's arms tightened around her. She clung to him, mist settling on her skin. Calm permeated the silence like the embrace of a mother swaddling her infant. Alexia recognized the presence as clearly as she'd recognize Ethel's soothing voice.

But what about the others?

Her heart stuttered, terror for Father, for Edward, Nelly, Lester and the priest, all still trapped in the church with those demons. What would become of them? Could they adequately fend off the Soulless without Kiren? And why hadn't he stopped the ravenous beasts?

The haze faded.

Kiren's head snapped up. He scanned the shadowed canopy of thick aspens, attention jerking to Ethel as she solidified in their periphery. "You should return," he said to her.

"I will not leave you until the crisis is abated."

Alexia recognized the lover trees from the same grove everyone had gathered in the previous evening. She caught Kiren's chin. "You should both go back to them. They need your strength." She placed a hand over the medallion beneath his coat.

He groaned. "I can only utilize that power under the dark moon, not beneath the sun." She frowned and he pressed a silencing finger to her lips, head bowed. "And I am far weaker than I should be after the conflict last night."

Alexia recalled the sallow hue of his skin the previous evening, and apart from the moment their bonding had begun, it had yet to regain its golden brilliance. Her grip tightened around the hilt of her sword.

Kiren placed a hand over hers. "The Soulless cannot taint anyone in the daylight. We have the advantage."

Ethel shifted from one foot to the other, hands clasped before her. All three of them had tasted death last night. It had been only too real, and it was only too real now for Father.

"We may not be strong," she whispered, "but we can still fight."

Kiren's eyes shot wide.

A high-pitched hiss zipped past Alexia's ear.

Ethel gasped.

Light glimmered off a dark prong embedded in Ethel's shoulder. A trickle of blood dribbled down her shoulder.

Kiren whirled.

Shadows streaked through the trees. Feet rumbled over the moss.

Kiren swung at the enemy.

A headache ripped through Alexia's brain, time slowing. Blackness reared before her. She blinked her eyes open, fingers pressed into stone-like moss, its dampness cool beneath her gowned knees, but strangely not soaking the material. She squinted through the pain.

Kiren crouched in front of her, both fists raised, his cheeks set like flint. A cloaked figure hung in the air, flying backward, aimed to crash into several assailants. A dozen more walled them in, an entire armada of stilled bodies.

Ethel had collapsed to her knees and was frozen, digging at the weapon in her shoulder. She'd freed it an inch, despite the bloodied barbs tearing at her skin.

Alexia's stomach heaved, burning bile racing up her throat.

How could she help them? Much more of this and she'd return to being bed ridden. Although her skills were meager, she would have to take her chances with a sword in normal time, or run.

She knew what Kiren would ask her to do.

But she was not Kiren.

She relaxed her muscles. Low growls hissed in her ears, movement writhing about her as she slipped the saber from its sheath.

Something smacked into her from behind. She stumbled forward, losing her grip on the weapon. She gasped as cold metal slithered across her neck.

The world shot back into sequence.

An arm looped around her waist, pulling her up, blade to her throat. The red-ribbed handle caught her periphery and she groaned, feeling like a fool. She couldn't even keep hold on her own weapon.

Rot hit her nose, so thick she expected to asphyxiate on it as her captor addressed Kiren. "I would not do that!"

Kiren was frozen, one hand wrapped around the chain at his neck. Four of the creatures latched onto him. One kicked the backs of his knees, the others throwing their weight on top of his shoulders and toppling him to the ground. His jaw smacked the dirt, eyes a smoldering pike fresh out of the bellows.

The men wrestled Kiren up onto his knees, arms twisted behind. Darkness hung over the creatures, leaking from their skin as a distorting haze. Decaying spots mottled their faces, half-violet—as though they were meant for the grave, but the grave had refused them.

Heat radiated through the body pressed at her back, another of these decaying corpses. Her skin writhed.

John had explained there were degrees of Soulless, and that he had escaped with most of himself intact. Some of the Soulless had been so drained they were merely intelligent corpses walking the earth—until the moonless night when they became something more. Alexia never could have fathomed his meaning, until now.

Kiren's chin lifted. She met his calming tides. *Be strong*, they said.

A man sauntered between them with spiked dark hair, sickly pale skin, and purple protruding veins. He turned on Alexia. His cheeks were hollow, flesh so thin his skull grinned through it. His eyes hid so deeply she questioned if they existed at all until they connected with hers. The pupils shone a brilliant crimson hue.

Seventeen

Relics

"Here she stands." The voice sounded as narrowly stretched as his skin, a hiss on the wind. "So nice to finally meet you, Alexia Dumont."

The tang of a tomb rolled over her. She gagged. The blade's edge scraped her skin, sharper than she remembered.

"What do you want, Amos?" Kiren's voice was calm, despite his ridiculous position on the ground.

"They tell me you have chosen a mate." The skull said over his shoulder while peering closely at her.

"Who tells you this?" Kiren huffed. "And more importantly, you believe them? I thought you were a man of reason."

The death grin swept away, although he still looked to be grinning through the natural arch of rotted teeth. "Even men of reason possess faults." He stepped closer, his face inches from Alexia's, acrid breath stinging her eyes.

She closed them.

"I tend to trust too easily, as you are aware." The rasp erupted in a fetid breeze across her cheek. "Lucky you do not seem to share that quality." He turned. "Or do you?"

Kiren's face revealed nothing, as unmoved as stone. The only indication he'd heard the accusation lay in his defiant glare. Alexia couldn't decide if she should applaud him for courage, or berate him for looking so dispassionate while a blade raked at her jugular.

A finger of bone lifted to her cheek and trailed down to her neck, uncomfortably warm, spiraling a burning trail toward her heart.

"You deny you care for this *child*?" Amos asked.

A tremor ran through Kiren's cheek, his mouth set. Part of her wanted him to shout and kick and profess his undying love. Another part recognized how perilous that could prove.

The skull tapped his chin. "She would make a fine snack."

"So she would." He had not just compared her to a meal, had he? Kiren's eyebrow twitched, reminding her to re-hinge her mouth. "As you will never have the satisfaction of discovering that fact, what is it you want?"

"Tell the truth—for once," the creature hissed. "Admit it! Have it out for the world to see. It is the least you could do to prove your love for her."

The corners of Kiren's mouth twitched upward. "You accuse me of having emotions? I thought you knew better."

"Infantile! Do not toy with me!" A sharp nail jabbed the underlining of her jaw. She sucked in a breath, trying to ignore the stinging warmth and drip of her own blood.

Ethel growled from somewhere behind her.

The skull continued, "You are your father's son."

Kiren's brows lowered. He spoke slowly, voice low. "What do you want?"

"Your charm."

A smile quirked Kiren's cheek. "I am afraid there are some things that cannot be shared."

The skull snarled. She jolted. The chilly sword grazed her neck, stinging like ice across the skin. Alexia could not believe this was happening.

A flicker passed through Kiren's frozen tidal waves. "You want it?" He bowed his head. "Take it."

The skeleton reached for the chain. He stopped. "What are you playing at?" His attention flickered between Alexia and Kiren, the skin-tight smirk returning. "Then it is true."

"You have the upper hand," Kiren whispered. "You had best take advantage of the *moment.*"

Any second the others might appear, if they'd survived the attack. Alexia prayed they'd survived.

The leader motioned for another of the living corpses to step forward, a white headed boy, maybe ten when he'd begun to rot.

The youth caught hold of the chain. A tremor rattled through his small frame—the same reaction she had witnessed the first time Miles handled iron. The boy tugged, but the links didn't move. Kiren was a marble statue and the chain may as well have been chiseled from the same block.

The young man pulled harder. No change. Panic widened his crimson eyes. He yanked again. He placed a foot on Kiren's shoulder and wrenched backward.

Snap!

His arm popped out of its socket and rattled hollowly across the forest floor as he thumped onto his back. The palm lay open, facing her, the fingers scorched black.

Do not look at it. Do not look at it. She demanded her stomach to stop roiling and focused on Kiren. A playful grin twisted his scar.

"You mock us!" The skull sneered.

"Try it yourself."

The leader's lip quivered.

61

"We have been through this before." Kiren's cool censure sent a shiver through her bones. "You cannot have what you cannot handle."

"Take it off," the skull commanded.

"And how am I to do that?" He shook his pinned arms.

"You take it off!" He seized the weapon at Alexia's throat and pulled her forward.

Sparks of pain lanced through her head. Her pulse quickened, palms beginning to sweat.

Standing over him, she met Kiren's stare. His shoulders drooped, an apology locked in his overwhelming gaze.

Alexia slid her fingers over the chain. A buzz of energy tingled up her arm, but no pain like she had witnessed in the boy's countenance. She locked her fingers about the links and tugged. A spike of searing whiteness shot through her brain.

A silent scream rocketed up from her core and she blinked free of the maddening pain to find a searing arm wrapped around her waist, the only thing keeping her upright. Her fingers still gripped his necklace, but it hugged his neck, solid as stone.

Had he caused that? Or did it come from her injuries? She had to believe the latter. Kiren would never harm her.

She let go.

Kiren's eyes lifted to hers, regret dancing across the surface. He shook his head at the enemy, anger crinkling the corners of his mouth. "Try to reason this through your impossibly thick skull: it *cannot* be removed."

One of his captors pulled a shock of his hair, wrenching his head backward. Alexia tensed.

Kiren's jaw muscles bulged, but no cry of pain escaped.

Cold metal bit her skin, like a pinch. She sucked in a breath. A coppery tang mixed with the cloying scent of decay as wetness slithered down her throat. She froze, unwilling to move, not even to breathe.

"You would rather spill her blood than feast on her?" Kiren jerked forward and was yanked back.

Fire spread across her neck, deepening with every instant. Her eyes stung, tears pushing their way through. Perhaps she and Kiren would never be married after all. Perhaps all of this was just a dream, a wishful fantasy neither of them would be allowed to realize.

The blade sliced deeper. Swirling white flashed through her. She gasped.

Kiren's chest heaved, the veins in his neck bulging.

The skull chuckled. "Not much more and she will be beyond your skill."

She choked, unable to swallow. Panic buzzed through her brain as warm liquid spilled freely down her neck.

This was it. She really was going to die.

"You want it that badly, let her go!" Kiren ripped against his captors, throwing one to the ground. Two more crushed down on top of him, slamming his chin into the moss. "I will not give it to you when you could slit her throat!"

The words sounded distant, like she stood on her balcony listening to them carry up from the yard. Warmth drizzled down her front. Her cheeks were cold. The trees shook about her. She leaned completely on the body behind her, unable to locate her knees.

"Spare her," Kiren begged. "On my word, you shall have it!"

Time was ticking. She felt it in the slowing beat of her heart, the dimming clouds at the corners of her world. She took a shallow breath and the weapon penetrated deeper.

"I swear!"

Everything was shaking. Fire shot up and down her throat.

"Damage her further and I will hunt you, one by one. I will bring your enemies—!"

The forest faded to black, her ears stuffed full of cotton. She forced her eyes open.

Kiren stumbled to his feet. Darkness crashed over her, slamming into her like a four-horse carriage. The ground trembled. She was no longer on her feet.

Emptiness.

Eighteen

Deal with the Devil

"I will bring your enemies down so quickly you have no chance to contemplate the waiting hell!" Kiren shouted, trembling.

A raucous smile widened across the Soulless skeleton's face. "I believe we have an agreement."

"Swear it!" Kiren's muscles coiled. Alexia's face was draining from peachy to porcelain, the very life seeping through the slit in her neck. Red hazed at the corners of his vision.

"On my eternal soul, you shall have her, as she is." Amos turned to his lackeys. "Release him."

Kiren jerked free, adrenaline coursing through his system. He slid a fist around the chain he wore, the weight that had been his far too long. He fought to steady his shaking hands, to not tear the chain links free. He lifted the charm.

Cloaked creatures fell back.

"Careful now." The Soulless leader cringed, crimson pupils wide as he dug the blade into her neck.

Rage blinded Kiren. Power surged up through every nerve, shaking his frame. He stomped. The ground trembled. Trees shuddered and leaned away.

The Soulless shrank into the woods, all but Amos. He stood firm, blade half an inch from permanently severing Alexia's airway.

"You are going to lose her." The hiss sent chilling shockwaves through Kiren's veins.

Not much longer. She had seconds, seconds and he would be too late.

Kiren lifted the chain, pendant dangling.

Sickly fingers opened wide to receive it. Kiren seized the medallion in one hand and shoved it into the palm of the thief.

The creature shrieked. Wisps of smoke rose from charring bone in a sickly-sweet aroma.

"This does not belong to you, nor will it ever," Kiren spat. "I will be coming for it." He let go, snatching the sword in the same instant.

64

Wind whooshed into the grove—either Lester's arrival or Ethel's movement—but Kiren didn't have time to confirm which. Beings tumbled over one another, trying to escape. Alexia collapsed in his arms. He clasped the neck-wound, inhaling as the life pulsed from his body into hers...

Nineteen

Running

A choked breath penetrated the silence.

Fire!

Fire against her skin!

Magma encased her, consuming her flesh until nothing remained but the sparkles behind her eyes. She breathed.

The sparkles glimmered into butterflies that flitted up and down her arm. She wanted to bat them away so she could sleep. They became angry bugs, biting into her skin.

"Alexia?"

She opened her eyes. A blurry outline hung above her, silhouetted by a leafy awning and snatches of sky. She squinted against the light. An arm slipped around her back and neck, lifting her upper body.

His countenance solidified into a straight nose that flared erratically, high cheeks, a jagged white scar.

"Alexia."

That this angelic being spoke her name made her happy, and then she remembered he was hers.

She threw her arms around his neck and he enwrapped her. Her entire body hummed for joy. He squeezed too tightly. She tugged at his shoulder, and his lips pressed into the crook of her neck. Alexia sucked in a breath, startled by the sudden intimacy and sparks of desire launching through her.

Lester harrumphed. She blinked up at him, standing a few paces back, scowling. He kicked at the forest shrubbery, rubbing his neck. Ethel stood beside him, both her hands clasped tight together, brows high in worry.

Alexia's entire body heated. She pushed Kiren back, but he caught her face, cradling it, rubbing her blazing cheeks, eyes consuming her in the pressing waves. They choked out all but the heat of his flesh pressed to hers, and a deepening need so vast it made the ocean feel small.

She smiled at him in confusion. He pressed his mouth to hers, bruising her, parting her lips.

She gasped. This was no innocent thing, but a kiss meant only to happen behind closed doors. She wanted to stop him, too aware of their audience, but he delved deeper and suddenly she no longer cared. She wrapped herself around him, fingers gliding up into his hair. The tension eased out of his shoulders as he rounded into her, pressing her closer.

He pulled away. Bright red smears stained the ivory embroidery of his suit coat and frock.

Her fingers flew to her neck. She drew a hand down her neck and bodice, horrified by the sticky dampness on her fingers, her wedding dress ruined, her very life almost...

Alexia turned her head. She couldn't face him, not in light of what had just transpired. "The pendant..." she whispered through a raw throat.

He caught her cheeks, turning her to him.

She focused on his ruined shirt, searching with her fingers for the chain that should be hidden there. No metal links bulged beneath his soiled vest. She bit back a cry. "What have you done?"

Kiren traced Alexia's jaw, mouth stretched tight in a frown.

She grabbed his hand and turned it over, her own blood glistening across his palm. "This is my doing—"

He lifted her to her feet, his breath hot across her cheek, lips tight and angry. They parted, and she expected chastisement, but he closed them again. His eyes softened into a starry night sky so tender, she was afloat. "No worries, love. Everything will be set aright."

She was grateful for the words, but her heart swelled with guilt. It was only because of her he was in this position. If she had been strong enough to do something more than stop time...

And what of the others they'd abandoned? "Father. Where is Father?"

"Safe in Nelly's care," Lester growled.

"We are best on a quick offensive." Ethel's fingers writhed together. "They are only a few miles out."

"You have an army in yer pocket?" Lester's head shook. "We ain't so invincible as before. We should bring in Elizabeth North and Mi—"

"Agreed." Kiren lifted a hand. "And if Elizabeth proves stubborn, remind her that she owes me a life debt."

Lester saluted. "On my way."

"Ethel, you will assist Lester." Kiren met the woman's stare.

"Of course." She dipped in a shallow curtsy before swirling into a cyclone of mist and disappearing.

Alexia took a deep breath, raking at the rawness of her airway. "This is because of me. I will help you retrieve the medallion, no matter the cost."

He crossed his arms.

She grabbed his shoulders. "I will not be your weakness. Do you understand me?" She shook him. "Either you will utilize my strengths, or—" Or what? She was far too weak to be of help to anyone. It would be best if she had never come into his life, never unmasked this vulnerability. She hated what had happened to him—to all of the Passionate—because she had been vain enough, foolish enough to embrace these desires. Had he ever been so vulnerable before his enemies? Had the Passionate ever been so defenseless before the Soulless? She squared herself. "Or I shall banish myself from you."

He looked away. "We have much ground to cover."

"Kiren."

He took both her hands and leaned down so their eyes were level, his burning. "You are to be my wife. Do you understand that?"

Her heart sped. His wife. She would belong to him, and solely him.

"No wishing, no silly thoughts of separation are going to change that—nor do I wish it so. You are the only thing I cannot lose, and the one thing they *will* target." He bit his lip. "Already I have failed you."

She shook her head, reaching for his cheek.

He drew a handkerchief from his pocket and wiped it across her neck. "It seems I condemn everything I care about."

"Kiren, stop." She grabbed his wrist. He met her gaze, his eyes startlingly vulnerable. "I will be your wife." She smiled with all the joy she had experienced but an hour ago.

Crashing pulled her around. Kiren's silvery stallion darted between trees, Edward low on its back.

Alexia laid her head against Kiren's shoulder. "You have not failed me. You saved my life, and I am only sorry I could not be strong when you needed me to be."

His arms wrapped around her, lips tickling her ear.

The horse skidded to a halt, tearing moss, prancing back a step and throwing its ivory mane. Edward dropped out of the saddle and handed the reins over. Kiren retrieved her sword, the very blade still stained in her blood, and aided Alexia onto the beast. He nodded a farewell to Edward, and mounted behind Alexia.

Twenty

Success

Amos pulled back the canvas and shivered. Energy pulsed off the metal, stinging his chin like the icy rays of a polar sun. He squinted, eyes watering. Even dimmed as they were by the ages, the power burned.

Hissing voices echoed through the cave, reminding him of those waiting. Nervous chatter.

Carefully, he rewrapped the prize, binding it shut with twine. Its buzz carried through the heavy canvas and rattled into his frame. Even with the stability of his many centuries, the bones of his fingers clicked while pulling at the string.

How many hundred years had they sought this prize? He'd succeeded. He was the only one who could claim victory, even if he had to admit the aid of a Passionate traitor, the child who had directed him to their point of ambush, the girl who strangely did not fear him.

He carefully laid the treasure atop two similar wrappings inside a satchel, decoys. Four other bags sat by, filled and ready with similar counterfeits. They would detain the factions of the Passionate, leading the groups in a wild chase. He hated to let this precious prize out of his control, but it was the only way to ensure its safety.

"Come now!" he called.

Five trusted allies entered the space, blacking out the light of day. He gazed into the decaying face of one then another, recalling the many years he had fought, scrounged and survived alongside each of them.

"You each know your task."

They nodded.

"Make your deliveries, and then we must deaden your minds so no one will perceive our plan at the sun's setting." That magic moment when their minds would unify, when their kind would be integrated in a cumulative hunger.

His lackeys stiffened. The youngest shifted from foot to foot, focused on the ground.

Amos lifted an amber vial. Its contents caught the sun and warmed like the nectar of the gods. "People *will* come after you. Upon delivery, drink this immediately."

Joseph stepped forward, skeletal hand extended, two finger tips missing where the ligaments had completely decayed. He had been but twenty and three, the young father of three beautiful girls when he'd been taken by the Soulless in rural France. Now, nearly five-hundred years later, he was the only one Amos truly trusted.

And Kingdom knew that.

Or at least, they would.

Amos repressed a grin as he handed over the poison, the strongest dose, to his friend. Four decoys to draw off the other factions and Soulless, one to lure Kingdom. He issued a satchel to each and dismissed them, all but Joseph. He grabbed his friend's arm as the others left the cave. "Yours is the one," he hissed.

Crimson pupils widened. Joseph's mouth cracked wide, head shaking.

Amos smirked. "Fly like a raven, my friend."

He watched the five disappear through the trees, each a different direction. A chill washed over his skin, the dense moisture of a traveling cloud.

"You are ready to play your part?" he asked.

The girl materialized next to him. "Are you?" Her soprano sent the hairs on his neck standing.

He nodded.

Her lips twisted up in a sneer-grin so wicked it ought to belong to Lucifer himself.

Twenty-One

The Future

Alexia had no idea how many miles passed below them, and she didn't care. She had Kiren. Somehow they would get through this.

The sun neared the horizon as they pulled to a halt, a mocking orb that reminded her of the ring circling her finger, the promise of eternity that neither of them had yet made.

So close. They had been so close!

A lighted inn waited before them, a splintering porch and square door with dual windows above it. Bays protruded from the upper floor and two large chimneys stood from a nearly domed roof.

Kiren slid from the horse and pulled a cloak from the saddlebag, tucking it about her. He took her hands and steadied her as she met the ground, legs shaky.

"Are you all right?"

She gazed into his startling eyes, lit by the warmth of an ending day—proof that even the worst days must eventually come to a close. "I am with you, am I not?"

He laughed. "Let us find you something to eat."

She loved that he was practical, that he could laugh, even in the face of so great a loss.

A simple room greeted them, four crude tables lining the back wall near the hearth. A young woman knitted next to the fire as the dog at her feet panted. The animal looked up and gave a curious whine.

The woman turned.

"Oh, oh my! I did not hear you there." She rose, setting her knitting aside. Brown strands of hair escaped her careful bun. Her round face might have been described as pretty, except for one drooping eyelid. "Come in then. What can we do you for?"

"Food please." He urged Alexia forward—something about his voice bothering her. "And a bed."

The woman's lip quirked up, spreading in a brilliant smile, crystal-blue eyes fixed absently and distant. "Who have you brought me then?"

Kiren cleared his throat. "Mae, allow me to introduce Dana's child."

A hand fluttered to the woman's pleated frock. Mae's head turned his direction, stare lost on his knees. She reached out, fingers panning the air. Kiren took her hand and guided it to Alexia's arm.

"Welcome. I have waited a long time for you, Alexia." The warmth of Mae's fingers seeped through her skin. Alexia turned a questioning frown on Kiren. Had this woman known her mother? Worked with her? Been told about the future?

Mae's nose flared. "But why do I smell blood?"

Kiren cupped Alexia's shoulder. "She will need a change of clothes, a bath, and a washboard."

The woman squeezed Alexia's arm, pulling her face to face. "What has he put you through?"

Staring into her blank gaze, Alexia found it difficult to resurrect her voice. "I am well."

Mae's frown relaxed. "Come. Have a seat. Allow someone less foolhardy to take proper care of you."

"Mae." Kiren crossed his arms.

She lifted a finger. "You have a horse out front to stable."

Alexia admired her hostess's handling of Kiren, but did not feel he deserved so blatant a rebuke. The woman pushed her into a spindle-legged chair and swept through a doorway on the far side of the room.

Kiren chuckled and pressed a kiss to her forehead. "You could not be in better hands."

"Unless they were yours."

He tipped her chin toward him. She squinted. The glow had leached from his skin. His scar stood out jaggedly down his cheek, a white zag against sun-kissed skin. He was abnormally insignificant—for him, almost...normal.

"Trust that I know what I am doing," he whispered. Even his voice held less...what?

"Placing me in the care of the blind?" she challenged.

A smile quirked his none-too-brilliant cheek, and he exited.

Strange. Maybe exhaustion had finally gotten the best of him.

Something wet touched her hand. She glanced down. She'd been so absorbed in thought, she hadn't noticed the dog pad over, or the way he sat panting.

"Hello, pup."

He gave a short yelp.

She patted his head, and as she did, Alexia fixated on the ring stationed over her left finger. It refracted light across the ceiling and walls.

Married.

One day.

Even after she matured into a beauty, the secret belief remained in her heart that she would forever be alone. She was so far from anything and everything she'd ever known. Her family. Her friends. Her home.

The animal growled. His hackles stood on end, nose pointed toward the exit.

The door creaked inward.

She turned.

Long dark locks spilled over a thin set of shoulders, face hidden in a black hood. Raven skirts swirled, ghostly-quiet across the floor, and pale skin caught the light against elegant long fingers, nails pearly white and curved.

She halted three paces in front of Alexia and the hood fell back. Olive eyes sparkled in the firelight, pupils a blazing red.

Sarah smiled.

Alexia screamed.

Twenty-Two

Recruits

Miles shivered and stiffened. The chill across his skin was one with which he'd grown all too familiar, one that meant he was being followed by a child of the mist. He hated it when they were in the mist. Impossible to get a solid read.

The brick alley shrank about him. If the Breeders had come for him, all they had to do was block off each outlet. He couldn't be this careless again. He should be out in the country, leading the Breeders and Soulless away from humanity, not placing the innocent in imminent danger. Still, he liked the salt air of the seaport, and finding work (the kind that kept his belly full and where his disappearance would make little difference) proved much easier in this Boston populace.

He reached out mentally, scanning the emotions surrounding him.

Worry sank into his gut like curdled milk, the fear of being unable to feed seven hungry mouths. He pulled away and fury drilled through his chest— outrage at the monarch's mandates on trade, his relegation of authority through hired bayonets, and the imbalance of justice afforded all citizens of the New World.

Miles shrank back into himself.

A shadow dropped across him, blocking the morning light at the end of the alley. He half turned, muscles taut and ready to run. He leapt forward mentally and hit a brick wall. Ricocheting back, he squared his shoulders for a fight.

"Bawdy langler! Put those punchers away. I ain't come to brawl."

Emotion squeezed its fist around his throat. "Lester?"

"Aye, laddy."

Miles's knees trembled. He wanted to run to the familiar face and cling like a needy child. Just hearing the man's voice was like coming home. But... "You should not be here."

The elderly man stepped into the alley, his familiar outline framed by sunshine. "The more apt response would be, why the shinny daylights are you here?"

Joy lifted Miles's cheeks. Count on Lester to strike at the heart of the matter—but he was right. If he was here, something had gone terribly wrong—or Miles was in immediate danger. He'd spent all last night forcing himself to see through the eyes of a fox family and he didn't think he'd let anything important escape through the link, but Lester's presence suggested otherwise.

"Tell me," Miles demanded.

Lester extended a hand. "We'll chat on the way."

Another shadow loomed in the alley opening. Miles shaded his eyes and gasped.

Ethel.

It was Christmas morning! His heart squeezed. He'd been able to survive this banishment by convincing himself he was on an extended observation assignment—albeit without the regular deliveries of meals or apple puffs—but the truth was far too devastating. He never thought he'd see his dear family again.

"How did you find me?" he asked.

Ethel's head tilted. "We never lost you, Miles dear."

He choked. "You were watching over me?"

Her smile answered.

How many times had he felt the brush of living wind? How many nights had he dismissed the awareness as his own wishful thinking, and how foolish he had been! If he'd just cried out, she might have appeared.

But she might not have. The Master had surely given orders not to make her presence known, but Miles knew how the man worked. He never left the safety of the Passionate to chance.

His lungs seized. The Master. Was he truly going to see his mentor and best friend once more?

Anxiously, he latched onto Ethel's hand. He was going home.

Twenty-Three

Dreams

"Alexia!"

Her eyes flew open. The world leapt in an erratic blur of color and motion. Lips pressed at her ear, arms clutched tightly about her, crushing her to a solid torso as the horse bolted beneath them. The reigns cut into Kiren's forearm where they looped, the beast slowing grudgingly to a canter, calming even less enthusiastically to a walk.

"Alexia, what is it?"

Kiren's brilliance robbed her of voice, his wild eyes eclipsing the blue of the sky. She inhaled his oaky musk and relaxed into him, clutching his sleeve. The stink of blood cut into her nose, and she turned her head away, not wishing to remember how close she'd come to death but a short time ago.

The open road waited, barred only by forests on the far horizon behind, and open rolling fields ahead. The sun hung at the apex of the sky.

He squeezed her. "You were dreaming."

She met his stare, intense concern in his azure depths.

"Sarah..." She trembled, recalling the crimson in her aunt's eyes.

He touched her cheek, his fingers a fire against her clammy skin.

She willed the terror to dissipate, wishing to forget as she leaned against his solid form. He stroked her hair, easing a sob out of her.

Sarah had been so real, so solid, alive—even trapped in the nightmare of her existence. Alexia's heart twisted, her lungs too tight, her whole world shards of shattered glass. Her sister was alive! But the hunger in her stare...

She cried, soaking his handkerchief and jacket, unable to stop.

"Was this a prophetic dream?" Kiren's chest rumbled with his words.

She smashed the heels of her palms into her eyes, trying to crush away the tears. "Is she truly dead? Entirely? She must remember me."

He stroked her arm. "I have not been to the other side, but the most dangerous part of this situation is that she will retain her memories." He turned her face up to his. "She may yearn to be reunited as deeply as you."

"I do not..."

He sighed. "I have lost friends, Alexia. They look on me as though nothing has changed, and if I allowed myself to believe that, I would be one of them."

Of course. He was right.

She exhaled.

But Sarah lived! Seeing her aunt had torn a gaping chasm in her soul, a hollowness not even Kiren could fill. She forced herself to breathe around it, kept it from entirely deflating her only by gripping the protective arm looped about her.

"Tell me—" Anything—anything to keep her from thinking, from the pain. "—about your childhood?"

He straightened. She twisted and reached for his cheek. His brows pulled together, accompanied by a slight pucker and downward curve of his lips. She hated that the request troubled him.

He glanced away. "There is not much to tell."

"Please?"

Kiren sighed, the lines smoothing from his forehead. "It ended sooner than most." The weight in his voice pulled her down with him, like irons shackled both arms and they'd been plunged into the sea.

She squeezed his leg and he came back with a smile, quickly looking away.

"I recall the forest, trees not so aged and a little brook where we caught frogs." He looped the tethers about her middle and tied them in a loose bow. She crossed her arms, and he tightened the knot beneath her elbows, with a quick peck on her forehead.

Her giggle escaped.

"Father taught me to use a sling. We practiced by targeting fruit we would take home for supper." He huffed and leaned back, fingers curling around the back of the saddle. "I used the skill to terrify a herd of cattle into a wild stampede and nearly destroyed our neighboring village."

Alexia twisted as far as the reins would allow and placed a hand on his thigh. "It could not have been so terrible."

The corners of his eyes squeezed, lips drawn in a frown. "But it was." He raked his fingers through his hair. "It seems no matter what he taught me, I always used it to get into trouble—not terrible mischief, but enough to cause my parents discomfort or misfortune." His brows lowered, gaze dropping to the ground. "You would expect he might stop teaching me so many dangerous truths. Not him. He wanted me to know everything, to experiment, to truly see the world in all its splendor."

She touched his hand. "He sounds wonderful."

With a nod, he closed his eyes. A sweet little smile pierced one cheek. "I remember the window above my bed bent triangles of light across the ceiling, and I imagined the shards a tangible defense against the night. If I could clasp one and tuck it under my pillow, monsters would run in fear."

She laughed.

He grinned with her. "I recall the book Mother read every evening—at my request, the tale of two brothers, one good, one bad. One would live until the end of time, the other would walk the earth as a ghost, haunting him for his murder."

"What a horrible tale!"

He cheeks dimpled with mischief. "But you must understand, she wished us to realize the importance of our decisions. She probably hoped it would persuade me to behave."

"Us?"

He cleared his throat, eyes squeezing with pain.

She caught his hand and cradled it between both of hers. "You will show me the memory, one day?"

"Yes." His brows lowered. He slipped from the horse's back and took the steed's bridle, walking alongside. "Occasionally, we took trips to the palace, a palace so magnificent I cannot find the words to describe it. You have never seen anything like it."

"Like the one in your mind?"

He blinked back at her.

"The crystal walls and seven towers?" She nearly burst into laughter at his shock. "They were glorious!"

His face lit, but it faded. "Yes, they were." His neck bowed. "While Father took care of his business, I explored the uppermost turrets, looking out over the entire island—"

"You were allowed inside?"

He shot her a smirk. "If you will recall what I said about mischief?"

Alexia reached out for his hand. He took hers, beaming back at her. Warmth flooded through the connection, the warmth of goodness inundating his soul.

"Let us just say, I saw more of that castle than the king himself."

She giggled. "And who was this king?"

His smiled dropped, face turned to stone. The darkness startled her. "He is long dead. Why should it matter?"

"What happened?"

He pulled away. She reached for him and he stepped clear of the horse. She waited for him to resume, to lighten and come back, but the droop of his shoulders weighed far more than even she could lift.

How many loved ones had he lost? Friends? Family? She truly knew so little about him, and he understood everything about her. One day. One day he would let her in, allow her to love away the grief in his heart.

This was not that day.

And he was not the only one aching.

She glanced up at the sun hanging in the west. The botched wedding had taken place near noon, and the day had passed on the road, some of it sleeping, some of it galloping. Only an hour remained before sunset, one hour before her dream came to fruition. She would see Sarah.

Kiren stepped off the road, pulling the horse behind and caught hold of a tree branch. A half formed apple plumped into a ripe, bursting fruit. He plucked it and lifted it to her. "I am afraid I do not make a very considerate kidnapper. I ought to take better care of you."

Wrapping her fingers over his, she pulled him closer. "You have not had much opportunity."

His smile froze. She sensed the need in his quietude, his touch against hers, the way their pulses matched, the heat crawling through her soul...

He let go. "Eat, dearest."

She lifted the fruit, and froze. "Would you like some? I can only imagine you are equally starved."

His head shook.

She chewed, thinking back to this morning. She had seen him take no nourishment—not a drink, not a bite of food, but he could have eaten while Nelly and Ethel dressed her.

"Kiren, if you are fasting out of consideration for me—"

He laughed. "Dearest Alexia, this may be a foreign concept, but I do not eat anything I have aided to grow."

"Why not?"

He gave her a squinty-eyed look. "The way I generate growth is by lending my own energy or life-force to a living thing. It is a gift, and I cannot reclaim the strength. I am not hungry."

"Not even a little?"

He shook his head.

"What you are telling me, is that in effect, I am eating a piece of you?"

His face screwed up into a mixture of agitation and humor. "The cells were dormant in the fruit's core—they all belong to the organism, but the energy I supplied enabled its quickening. I gave it the push."

She sat back. "I do not understand how you cannot be hungry."

He shrugged. "I suppose it is part of my...talent. I naturally regenerate, making my energy requirements a minimum. I do not take more than I need."

"Which is?"

"One meal a day? I often go as long as three between dining."

She stared, bewildered. "Three days?"

He shrugged. "Once as many as seven."

"Without issue?"

Kiren scratched his head. "I was quite fatigued, but that is because I had not slept."

"Tell me about this sleeping thing. You seem to do it so rarely."

He laughed. "That scares you?"

"Tell me."

He laughed harder. "I sleep when it is needed, a few hours here, a few hours there, but like food, I do not typically require much, unless I have employed my skills."

She gulped. "And then you act normally?"

"What is normal but a perception?" He glanced at her quizzically. "What you are accustomed to by way of living is completely different than, say, Ethel's way of life."

Her fists balled and she tucked them into her lap. "That is because she is married."

"Alexia—"

"Well it is."

He gave her a frown. The silence between them widened. The sun dipped lower.

Kiren's shoulders heaved. "Is that what you want of me? To find the next church and bribe the clergy to marry us like a couple of vagabonds?"

She blinked, slapped by the animosity in his tone. "Yes."

His brow rose. "With no record of your marriage having taken place? No family, friends or loved ones to share in the occasion? You would have me treat you no better than a common barmaid?"

She bit her lip.

He crossed his arms. "These things only happen once, and I am determined *my* bride will have every privilege her heart desires. There will be no dread of being overtaken, no rush to make a hasty attachment."

She backed down from the warning in his eyes.

Kiren exhaled loudly and slid a hand across hers. He met her gaze, his lighted by the late sun. "It is all I can do not to run away with you. Even now— now when they are expecting me to join them, to lead them—it is all I want."

Had a more romantic suggestion ever escaped his tongue? She wanted it. She wanted that adventure, that excitement, that freedom.

He groaned. "And then I think of those who serve with the belief I would sacrifice everything for them." Both hands combed through his hair. "Why can we not live in a world free of warfare? One where I could convince your father to surrender your hand by proper means of etiquette? One where you do not have to give up your home and dreams for me?"

"I have not given up my dreams for you." She placed both hands on her hips. "You are my dream."

He laughed. "More like a nightmare. Now are you ready to tell me about yours?"

Alexia glanced at the sun, nearly touching the horizon, at the building coming up on the skyline. "I...I saw Sarah."

"I discerned as much."

"It was just a dream."

He stopped the horse. Taking her hands, he met her eyes. "Tell me."

He was hiding much from her, and perhaps he dreaded a stronger connection between them for fear she would discover his mysteries. She deserved her own secrets, didn't she? She deserved to see Sarah again.

"There is nothing to..." The inn hung in her periphery, a testament to her lie.

He looked, then back to her. "She is there?"

She bit her lip. Miles had once warned her about trusting too easily. Kiren himself had warned her against laying herself entirely at his mercy. This once she would use her own discretion.

She would face Sarah.

Alone.

He volleyed into the saddle behind her. The reins snapped and wind howled past her ears. He crushed her to him, the rhythmic knock of his heart heightening her own. The sun dipped toward the horizon.

The exactness of her vision stole her breath—the rickety porch and added gazebo off to the east, the scythe and cracked wide stump out front, the square door with two small glass panels above it, the framing widows to either side and bays protruding from the upper floor, the two very large chimneys and slatted-wood roof that nearly domed rather than slanting... Mae would be inside, knitting a brown scarf to match her apron and the dog at her feet would be panting quietly.

Kiren pulled to a halt. Her chest ached from the hammering within as he slid from the horse, and she couldn't decide if he was pretending at a sudden calm to ease her nerves.

"Come now, Alexia." He took her hands, steadying her when she met the ground, legs trembling. "Are you all right?"

She looked at him in horror, his words the very tone of her nightmare.

He slipped a cloak about her shoulders. "Let us find you something to eat, shall we?"

The door creaked open. Mae's needles clicked rhythmically and the dog on the floor lifted his head. Flickers of light romped across the room from the fire, elongating the distance with ominous shadows.

Kiren guided her in. Instant gloom—an absence of warmth she'd never known—filled her lungs. She turned to him.

The healthy glow of his skin had paled and tired lines hung under his eyes. His grip felt less stalwart. His hair held less body, his lip cracked from dehydration, but his eyes—they remained true.

"Wh-where are we?" she whispered.

"Scorched earth." He smiled. "Here all beauty, all strength, all extremes of emotion or hunger are diminished." His eyes touched hers. Something more hid in the strain of his tenor.

She grabbed his arm. "The Soulless are powerless here?"

His smile soured. "And they are not the only ones."

Her fingers bit into him. "You are saying I cannot halt time here?"

Severe sapphire flashed at her. "Trying could kill you."

And by extension, him. She shuddered. "How did you find this place?"

He waved at the room. "We built it."

The structure was an echo of his home in Wilhamshire, the elegant use of windows to produce an airy feel, lighter woods, and a hearth at the heart of the building which must warm the entire place. Above, a balcony curled around the great room, a narrow staircase along one wall leading upward.

Mae's gingerbread bun bobbed and she turned. "Have you finished in the doorway, or shall I ignore your presence longer?"

Her needles had long since ceased to move, scarf set aside. Brown wisps framed her smiling cheeks, eyes blankly fixed their direction, one lid nearly closed.

Kiren squeezed Alexia's shoulder. "Mae, you are looking well."

Her grin widened, crystal-blue eyes crinkling at the corners. "Who have you brought me then?"

Kiren cleared his throat. "May I introduce Dana's child."

She reached for the chair arm and missed. Catching it the second time, she pushed up and tottered forward, arm extended. Kiren took her hand and guided it to Alexia's.

Mae's warmth thawed through her skin. "Welcome. I have waited long for you, Alexia."

"For me?" She turned a questioning brow on Kiren. Had he intended to bring her here all along?

Mae's nose flared. "But I smell blood?"

Kiren exhaled. "She will need a change of clothes, a bath, and a washboard. Oh yes, and a meal. What would you have me do to help?"

Their hostess waved a hand. "You are exhausted from the ride." His mouth opened and she lifted a finger, silencing him. "I can always detect the exhaustion in your voice, and if you do not relent, I will tell her what else I hear."

His nose twitched.

"What else do you hear?" Alexia asked.

The woman squeezed her arm, drawing her face to face. "What has he put you through?"

"It was not him."

Mae's frown relaxed. "Come. Have a seat. Allow someone less foolhardy to take proper care of you."

"Mae." Kiren crossed his arms.

She pointed that finger at him again. "You have a horse to stable."

Alexia couldn't help her grin, adoring Mae already. The woman pushed her into a chair and swept through a doorway.

Kiren's chuckle lightened her heart further. He placed a kiss to her forehead. "You could not be in better hands."

"I could be in yours."

He tipped her chin toward him, his white scar standing out starkly against tanned skin. Alexia followed each zag. Had he obtained this cut while saving someone's life or while battling for his own? She ached to know.

"I will only be a moment." He rubbed a thumb down her jaw. "You cannot be harmed here."

"They know you do not have your pendant, or they will soon." She glanced to the dimming daylight through the windows.

His head shook. "You are safe on scorched earth." He straightened, rising. With a glance back from the exit, he winked and slipped from view.

Something wet raked her hand. The dog sat panting at her feet.

"And what are you? Some kind of guard hound bred by our kind?"

His head tilted.

She patted him, the mutt was as benign as in her dream. Her gaze landed on the ring stationed over her left finger. It glittered marvelously in the room, scattering twinkles over the furniture.

She inhaled. Why had she let him go? Any instant Sarah would appear. Somehow she would slip by him.

The dog growled, nose aimed toward the exit.

The door moved.

Alexia pressed back into her seat, gripping the wood, wishing for the strength to slow the minutes.

Long dark curls spilled over the proud set of shoulders so well known to her, face obscured by a hood. Flowing black skirts dusted across the floor, pale hands illuminated by the fire. A chill followed her in, and a paralyzing silence.

"Sarah," Alexia breathed.

The cloaked woman halted in the middle of the room.

Her hood fell back. Olive eyes sparkled in the firelight, unadulterated surprise the only emotion in her blazing red pupils.

Twenty-Four

Bread Crumbs

How Lester did it, Miles would never know.

He nodded to the old man in the crimson light. With the elder's speed and bizarre foresight, they had discovered the cave far faster than he'd thought possible. His palms were damp from the anticipation of entering the Soulless consciousness. He'd had glimpses: the call of people claiming to be his parents, the recognition of a hundred hive-mind creatures who mimicked that fondness for him and lusted after both his health and his reunion with them...

Miles shook the thoughts away. Tracks scattered dirt in front of the cave entrance, eleven sizes and weights, all aimed in different directions.

Lester stepped into each scuffle pattern of steps, gauging height and speed from the lengths—something Miles only knew because the elder had educated him.

He liked the runner, how easily he kept everyone out of his head. There were so few people who could. It was a relief to not be overwhelmed by his companion's thoughts and emotions. Even though he'd developed a means to block out most distractions, there were just some instances where he got sucked in.

Like Alexia.

"These be the ones what were carryin' more than their own hides." The old man traced five separate paths with the stick clasped in his hand. Glancing at the sky, he grunted.

Miles leaned back, crossing his arms. "You mean to run them all down and figure out which one has the medallion?"

Lester grinned a toothy grin and tapped his head, then pointed at Miles. "You'll be the one what does the askin'."

He groaned, trying to ignore the chill of mist across his skin, the living kind that whispered in his head as it passed. He expected Ethel's thoughts, but suppressed rage smacked him like a tidal wave.

"Lester—"

The old man lifted a hand in a shushing gesture. He crouched forward and stepped gingerly into the darkness of the cave. Miles glanced warily at the sky before following. He didn't like this.

A desperate hiss refracted off cave walls, startling him. How had he not heard it before? He squinted into the pitch, then closed his eyes. Reaching out mentally, he stepped in and sent his mind spinning toward any consciousness present.

A bug. The cave wall beneath him clung to his six feet. Large shadows blotted out the light. He tasted the air with his antenna, scenting sweat and anticipation.

Miles abandoned the crawler and skimmed further.

No light. Agony! Acid slithered through her veins, tearing at her inner organs. Every muscle tensed, frozen in blazing pain. She was going to burst!

Ripping himself from the sufferer's mind, he landed on his knees, gasping.

Lester gripped his arm. "What is it?"

Miles stumbled to his feet. "Hurry."

They groped into the darkness, halting when raspy breaths filled their ears. Miles hesitated and reached out mentally, brushing just over the edge of her misery. He staggered under her agony, grabbing her around the waist and lifting the girl off the cave floor. He sped toward the cave exit and remaining day.

Sunset caught her hair, painting it pink. Her fingers grappled inwardly, crooked and tense. Glittering metal ringed her wrists—a thin gold chain.

He set her on the ground outside the cave, and her knees crumpled. He caught her and laid her down. Wrapping the edge of his sleeve over his fingers, he tore the links free. They bounced in all directions, refracting sunlight as they spun away.

Bellezza's little body collapsed, panting, eyes drooping.

Why hadn't he felt her sooner? That kind of desperation should have smacked him over the head and dragged him into the darkness. But she had a way about her, a hush, all of her pain coiled so tightly inside.

It was swimming around him, swimming through hazy images of night skies, screaming, running, the bitterness of desperation, despair...

Blinking his vision straight, he startled at the sweat doused curls beneath his fingers as he finished smoothing them back from her face. Had she heard him through her misery and somehow mustered enough strength to call upon even a fraction of her gift?

Her eyes fluttered open, the chocolate swirls so innocent and vulnerable. He wanted to ask if she was all right, but the question would anger her. She wanted pity from no one.

With a smirk, he nodded.

Her lip twitched.

Curling his fingers into her hair, he delved into her mind.

Little sparkles glittered on the outskirts of her consciousness, quickly snuffed out. Blackness bubbled up, obscuring everything in inky rage. A grinning skull emerged from the pitch, scarlet beads for eyes. Bellezza laughed inwardly as she imagined gouging out each eye with an iron dagger and then tearing his smiling head clean off. And she would.

As soon as she could lift her arms.

A deep chuckle startled her. A luscious sound. She forced her eyes open and stared into gray eyes, instantly aware of his touch at the back of her head.

Bellezza jerked free.

Miles jumped out of her head.

"Stay out," she mouthed.

He nodded and rose.

Lester uncrossed his arms and approached. "And?"

"The Soulless," Miles muttered.

The old man waved for him to continue.

Miles turned. "Bellezza?"

She rolled her eyes. "They were lucky enough to capture me," her whisper was hoarse, tremors shaking through her thin frame. "They found out about the wedding. Attacked. Left me to die."

Lester grunted, disbelief clear from his shaking head. "Here's what I think happened. You made an accord with them what exacts yer whims, and they turned on you."

She bit down, nose crinkling. Her rage permeated through Miles like a dense, overly-sweet smoke.

"Kin you tell us anything more?"

She rested on her side, quiet. Miles was ready to dive back in when she spat, "The one they call Joseph—he had the weapon."

Miles knelt next to her. "Which direction did he travel?"

She pulled in a long breath, her chest rising. "Oxford."

He met stares with Lester. The old man nodded. "We'll go after we retrieve the Master."

The Master. Miles pulled a hand through his hair. "What about her?"

Lester's head shook, voice lowering. "Ripe lot of lies. Coddle her and she'll bite yer hand off." And Lester would know.

Miles sighed.

"Ye'd be best t' put her back where you found her, gold 'n' all."

Miles knew the two had some history, but he'd never heard the old man so insensitive with anyone. "You can't be serious."

"We haven't the time or manpower to punish her proper. Set that chain 'bout her and I'll send Ethel to fetch the wily nixie."

Twenty-Five

Soulless

"Alexia?" Sarah covered her mouth.

Alexia clung to the table. Her aunt's voice, like the flow of honey over glass paper, had not changed. The relief-joy-terror in her aunt's single pronouncement summoned her like the siren call of fresh baked bread. Moisture pooled in Alexia's eyes, but she could not move under the power of that crimson stare. She remembered a night—had it only been a month ago?—when similar eyes encircled her with promises of love and fulfillment, their appetites bubbling below the surface.

Alexia's cheeks were wet. "You are alive."

"*You* are alive!"

"Of course I am alive." Alexia blinked, confused.

Sarah deflated to her knees, knuckles white against her clamped fists. "You are injured?"

Alexia glanced down at the stains, now almost black in the firelight. "I am not harmed."

Sarah covered her nose with the corner of her cloak, looking away. "How did you find me?"

The pressure holding Alexia immobile vanished, hairs on her arms standing at full length. "I found *you*?"

Crimson pupils turned back on her. Alexia's heart halted, then resumed with a tremor.

"Did you not?" Sarah asked, her brows puckered.

Alexia hesitated. Her aunt belonged to the opposing force. Even now she could see the restraint in Sarah's every effort, and anything Alexia said would be used against her once the her aunt joined with the collective consciousness of the Soulless.

She bit down. "John did this to you."

Sarah's head shook. "I did this to me."

87

Her aunt had had no comprehension, no warning about the persuasive powers of the Soulless previous to her association. It could have been prevented, all of it!

"*John* will pay." Alexia couldn't hide the loathing his name inspired.

"No, Alexia, he is my—"

"Husband. I know."

Sarah nodded. "And he is good to me. He did not want this, but circumstances—" Her eyes darkened and Alexia could almost hear her unuttered curse against Bellezza. "—determined otherwise."

"*Is* good to you? You call *this* good?" She motioned to her near-sister's tensed frame.

That scarlet gaze paralyzed Alexia, but not in fury. In empathy?

"Oh, Alexia. John said they would hunt you, that they would kill you, that I..." Her head bowed in shame.

"Where is John?"

"Not here."

"Then where?"

"Searching for you."

Alexia swallowed. "Why would he be searching for me?"

Sarah slid the tiniest bit closer. A tremor rattled through Alexia. "He wants you safe," her aunt whispered.

"No, he wants me dead."

Sarah's locks shook. "He fights too. Lexy, he has told me things... I do not know how much I believe, but there is more to this than simply a war between the Soulless and Passionate. There are factions, there are plots and schemes and"—her eyes grew wide—"so many of them circle about you."

Cold air threatened to close off her passageways. "Because I will one day marry the leader of the Passionate?"

Sarah blinked and clasped her hands together as though she wished to congratulate her niece. Her face fell, head bowing. "Because you can...can change time."

The intensity in Sarah's stare communicated a wish she didn't appear bold enough to state, and yet to watch her near-sister hesitate took Alexia off balance. Thank goodness for the solid seat beneath her. Her aunt wanted her to fix things, to go back, to stop it from happening. Oh that she could! "I cannot *change* the past."

Sarah's eyes closed. "John said you could. That is what they believe—the others, the Soulless who rule m-my kind."

Alexia leaned closer. "There are rulers?"

"Groups, Lexy. Factions. Some are good, some are bad. They are all looking for solutions, or power, or ways to fulfill their...lusts." Her focus remained fixed on the floor. "The strongest hierarchy has hired mercenaries and promised favors and power to any who can bring you to them."

"Because they think I can change time?" she suggested incredulously.

"Perhaps. Maybe that is simply what they wish us to believe. They may only wish for you as leverage over"—she scowled—"*Arik.*"

Alexia frowned. The alias was one Kiren had allowed Sarah to use for him, and her aunt had adored him, even expressed hopes of marriage.

"It is not his name," Sarah spat. "It is simply one he gives to persons like me."

Alexia twisted her fingers over her skirt.

"You are not surprised?" Sarah's lip drew upward.

Alexia sat back. Her aunt moved forward in the same instant. Alexia nearly fell out of her chair.

"Do not!" Sarah squealed and grabbed at her ears, face squeezed in intense concentration. "Do not pull away. Do not run from me! I will give chase, whether I wish to or not. I cannot stave the instinct!"

Alexia froze.

Her aunt retreated a couple steps, hissing as she went. A strange rattling echoed through the chamber. Sarah's crimson stare burrowed into Alexia. "He is not who he says he is, and I am not convinced he is entirely good." A rasp filled her tone with fire.

Did this come as a result of her Soulless state or true wrath? "I love him, Sarah."

"Please, Alexia, nothing is quite what it seems!" She closed the distance.

Alexia held still—terrified to run and draw her aunt after. Uncomfortably warm fingers seized her shoulders, severe pupils consuming the whole of her attention. "He took your memories. He took mine. He has deceived us both, and how many others, I cannot say." Sarah's grip tightened. "Trust only yourself. Be so careful!"

A wild shudder ran through them both. The fire dimmed. Sarah pulled away, backing out the doorway, fierce belief in her terrified expression. She whirled and escaped.

The room warmed. Flames leapt to life.

The dog cowering under Alexia's chair emerged. Her knuckles turned from white to pink and the chill slowly dissolved from her bones—except the one Sarah's words had left.

Kiren had taken her memories when she was a child because she'd been terrified from a Soulless encounter. Father had begged him to do it, and he'd complied out of a sense of mercy. How much more had he taken, and would she ever know for sure unless she dug the memories out of his mind?

She shivered. Why else would he fear her diving into his past, if not for some memory he dreaded she might recover?

Alexia twisted her ring. Did she trust Sarah? Could she afford to believe her, or had this been a play, an attempt by the Soulless to weaken and confuse her—as Kiren had counseled they would? But even he had warned her against trusting him entirely. If she couldn't recall her past, she couldn't recall it and there was nothing she could do about it.

Or was there?

"Dana..." Her mother waited in the absence of time, a dimension without physical limits, and surely she had seen all.

Hinges creaked. Kiren knelt suddenly at her side. "You are pale, dearest." He took her hands.

She cringed. How could he bear to kneel so near, to stare openly into her eyes or pledge his love when he was hiding things—more stolen pieces of her? She turned her gaze to the dog, wishing the animal would move and validate her change of focus.

"Alexia, no one can hurt you here."

She bit down. "You intend to leave me here, do you not?"

"Love—"

Mae stepped into the room, carrying a steaming bowl and wedge of bread. "Hope I am not disturbing a lover's conference."

Alexia flinched. How did Mae know about them—a woman she had only barely met, one who had been too distant to possibly hear about the wedding?

Mae placed the food on the table before Alexia, turning to Kiren. "And now I will see to that horse."

He rose and slipped a pouch into her hand. "Fed, watered, and ready to rest in your care. Take care of my Alexia?"

Alexia huffed.

"You doubt me?" Mae placed a fist on her hip.

A grin spread across his face. "Never."

The woman's brow pleated. "I suppose there will be no convincing you to rest the night?"

He grunted.

She lifted both hands in surrender. "Not my place to tell you what a fool's move it is to travel on a moonless night, but you protect that neck of yours. I know someone who will be a might bit troubled if something should happen to it." She winked Alexia's direction and turned to climb the stairs.

Alexia picked up her spoon and prodded at her stew. "She is right, on all accounts."

He scowled. "Eat your dinner."

She ate, conscientious of Kiren's dulled visage, and yet breathless for how close he sat—as if he needed to monitor her every bite to be certain she obeyed. She had but to shift and her hip pressed against his. She forced herself not to look up for fear his adoration would freeze her appetite, and that he might apprehend the curious mutinies she'd stowed to debate.

His fingers drummed across the table. "This building and the yard to the rear are protected, but move beyond the line of blossoms and you leave safety."

"You marked the space?"

A smile quirked his cheek.

"Then why is it you did not bring me here to marry me—if it is safe?"

90

He sat back and pulled both hands through his hair, gripping his ginger waves and sighing through clenched teeth. "A proper wedding in a proper church, is that too much to hope for?"

She reached up and caught his hand, laying it tenderly between hers. "You are not going without me."

"I will not have this argument." His fist slammed into the table. She jumped. "Our offensive will be hard and fast. You are not able to travel as I do, and I cannot be worried for your safety."

"Yet I am not afforded the same courtesy?" She glared back, angry. "And what will you do if they discover I am here?" She waved toward the door. "What if they drag me away—beyond the safety of these borders?"

"I will not be gone long."

"Sarah is here."

His jaw clenched. "Where?"

She couldn't meet his stare. "I do not know, but I saw her." She curled both hands in her lap, too angry to touch or be touched by him. "Do not leave tonight."

The hunger in his world-consuming gaze stole her breath. She wanted to throw free all barriers and embed herself in his starry sky—who cared the consequences!

He leapt back from her, rising. "I must go, and quickly. We can only track the Soulless during moonless evenings." His frown spoke of a deeper depression he'd been concealing—or perhaps one she perceived only because of his diminished glow. A sigh rattled out of him. "Your room is ready."

Mae emerged from the upper hall, bracing against the white-washed wall for guidance. "I lit the tapers and turned the sheets back. I will be around to gather you, once I have water boiled for a bath."

Alexia took Kiren's offered arm, glancing worriedly at the windows. Was Sarah watching? Did she know about his amulet's absence? And if so, would her aunt attack him the instant he left safety?

She had to convince him.

His lips made a tight line as they ascended to the upper floors. She took that as his signal to keep quiet while other ears might overhear—though she desperately longed to apologize for her omission.

He pressed the door wide and waited for her to enter. Beyond stood a double-wide bed, covers open, large enough for—dare she think it—them! Arched planks walled in the far side of the mattress, a window blinking against two candles that bathed a portion of the aging floorboards, giving the room a rustic feel.

Kiren followed her in, pulling the door nearly closed, sealing them into the confinement alone. His arm looped around her waist, crushing her to him, lips madly engaging hers.

Her barriers tumbled, welcoming him in, aching for more of him. Bursts of light flashed behind her eyelids, an ecstasy and wonder that any emotion so

91

powerful could exist. The caress of his consciousness skimmed through her mind, setting every nerve on fire, every memory racing to the surface and openly offering itself to him. She ached for his flesh to touch hers, for their bodies to merge, to truly be one!

His lips were no longer on hers. She leaned after him, but he held her back by the shoulders. His head tilted. "You actually spoke with her?" He pulled away. A subtle wall appeared between them—one overgrown with bewilderment.

Alexia hugged herself against the guilt. "But you said...our gifts, scorched earth..."

"You intended to deceive me?"

Her hands writhed over one another. "Sh-she did not harm me."

"She cannot here, but she wanted to." His stare burned into her, still laced with suspicion. "Scorched earth suppresses our strengths. It does not erase them." He paced slowly about the chamber, aggravatingly so. She could almost hear the questions pulsing through him: would she be safe? Had he made a mistake by bringing her here? What other option did he have?

"I am an entirely selfish creature." He stopped with his back to her. "Here I am romancing you beyond reason, attempting to say goodbye, while you undoubtedly sought opportunity to speak." He twisted, eyes spearing her through like the prongs of an azure trident.

Looking into his aching stare would only affirm the masked accusation, so she kept her gaze down—innocently, she hoped.

His words were pointed. "I fear you as I fear no one."

And with good reason. She frowned.

"And you, dear Alexia, ought to fear me." Something deep within his pigmentation had changed, sharpened, intensified. "At least the portion of me you do not yet understand."

Her heart trembled.

His fingers slid over top hers, interlacing, sending a quake of desire up her arm. She fixated on the loop of their hands as his grip tightened, almost worried he might snap her wrist in an instant of passion.

"Alexia?" The word drew her back to his fearsome sea. "Dead or alive you dictate my existence. Dead or Alive."

She did not need the conviction in his eyes to reinforce the words, but it did. Her knees shook.

"I need you." His whisper thrummed, low and ragged with desire.

So much for air.

His fingers glided up her arm. She leaned in to gather his oaken musk, ready and willing to surrender all.

The hard mask of duty returned. "But others hang in the balance. Their needs are no less important than my own. *We* must be conscious of them in our decisions, all of them." His eyes begged her to understand, to confess her deception.

She swallowed down her raging passions. He was right. Ethel, Edward, Nelly and so many others needed him. She mustn't keep him. "You should go."

His head bowed.

"I can defend myself, even against Sarah. I will think first and always of you." She traced her ring. "Always."

He groaned.

"Recover it for me, for us." She slid around so that his arm looped her back once more. "I need you as terribly as you do me."

He brushed a curl behind her ear. "Mae will not tolerate weapons in her inn, but I left your sword in the stable out back, should you need it."

"And Father?"

"He will be kept safe, but I do not think having him near Sarah would be a wise decision."

She bit her lip. Of course not. Father didn't understand what it meant to be Soulless.

Kiren kissed her, gently. She tasted the farewell on his lips, but didn't want to let go. Their arms entwined. Tears slid over her cheeks. He would come back to her—she had to believe. And in so believing, she had to let him go.

He brushed her cheeks, lips separating from hers. "I trust Mae, but even so, lock yourself in when you slumber." He slid a heavy key into her grasp. His brow crinkled as though his very heart were breaking. "Goodbye."

Twenty-Six

Motives

Kiren exited through the back of the inn, eyes instantly drawn to Alexia's window. She would be safe. He had to believe that.

A thin shadow shifted in the yard, within the white ring of blooms he'd used to mark the perimeter. The graceful woman rolled her shoulders, trembling as she stared at the same glass.

"I trust she will come to no harm?" he asked Sarah.

"I would give my life to protect her." The woman scowled at him. "You have always known that."

"I have, but you have not always been her enemy."

The corners of her mouth dropped, late sun glinting off the hurt in her stare. "Is that what we have become? Enemies?"

He reached for his absent medallion. "Protect her, Sarah. Mostly from yourself."

He felt the weight of her scowl as he stomped away.

Twenty-Seven

Reunion

Miles's legs weighed like anvils. He stood rooted in front of the inn as that stalwart figure—the man he'd known, trusted, and loved all his life—paced toward him.

The Master answered to so many names. Miles didn't know which fit him best, but the one Alexia accidentally revealed felt the truest: Kiren. How strange that only when he'd lost the man did he truly come to know him.

Lester greeted the Master with a nod. "We know where it be."

Kiren brushed past the runner and threw his arms around Miles. They were warm and encompassing, as they had been when he was a child, yet they didn't feel quite so unbeatable now. The Master had been bested. He was being forced to rely on others, and although Miles knew better than most how much Kiren depended on them all, his role felt heavier than a mountain.

Kiren pulled back and clapped his shoulders, beaming with pride. "You have done well."

"And you should be married."

Kiren's brows shot up.

"Bellezza told me, accidentally." Miles rubbed the back of his neck.

Kiren chuckled. "We have all missed having someone around who knows more than he should."

Miles smirked.

"Where is Bellezza?" Kiren asked, looking around.

Lester shrugged. "With Nelly—if her heart don't get the best o' her. I'll bind that imp proper when we have the time, but we had best be runnin' if we wants to catch these devilry prigs." He turned a kindly wink on Miles. "Not meanin' to cut yer reunion short."

Mist solidified into Ethel's form. "Elizabeth awaits us."

Miles reached out to her. "Enough talk. Let's go save the world."

Twenty-Eight

Double Cross

It felt like blisters covered every inch of Joseph's feet after running all day. He shifted the pack on his shoulder and pounded at the cottage door, the echo carrying back to him from inside like the hollow pulse of his own clock, one that would cease ticking if he were caught. A candle flickered in one window—burning before dark—his signal that this was the right house.

He glanced back over his shoulder, tapping a nervous hand against his leg. The twist of shadows across a dipping field tightened his throat.

The Kingdom faction could be out there, just waiting for him to make his move, and as soon as the sun disappeared, the others would be in his head. Wind whistled past his ear and he jumped, scanning the hollow.

Grass rustled. He whipped toward it.

Nothing.

A razorblade of orange hung over the horizon, coloring the tips of weeds from dusky to flaxen. The hue reminded him of cork-swirled pasta, a dish he used to consume with gusto.

Joseph lifted his shaking fist again.

The hinges creaked, and a large, square man filled the frame, his bald head glistening with sweat. Putrid waves rolled off him.

Joseph wrinkled his nose and shoved a twine-wrapped bundle into his hands.

The man grunted and turned. He disappeared into the house, slamming the door shut.

Joseph sprinted back down the lane, as light as a gelding in a summer prance. The last sliver of sun glimmered over the horizon. He'd done it in time!

Letting out a heavy sigh, he slowed and hefted his pack from a weary shoulder. Three deliveries since Amos wrangled the necklace from their enemy, and now it was time to ensure his knowledge would not reach the others.

He slipped a golden vial from the bag, wondering if his companions had reached their destinations. Five of them had fled, each with the same number of packages—one of which contained the stolen medallion. His. He had no idea which of his deliveries it had been, or what would become of it now, but he believed it would return to their hands after the moonless night—when the boy, Miles, could not tap into their shared thoughts and glean its whereabouts.

He lifted the vial to his lips, pausing. This was going to hurt. The poison would cause damage he may never recover from, but it was worth the price—keeping the medallion away from their foe.

He tipped the glass back.

A hand wrapped around his, pulling the glass away. Liquid lapped at his lips.

No! He pulled harder. The vial was torn from his grasp. It spiraled through the air, its contents glimmering in the last of the light. The glass smacked into the hard packed road and exploded.

He lurched forward, but fingers bit into his arms. Dropping to his knees, he scuffled as far forward as he could, fixated on the disappearing venom. If he could lick up some of it from the dirt, it might be enough!

"Hold him."

The cold words sank into his core. He knew that steel voice—one he'd heard a hundred times echoing through the collective conscience of the Soulless right before his allies were destroyed by light. Dread melted into his bones.

He swallowed dryly. Three shadows draped over him as the poison seeped into the earth. He leapt toward it, but a grip of iron held him.

"Have you absorbed enough?" the Kingdom leader asked one of his compatriots.

Joseph's muscles clenched. He turned his head, pinned to the ground by a stare that carried the weight of the ocean.

The boy, Miles, held him firm, cheek twitching. Behind him the would-be king stood, and to his right the gray-headed runner, Lester, clenched and unclenched his fists. Joseph's limbs shook.

But wait! The Passionate ruler no longer possessed his weapon.

The last glimmer of sun remained on the horizon. Another minute and they would be the ones at Joseph's mercy.

He barely contained the grin.

"He does not have it." Miles's voice reminded him of the Christmas fiddle his uncle used to play, deep and sorrowful, impossible to ignore. "But I know where he has been."

His captor threw him to the ground. Joseph twisted and glimpsed the young man, his skin sallow and sunken, his eyes too deep, his teeth uneven and wide.

"Elizabeth?" Their blue-eyed leader turned.

A woman with flaming hair stepped forward, a scowl on her pretty face. Her damask dress looked to belong in the high courts of London.

Joseph scrambled backward on his elbows. *Red Pain.* They all knew of her. Ten years ago she'd been attacked on a moonless night by four of his suffering brethren. She'd turned her gift on them, and he still remembered the vise-like agony seeping through their shared consciousness.

No one dared approach her.

She glared at him and touched her temple. Daggers sliced into his brain.

He shrieked and tumbled back. Invisible blades chiseled through his nerves, shredding them, the claws of a leopard raking over sinewy cloth. Nothing remained—nothing but the frayed illusion of draining arteries. He tried to lift his arm off the road. It didn't move.

The party turned and walked away, the leader and youth nodded back and forth as though carrying on a conversation without words. The glow of the sky was fading. Any moment the change would happen and his companions would know he'd failed.

He closed his eyes and welcomed the sting that should preface tears, if tears were possible.

Footsteps ground toward him.

His eyes snapped open. The bald man who'd accepted his final delivery stood over him, a dagger in his fist.

Joseph's pulse quickened.

"Sorry 'bout this, mate." He knelt and lifted the dagger over Joseph's chest. "She said this dagger were blessed. Straight to the heart, she said."

Joseph wished he hadn't looked.

Twenty-Nine

Mae

Mae led Alexia into the kitchen. A corner of the room with the fireplace had been cordoned off by a clothesline and a wide sheet. Behind the screen waited a tub filled with reflective ripples.

Burning wood popped in Alexia's ears, no scampering of feet, no distant snoring. "Are you alone here? Have you no house-hand or husband?"

"I have a dog."

"But none of the others?" A woman who functioned without a man dictating her life, Alexia marveled. She nimbly unbuttoned her overdress and slid it off, cringing at the crusted blood. "I do not mean to pry."

"By all means, pry." Mae circled around and assisted Alexia with her skirts, pulling the silky material away. "I should like it a great deal more than silence." She paused, gathering the material together and searching the bloodstains with her fingers. "Some things are not as timeless as others."

Sadness welled up in Alexia's heart. Then Mae was one of the lasting creatures, like Nelly, like Ethel. "Have they been gone long, your family?"

Mae smiled, her head down. "I am not lonely here. Why, our brothers and sisters visit from across the globe, and I have housed more than a few children. You may have met my most recent boarder." She draped the dress over the privacy line. "He appears but a boy, wee in size, but he is a young man who carries messages for your sweetheart."

Images of a boy on horseback danced through her head, the lad who had visited Kiren's house in the woods with regular news.

Mae loosened Alexia's bustle and corset. "Your mother came to stay here. Helped me for a time."

"*My* mother, Dana?"

"It was because of the nightmares." Mae set the stained undergarments aside. "Poor child was plagued by them. She hoped they would fade on scorched earth."

"And did they?"

"Aye."

Alexia stepped into the warm water, shivering. She would have given most anything for the nightmares to disappear when she first came of age—to not see people's imminent death. She appreciated her mother's need. "And this is where she met my father?"

Mae handed her a bar of soap and a wash rag. "He was a dashing young rogue, but she seemed to know him the first time he stepped through that door. My heart broke for her when he left."

"But he returned."

Mae nodded and sat down on an over-turned barrel. "They always return."

Thirty

Compelled

Charles paced the upper hall, pausing once to glance out the window at the moonless sky. This secret house had been empty most the day—since shortly after his daughter disappeared. He didn't like it.

Alexia was not yet married, which meant she should be under his care, and the eerie silence, the hushed voices, and rushing to and fro left him uneasy. Worst of all was the lack of answers.

A door in the hall slammed open and the woman with white hair stumbled out. Her eyes lit on him. "Baron Dumont, do you know where Nelly is?"

"Who?"

Her shoulders dropped. "The cook. And my name is Ethel, as you have clearly forgotten."

"Right." He scratched his head. It was not that he intended to be rude, but they were below his station, and his chances of speaking with any of them again—well, they were apparently increasing by the moment. Regardless, he intended to divorce all connections to them the instant this conflict ended.

At Ethel's scowl, he smoothed the disdain from his face. Here he was not the man who possessed land and governed. He was merely a guest and it was his duty to deport himself appropriately until such time as he could resume his proper place in society.

"You would do well to remember some of us can read minds." Ethel winked.

He tensed. "You read my mind?"

"I read your face, but you had best exercise caution. Not all of us are forgiving." Her smile communicated her good intentions in informing him, but the warning shot a panicky need through his knees to carry him far, far away from here.

"Your assistance is needed in the kitchen." Ethel pulled the door shut.

His eyebrows shot up. "My assistance?"

"That is what I said." She burst into a cloud of mist, the haze evaporating.

He crinkled his nose. It was not natural, not right, the way they moved through this world—even if she had saved him only a day ago.

He begrudgingly turned toward the stairs, but a muffled whimper carried through the closed door. Returning to the wood, he placed an ear against it.

A wisp of voice struck him, a groan.

"Who is in there?" he called.

A gasp. "Help me." The pitiful whimper grabbed his heart.

A girl. A child.

Charles twisted the handle. He pressed the door back, revealing white oak-paneled walls and a solid-framed bed. Golden curls spilled across the covers, a small body curled in on itself.

He stepped closer. Gaunt lines cut across the child's porcelain-doll face, her limbs trembling beneath frayed velvet. Charles remembered the days when Alexia was so slight, when he used to watch her run and play in the yard.

Brown eyes fluttered open and closed again. The girl (could he even think of her as a child?) possessed the most brilliant red lips he had ever seen, her lashes long and thick, the width of her broad cheekbones both sensual and appealing. The spice of nutmeg pulled him in, rooting a hunger for physical intimacy—the need to know if her flesh was as soft as it appeared.

Charles froze. What was wrong with him? He had not looked on a woman this way since Rosalind's passing. And to view this girl in such a fashion...

Bewitched. It was the spell they cast over mortals. How he despised them! All of them.

And yet he couldn't turn away.

"You are Alexia's father." The brazen soprano left his ears tingling. Her chocolate stare swallowed him, bitter and addicting.

Do not speak to it and it can have no power over you.

The girl laughed, her throat catching in a cough. Her little body shook as she lifted her wrists into view, dual golden bracelets linking them together. Her lashes lifted, eyes pleading. "Help me."

A hint of cinnamon—but softer and sweeter—breathed over him, leaving his mouth watering. His fists clenched. He needed to get away from her, to flee from this bizarre craving.

"Help you?" he asked.

"Remove the gold."

Charles stood back. There must be a reason she wore the bracelets, but how could a little decorative jewelry make any difference?

"Please." Her voice caught, nearly breaking in a sob.

Charles couldn't help himself. He reached out to unlatch the bangles, but there was no release mechanism.

He slipped a finger between the thin metal and her skin. Her breath caught. He met her consuming stare.

It was an avalanche and he'd been buried, pressed under layers of sweet earth, an interment he never wished to escape.

"Free me," she whispered, lashes batting in slow motion.

He bent the bracelet, pinching it into a point and then twisting it in the opposite direction.

Snap.

Tears spilled down the girl's cheeks as the metal fell away from her arms. Charles gasped. Her skin was charred black, two ribbons of ash around her wrists. Her fingers wrapped about his, warm and small. A trill of need rang into his veins, echoing in his ears and blocking out all but her.

Color had returned to her face, her cheeks rosy, her skin begging to be caressed. "I will never forget this, Charles Dumont."

He swallowed.

She melted into a gentle haze, the fog embracing him before skittering away and leaving him cold.

"No!"

He twisted to the doorway where Ethel stood.

"What have you done?"

Thirty-One

Family

The mirror hung before Alexia, returning a countenance much less grand than expected. She possessed foibles: skin imperfections, one eyebrow slightly higher than the other, cracked, dry lips, colorless cheeks. Not the ghastly creature she had been all growing up, but neither the impossible beauty she'd come to recognize. This was the real her.

She grinned.

The eyes remained the same. That jade hue she'd always liked caught the late afternoon rays and reflected the window at her back.

She had slept nearly the whole day and was thankful for no disturbances from the Soulless in the night. She'd roused this morning to the noise of new arrivals, hoping Kiren had changed his mind and returned with Father. The newcomers were a family, but not hers. She'd had every intention of greeting them, but had sat back down in bed. The next thing she knew, she'd opened her eyes to near-evening light stretching across the wall.

Kiren had been right to leave her behind. She was in no shape to assist him, no shape to help anyone—not even herself. Even now, a dull ache hung at the back of her mind.

A girl's squeal drew Alexia to the window. The child of five sat drawing with a finger in the dirt between a garden and the stable. To be so young, so carefree... Alexia envied the girl. That kind of innocence needed to be preserved.

As promised, Kiren's ring of white blossoms dotted a line across the yard, marking a perimeter that encompassed only the inn and a short stretch of grass. Glimmering caught her eye, something in the off-road fields.

A distant silhouette trundled through the grain. The wheat grazed at his beltline, his shoulders square, strong looking, his dark curls catching the breeze.

She squinted.

Another flash. An earring...

John!

She stumbled backward. How could he have found her so fast?

Sarah.

Straightening the bed and gathering up all evidence she'd occupied the chamber, she grabbed her shoes and hastened out the door barefoot—to keep from making too much noise. John could easily drag her out of the building, away from safety, and carry her helpless to his masters—if he didn't consume her first!

He had been respectful to Sarah and always honest with her, but could she ever forgive him for engaging her aunt's affections while carrying the Soulless curse? And more importantly, his knowledge of her location would bring the other Soulless.

The hall waited dark and empty. She hurried across it, cautiously tiptoeing down the stairs. The gathering room waited silently.

She scampered through the chamber and into the back where Mae had disappeared last night. Certainly the building possessed a cellar somewhere in the vicinity of the kitchen—or a back door. She could hide in the shrubs outside.

Alexia flitted into the kitchen, glancing at the iron kettle hanging over the flames of an open spit. Next to it, a floured working space proffered brown feathers and the trimmings of a pie crust. A single chair sat in the corner, directly over a cellar door with a metal handle. She shoved the chair aside and pulled back the hidey-hole covering.

"Mae?" cordial bass rang from the entry. Shivers tickled over her arms.

"John?" the innkeeper replied from a room over.

"I am very pleased to see you in good health. How are you weathering?"

Down Alexia stumbled, into the darkness, recently sanded steps smooth against the soles of her feet.

"Seasonable and tired." Mae's voice dimmed behind heavy planks.

John's muffled bass only carried through for its weight. "Seasonable? No, seasoned, and well-spiced."

"Oh, John."

Still a flatterer. All Soulless were from what Kiren said.

Alexia pulled the trap shut as the kitchen door opened. She sat. *Don't breathe. Don't think.*

Slivers of light trickled through the boards, revealing the tops of crowded shelves in a cellar pantry. The bitter taste of herbs scented the air, and a narrow path led between racks to a deeper bowel of pitch.

Thump.

Dust dropped over a distant shelf.

"Certainly a different *scent* to this kitchen today."

Alexia's heart froze. He knew.

"Smells *delicious*."

Mae laughed. "Chicken pie. Be ready in an hour if you would like some."

"You are too kind."

"I know it."

More footfalls, aimed to the door above her head. Alexia felt her way forward, noiselessly fumbling between racks toward the back of the cellar, heart drumming. There had to be a way out! If John found her, she was a good as Soulless.

"John, you are shaking my inn to pieces. Do not stomp around like an unlicked cub."

"Or you will do the licking?" He chuckled.

Alexia remembered the days she'd liked that laugh, the days it had brought her comfort, the days before she knew what he was. She needed a place to hide or an escape. Perhaps if she wound through the shelves she could circle back and escape before he caught her.

Her foot slid over a ledge. She threw herself back and crashed onto her rump, shoes flying.

Ouch.

Dragging her fingers across the dirt, she halted at a drop off. Emptiness gaped before her as though someone had intentionally dug a pit in the middle of Mae's cellar. Why would she have a gaping chasm down here? Could this be a trap? Was Mae working with John?

The innkeeper called, "Do not disturb my stores, John."

"And risk your wrath? I would not dream of it, fair Mae." The cellar entry opened, dropping a rectangle of light across Alexia and brightening the top rung of a ladder leading into the hole before her. She peered into the circular cavity, as far across as she was tall, a tunnel that disappeared into darkness, perhaps one that exited the building, or maybe simply a cubby deep enough to hide in. Why did Mae need a tunnel into the ground?

"I noticed the missing jar of preserves last week, John."

"It went to a good cause, I can promise you that."

Grabbing the raw wood of the ladder, she slipped into the darkness. John's boot thumped the first stair.

Alexia scrambled downward.

"Now out of my kitchen." Mae's rebuke carried from further and further above. "I have important work here."

"Very well, madam," John's voice boomed closer.

Pitch engulfed Alexia.

John was going to discover her unless she froze time to escape him.

Cold washed down her spine as she recalled Kiren's warning. She couldn't use her gift here. If she tried, it would kill her.

Heavy footfalls thudded toward her.

Discovered by the Soulless or killed by her gift, which was worse? She descended faster.

If she was lucky, he would stumble into this hole, slip over the brink, and snap his neck when he hit the bottom. He wouldn't die. The Soulless could not die. Perhaps he would be eternally immobilized by the fall and unable to escape the hole? It would serve him right for what he'd stolen from Sarah.

Alexia gasped mentally. What was she thinking? She'd never harbored so malignant a wish toward anyone—not even the man who had nearly raped her and then blackmailed her father into a marriage arrangement.

But John had courted Sarah, knowing his state of being might ultimately prove her damnation. When Alexia confronted him, he'd admitted it and yet swore his love for Sarah. A love he should have proven by letting her go.

Boots scraped the rungs above her. She bit down and doubled her efforts.

A jingle carried up from below, like iron rings grazing across one another.

She glanced down, startled by a splinter of light on a distant floor, so thin and gray it had escaped her previous notice. Who—or what—waited down there? And if light, might she discover an exit? Right about now, slowing time would be only too convenient. Why had Kiren brought her to a place her abilities were useless?

Because he loved her. Because he feared for her. Because he knew she would overdo if given the least provocation.

And John was certainly provocation.

The ladder ended. Solid earth pressed beneath her feet. She glanced up for John, but he was lost in the blackness.

Rattling metal.

She knew that sound. Two days in the darkness with a cell mate who both terrified and bewildered her had cemented the jangle into permanent recognition. Two days of pitch blackness with nothing but Bellezza's cruel cackle and the rhythm of iron chains.

A prisoner? A tasty morsel John was saving for later?

She stepped forward, hands out. Two wooden doors fell back at her touch, whining on rusted hinges—hinges set into earthen walls. The chamber had been chiseled out of the ground, rounded walls plastered and whitewashed, but blemished where rivulets of dirt had bled through. The uneven ceiling domed far above her reach. Wooden planks had been laid and polished into a balmy sheen beneath the pool of radiance—an oil lamp. It brightened the oval cavern, outlining a crude table, a rocking chair, a framed bed, a chest, and a body dangling from the wall.

Alexia gasped. "Sarah!"

Her near-sister's face was pale and ringed in shadow, strained but triumphant. Sarah twisted in her irons. Her feet barely scraped the floor, just enough to keep the shackles from pulling her shoulders from their sockets.

"A-Alexia?"

Hundreds of questions formed at her lips as she closed the distance, but only one escaped. "Did John do this to you?"

"Lexy, no! Stay away." Her aunt turned her head, cringing.

"It is day, Sarah. The New Moon is over. You cannot hurt me now and I am not going to leave my family to perish." She poked at the shackles, searching for a weak link.

Sarah's crimson eyes burrowed into hers. "It does not lessen the hunger."

Guilt tightened her chest. Sarah had given up joining the Passionate to remain in Alexia's life, as a true sister might, and Alexia had spat on so generous a gift, ready to abandon her dearest friend the instant Kiren appeared. She touched Sarah's pale cheek. Heat seared into her skin, as if her near-sister might spontaneously burst into flame.

Alexia jerked back and inhaled.

"This is my fault." All along she had blamed John or Bellezza, but she had known what would happen to Sarah. She had permitted her best friend to love a devil. Tears pooled in her eyes as she searched the nearby table for a key. This change could have been prevented. "If I had only arrived sooner that night—"

"It was her choice."

Alexia whirled around.

John stood at the foot of the ladder, arms crossed, wearing a squared grin, and blocking the only exit.

Thirty-Two

Warfare

Kiren pulled his horse to a halt as Miles doubled over, holding his head. Miles screamed.

Kiren's horse stamped backward. The buildings of Wilhamshire echoed the lad's shriek, and dozens of voices rasped in harmony, mimicking his cry. Kiren spun, searching for the hidden creatures. They were surrounded, but not boxed in.

Miles glared at the horizon where the sun had just disappeared. No moon graced the cloudless heavens—the third night of lunar absence.

Kiren's heart stopped. It occasionally happened, an additional night of continued horror. He'd not planned for this. How many of his friends had he sent directly into danger's path while seeking out his missing necklace?

Miles tore at his hair. "Get away! They can see you." His eyes turned up, a dim glow at the center. He licked his lips.

Kiren whipped his horse and it bolted.

Another scream assaulted his ears, a child's. He turned his beast that direction and kicked hard. The animal lurched between two buildings.

A black-robed creature pulled a boy out of a window by his collar. Kiren charged straight into the thing, bowling it over. Bones crunched beneath the horses' hooves as Kiren caught the lad.

William.

The wail of a woman burst through the same building. He rounded the back, leapt off his beast, and kicked the door open. Shrouded wraiths tugged at Phoebe Ann, William's mother.

Kiren tore a dagger out of his belt and launched himself forward. He slashed the blade across one creature's throat, and it burst into black mist. Without looking, he jabbed the weapon into the other sufferer's gut and grabbed Phoebe's hand, dragging her through the blinding mist, her breathing ragged.

Kiren's stallion pranced uneasily at the back door, William holding it fast. A quick assessment told him the beast could not handle their combined weight.

The Soulless would remain between states for but a few moments, no time at all to escape on foot.

He hefted Phoebe into the saddle behind her son, wrapped her hand around his dagger, and slapped the horse. "To the inn!" he shouted after them. They would be safe there—if Mae could keep the Soulless at a distance. She'd never failed thus far.

Kiren pulled a hand through his hair. Phoebe knew the secrets of keeping herself and family hidden from these enemies. How had they found her? Or were they breaking into house after house now that he couldn't stop them?

Kiren's blood froze.

Miles.

The young man knew nearly every Passionate on the registry—where they lived, what their weaknesses were—and the Soulless were in his head!

He bolted for the Thompson house, hurdling a discarded wheelbarrow, pulling himself up over a fence, two streets over, one block up...

He stopped.

Firelight danced in the second story window, smoke curling heavenward. Kiren sprinted for the building, sending up a prayer.

A man tumbled down the front step and landed on his side.

"Robert?" Kiren called.

The man crawled up onto his knees. Ash darkened one side of his face a stark contrast to his blonde shock of hair, a knife clasped in his hand. "Thank the Lord!"

"Do not thank him yet. I cannot help you this night." Kiren lifted the man to his feet while Robert's face twisted in confusion. "You lit them on fire?"

"That I did."

"Then fly, to the inn." He pushed Robert toward the town's limits.

The man shook his head. "But you are here."

"And I cannot protect you. Flee!"

Robert sprinted for the woods. Kiren turned back the way he'd come. If the Soulless were in Miles's head, then he had only one choice. He sprinted his fastest.

Kiren skidded to a halt in the town square—where he'd left the lad.

Miles cringed into the neck of his steed, burying his face. The animal whinnied, prancing uneasily. Four wraiths circled in. Kiren glanced about the square for ideas. Hesitate a second too long and they would take the boy.

He'd never let that happen.

Kneeling, he placed a hand to the hard-packed road, searching below the surface. There! A set of trampled roots.

He dashed forward. The creatures whirled in unison, Miles's head lifting at the same instant. Kiren dropped to his knees, glided to a stop, and slammed his palm against the ground, hurling energy downward.

The shrouded figures stood immobile.

One hissed.

They broke out of their trance, rushing him in a flurry of darkness.

Vines broke through the dirt. They looped around the creatures' feet, pulling them to a halt. Kiren leapt up and caught the dagger sheathed at Miles's hip. He spun and slashed. Black haze blinded him.

He vaulted onto Miles's horse and seized the reins.

The boy's head shook. "Please, you have to—!"

He punched Miles in the temple. The lad crumpled and Kiren looped an arm around him, kicking the horse and aiming away from the city.

The only way to stop the Soulless from seeing was to keep Miles unconscious, much as it pained him.

Morning was too welcome. Kiren leaned back against a tree, finally able to relax. Miles's horse had been lost in the course of the night, but it would find its way to the inn. Of that he was certain. The last time he'd knocked Miles out, he had to carry him over one shoulder and run for a new location, hoping the Soulless wouldn't recognize the terrain Miles had briefly glimpsed. He prayed Phoebe and William made it to safety, and Robert—he was a fighter.

"You worry loudly, old man." Miles shifted onto his elbows.

Kiren pulled his thoughts inward, lifting his usual barrier. "How many did they catch?"

"Not sure." Miles rubbed at the back of his neck, grunted, and settled back down. "My head..."

"Sorry." He rested a hand over Miles's temple and focused on healing the multiple bruises.

Miles breathed easier. "I glimpsed Joseph Gregory—I think they, well, I think he's one of them now. And I'm pretty certain they took Margaret Shaw and Regin."

Kiren's head swirled, sickness building in his throat. "Regin?"

Miles covered his face. "My memories are... Edward should have taken them—"

Kiren placed a hand on his shoulder. "You are you because of what you know, and I'll not take that away. We need you in the war." *Or all is lost.* Kiren didn't say the words, but they echoed through his soul. Until he had the medallion back, every person he knew and loved was in danger, and Miles was the key to predicting their enemies.

All of them.

Thirty-Three

Brainwashing

Alexia landed against the earthen wall, heart hammering against her ribs. She needed her sword. Where was her sword?

"To what do we owe the pleasure?" John asked casually.

Her gaze bounced to the ladder at his back. Again she wished she wasn't standing on scorched earth or that she had a weapon. Nothing on the bed, the table, Sarah, or the rocking chair. She leapt forward and seized the gaslight, holding it in front of her.

John stalked forward. She backed away. Her legs hit the rocking chair and she toppled into it. He strode past, digging a handkerchief from his pocket. He unwrapped a heavy key while keeping the fabric between his fingers and the dull metal.

Metal—poison to them—and yet Sarah was covered in it. Did it burn her as it did the Passionate? Alexia could only imagine her aunt's agony, having never experienced the burn of metal.

The exit. She could escape while John's back was turned, and remove the ladder, trapping him here. But what about Sarah?

The key clattered into Sarah's irons as John wrapped an arm around her.

Alexia blinked in confusion. He'd come to rescue Sarah? But then, who had locked her up?

Go or stay? Could she ever abandon her sister again?

"The temptation grew too much?" John questioned softly, freeing the manacles from Sarah's arms, and supporting her weight as her knees bent limply. Alexia was not meant to hear it, but the phrase stopped her debate. She set the oil lamp down.

"Better to be safe," Sarah replied.

John rubbed a gentle hand over her aunt's wrists, and lifted them to his lips. Alexia tensed as he kissed the discolored skin. "You are far wiser than any mate I could have hoped for."

Sarah embraced him.

112

Alexia stared. Her aunt loved him—even after all he'd done to her? And how could he even pretend to care for a woman he'd so selfishly damned to this eternal state of misery?

Her heart pinched as she recalled those last weeks together before she'd left Sarah's care—how frequently John had called, how sweetly he spoke to and of Sarah, how he'd vowed his deepest adoration and love for her, promising to marry her.

And he had.

"How is he?" John whispered, placing a hand over Sarah's center.

"Quiet today."

Alexia looked again. Sarah was wide about the middle, nearly twice her normal girth, but her near-sister couldn't possibly be...could she? How could Alexia have missed that detail?

John bent and leaned an ear to Sarah's belly. "He is going to be a strong one."

Alexia covered her mouth and pushed out of the seat. Sarah looked up. She smiled.

"Is that possible?" Alexia wondered.

"Mmm," John hummed. "Possible indeed."

Alexia glared at him. How dare he do this to Sarah? Was it not enough that he'd destroyed her—must he also put her through the torture of childbirth? And for what? To bring a monstrosity into the world?

But then, Sarah had not been Soulless long. She must have been in this fragile state before John destroyed her.

That her sister could bear the thought of raising a child turned Alexia's stomach—after all they'd experienced: ruined marriages, jealous lovers, children birthed out of wedlock, lives fragmented around the notion of family. John must have forced her. That could be the only explanation.

But then, had she not been considering the same idea just yesterday morning? Bearing Kiren's baby?

She glared at John. "Will the babe be Soulless or Passionate?"

He straightened. "He possesses the pulse of one untainted."

Alexia crossed her arms, stepping backward as he rose to his full height. "What do you want with a Passionate child?"

He scowled. "I want to be a father again, Alexia."

She shook her head. He wanted something else. This had to be another attempt at recovering himself, at returning to a state of health. Somehow this little one figured into his twisted plan—as Sarah had before he'd ruined her.

She had to stop this, somehow, and find a way to save the infant. Where was Kiren now when she needed him, when his wisdom would calmly assure her how to act?

Sarah rubbed a hand over her belly and settled into the rocking chair. "He is going to be beautiful."

Alexia whirled and stalked toward the ladder. There was nothing she could do for Sarah if she was so deluded as to believe all would be well. Her aunt couldn't raise a Passionate child. She could barely stand to be in Alexia's presence—let alone the presence of a powerless infant.

Dual growls reverberated about the room.

Alexia froze. Hair on the back of her neck stood on end.

The two Soulless stood at her back watching her flee a tiny confinement with only one escape. Who cared that they couldn't *drain* her on scorched earth—it would only take John grabbing her too tightly around the neck or throwing her down with enough force to break her. What could she do, turn around and profess she was not trying to flee them?

The sword. She needed her sword.

Alexia leapt up the ladder. Heavy footfalls echoed after her. She squeaked, fingers slipping as she lunged, skipping rungs.

"Stop!" John roared.

All his benign behavior had been a show. He would rather consume her than love her like a niece!

The ladder shook. She gripped tighter, cursing her sweaty palms. Wood vibrated beneath her fingers, groaning as he mounted below her.

Faster.

The dim outline of light above beckoned. She reached for it with every handhold, deafened to all but the rasp of her pursuer's loud breathing.

The ladder moaned and bowed. She gasped and glanced back. Sarah ascended below John, two sets of bleeding bright eyes in the darkness. Alexia missed her next handhold and reached again. John's fingers skimmed her heel. She yanked both feet up to the rung under her fingers and pushed up, grasping at earthen floors.

Indistinct shelves lined a corridor to safety.

Something brushed her heel. She jerked a knee up under her and lunged forward. She jolted to a halt, landing on her face. He had her hem! She rolled, kicking at his hand. He rose out of the hole, eyes open in a ravenous red.

John stood over her, a hunkering silhouette of darkness.

She kicked his knee. He crumpled backward.

Alexia threw the kitchen hatch open wide, launching herself at the backdoor before her pursuer rose from the cellar.

The barn wasn't far.

She sprinted into the burgeoning night, dancing around thorns and twigs. White blossoms crumpled underfoot as she crossed the safety line.

Warmth burst inside her, a natural geyser of inner fire that had been iced. She stumbled from shock. Her palms smacked into the weeds, knees thudding in unison.

Power coursed through her limbs, pulsating, hungry to escape, waiting to be called. She lifted a hand and examined her arm. Did she imagine it, or did she actually glow, so saturated by the excess of energy?

A shiver of strength shot up from her toes, tickling the skin as it traveled.
What was happening to her?

A huff.

She pulled her feet under her and twisted.

John stood in the doorway, arms splayed, frozen. She smirked at him. Let him come now, see who fared better.

He shook his head, eyes wide, and backed into the darkness.

Coward.

A high-pitched scream tore the wind.

She spun around, turned toward the stables. Her feet were moving before she'd given the command. The building's gray-brown walls reared up and she circled to the doors. The breeze died. A chill launched up her arms, raising hairs.

Oh no.

The sky—there was no moon. It was not supposed to be like this. They had passed two moonless evenings already! The cycle should be ended.

A ring of black shrouds blocked the barn's exit, six of them, and an unattractive girl crouched in front of the doors, covering her head—a Passionate child.

Alexia's heart clenched.

The world stopped.

Ice solidified in the air. She took a step. Her dress weighed like it was made of shale, the muscles at the back of her neck tensing with strain.

Kiren was not here to save anyone. They knew. They all knew, and this child was outside the ring of safety.

Frustration fired through her gut. She might be able to freeze time, but what good did that accomplish? As much as she wanted to rescue the girl, it was impossible to move anything but herself in this state. By the time she retrieved the weapon waiting beyond the doors, the girl would be lost. The best she could do was place herself between the wraiths and their prey—and risk not only her life, but Kiren's as well.

Or she could run for help. She turned back to the inn.

And once she crossed back onto scorched earth, what then? Time would resume its natural progression, and she would be far too late to assist. What good was her gift if she couldn't use it to save people?

But maybe she could.

Her nails dug into her palms. The muscles in her shoulders tightened, her strength draining by the second. It only took one touch. A single fingertip grazing her skin on a moonless night would forever taint and damn her to a Soulless existence—so she'd have to be careful.

She sucked ice into her lungs and shimmied between the immobile demons, placing herself next to the child. Carefully, she released the tension in her muscles, a little at a time, but not completely.

The Soulless held their stances, shocked by her sudden appearance. She must look like a blur to them. The thought made her grin. She grabbed the girl, tugging her toward the break in the line, keeping time slowed.

The nearest wraith reached for them, his fingers shedding slow wisps of ebony, like obsidian flames. Alexia shoved the girl's head away from its touch, saving her by an inch.

The others surged forward. She pulled the girl toward them, dodging around an extended arm. One bounded over top of them. She stilled time further and hurried beneath the ominous blackness, a death bird, tugging the child away and flattening her to the ground as the enemy's body descended. The creature's feet slammed into the earth only a second after the girl vacated it.

Black bodies walled them in. She slipped between them, twisting to avoid their touch like angling through a real-world jigsaw puzzle. The passages between wraiths narrowed, but with the child suspended in mid-air, she could manipulate the girl's every move, shaping her safely through the pitch.

Her head pulsed.

Panting heavily, she caught a glimpse of the inn between the last two demons. They were going to make it!

Alexia dodged around them, heart soaring. She pulled the girl after her, fixed on the inn, and was jerked backward.

Half-decayed fingers wrapped around the child's skirt.

Alexia's brain screamed as she yanked time completely to a halt. She stepped back through the ice-air and gripped the solid skirt, right above where the Soulless had it, ready to tear the material free as soon as it was pliable. She released the seconds, her head heavy as a brick, and yanked the fabric free from the enemy's grasp.

Creatures surged forward. Darkness swallowed them. Alexia tumbled to the ground as wraiths converged, lifting the girl out of her grasp.

Forcing the world to stop, Alexia crawled forward on her elbows and knees. This could not be happening. She could still make it right. It wasn't too late! One of the wraiths had wrapped its bony hand around the child's wrist.

Thirty-Four

The Sands of Time

Dizziness sent Alexia's head spinning. A tear slipped down her cheek. It *was* too late. She had failed.

Kiren would not have failed. He would have found a way, but she was not like him. She was weak. And short sighted.

There was no way to make it better. The girl was lost. Alexia could only use her gift to benefit herself.

Turning back toward the inn, she trudged forward.

Why could she only slow time? If she could go back in time—only a few seconds—the girl would be saved! The Soulless believed she was capable.

And why can't I go back in time?

The world fractured about her into particles, like sands. She swam through them, using all the strength in her arms and legs as they shifted around her, stubbornly, focused on that moment when she had broken free from the Soulless, when only a single creature clung to the child's skirt. It was like grabbing a fist full of water that solidified as her fingers wrapped around it.

Nothingness washed before her eyes and she blinked them open. Her very essence ripped from her chest, like a fish who'd been gutted. She blinked her eyes and stumbled, head throbbing, gasping for breath.

Something was different.

Something had changed.

The girl hung behind her, frozen, skirt gripped by one of the creatures.

She had done it! She'd reversed time!

Alexia grabbed the girl's hands, pulled forward with all her might, released her hold on time, and shot forward.

Material tore. The child flew with the force of Alexia's time-altered yank. They crossed over the safety line, right past someone, and Alexia caught the girl, cushioning the little one and twisting until her back slammed into the inn. She slid to the ground.

Mae. Mae stood on the brink, arms crossed.

117

Alexia's head felt like a pillow full of down, a soft buzzing in her ears, the taste of sulfur at the back of her tongue. "The Soulless—" she warned.

A wicked smile crept over Mae's face, her blind eyes crinkling at the corners. "I can hear them." She stepped over the line of white blossoms.

The grass reached for her foot—like iron shavings drawn to a magnet. The stretching plants shriveled and blackened, desiccating and writhing into the dirt. Deadness bled out from the innkeeper across the foliage, spreading like the black fingers of an inky night, but halting along the perimeter Kiren had marked. Like a giant sucking breath, an invisible force drew the color and life out of the earth, pulling it into Mae's body. Her eyes closed, nostrils flared, chest lifting as though she were breathing for the first time. Death ringed her foot, extending twice the woman's height in all directions and growing while her skin gleamed and brightened.

A shriek rent the air. The creature nearest Mae collapsed. Those on either side dropped. A fourth and fifth toppled.

Hesitating, Mae retreated back over the line. "Go away. The girl is under my protection."

The one still standing trembled and disappeared in a blinding blur of motion. A wide berth of shriveled nothingness remained, five immobile lumps littering the ground, not a whisper of life stirring them. Mae turned and faced Alexia, her innocence a halo of light against a backdrop of devastation.

"She is so powerful," the small girl whispered at Alexia's side.

Alexia blinked at the child, fighting to find the strength to merely open her mouth. "You should go inside."

The child nodded demurely and disappeared through the door.

Alexia felt as though her body had been bled dry, a limp shell, but something was different. Her muscles buzzed as if they'd been aching for use and had finally seen exertion. Warmth seeped through her, an unexpected high lifting her from the devastating exhaustion.

"Are they dead?" Alexia asked Mae and shoved up onto her knees, the world spinning.

"Soulless cannot be killed." The woman stepped around her and started back to the inn. Alexia knew differently. She had slain one once.

"These will not be harming anyone anytime soon," Mae said.

"We are going to leave them there?"

"Their friends will retrieve them. Not to worry."

John stood in the doorway, mouth a tight line.

Alexia stumbled to her feet, certain the power of gravity had doubled in the last hour. "And what about the enemy within?"

Mae paused. "Who do you think alerted me to the situation?" A smile lifted the corners of her lips. "John is my friend and guest, just as you are. I have provided him safe haven on moonless nights to stave his hunger, and while he is on these grounds he can taint no Passionate—intentionally or otherwise."

John cleared his throat. "Unintentionally. It has never been my desire to harm my fellows, as you fully know."

Or so he'd professed. Alexia scowled. "And yet you chased me toward them."

He shrugged. "You ran. None of my kind can resist the chase."

Kiren could not possibly have known John resided here, but Mae did. How could she not have warned them?

Mae shuffled toward the entrance. "He is awfully brave to stay here in my presence. Is that not so, John?"

"You are a woman to be feared and honored." He half bowed and stepped back for them to enter.

Alexia plodded after them, catching herself on the wall to steady her trembling knees. Propping herself on the doorframe, she crossed her arms and shot John a glare. "You would rid yourself of him if you had witnessed what I have. Was there no harm in raping Sarah of her gifts, in robbing her of the life she should have known?"

John stiffened. "Sarah is the only one I..."

Mae touched his shoulder, and his head bowed. "We all do things we regret." Her blank gaze lifted. "Except for those of us who are able to change the past."

Alexia tensed. What did Mae know? Could she see despite her blindness? Had she witnessed Alexia altering the child's fate?

John stepped forward, offering Alexia a chair. "Perhaps you would hate me less if you knew my story?"

She scowled but took a seat, gratefully. Mae bustled about the kitchen, a comforting presence to counter his.

"Before all this"—he motioned down his form—"I was like you—raised among humans, oblivious to our differences. I had a family—a wife, sons, even a daughter, all human, or mostly so." He rubbed a hand over his mouth. "*He* did not find me until well after I came of age, for I did not possess enough of the blood to be noticed. What I did have was a gift for healing—not as strong as his, mind you. It started as a talent for seeing what was wrong, and thus an ability to prescribe the correct treatment." He dropped into a chair across from her, elbows landing on his knees. "I served a small community as their doctor." A sad smile tugged at his cheeks, eyes far away. "In Wilhamshire."

She closed her eyes. The bustling town reared up in her mind, the winding streets and shop fronts, the tavern where she'd once weathered a night after Miles saved her and Sarah from the Soulless, the house on the hill where Kiren had imprisoned Bellezza—Haunted House of Stark.

"My given name is John Stark, after my father, and after his father."

Alexia gasped and sat back.

His brows scrunched down. "I met *him* over a patient one day. He observed my treatment and informed me I had rare gifts. I belonged to a secret race. To prove his point, he healed the child I had been treating, and proceeded over the next many weeks to teach me how.

"His home had been discovered by the Soulless, and he had been forced to vacate. While passing through Wilhamshire, he heard stories of my successes, and came to investigate. For a time, he resided in my home, until he was able to establish a new residence I have yet to discover. He became my…my children's godparent."

His fingers clasped into his knees. "But one day, after spending the night at a patient's sickbed, I returned home to find my wife and children murdered in a most brutal manner." His eyes darted from one wall to the other, cheek twitching. "The Soulless had come in search of *him*." He met Alexia's gaze. "My entire life was gone."

She shivered. It couldn't be true. John's family had not been massacred because of Kiren, had they?

"I went after them. *He* told me not to"—his head shook—"but I was determined to have my revenge."

She straightened up, but couldn't look at the man, the person who had lost everything because he showed kindness to a vagabond.

John mimicked her. "He spared my life even after I became one of the Soulless, and we have danced the dance ever since."

Mae placed a hand on Alexia's shoulder. "John is a good soul."

He rose and extended a hand of truce. "We are family now, whether you like it or not, and I will not make the same mistake twice. I protect my own."

She glared at his offering. "Is that what you did to Sarah?"

His brow scrunched.

Her fists balled. "You destroyed her."

He bowed his head. "While at your father's home, I chained myself in the cellar on moonless nights, but the child sabotaged my restraints and set me free."

Alexia's teeth ground together. Bellezza and her selfish whims!

"I had only enough time to warn Sarah and flee, but before I could escape, your fiancé arrived. The standoff ate my final moments of sanity. Desperate to escape, I shot a blind bullet and the next thing I consciously recall, Sarah lay in my arms, her transformation complete."

Her fury gave way to trembling. Again he had lost, because of Kiren. No, because of her. She did this to Sarah. To John.

Her chest felt hollow.

"Forgive me, Alexia." His extended hand dropped to his side. "You know how dearly I love her."

She gave a stiff nod. She had watched their relationship develop, the first truly healthy romance she'd observed.

Mae delivered a meal to John and shooed him below. He went with an exhalation of thanks and a few brief exchanges.

John and Sarah both suffered because of Kiren, because of her. Her eyes stung with waiting tears. She had done this to them both.

Mae settled across from her, silently waiting. Alexia brushed a sleeve across her cheeks. She just wanted to sleep, to let all this settle, and to really understand what she'd done only a few moments ago.

"I felt the shift." Mae's voice startled her. "Maiden of Time."

Thirty-Five

Fall Out

Kiren pulled his hands through his hair, working again to process Ethel's report.

Bellezza had escaped.

With Charles's assistance.

This was just one more headache he didn't have time to process. What was he supposed to do about Bellezza—especially now that the Soulless had knowledge of the Passionate's hiding places?

Ethel's head was bowed. Lester scrubbed a hand over his face. Miles was seated, picking at the grass between his feet, teeth grating back and forth silently enough no one else could hear it, but it set Kiren's nerves on end.

"I can go after her." Ethel straightened up.

"We cannot spare you," Kiren said. "Not with this new threat."

Lester nodded. "Agreed. We have to warn the others o' what's comin'."

Miles pounded the ground. "The only safe place is scorched earth, and we can't possibly bring everyone there."

"Or across the great waters." Lester cocked his head.

Kiren let out a heavy sigh. "We must again unite our kind and pray our unified strength will be enough to repel the enemy."

"But what about them Breeders?" Lester grated. "They ain't be willin' fer to join forces."

"Elizabeth North was," Kiren reminded. He didn't mention that she'd fought him every step of the way—until he'd revealed the identity of her father, a man who had been most anxious to reunite with her. Edward had never dreamed his daughter would know him, and Kiren had granted them some time to bond, even amid the crisis.

Tight expressions and worry filled each face.

"If they recognize the direness of the situation," Kiren continued, "perhaps they will cooperate peacefully. Last night, terrible as it was, may have been the very incident we needed to persuade them."

Miles shoved to his feet. "And if they decide to fight us instead?"

"You will know it." Kiren nodded. As much as he hated placing so great a responsibility on the lad's shoulders, it was what he'd been groomed for. Kiren had only hoped he could shelter Miles a few more years.

Ethel wrung her hands. "I do not like it."

"Aye," Lester agreed. "But it be time."

They all turned to the elder, Ethel's face a mix of terror and shock. Miles's brows tweaked, his mouth a tight frown.

Kiren blew out the breath he'd been holding. He'd been worried Lester might disagree, and as the oldest of them, his opinion carried the most weight.

Ethel pushed her sleeves up. "Then let us be to our business."

Miles tugged a hand through his hair, shuddering. Pity tightened Kiren's gut. Oh that he could spare the boy!

Kiren rolled his shoulders back. "Lester, Ethel, gather them in. We will converge at the inn and make our plans with equal say among the factions, see if we cannot unite as a nation."

Those words remained in his ears. *A nation.* Had the Passionate ever been fully united since the crusades? And would they welcome another war with humanity by coming together in their strength? He prayed not.

"Gather them in."

Thirty-Six

Purpose

"Maiden of Time?" Alexia's fingers curled in a tight ball. She hadn't told anyone—not Kiren, not Sarah. "How do you know about that?"

"You went back, did you not?"

Alexia nodded, her head a wide, cottony ball. She realized Mae couldn't see her motion. "Yes."

"You saw what I did to the Soulless. Have you met any Passionate more powerful?"

Alexia held her downy-stuffed head still. "No."

"But I have." The blind woman reached across the distance. "And she sits before me now."

"You are mistaken." Alexia rose and pulled back, stumbling into the wall, knees threatening to fail her. Her muscles felt like jelly.

Mae smiled. She seized Alexia's hand, her skin pulsing, bursting with life. "You have the power to shape the world."

Alexia swallowed, her voice small. "And you, the power to destroy it?"

Mae's smile remained although her head bowed. "Some give life. Some take it."

What a terrible gift! Alexia's heart tore in two. "And that is why you occupy scorched earth?"

The woman's mouth tightened.

"I rescued the child tonight, but I could not save Sarah. I was not strong enough." Alexia took a deep breath. "If I could have reversed the minutes, only a few, I might have delivered her from this fate. Why did it not manifest then?"

"Our gifts develop as we do, strengthening as our power to wield them increases."

Alexia blinked. "But if I can go back, we never need lose the medallion." She jolted toward the door, blackness inking out the room. Fingers held her firmly in place, the back of her knees smacking into a chair. She blinked her vision clear.

The woman's smile had shrunk. She squeezed Alexia's hand. "Do you trust me, Alexia?"

"Yes."

"Then allow me to help you."

They spent the evening discussing strength, motivation, and how to trigger one's ability. By midnight, when they retired, Alexia had a greater sense of how to access her talents and how they drew from her body's reserves. She could decide where the energy came from rather than destroying her brain—as seemed her default—but it would take practice and focus. Still, she had no greater understanding as to why this door had opened now instead of when she needed it most.

Dana. Her mother. She would have the answers Alexia needed.

She closed her eyes. All she had to do was want it, stepping out of time to the absence where her mother waited—a woman she'd never had the privilege of knowing.

"You have questions for me." The soft voice eased Alexia's lids open.

Too-green eyes, like her own, peered back around raven locks that curled freely down the breathtaking woman's back. She knelt next to Alexia, only a couple years older than herself, head cocked, half-smile welcoming.

"I am sorry that I have not been to see you since—"

"Time does not exist here, Alexia. You go, and the same instant you return. I am here for you."

"As you were there for my father?" She couldn't help the smart. Even so, the hurt in her mother's lowered gaze sent prickles of guilt into her stomach. "Why did you allow him to marry another woman when you so ardently adored him?"

Dana's brow twisted. She sat back and heaved a great breath. "I begged Charles not to leave for the university without me, but he felt to honor his father, he must. I intended to follow him..."

"You were prevented?"

Dana rubbed at her nails, focused on the cuticles, but far away. "It was the middle of the night when he came to me. I did not question it. He would leave in the morning and we had often been quite intimate, though not entirely." She hugged herself.

Alexia placed a hand on her mother's arm.

"It was not Charles in the darkness."

Alexia pulled back, shocked.

"His father, Benedict, claimed me." A single tear glistened down Dana's cheek. "For years I endured his accosts, even bore him a child whom he would claim belonged to his wife."

Alexia blinked and shook her head clear. "A child?" A shiver crawled down her arms. "Sarah..."

She had a sister, a true sister. Sarah was her sister!

Dana clasped both hands before her, and pressed them to her lips. "May she forgive me, when I learned of Charles's marriage, I could abide the union no longer. I forced Benedict's carriage off the road."

Alexia knelt. "Using a gift like Sarah's? To control wooden things?"

Dana's cheek twitched in a sad smile. "Not like Sarah." She rubbed a finger along the smooth black nothingness of a floor. "I had greater command of the world than she. For me, all elements obeyed, which is likely why my time was to be so limited."

Multiple gifts. They could possess multiple gifts like Bellezza's scream and ability to mist and her strength, or Kiren's healing and thought reading and adept hearing... Might she have more than one talent? She had not only slowed time, but leapt back and altered the outcome.

Dana's eyes flashed up, dark under her brows. "I would have moved all the elements to be with your father, and I did."

Alexia knew the rest of her mother's story. Her grandparents had died in the accident and Sarah became an orphan. Father had returned from Cambridge with his new bride, Rosalind, and Sarah fell into his custody. He returned to Dana's arms, his one true love—whom he had believed dead from his father's communications—and Rosalind discovered them. Their wedding bliss evaporated, but Rosalind still took Dana's child from Kiren's arms rather than sending her away after her husband's mistress died in childbirth. No one knew the deception, and Alexia had always been Charles Dumont's sole heir, until she could stand the lie no more and left to be with Kiren.

"I am so sorry." Alexia wiped at her own tears.

Dana huffed a single, sad laugh. "It was always meant to be this way. I should never have lived to raise you, but Rosalind did well."

Alexia's heart pinched. Her surrogate mother had given what love she could, constantly forced to face the evidence of her husband's betrayal. Alexia ached with longing for the woman.

But Alexia had gone back—only a few moments—and she had saved a child. Couldn't her mother have prevented this fate?

"You could have changed it," Alexia realized.

Dana looked up. "It is one of the gifts the heir of time possesses."

Alexia settled next to her mother. "One of them?"

Dana placed both hands flat on the ground. "You can mold time, but there are dangers. You can hasten the moments—though you cannot alter your physical placement." She lifted one hand and shook her head. "If a wagon should be driven through the space you occupy while speeding time, it will kill you." Her brow quirked, voice lowering. "Slowing time or jumping back is safer. You can alter the events around you, only a minute or two at a time. You can even evade death. Why, I escaped my own death many times."

"You what?"

Dana's fingers curled into loose fists. "You must start slowly—a few minutes at first, eventually an hour, only as far as is needed."

"Two days?"

Her head shook. "You cannot control the outcome of altered days, weeks, months. The danger of changing things..." She drew in a shaky breath. "The first time, the very first time, your Father and I were married."

Alexia's jaw dropped, words escaping her.

Dana smiled. "A simple wedding. He abandoned his family and wealth for me, fleeing to dwell among the Passionate. We lived peacefully in a cottage where he slaved day in and out, working the land to provide for us, labor that had never been demanded of him before." Her cheeks twitched. "He did not complain, but I could see the toil wearying him, and how he thought about all he had abandoned time and time again."

Alexia peered at her mother, too bewildered by the image of her father, high and noble, working the land with his own hands.

Dana bowed her head. "I thought I could make it better. I reversed the years and started anew. This time Charles took me to his home and informed his father we would marry. No argument could change his mind. We were in love." She nodded to herself. "And so we married. His father did not like it. He cut Charles off. Thankfully, we found mercy in a neighbor who housed and employed us.

"Charles made a minimal wage as a clerk and he was looked down upon by all he had formerly known. I became a blight and shame—the fortune hunting girl who had seduced a nobleman's son with her charms." Her pained smile broke Alexia's heart. "Men of money and breeding heard of our circumstance and began frequenting our benefactor to catch a glimpse of the 'gypsy child'—that is what they called me."

"How awful." Alexia hugged herself.

"In course of time, I had admirers, and it was more than Charles could do to keep them from harassing me." Her head bowed. "I kept the incidents hidden from him, or jumped back to erase them, but when one—" She shivered, her cheeks flaming red. "When one man *assaulted* me..." Her shoulders curled inward. "Charles happened upon us. He attacked the man, and in the struggle, he snapped the nobleman's neck." She glanced up and back down. "I was in no state to fix it, and we ran to escape a hanging."

Alexia could barely find a voice. "He actually killed a man?"

Dana's glistening green eyes met hers, brows low.

Married. They had been married. Alexia bit back tears as they pressed forward.

"We were chased and hunted, and finally I decided I could make things better. I went back. All the way back." She rubbed her hands as though cold. "The third time, I insisted our wedding be a secret, so Charles might retain his wealth and status. He agreed, reluctantly. We spent what time we could together without rousing suspicion, and in the course of months, I found myself with child. Charles was ecstatic.

"Of course I should have been also, but no one knew of our union. To the world I appeared a lewd woman. I returned to Mae's care and worried. Would this baby inherit my talents? And if so, what would become of me—for there can only be one, one to govern the flow of time."

Alexia leaned forward. "And if your child had bourn that power, you would have died?"

Dana nodded. "My time neared. I felt it coming, and at the end I knew I should not live through the experience." Again she looked at Alexia, her brows creased. "Cowardly, I tried again, the fourth time.

"This time, Charles did not want to marry me secretly. He demanded that we openly go to his father or we not be bound. I chose the latter, knowing what the former would mean. I regret that our relationship progressed. He came to me every night, and I could not refuse him.

"Again I found myself expecting, and this time with no husband to validate my condition. I was shunned by the Passionate. I was turned out and hounded. In his eyes I saw resentment and anger—both consequences of our sins. He stored me in a house with other expectant women until the time came for delivery. I kept thinking I could make it better—like the first time. We were poor and tired, but we were happy. If he chose that path once, surely he would choose it again. But I was mistaken.

"Each time I returned to the beginning, it changed—for the worse. I became a stop on the road, then servant in his house, then the mother of a bastard child—one who did not inherit time—then a murderer...

"Finally I conceded. I had dreamed of you so often, I knew you must eventually come into the world, and the last time, the worst time, I stopped trying. I did not have the heart to do it again. I could not make it better."

Alexia reached for her mother. Her fingers curled over Dana's peachy hand.

Dana smiled at the ground. "Start slowly—seconds, minutes, an hour perhaps, only as far as is needed."

"But you have gone back years!"

"And paid dearly." She turned up her large eyes. "You cannot control the outcome of altered days, weeks, months, and it will destroy you. Do not sacrifice all, like me."

Alexia clasped both hands in her lap. She ached for her mother, the pain she had experienced in trying to make a better life for her husband. Alexia would have done the same. And if anything happened to Kiren... "The Soulless think I can prevent their curse."

Dana's eyes widened, their lively green brimming with terror. She grasped her shoulders. "You cannot. We are given only our lifetime through which to navigate our gifts. You can return to any point in your existence, but to step beyond?" She shook Alexia. "It is not possible." She blinked away, as though calculating something more. "And even if it was, there can only be one. Do you understand? Only *one*." She leveled so they were staring eye to eye. "If you were to step into another time, what would become of your grandfather, of me?"

Alexia's mouth worked, no coherent reply forming. Could she destroy her ancestors by jumping beyond the bounds of her own timeline?

Dana's hands came together supplicating. "You have your own time. Do not ruin ours."

"You said it is not possible."

"It is not."

Her insides curled from the selfish wish, the guilt withering her heart. She wanted to do the impossible, to save them all.

"If I cannot go back, then we have no issue." Alexia shook her head.

"Good." Dana smiled. "Now go and learn. Practice your gift, but do not push too far too fast."

Thirty-Seven

Complications

Birds twittered free from their branches, launching into the sky, the only movement in the still lane. Amos pulled his hood closer, shading himself from the offending sunlight and focusing on the cottage ahead.

He glanced back over his shoulder. It was too still. He hissed as daylight scraped across his lower cheek, further frustrated by the empty lane behind him. Yesterday he snuck away from the others, found his way across the province, and reached the signal point. He had no indication as to what the signal would be, except that he would recognize it.

A breeze chilled his skin and he turned.

Amos froze.

The child, blonde ringlets, eyes thick enough to be buried in, dressed as finely as any king's child stood in the lane, grinning. Her delicately gloved fingers were clasped in patience, chin high.

He jerked about, searching for another set of eyes, a body, some evidence that this was wrong. She should not be here. She should have been apprehended by the Kingdom faction and carried off to prison for her betrayal.

Bellezza grinned widely, but smugly—as though her father had just given her a pony she'd manipulated him into offering. "The victor returns."

"What are you doing here?" he hissed.

"You did not believe I would allow you to have it, did you?" Her hands turned over, revealing a canvas wrapped package, and the hairs on his arm stood on end. "After you left me for dead."

He could still salvage this situation. *Think. Think.* "It had to look convincing."

Her grin deflated to a flat line, her voice lowering. "What an excellent idea."

Cold mist exploded about him. The girl was gone. Fog hovered over him, a suffocating weight muting the sunlight to a hazy orange, the hue of rotted fruit, the stench of death, the heaviness of suppressed rage.

Pain exploded through his chest. Fingers curled about his heart, crushing down with a teasing squeeze. "How about this?" The whisper hovered at his ear. "Is it *convincing?*"

Mist curled about his chest, an embrace from the demon child. Misery reddened the corners of his vision. He couldn't respond even if he wished.

Her cackle stained the air. "You poor, pathetic sod." Her wrist twisted.

White lightning shot through his body. A scream ripped from his lungs.

"No one crosses me and lives." Her grip tightened. "But as you cannot die, I promise, your torture will be excruciating, ingenious, and eternal."

Amos wished death would present itself and take them both.

Bellezza screeched, the shrillness burning his ears. She released him and Amos tumbled to the ground, vapor sucking away from his skin. He clutched at his chest. The girl stood, legs wide, shrieking.

He covered his ears, begging them not to burst.

Light glistened off the golden tip of an arrow that speared through her palm. The wrapped necklace lay on the ground at her feet.

Amos scrambled forward.

Shadows fell over him. A line of hulking silhouettes walled them in.

Bellezza tore the arrow out of her flesh, blood staining her satin glove, and dribbling down her elbow to drip on the packed dirt. A boot landed over top the pendant, a crossbow aimed right at the girl's head with another arrow nocked.

Bellezza dropped the bloodied arrow and burst into nothing. Mist cleared, and a ring of crimson eyes followed the half-rotted hand that plucked the necklace from the dirt.

In unison, the Soulless turned their backs on Amos and walked silently away.

He fumbled to his knees, ready to spring after them.

Pain sliced through his ribs. He gasped and looked down. Blackened blood oozed around the strange dagger protruding through his flesh and spearing his heart. He lifted his eyes to the bearer of the weapon, a woman with a delicate facial structure and crimson pupils. The red in her eyes faded, leaving a piercing green.

Had the red been an illusion?

Her short-cropped hair was reflective of Soulless style and near black, but the taint of rot didn't cling to her.

He gasped. "Deiliey."

She twisted the weapon and he toppled to one side.

Bellezza solidified in the bushes off the road as the woman straightened and removed her dagger, wiping it on his clothes. She tucked the weapon into her belt and followed after the Soulless.

Bellezza hazed to the miscreant's side and felt for a pulse.

Dead.

She stared after the woman. There *was* a weapon that could kill the Soulless. She'd heard rumors, but it was true.

Thirty-Eight

Learning

Sunlight pooled over the drooping line of flowers, the first clear day Alexia had seen all week. She shook her mind clear and eyed Mae who was ready to spar, poised on the safe side of the line, rolling pin raised like a club.

Alexia focused, recalling the instant exactly ten seconds earlier when Mae had batted her arm with the kitchen baton. She rubbed the tender skin and called her energies. They bubbled up inside, rising to the surface like a geyser ready to break forth. One of her greatest mistakes at first had been expending too much strength at once. Mae had taught her to envision and utilize only what was needed. Alexia lifted the lid and freed the inner steam. She focused on *when* she wanted to be in the timeline and reality twisted away—like a curtain being dropped over the present.

She blinked. Blackness cleared and Mae hefted the rolling pin.

Alexia tensed and sprung, dodging left, knowing her mentor would fake left and swing right.

The rolling pin whizzed by. She stilled as Mae hoisted the blunt instrument. "Again."

Must we? Alexia rubbed her arm reflexively and gasped. It didn't hurt. Not only that, she didn't feel ready to pass out. Rather, she felt invigorated, like she'd just taken a quick jog across a room.

Mae jabbed her in the ribs.

Alexia wrapped her arms around her aching bones, groaning, and focused again, calling the boiling wellspring to the surface. Three seconds back would do it. She released the energy and willed the change, watching as that curtain blanked out the present once more.

She blinked, and blackness dropped away like a stone.

"Again," Mae said. Alexia leapt back. The innkeeper stabbed the air with the rolling pin. She straightened. "Ah, you have figured it out."

"Finally," Alexia muttered, but she couldn't help a grin at the pride in her hostess's face.

"Now we must practice until it becomes a reflex."

Alexia grunted and readied for more pain.

Thirty-Nine

Gathering

Mist pulled together in the thicket where Kiren and Miles had made camp, and Ethel collapsed at Kiren's feet. He knelt and lifted her up. Her body heaved with the force of panting, limbs shaking. The tang of sweat and copper hit him, the front of her smock riddled with dried blotches.

"What happened?" he asked. His horse stamped and shook itself, obviously scenting the blood staining Ethel's smock. Miles woke, uncovered his face and lifted onto an elbow.

She leaned against Kiren. Salt scented the wind, the saline of tears. "There were too many."

"Too many?"

He, Ethel, and Lester had parted ways three days ago and gone different directions to gather in the Passionate, carefully following Edward's map of the known persons. Lester took the north and west, being the fastest. Ethel took the South. He and Miles took the road to London.

Ethel lifted a hand, offering her palm.

A sharing. It was easier than relating the experience through words. He shot Miles a silent invitation and took her hand. Closing his eyes, he welcomed the vision.

Ethel pulled herself into a solid state, feet touching down in the muddy lane. She'd been to three villages today and informed the Passionate residents of the gathering. The news was received with a mix of fear and excitement. She'd been welcomed and fed graciously in two households, but the others... She saw one man's determination to stay in the set of his chin, regardless of the directive, and she'd actually been chased away from another home at rapier point.

Despite that, this was the visit she'd been dreading most.

She lifted her gaze to the hamlet. The little town had hardly changed a day since she'd left two hundred years ago. They still built with the same shoddy

135

thatching for roofs, and the permanent perfume of cherry blossoms clung to everything. The orchards surrounding the place were in full bloom, a flush of green and red setting off the rural settlement.

A soft whisper of wind carried past her ear, one she knew. "Hello, Sybil," she said.

"Felice." Her mirror image appeared beside her, except where Ethel's white hair was neatly gathered in a braid, her sister's was wild and free, swirling on the wind.

"I no longer answer to that name," Ethel reminded her.

"Casting off your name will not change who you are." The flatness of Sybil's tone didn't surprise Ethel. Her sister knew only one way to be—frank and forthright.

"And that is where you and I shall never agree." Ethel faced her twin, arms crossed. She had abandoned so much more than a name when she left this place.

Sybil twirled a dismissive hand in the air. "If you are not here to resurrect an old disagreement, why did you waste your strength?" She leaned forward, entering Ethel's space. Fruity tartness taunted Ethel's nose—the familiar scent she had grown up with, the perfume of a sister she'd snuggled with on chilly nights and turned to after nightmares.

Sybil's face fell. "This is not an unplanned visit. You are groveling at that king-lover's feet and bending to his every whim."

Ethel's toes curled in her shoes. She hated that Sybil uprooted her calm so easily. It was what her sister wanted, for her to have returned permanently, but it would never come to pass.

"Well, what message have you to deliver this time?"

Ethel's visit here was pointless. Sybil and this Breeder community would never join with the others. She may as well be offering hay to a lion. "The Passionate are gathering."

Sybil huffed. "You mean to say, the Kingdom faction is demanding for people to gather. I had heard."

For all their years apart, her twin had yet to grasp the depth of her commitment to the would-be king. Ethel lifted her chin. "You should come with me."

Her sister scowled. "Have you gone mad?"

She let out a loud sigh. "Whether you choose to follow him or not, he has protected our young and allowed us to thrive in this land."

Sybil's mouth puckered.

"He cannot do so any longer."

Her twin's eyes widened.

A shriek carried down the thoroughfare. They both whirled. A boy of six charged through the street as shapes flooded out of the trees, fluttering, black, upright.

136

Ethel's heart stopped. They would not attack in the daylight, not when they had no power beyond brute force! The sun still hugged the sky!

But she couldn't dismiss what she was seeing. At least fifty bodies charged down the street and swamped into the meager buildings. Passionate burst from the confines like birds between trees.

She took a stance, prepared to fight. Sybil crouched in her periphery. The Soulless had made a grave error taking on a village with almost twenty full-blooded Passionate. The enemy was out-manned, no matter their numbers.

Something flashed silver as it whirled through the air and wrapped itself around a man's neck.

A chain.

Metal! They were wielding metal?

Light flipped toward her. She misted. A dagger sliced through the space, stealing the air from her lungs, but passing through without damage.

Sybil disappeared.

Not only were they wielding metal, they had recognized her as a child of the mist—else why would she have been one of the first attacked?

Glimmers of alloy blinked all through the skirmish. Ethel begged Sybil silently not to do anything foolish. This was no crazed scuffle. Soulless attacked in ranks, sticking close together and focusing on one enemy at a time, their limbs masked from the sun and from the metal they wielded.

The boy who'd first screamed hid behind a trough. Ethel materialized enough to wrap her arms around him and break into the void. She deposited him out front of the inn on scorched earth.

"Me da!" He turned on her. "Don't let 'em take me da!"

She leapt back through space and perched precariously on a roof. Chaos filled the street.

Mist broke and bent in the form of her sister, robbing a scythe here, beheading a Soulless there. She popped in and freed the chain from a woman's ankles, rocking back a second before a blade twirled through her space.

Ethel grabbed the woman and misted, whisking her back to the inn. She left the woman wobbling on her feet and returned.

Sybil threaded through the mass, dispatching the enemy with precision. A gray-bearded elder bent the light to blind his enemies while a soot-covered man pounded the ground with a fist, knocking the creatures off their feet. A short-haired woman faced two Soulless who crashed to the ground unexpectedly, pinned by an invisible weight.

Sybil appeared next to Ethel and threw a teenaged girl into her arms. Gaunt hollows cut into her sister's face. She was exerting herself too much. "Go!"

Ethel zipped back and released the girl, returning empty handed and grabbing the nearest Passionate. Twice more she whisked someone away, taking two on the last trip. Seven now. She returned.

A sickening cheer deafened her. The light caster had disappeared. The dirty man who rattled the earth was missing, and Sybil...

Her sister stood in the street, a chain wrapped around each arm, being pulled both directions at once.

Ethel shrieked. Heads turned her way.

She misted and grabbed the nearest weapon, pruning shears. Without thinking, she solidified in front of the Soulless creature holding one chain. She slammed his arms with the shears, knocking the chain free and fazed. The second guard tensed, waiting for her. She appeared, skidding across the ground on her hip, and smacked his knees. He crumpled.

She misted.

Sybil dropped to her knees, tearing at the links still squeezing one wrist. Her skin was a sallow yellow. Shrouds swooped inward.

Ethel popped between them, grabbed the dropped chain with a sleeve-wrapped hand, and whacked a line of them in the nose. Barbs cut through the cloth and into her fingers. She dropped the chain.

The creatures tumbled backwards. Metal links shot past her ear as she bent away. She misted across the ring, called the winds, and rocketed five of the Soulless onto their backs.

Panting, she emerged next to Sybil who dug clumsily at her manacle. A blade flashed overhead.

Ethel misted out.

A Soulless creature swung the weapon downward.

Sybil lifted her gaze.

The blade glistened, reflecting Sybil's surprise.

A scream tore from Ethel's lips. She popped in on the creature's back, but her weight wasn't enough. A sickening crunch rang in her ears. Fueled with rage, she locked an arm around the enemy's neck and yanked. Its neck snapped.

Black cloaks descended. She fazed away. She leaned on a chimney, unable to process what she was seeing. Sybil lay in a pool of growing crimson, metal piercing her stomach as she gasped and choked.

The Master could heal this.

Ethel misted to her sister and tore the weapon free. She wrapped Sybil in her arms and tugged toward the void.

It wouldn't open.

Creatures turned on them. Iron links still anchored Sybil's wrist. She locked eyes with Ethel, hers wide with the love they had always shared, no matter the disagreement. "Go," she whispered.

"Never."

Sybil shoved her away and cried out as blood oozed from her center, curling in on herself.

A hand came down on Ethel's shoulder. She misted and landed on the other side of her sister. The links had cut into the flesh.

"Go!" Sybil shouted.

"No!" Ethel reached through the mist for her shears. She latched onto them and pulled them to her. Soulless creatures jumped away to avoid the weapon as it shot through the air.

Ethel drove the sheers into the metal links. They dented. She felt the presence behind her and burst. The creature landed on the shears, carrying his weight and momentum downward.

The links snapped.

Ethel seized Sybil and shot away. She didn't know where the Master was, but it didn't matter. She would find him.

She emerged on a mossy bank, the place she and Sybil had spent many a day dreaming about their future. Never had they imagined, as best friends, their paths would diverge. How many years had she been begging Sybil to join the Master? If she had only listened!

Lazy branches shaded them from detection, the soft gurgle of a stream filling the air. They would shield Sybil until Ethel could return with the Master. She rose, but Sybil grasped her skirt. "Do not leave me."

"Sister."

Sybil choked and coughed up blood, her entire body seizing.

Ethel caught her and held her steady against her chest. "Hush. He can heal you."

A halted chuckle. "Not this time."

"Sybil—"

"Felice. You were always smarter than..." Her body shook, every limb trembling. "Promise you will..."

Ethel lifted Sybil's hand and placed it against her own cheek—the way they had done as children, always when words failed.

Bury me with our parents. The request sent shivers down to her toes. Tears spilled free.

Sybil's head tilted back. She sucked in half a breath. Her chest lifted. Her mouth widened to pull in more air, but never did.

Pain speared through Ethel's body, a ripping as her very soul tore in half. Wind gusted about her, ripping her hair loose from its braid.

She couldn't feel it.

It whipped and spiraled, slashing the branches above her head and tattering the ends of her gown.

She didn't care.

The torrent launched into the sky. Dark clouds gathered overhead, drenching the moss in shadow and blacking out the sky.

She wanted nothing more to do with sunlight. Her sister was dead.

Kiren held the listless woman. He didn't need to know how she'd spent the afternoon digging a grave, or how she'd laid her sister's body to rest with nothing more than a silent vow for retribution. She was changed. That much he understood.

"I am so sorry." His whisper was futile. She had needed him, and he hadn't been there. They had all needed him, and he was too weak to answer the call.

The Soulless had never attacked during the day before, and certainly not with such unity, but was it only his medallion's capture that had spurred this brashness? If they were attacking with weapons in the sunlight, what was next?

The loss of Ethel's sister was one they would all feel. Sybil had been the guardian of her settlement, the rock for twenty Passionate lives. She had given the others a reason to believe—no matter what her affiliations. More than that, she had been his friend before she learned of his true heritage and sided with the Breeders.

A hole opened up in his chest. One more empty space. One more loss.

He tightened his embrace around Ethel. Tears slipped down his face, and he prayed for strength—for them both. How could they survive another death? How could they continue when he no longer had the power to save them?

Because someone else has that power now.

He swallowed a lump. The stray thought was far from welcome. He'd known this was coming, but he didn't want to face it. *Not yet. Give me more time, just a few more precious days with her.*

Life was too short.

He straightened up. "It is time. No more running."

Ethel shifted in his arms, silent.

Miles tensed in his periphery. He nodded at the boy. "You and I will discover what intelligence we can, and the Soulless will have their war. We will utilize those who are assembled at the inn to spread word of our gathering and launch an offensive. There is no more time for us to be a separate people."

And there was no more time for him to be a separate person.

Forty

Sisters

Alexia leaned back on her pillow, unable to slow the pounding of her migraine. With the arrival of so many guests and refugees there was no quiet. Mae was a sergeant right out of hell, demanding, never compromising, pushing, and constantly barking new commands. She did achieve results, however, and Alexia could leap twenty seconds without thinking about it. It was how she'd avoided John all morning. Since learning of his sad story, she couldn't see him without aching for all he'd lost.

This morning Mae demanded that she jump back to before breakfast, nearly half an hour, and here she lay, paying for it.

The door creaked open, and she pulled the blanket tighter over her head. She didn't need Mae teasing her about being lazy with her head threatening to hammer a hole into the floor. And heaven forbid the woman should start in again with that abhorrent old English. It was nigh impossible to discern her meaning when she started snapping with the rough Germanic brogue.

The mattress dipped, shifting her. New agony burst through her temples, like the stampede of a hundred horses. She groaned.

A hand brushed over her curls. "You are so brave."

She flipped the blanket back. Sarah's bulbous form weighed down the mattress, her head tilted, eyes a wreath of Christmas contrasts.

She wanted to embrace her aunt—no, *sister*—and pretend nothing had come between them, that Sarah had not joined the Soulless, that their lives had not been turned upside down. She yearned for the simplicity of the days when they'd walked Father's grounds and laughed about pranks they'd pulled on their nanny, or the calm that had encircled them after Mother's loss, as they embraced and pledged to be ever constant to one another—when their greatest concern had been keeping Father from drinking or finding Alexia a suitable match.

And here they sat. Enemies.

"What is it?" Sarah's brows squeezed together. "Have I lettuce between my teeth?"

Alexia laughed and groaned, pressing her forehead against the pillow. She had missed Sarah's wit and good humor, but laughing was not a wise choice. It killed her that her nearest relative must be so close, and yet the very object of her constant worry and fear.

She loved Sarah.

She could not afford to love Sarah.

Her sister's brow lowered, the hopeful smile disintegrating. She sighed, placing a hand on her belly. "You will not shun your cousin, will you?"

Alexia grated her teeth, forcing the pain to dim. "Nephew."

"If you insist." Sarah beamed.

"How can you know it will be a boy?"

Sarah shrugged. "I am always right, as you well know."

Always—so intuitive about people and their behaviors, so observant and ready with the right word. But she had been wrong once, and that single choice had taken everything.

Her sister's lips trembled. "I am scared, Alexia."

She scowled. John had no right to impregnate Sarah owing to his Soulless nature, and she had no words of comfort to offer, because Sarah should be scared. She should be terrified.

"What if I should not live through this child's birth?"

Alexia sat up. Pounding spots slammed through her head, but she spoke through them. "But you will."

"And if I do not?"

This was the thing killing Alexia most. Her sister had become so serious since John took her, naught but the mere appearance of her best friend who laughed at the idea of ghosts and taunted her with horrible nicknames.

Sarah hugged herself. "Will you take him, if I do not—?"

"Sarah, stop." Alexia placed a hand over her sister's mouth. "You are going to raise this child, and he will be the sun for you."

Sarah bit her lip and nodded. "You are right. Dumonts are made of sturdier stuff." She huffed and wiped away a tear. She was no longer a Dumont, and apparently she'd forgotten that fact. Her face crumpled as though the realization had hit. "And you, are you worried?"

Of course she was worried. Alexia shook her head, jaw clenched. She watched the sky and hoped for Kiren's safety. He had not sent word of his efforts, which meant either he had been unsuccessful and captured, or was too far away to reach her. She tried not to think of it.

Sarah laughed. "All we do for them, and the men in our lives bring us nothing but turmoil." She sobered. "Perhaps we would be better off without them."

Alexia patted her sister's hand. Knowing what she did now, she might be able to go back and save Sarah from this fate. Why did that no longer feel like enough? Sarah was her sister, and the person who mattered most in the world, but John had been a good man. He didn't deserve this eternal hunger. And

Miles's parents? Countless others she did not know? How could she feel indifferent toward them—all victims to nature's cruelest trick?

But it was not possible to right this wrong.

Alexia seized her sister's fingers. "If something should happen to you, I will protect your child."

"Then he will be safe." Sarah's shoulders relaxed, as though she'd been holding up the weight of the moon with them, and it now slipped free. "How did you do it?"

"Do what?"

"The night I..." Her voice choked off. "When I changed, how did you defeat the Soulless?"

Alexia scowled. "My future husband was the one who defeated them."

Sarah frowned.

"But..." Alexia recalled that evening, black wraiths flooding into her father's estate and the seemingly normal sword in her hands. "I hear tell it is not possible to slay the Soulless, and yet..."

"And yet?" Sarah leaned forward, her eyes bright.

"The sword mounted in Mother's room, you remember the one—with the red ribbing about the handle?"

Her sister nodded.

"I slew one of them with it. I have relived that night a hundred times trying to decipher the reason, and it must have been the weapon."

Sarah blinked. "You are saying there is a weapon that can slay the Soulless?"

"I do not know. Not for certain." She almost confessed that the very blade was hiding beneath her mattress, but stopped short. Mae would not approve and she'd been so careful to keep it concealed. How would Sarah feel about such a thing in her presence?

Hands wrapped around Alexia's, Sarah's eyes wide. "Then we have hope. Do you know where it is? I pray you have it near—for all our safety."

That was right—her sister was hiding from the Soulless as well. How would those creatures feel about her child?

Still, Alexia hesitated. "It is here."

"Here?" Sarah gasped, leaning forward, a grin stretching her beautiful face. "Can I see it?"

Alexia slid the sheath from under the bed. Her sister bolted upright, emerald eyes widening.

"It is not a weight I like in my hand or life," Alexia admitted. "But if it means the difference in our survival, I will use it."

Sarah's head bobbed thoughtfully and she slid to her knees, a wicked smirk puckering her cheeks. "May I see the blade?"

Alexia hesitated. It was a weapon against the Soulless, against Sarah. Although she hoped her aunt's motives were nothing more than curiosity, she didn't trust her entirely. Alexia slid the weapon out of its covering and lifted it.

Sarah's eyes glimmered. "It is beautiful."

Alexia scowled and looked the blade over. The metal was blemished and the blade chipped in several places. To call it beautiful was to admit a loss of sanity, but it was hers.

Sarah reached out and ran a finger along the edge. She gasped and pulled her finger back, sucking on a cut. "Well, it did not kill me," she uttered around her finger.

Alexia had to believe she imagined the glimmer of madness in Sarah's eye, but the fact she'd sliced her finger… Was she attempting to end her own life?

Alexia lifted the weapon vertically, away from her aunt. Why did it feel so natural in her grasp? "I think it must be plunged right through the heart."

"I will *not* be testing that theory." Sarah laughed.

It was just her imagination. Alexia chuckled along, needing the laughter, but also more relieved than she dared admit. But of course! This was Sarah, the woman with more life in her than anyone Alexia knew!

Sarah nodded. "You should name it."

Rising, Alexia gave the blade an experimental swing. "It seems wrong to name a weapon."

"Then I shall name it." Sarah got to her feet and curtsied at the weapon. "I hereby dub thee *Slayer*."

"*Slayer?*"

"What else would you call a sword?" Sarah shrugged. "May I?"

How rare it was that Alexia had something her aunt wanted. She tucked the weapon behind her back. "No."

"Oh come, Alexia." Sarah rolled her eyes and reached for the hilt, her sliced finger catching the light. "I just want to feel its weight."

Alexia jerked it back, laughing as Sarah missed. "And cut yourself again? What kind of friend would I be, allowing you to come to harm?"

Her aunt giggled and faked right, swerving left and catching the hilt.

Alexia's grip tightened. "You cheat!"

"Just let me hold it."

"No!"

Sarah yanked, pulling Alexia off balance, but she didn't release her hold. Her grip slipped as laughter shook her frame. Her sister jerked again, both of them losing their clutch. The blade whirled free.

Smack!

It ricocheted into the bedframe and slammed into the wall. The metal crashed to the floor in two pieces.

"Agh!" Alexia dropped to her knees, pulling the pieces together, heart crumpling. It split almost exactly down the middle, leaving a jagged dagger clinging to the too-large hilt. It had been old, the metal brittle, but…

If she wasn't on scorched earth, she would jump back in time and keep it from happening. It shouldn't matter to her—it was a weapon after all—but it was almost like a piece of her had just broken.

Sarah knelt next to her and offered the sheath, head bowed. "I am sorry."

Alexia accepted both, the sheath and the apology. It was just a sword, after all. She had her sister back.

She picked up the broken portion and halted. "Now there are two."

They met gazes.

Alexia lifted the broken end. "You should have this, to protect your child."

Forty-One

Moonlight

"...two weeks of travel is not enough? Someone else's rump can take a horse-beating for now."

Alexia sat up in bed. She threw the covers off and raced to the door, halting as she remembered her dressing gown. Her fingers shook as she wrapped herself and threw the door open, halting at the balcony rail.

Kiren stood in the great room below, gaze snapping to her. She gasped at the strain of material across his broad shoulders, the added color in his countenance, the wisps of hair that had fallen free from its tie and framed his pointed chin, the crushing wave of need sweeping over her from his oceanic eyes.

He was the day she'd been stumbling toward while wandering through midnight lands.

They moved the same instant—he to the stairs, she along the balcony rail. He mounted the steps two at a time and reached the top as she arrived. He threw his arms about her waist and lifted her off her feet. Sweetened oak overwhelmed her senses and she looped her hands about his neck, burying her nose against his honeyed skin. He lowered her, one arm gliding free, his fingers trailing warm tingles down her cheek.

"How I have missed you!" he whispered, cupping her cheek.

"Not nearly so bad as I have missed you. Did you recover it?"

His smile faded. "I will." His lips silenced her, carrying the fervor of a smoldering bonfire. She opened to them, adding her own dried logs to the flame. His mouth traveled down her neck and back up, pausing at her ear. "How have I survived your absence?"

Sparks shot through her limbs, feeding the primal desire at her core like a parched desert begging for its first drop of rain. "No more surviving. It is time to feast."

His nose grazing her ear as he turned, glancing down where Mae busied herself sweeping, very obviously ignoring them.

Alexia kissed him briefly, and tugged him forward.

146

Mae cleared her throat from below. "No unlawful business up there, you two."

Heat flared in Alexia's cheeks. Kiren laughed and followed her into her room.

Alexia said, "She is not insinuating—"

"Mae loves me and could never believe ill of us." He winked. His scar, she loved how it caught the light with every word. His lips, she admired their cheery color and extreme kissability. His soul, she ached to possess it as her own.

She wrapped her arms around his waist beneath the suit coat, seizing control of his mouth before he could protest. He groaned deep in his throat, a ravenous wolf. His hands pulled at the material around her shoulders, gliding down to her hips. Her own inner wolf rose up to meet him, fangs bared. Her back slammed into the wall and awareness melted into their shared space. Kiren's need crashed into her like waves against a coral reef, penetrating the pores, seeping deeper, demanding for this battle to be over—to have her entirely.

They should be married already.

He pulled back, his hands trembling against her cheeks. She trapped his skin to hers, lifting her lips to dive back into him.

"Alexia, stop."

She ignored the warning in his voice, grazing her mouth across his. "I do not want to."

His lips followed hers, barely restrained as fiery breath raged across her chin. "And that is precisely why we must."

He was right. Of course he was right, but still...

She brushed the loose hairs behind his ear and traced the dark circles below his eyes. "Have you eaten recently? Slept?"

"Enough."

She pushed him back and placed her hands on her hips.

He chuckled, yanking her into his arms. "Your sternness may prove enough to break me. You must stop looking so adorable." Ominous swells crashed over her from his marine tides, almost more than she could bear.

She tugged at his collar. "I warn you, I am not the helpless girl you left behind, sir."

"Sir am I now?"

She giggled with him.

Kiren lifted her fingers to his lips. "I have so much to tell you, but there are too many ears here. Retrieve your shoes and let us away."

"But I am not dressed." She lifted the corner of her gown to illustrate.

His hands looped her waist. "You are dressed enough for me. And just for me." Her cheeks burned. "Come now, love."

She slid her feet into shoes and allowed him to drag her out the door and down the stairs. They tiptoed past Mae, into the kitchen, and out the back door.

Someone stood in the moonlight outside the protective circle, a shimmering white silhouette—long ivory hair floating loosely on a breeze, gaze averted.

Alexia turned a questioning look on Kiren. Why would he drag her out in the middle of the night to witness her mother-figure undone? Kiren smirked, winked, and drew her forward.

Placing a hand on Ethel's shoulder, he whispered, "We are ready."

The woman extended a hand and blindly took his. His fingers slipped between Alexia's, and the world disappeared behind a wall of mist. A swirling breeze raced over her skin as the ground dropped away beneath her feet. She squeezed Kiren's grip tighter and clamped her eyes shut, anxious for the wind to fade. It did. Her eyes popped open as Ethel blurred into a cloud and disappeared, leaving them alone.

The hum of crickets filled her ears. Leaves whispered in a night symphony, blocking the moon and stars above. Kiren tugged her forward, into the black.

A glimmer of light broke through the trees. The gurgle of a stream welcomed her forward, and he pulled back a veil of moss to reveal a single lamp perched on a rocky surface, water burbling below. Brilliant flowers flooded the small clearing, foreign pinks, purples and oranges she knew Kiren had taken great care to preserve. Trees he had fashioned into the likeness of past friends circled this woodland haven, living wooden sculptures.

At the center of the grove waited a bed, an actual bed—four posters, a feather mattress, several luxurious looking blankets, pillows—all safely tented within a mesh canopy.

Her breath caught in her throat.

She stepped closer. Thin twined tree limbs formed the bedframe, periodic leaves sprouting off in random directions. Each post supported the white gauze, illuminated by the single lamp like a cloud against a dark night.

She swallowed.

"Are you surprised?" Kiren's fingers slid around her hips, his mouth pressing to her neck. She lost herself in the simmering stir of slow kisses, traveling downward.

"I do not understand," she barely voiced, too conscious of the volcano within, brimming to explode.

His lips traveled back up to her ear. She turned, seizing control of his mouth and raking her fingers down his chest. Shimmers of sunlight shot through her body, like she'd been trapped on a polar icecap and the fingers of day were tickling through her chest, filling her with so much radiance she might burst.

He pulled away, forcing some distance between them, panting, his eyes fierce with a fear she didn't understand. He straightened up and pulled a hand through his hair. "This was to be your wedding night surprise, but as that may not happen for some time..."

Who needs a wedding? She blushed at the thought. Of course Kiren couldn't break one of the fundamental rules governing their society, and she felt dirty just for considering the possibility, even if he should already be hers. Averting her gaze, she asked, "And why have you brought me here?"

"Dearest," his knuckles locked around his ginger waves, "I should have told you this some time ago, and I tried, but..."

She lifted her gaze.

His lips trembled apart. "It is possible to be prematurely bonded, even without a physical union. The instances are rare."

She blinked up at him. What was he saying?

"I hope you understand, but I believe the night you came of age, when I kissed you in that heightened moment..."

Alexia gasped, covering her mouth.

"I have been so careful with you because..." His shoulders rolled back. "Because I am yours, entirely." He reached for her fingers. "And I hope you are mine."

She bit her lip.

Kiren pulled her toward the bed and she settled onto the mattress. He sat beside her.

"Is it possible," Alexia asked, "for you to be bonded to me, and I not to you?"

His lips pursed. He shrugged. A twitch in his cheek suggested he knew, but the set of his mouth said he would never reveal it.

Both hands came together in front of him. "The point is, very soon our calm will end, and this knowledge may prove necessary for your survival."

"Will it?"

He sighed. "Miles has apprehended intelligence from one of the Soulless that suggests Bellezza knows where they are keeping my pendant. He and Edward are searching for her."

Alexia whirled on him, her throat tight. "You are working with Miles?" How could he have not told her? He knew how dearly she loved Miles, how tormented she'd been by his dismissal. "Where is he? When will I be able to see him?"

Tugging a hand through his hair, he hissed in a breath. "Soon."

The hesitation shocked her. Had he been keeping Miles away from her intentionally? That was silly. "Would Miles not know the pendant's location from seeing into the consciousness of the Soulless?"

"They were cunning." Exhaling loudly, he continued, "They covered their movements. Even so, Miles has worked to keep his mind free of theirs each moonless night. What little information we did gather on our return to the inn was disjointed, but we now know Bellezza conspired with the Soulless to steal my pendant."

Alexia shouldn't be surprised, but disappointment collapsed her chest. She had hopes Bellezza could be redeemed. Perhaps that too was madness.

"Miles and Edward will find her." He wrapped one of her curls about his finger.

She lifted her gaze to his. "What of Father? Is he safe?"

He nodded. "Would you like to see him before we return?"

"Please." She clapped eagerly.

The warmth in his stare fizzled to gray. "Why is it I take you away from everything you love?"

Alexia caught both his hands and brought them to her lips. "Kiren, I did not know what it was to love until I met you."

His brows lowered. "You have loved more deeply than either you or I know."

She touched his cheek, confused.

"I will be called to my duty in the coming days, far away from you."

She bit down. "Why do you assume you must do this on your own?"

He sighed and a cloud of sorrow dropped over them. "There are a few more things you should know."

Alexia lifted her head and met his tired gaze, afraid to say something and interrupt. He closed his eyes.

It was there, on the surface. She could feel it, like an egg on the brink of the counter, teetering and ready to topple, terrified that it would plummet to the floor and shatter. She wanted to utter the words, "*I will catch you*," but didn't dare. If he was finally ready to reveal his ominous past, she would stand back and give him as much breathing space as needed.

"What is it you fear to tell me?" she whispered.

His brows scrunched together. His lips twitched, twisted, and pulled downward, voice soft. "You see me more clearly than anyone."

Alexia placed a hand on top of his.

He stilled. "My parents are dead." He stared up at the bed's canopy, the pulse in his neck the only indicator of his distress. "And it is because of me."

She counted his heartbeats, waiting for him.

"The necklace belonged to my father." His lashes trembled against his cheeks. "My mother had one as well. They were ancient relics, tied to an inexhaustible power source: one charm to defend, the other to protect."

She touched his knee. "Your father worked for the king, protecting him? And your mother as well?"

He scratched his head, sliding his knee from beneath her grasp. "My father was the king."

Alexia leapt to her feet.

His mouth twisted as he met her stare. No deception hung in his gaze, more of a tremulous fear she'd despise him for the news. The king. His father. A king!

"You are a prince?" She gasped. "An heir to a throne?"

Rubbing his brow, he gnawed at his lower lip. She wanted to trace the curve of his mouth and draw him back to her, but he was royalty. Should she touch him at all? She was so far below his station—a half-breed and bastard child. He ought to shun her.

Kiren's whisper startled her. "They are dead, and their kingdom with them."

She shivered against the sadness laden in his tone. Not only had he lost his empire, but his family as well. "You blame yourself for this?"

His shoulders dropped lower.

"Please, Kiren." She caressed his arm. Whether she was worthy of him or not, he needed her. "Tell me?"

His head fell into his hands. "Our parents bestowed the medallions on us. They should not have. They needed the protection far greater than we."

"We?"

He lifted a staying finger.

"You cannot help that they made their decision." She resumed her seat beside him. "This is not your fault."

He gave a mirthless smile. "Perhaps not, but the rest is." Bending his neck, he picked at the blanket, his voice a resigned sigh. "Father had been ruling for ages, and because of his many powerful enemies, he kept my birth a secret." The fidgeting stopped, his hands flattening out. "He would have revealed me to the world when I was strong enough to withstand the dangers."

She slid her fingers over his, but he snatched them away. She flinched, stung.

Kiren wrapped his arms about himself. "I took it." His head bowed, eyes closing. "Father explained the relic, the seemingly ordinary overturned bowl that would make our home invisible to our enemies, its magical properties shielding us from detection." He groaned and rose, pacing away from her. "The source of their safety, and I took it."

Her heart was breaking for him.

"I only went as far as the brook," he muttered. "If it could hide our home, surely it could hide a frog."

She went to him, placing her forehead against his back, listening to the tragic stutter of his heart.

"I was only a child. It was an act of curiosity and yet..."

She slid her arms about his waist.

"The roar of fire drew me back home." His muscles tensed, and she questioned if he'd pull away from her again. She could feel the tremor building from his heart outward. "The flames, the cottage..." He swallowed loudly. "They are dead because of me."

She nuzzled his shoulder, wishing she could ease his agony.

His chest expanded, his body shaking. "They are gone because of me."

She pulled him around, cupping his cheek and drawing his gaze. "Did you set the fire?"

His head barely shook.

"Kiren, my dear, sweet, overly-responsible man, you are not to blame." She brushed the hair back from his face. "It may have simply been the result of an overturned lamp or stray ember."

He seized her fingers, eyes dancing wildly. "Oh, that I could believe such a possibility, but it was one of our enemies, the man who..." He bit his lip.

"Who what?"

Kiren's head turned away, eyes closed once more. She brushed over his scar. "I have a twin sister," he confessed.

She blinked. "You what?"

A tortured smile crooked his cheek. "She was with me when they died, but we became...separated."

She pressed on his chest. "Who is she? Have I met her?"

He ran a hand through his hair. "I have searched, you do not know how far and wide I have searched, but I cannot reach her."

Of course he had. How terrifying, to know your own flesh and blood wandered the world somewhere, to realize they haunted some hidden corner you could not penetrate.

Alexia placed a hand over his heart. "Is that why you gather the Passionate? Hoping she will come to you?"

His lashes trembled closed. He captured her fingers, locking them against his breast. "I gather them to protect them. I gather them for you." A hopeful quiver shook his voice. His eyelids lifted to reveal a hint of sunrise against a beautiful blue sky.

"Me?"

He cupped her cheeks, gazing deep into her eyes like he hoped some recognition would suddenly appear. He exhaled, dimming. "You are my family, Alexia."

His words struck her like a mallet. She bit her lip. "I will be. But what about your sister?"

"She is protected by a medallion. My parents and their kingdom are gone, and I am not inclined to resurrect the order set in place by my father. It is a heavy burden, one I am not certain I shall ever feel worthy to bear. Not in this world."

She tried to interrupt, but he placed a finger to her mouth.

"The Passionate are weak, and my family's enemies still roam this land. It is enough that this war is driving us to unite, something I have long hoped for."

She nodded.

"One day we shall rise to power." He gazed into the trees. "But that day is still far distant. For now it is much easier to cling to what is good, nurture what is young and fragile, and pretend I am nothing more than a man in love."

She traced the pleats of his suit coat. He was a prince, the heir to a throne, a leader and champion of the Passionate, a healer and friend to all, the eternal possessor of her heart. "You will always be so much more than a man in love."

He grinned. "And you, so much more than my distraction."

The Maiden of Time. She couldn't forget that. Did that place her in the same realm as royalty?

His blue pools wept in a misty morning sadness, his earlier depression weighing over them both. "Judge me tomorrow, when you have digested the information. I would have no secrets between us, Alexia. I would have you for my equal."

She grinned, attempting to lift the sadness. *His equal.* "Will that make me a princess?"

"If I am ever restored to my parents' throne, you will be queen."

Her heart squeezed. She had studied the obligations of royalty, how their lives were dedicated to the people they served, how they were always watched, scrutinized, held to an impossible standard. Such a public call had never appealed to her, not even as a child. What made it worse was that he could read her displeasure. "You know I abandoned my family's prestige, never anticipating the obligation should again be mine."

His eyes turned down. "I know, and I am sorry."

The regret in his frown twisted her heart. She caught his face and lifted it. "Well, I should not mind so much having servants to do the laundry or clean the chamber pots."

He broke into a low chuckle.

She pressed her forehead to his and kissed him lightly. Her equal. "I will have you for my husband, no matter how many complications are involved, no matter how many things for which you hold yourself accountable. I love you."

A bird twittered from a branch overhead, the distant glow of sunrise painting the sky a lighter shade of blue.

Hope.

Kiren grabbed her, eagerly aiming for her lips.

The ground shook. They both stumbled, and Kiren caught Alexia, grabbing hold of the bedpost.

Forty-Two

Infiltration

A chill tickled down Charles's spine. He halted mid-step and counted to five. It was his imagination. How many days had he spent in this hidden estate, and despite the strange breezes and occasional disembodied whispers, he and that cook remained the only two occupants.

At first he'd felt like a prisoner. After Nelly explained the situation, how his being out in the world would place Alexia in danger, he'd resigned himself to their strange library, hourly walks through the halls, and the occasional raid of the wine cellar. The chatty woman keeping him company would speak of the weather, maintenance about the house, and odd facts of nature, but never a word about his daughter or her soon-to-be husband. The quiet was driving him mad!

Early morning light trailed across the hall, bars of gold against a figurative jail.

Panting rasped in his ears. He spun.

Two shrouded figures stood at the top of the stairs, their robes robbing the hall of light. Ice raced up the back of his legs. He gasped and reached to his hip where a sword would have been mounted in his soldiering days. His fingers wrapped around air.

The creatures turned toward him. One stepped into a streak of light, and crimson pupils pierced through the darkness of its hood.

Show no fear in the face of the beast.

His breathing slowed. In the room to his right he would find furniture he might mangle into a makeshift pike or shard, but to buy himself time he'd have to barricade the door and he couldn't think of anything substantial enough to keep two grown men from breaking through.

They slunk closer.

The floor trembled. Things clattered over in the rooms, echoing into the hall. A vase crashed. The creatures halted and widened their stances to remain upright.

Blinding whiteness whipped out of nowhere.

Forty-Three

Quake

Kiren caught himself on the bedpost and steadied Alexia. The rumbling faded.

How strange. England had never been prone to earthquakes.

An avalanche of crashes echoed through the branches, a distant clattering. Birds skittered free, launching into the sky like dust motes from a disturbed drapery.

Kiren's blood froze. This was no freak quake.

Nelly.

He launched through the trees, stretching his senses beyond the branches. *Shouting. Deep voices. Hissing.*

"Kiren, stop!"

Vertigo tore at his insides, spinning him mentally back toward the little woman chasing after him, his match, his perfect other half. He bit down. How was he supposed to keep her safe and rush to his friends' aid? Why did it have to be one or the other?

"Go back, Alexia," he called over his shoulder.

"Ripe chance of that happening." In a blink she was sprinting at his side.

He almost missed a step. "You just jumped."

"Slowed...time," she panted.

His fist tightened. She would kill herself from overexertion given half an excuse. "You should not be following me."

"Then make me stop."

He grinned. He could do it, but she would find means to punish him later as payment. His smirk dropped as he glimpsed her white skirt. "You are not dressed."

"I am enough for you."

He ground his teeth. "Alexia—"

"It was the estate, was it not? That noise?"

He clenched his lips, focused on the careful placement of his feet. She jogged at his side, eyes straight ahead, brows low. He wondered how she had the energy to keep up with him until she blurred in his periphery. He was out pacing her, and she kept taking breaks, then catching up with him.

Such a strange reality.

The trees thinned and he reached out to slow her, scanning the horizon. Where there should be a building, sky met his view. Rubble covered the ground.

He swallowed.

Alexia's jaw hung. He waved for her to stay as he moved forward. Dust covered the ground like powdered snow, layered in a wide circle well beyond the collapsed timber and stone. Decades of work in ruin.

He snapped to attention, scouring the grass for signs of passage.

There.

Dusty footsteps converged at the east end of the grounds. He hurried over and bent to trace the debris.

Nelly had been here, just before a struggle. Or Charles.

The tracks bled away south in snowy prints. Two grooves lined the trail, likely the drag of an unconscious person's heels.

Captured. One of them was a prisoner—like so many missing others—and would become a feast on the next new moon.

He would stop them this time.

Kiren followed the confusion of prints, trying to discern which of the two had been taken, but it was useless. How had they discovered the location of his house? Granted, Ethel had not been here to obscure it with the mist, but the only way they could have known of its location was if...

Miles.

They must have gleaned it from Miles the night they learned of so many Passionate hiding places. How many had been taken because of that single night?

He glanced back at the rubble, his chest constricting with tightness.

If Charles hadn't escaped, if instead he lay buried somewhere in that mess... Kiren couldn't swallow the lump.

A hand landed on his shoulder.

He whirled. Alexia jumped back.

He slowed his breathing and reached for her. Her fingers slipped between his, tightening and pulling him closer.

"Kiren?"

"I have failed again."

"You have not—" Her mouth remained open, eyes widening, fixated over his shoulder.

He turned.

Two scarecrow forms stood on the edge of the clearing, their ragged cloaks flitting in the wind like the black flames of a dying world.

He threw Alexia behind him. They couldn't taint anyone, not in the daylight, but they would attempt to overpower him or injure them both, and what if there were more in the trees?

The accursed sprinted across the distance. Alexia grabbed his arm and stepped forward, assurance and steadiness filtering through her grip. She met his eyes. Urgency flashed in her depths, and a warning: *Go to safety. Meet me back here when you have help.*

She vanished.

Kiren whipped toward the Soulless and gasped. Alexia stood behind the creatures.

He blinked his eyes clear.

"You!" she yelled. The Soulless stopped and turned. "I hear rumors you are searching for the Maiden of Time."

Kiren tensed. What was she doing? He raised a hand, begging her silently to stop.

She lifted her chin. "Here I am."

Their heads swiveled, leaning one direction, then the other.

"What are you waiting for?" she called.

They turned on her. She blurred, appearing half a second later at the edge of the trees.

He stared, unable to move. He knew she had the potential, but seeing her use her gifts with such strength! How had he found himself a companion so gifted, one who put even him to shame?

She blurred and disappeared entirely. He wanted to go after her, but she was right. There was nothing he could do for her, and Ethel would be waiting by now. He sprinted back the way he'd come, shame filling him with every step. He should be the one protecting Alexia, not the other way around.

A strange bubble formed in his gut. It wouldn't settle, and it irked him.

They were not equals. She was his better—in every way. Why should that bother him?

Ethel waited for him at the designated spot, mist whisking off her arms and hair in a nervous haze.

She rushed forward. "Where is she?"

"The wooded estate."

Her eyes shot wide and she seized his arm, instantly sucking him into the cloud. His feet touched down over the uneven rubble of his demolished house. Ethel was gone before she'd fully materialized. She appeared a second later, holding Alexia's arm.

Kiren threw his arms about Alexia. His mind screamed the number of things that could have gone wrong. He would never put her at risk again.

Never.

Ethel's shoulders slumped, her knees crunching into the snowy debris. "The Soulless are not far." She reached out, and Kiren caught her elbow before she toppled over. Dark rings hung beneath her eyes, skin a gaunt white.

"Do you have enough strength?"

"I do."

Kiren frowned. She was getting old, and the strain of recent days had been so great.

Ethel looked him right in the eyes, head bowed knowingly.

He took Alexia's hand and nodded. The world faded into mist.

Forty-Four

Favors

Charles batted at the mist, the hall clearing. The golden-haired child crouched before him.

He backed away across the shaking floor, raising his hands, unsure if he should fist them or flatten them in surrender.

Behind her two dark figures staggered forward.

She burst into smoke and appeared right in front of Charles, seizing his wrist. Odd warmth swarmed into his skin, intoxication far deeper than that found at the bottom of any bottle. His eyelids drooped, her nutmeg aroma the only thing he craved.

"Charles Dumont." Her soprano stole his breath, so like the hymn of tinkling bells. Who cared that the world was quaking around him! "You saved my life. Now I save yours."

Plaster from the ceiling crashed next to him. "What the—"

"Hold your breath."

She had cast her spell on him. Rage pumped through his body. How dare she touch him! How dare she exert her influence and cloud his brain! "I am not—"

White mist wrapped itself about him. He choked and gagged, closing his mouth. He hung suspended, like in a dream, surrounded by nothing but silence and the distant rumble of angry winds.

Weight returned, his feet touching down. The fog cleared, sucking inward as Bellezza formed in the center.

He ripped his wrist free, disgusted, terrified. "What are you?"

Her head tilted and she mimicked his bass, "Thank you for saving my life, Bellezza. I am eternally indebted to you." Her lip lifted in a snarl. "And here I thought Alexia learned her manners from you."

Alley walls locked them in, tight enough he could touch both sides without extending one arm fully. He peered over her head as wagon wheels rattled across cobble. Fresh bread and grime mixed in the unmistakable stench of a small town.

"Where have you brought me?" he demanded.

"My, my. Temper." She smirked. "I knew I liked you for a reason."

His nostrils flared. "The Soulless, how did you know? Why did you come?"

She shrugged and took a little hop skip toward the alley exit. "I was tracking them."

He grabbed her shoulder and whirled her around, bolting her down in his grip. Her teeth locked together, lips peeled back, eyes a quagmire of murder. He had seen her like, angry lads on the battlefield who had something to prove, and he would not be intimidated by the act.

"Why?"

She shrugged him off, his fingers sinking right through the mist of her shoulder. Her chin tipped downward, a teasing little smile lifting her lips. "Despite being a man of leisure, you freed me." Her nose crinkled. "I would go so far as to suggest you did so against your inclinations."

He took a step back, shaken to his core.

She giggled, her eyes sparkling. "I could see your desire, sir. I am no stranger to wantonness."

"You are a child," he barely voiced.

"I am no more a child than you are a gambler," she hissed, advancing. "You and I are much alike. You prefer shooting to thinking, lock yourself in with your memories at odd hours, and indulge in a fondness for anything that may drown your sorrows." She slipped past him, dragging a finger along his bicep. "I share those loves, but prefer to exact revenge on those who cause my sorrows."

He reluctantly pulled away from her touch. "Why have you brought me here?"

She giggled and clapped. "I would like to propose another exchange, as our first one has concluded so nicely." She curtsied. "You give me something I want. I give you something you want."

Charles prickled. "You have nothing I want."

She rolled her eyes. "To know the real Benedict Dumont?"

His father's name rang in his ears. His estranged father. Their relations had become strained after Charles returned from military training, when his father denied him the one thing he desired most: Dana.

And then Father died in a carriage accident.

Charles shook himself.

A grin widened Bellezza's mischievous face. "I shall tell you precisely why your precious Dana could not come to you at Cambridge, and I do believe you will be adequately motivated to assist me."

"Why should you need me when you can simply—" He whirled his fingers outward to illustrate her poofing.

Bellezza tugged at his lapel. "Because it is so lonely doling out revenge."

He pushed her back, reaching for a weapon that was not docked at his hip. He couldn't afford her touch if he hoped to make it safely through this, and he suspected part of her wanted him to crumble, that all this was a test.

She shook her head. "Whether you like it or not, you are the son of a Collector. I should be inclined to end your life, except you seem to have saved mine. I propose a truce. An alliance."

"Is that all?"

Her grin faltered. "Do you know what the Collectors collect?"

"You speak in riddles, girl."

Her fists balled, her lip twitching upward to reveal teeth. She stepped back, the rage bleeding from her eyes. "Passionate. They collect the Passionate—like your precious Dana who was collected by your father."

The words jangled through his brain, a discordant collapse of bells in the tower that had been his mental fortress. Charles's knees quivered.

All those years ago when he left home for Cambridge, Dana promised to meet him on the road and then never appeared. He hadn't understood. Had she been unwell? Unable to follow? He wrote home and inquired on her state of health, only to be informed by Father that she had died from scarlet fever. He mourned his beloved for three full years, unwilling to return home for his anger with Father. At last Rosalind tamed his perpetual sorrow. He married her, received word of his parent's death, and returned home to find Dana alive.

He had always seen it, the shame in Dana's eyes upon his return, the way she refused to speak of his time away, the way she clung to Sarah—a child who bore far too many physical similarities for having merely been *nannied* by Dana.

He had struggled to reconcile his jealousy and rage, but Father had been dead and Dana had been a victim trapped by Charles himself. He was warned, and he still carried her off to his home. Charles had sought to apologize to Dana, to comfort her, to make amends and somehow compensate for her loss and pain, but those efforts resulted in his own fall and the birth of a child who had given his life new purpose and—in the same blow—robbed him of both his lover, and his wife's trust.

He could do nothing to punish his father, no matter how hot his blood burned, but if there were others...

Bellezza grinned. "I should like your help in dismantling their network, Charles Dumont. Being the son of a collector, you can infiltrate their inner circle, learn all of their names, and bring that intelligence to me."

He crossed his arms, but his voice wobbled. "And why would I play your game?"

Bellezza walked her fingers up his chest. "Because I will make each of them suffer the way your father should have suffered."

He slapped her hand away.

Her grin widened. "I will hide you here two days while you decide, during which time I must obtain some much needed information from a Breeder informant."

He ground his teeth together. "You forget, I am not a gambling man."

"I forget nothing." She touched his cheek, toxins swimming instantly through his brain. "One thing you may learn about me, I will never kill someone who has set me free."

Charles could not believe he had agreed to this. He stood at the back of the room with his arms folded as the visitor took a seat across from Bellezza. She had introduced Charles simply by stating to her company that he did not wish to find out the extent of Charles's power. He felt more comfortable with the loaded pistol hiding within arms' reach, but not pleased by this circumstance. Who knew what strange talent the young man possessed?

"Tell me of Deiliey," Bellezza demanded.

The visitor shook his sandy head. "She is dead by all official accounts." His Irish accent surprised Charles.

Bellezza sat back, waving an encouraging hand.

"Nigh three hundred years ago, she led our division. She was contendin' against the Kingdom faction for dominance, and winnin'." He crossed his legs at the knee. "She had infiltrated the church and was posin' as one of the Cardinals with much influence. So much influence we got nigh whatever we wanted." He leaned on the arm rest. "Until Kingdom reared its braided mane."

"He overtook the church."

"Right bloody through. He ousted her for bein' a woman." He nodded. "There was an execution, there was."

Charles loosened his fingers from cutting lines into his arm. What was it to him if one of the Passionate had been put to death?

"But it was a show," the visitor continued. "A private thing for only the clergy. It's said Kingdom loved Deiliey and banished her from civilized lands on penalty o' death instead of plunging a sword through her. She ain't nothin' but a ghost."

Bellezza leaned forward. "Is this ghost in possession of a blade that can slay the Soulless?"

The man rubbed the back of his neck. "It's said that she was. Then, it's also said she was able to look into a man's brain and addle it all about, so what be true and what ain't are nigh but impossible to decide betwixt."

"Any recent sightings?"

His head shook. "Not in well past a century. My guess, she died in exile."

Bellezza grinned. "Fascinating."

"Now, you pledged a favor."

The girl's grin dropped. "I let you live. How is that?"

He yawned. "I was thinkin' somethin' a wee bit more enticin'." His eyes scaled up and down the girl.

Charles cleared his throat loudly.

The young man jumped.

"I think you are finished here." Bellezza batted her eyes.

Forty-Five

Gold

With the Soulless growing so bold, Kiren thanked heaven for Miles and Edward's quick success in locating Bellezza. Intelligence among the Breeders had led them to this location, and while he regretted leaving Alexia so soon, she had insisted on attending to Ethel in her grief and exhaustion. His precious woman had such a good heart.

"For the fiftieth time, the food was atrocious! How can you expect anyone to survive that *merde?*"

Kiren rolled his eyes. For manners, even the poor put Elizabeth North to shame. He'd have to wash his ears with lye to ever consider them clean again. Lifting a finger to his lips, he shushed her and leaned around the corner of the building.

The town square was still too full from market day, but he couldn't risk waiting a moment longer. Most of the vendors had closed down their wagons, barrels, or display quilts, and gone off to find some dinner in this rustic province, leaving just the stragglers in their festive but still drab attire.

A royal blue gown and golden curls drew most eyes, as intended. Bellezza did always have a flare for the bold.

Miles's head appeared around the butcher's shop across the street. He met gazes with Kiren and nodded. The girl didn't suspect a thing.

Kiren pulled back into the shadows. "Are you ready, Elizabeth?"

She sashayed forward, brushing him with her ample breasts. Again he rolled his eyes, asking why God had plagued him with so promiscuous an ally.

She held up the handkerchief-wrapped bracelet, the dulled gold visible through the cloth, readying it for her attack. Kiren shuddered, hating that this was necessary. Gold was the worst torture for their kind, like a live parasite gnawing at the flesh and infusing the bearer with fiery, if not deadly, poison. You did not employ gold unless you were aiming for a kill, which meant he'd avoided it all but this once. Bellezza had overcome the effects of iron and gold was the only prison left to restrain her.

Lady North reached up and touched her temples. "For your pain, I am sorry," she whispered.

Blinding misery shot through his head.

Blackness rushed in.

Dirt pressed into Kiren's cheek, a subtle ache forming into bruises along his ribs and calf. He blinked his eyes open. He shoved up onto an elbow and knee, heaving himself forward. Wooden planks brushed beneath his fingers as he leaned on the building, recovering his feet.

Rustling pulled him around the corner, and he froze. The dozens of people who occupied the square lay on the ground in graceless heaps. Elizabeth knelt over Bellezza's inert form.

Clink. The golden bracelet snapped into place.

Elizabeth turned and jolted, clasping a hand over her heart. "You recover so quickly!"

He cut across the square. "How far does your range extend?"

"Only as far as you can see."

He nodded and caught Bellezza under both arms, hauling her up and crossing to the butcher shop. Miles lay against the wall, his neck kinked to one side. Kiren slapped his cheek lightly, twice. The boy jerked awake.

"What was...?" His eyes turned on Elizabeth.

She straightened, lifting her chin. "Shall we away?"

Miles climbed to his feet, gaze warily sweeping over Bellezza's unconscious form. He met Kiren's stare, the question in his eyes. *Are you certain we have to do this?*

Kiren nodded. The trepidation in the boy's stance gave way as he resolved to play his part. Kiren despised that they must now resort to underhanded tactics, but Bellezza sprang this mess upon them, and she would be the source of its undoing.

Forty-Six

Interrogation

Bellezza's shriek carried down through the ceiling.

Kiren shifted in his seat and glanced up, pitying Edward who had the unfortunate duty of questioning her after she'd awakened. He turned to Miles. "Is she in pain?"

The boy lifted an eyebrow and shook his head, muscles bunched as he braced himself against the wall. From his posture it was a clear lie. Through clenched teeth Miles hissed, "She's not very happy."

Her screams elevated, curses ringing into the rafters.

"Miles?" Kiren extended a hand. The boy hesitated. He shoved off the wall and touched palms. Kiren closed his eyes and dove through the connection, into Miles's perception, into Bellezza's head.

Her vision seethed red. "Where is he hiding? The hen-hearted boor!"

"Where is who hiding?"

She cracked her neck from side to side, glaring at Edward through the iron bars of her prison. Men were vile things, and this one, with his delicate posture and fine, aged features, reminded her all too clearly of the "gentlemen's club," or Collectors she'd already taken the privilege of destroying. His calm demeanor sent hot prickles of fury racing through her veins, and she was determined to rile, if not murder him.

"Your pristine master." She grinned, giving him an innocent batting of the eyes. "The would-be king who orders you away from your home and bed to torture young girls—the one who uses you like a defiled serf."

Edward crossed his arms, his brow pinching. "Let us start again. The water you drank earlier possessed trace amounts of gold which will prevent you from traveling by mist for some time."

"You are a monster!"

"I am Edward, and I wish you no harm."

166

She bit down. No harm? No harm indeed! After stealing away her most precious gift? All men everywhere wanted something, and he was no exception. Why, he was probably formulating how best to use or dispose of her this very instant. She lifted an arm, exposing a gold encrusted manacle, its iron chain dangling and fastened to the floor—the very shackle she'd worn for months, only now coated in gold. "Prove it. Remove this vexing cuff."

He nodded as though considering it—which she knew he wasn't. "I do not believe you comprehend the trouble you have caused, young lady."

"I am not YOUNG!" The room shook from her shriek. Her arms trembled, nails digging into her flesh. She would bring the building down on top of him if she could, bury him in his ignorance. Wouldn't that be a fitting death?

He took a seat across from her, separated by the iron beams. His cornflower-blue eyes smiled at the corners, mouth twitching upward to match.

How dare he mock her! She imagined the cuff falling free, his shock as she plunged a fist through his chest and watched the light seep out of his eyes.

He plucked a thin wooden wedge from his pocket and began cleaning out from under his nails. Nails blackened by ink.

A scribe. The kingdom-monger could send no better than a lowly scribe to torment her? She'd apparently not done enough to exasperate him. Once she was free, she'd have to go after Alexia again, see if finger bruises across his future wife's neck would be enough to earn her more than a cursory jailer.

She growled. Edward didn't even jump, but continued to work as though he was alone in the room.

She flumped down on the hard stone and seethed, fingers slicing into her knees. Perhaps that's why he'd been chosen. He was deaf or completely numb to terror. He should die. She should find the perfect way to kill him, something that spoke to his dignified poise and inability to ruffle. Perhaps something involving ice—

"Indeed, I believe you are old enough," he said, "to comprehend the number of innocent children who have lost parents, homes, and much, much more because one woman put a powerful weapon in the hands of brutal creatures."

A lump formed at the back of her throat, one she couldn't swallow. She had once been one of those innocents, long, long ago...

Rage pulsed through her.

Where had *they* been when she needed assistance? Off pursuing their own selfish pleasures—the growth of their shiny Passionate community and the grooming of a perfect bride-queen. They were not concerned with outliers like herself.

How dare he turn this on her? Edward's master knew she'd been promised a place at his side, a future and an important role among them. The instant she had begun to believe it might be so, he'd fallen madly in love with Alexia and forgotten all but his own lewd desires.

167

She blinked back a tear, furiously determined to show no weakness. "Pawns. They are only pawns for your master's pleasure." Those clear eyes met hers, and she had to look away. "I have freed them from future enslavement."

"Bellezza?"

Her gaze slid back to his.

"You have damned them to unknown suffering."

Damned them? She'd damn him!

A hiccup burst through her lips. She covered her mouth. No, not now! Why must this always happen?

"And when you interposed as an ambassador between Passionate and Soulless, you ignited a war which has caused yet more suffering and loss."

She tensed. That had been justified, and necessary—to keep them occupied while she dealt out revenge and freed several suffering souls. She'd known there would be a price. Hard decisions had to be made, and if the would-be king couldn't make them, she would. Could they really complain? They were getting the war they'd desired for ages.

Edward leaned forward. "Where have they taken the medallion?"

She rubbed her arm. The dark night came back, the constant strain and exhaustion of remaining in the mist, watching, following the clan of Soulless into the woods near Wilhamshire and around a cliff of stone to the place where two trees leaned in and became one. They had fished in the grass and lifted a wooden loop, yanking up a hatch covered by vegetation that grew throughout the wood. She'd followed them down and through a series of black tunnels to arrive at one great cavern where starlight seeped through pinpricks from far above, and hundreds of Soulless loitered. It had almost been too easy, except for the way her heart had threatened to rupture from her chest with every breath.

She turned away, disinterested. "I cannot fathom why you think I should know."

Kiren released Miles grip and sat back. "Right beneath us, all this time."

The lad nodded. "And now we know."

Forty-Seven

Shredded

Alexia rounded the corner of the barn and froze.

A silhouette leaned against the wall. His frame towered over her with deep-set eyes, hollow cheeks and wide, angular teeth. Brown hair landed in thin wisps, obscuring half his timid face, but Alexia couldn't be deceived by the appearance as when they'd first met. Although they shared a birthday, she felt he'd aged years beyond her for the audacity of his gifts.

"Miles!" She dropped her bucket of oats and threw her arms around him.

He gasped, arms lifted awkwardly as if unsure where to place them. She didn't care.

"This is where you hug me back, you oaf."

His bone-thin hands patted her shoulders.

Alexia rolled her eyes and freed him. "It is about time you came to see me."

"I'm not really supposed to..." His velvety voice melted her, leaving her knees weak. It was easily the most beautiful voice she'd ever heard, one she had missed so desperately.

An uncertain smile twitched up his cheek.

She stood back and huffed. "Are you listening in?"

He lifted his shoulders, focused on the ground, cheeks reddening.

She laughed and forced up the mental barriers Kiren had begun teaching her when she was a weakling prisoner recovering in Father's home. "Supposed to or not, you are my friend, and I expect to see my friends when they are nearby. Is that understood?"

He bit his lip and gave a single nod.

"And I anticipate you will tell me all about your adventures while you were away."

He rubbed the back of his neck. "All of them?"

An arm slid around her waist. She jumped. Soft lips landed against her ear. "In good time. For now we have more important matters to address."

She shivered and turned to embrace her fiancé.

"Their hive is here." Kiren pointed to the map, slightly east of Wilhamshire, just as Bellezza had accidentally told them. "And it resides underground—which is why we have never been able to locate it."

He glanced across the table at Lester and Ethel. The mist maiden bore deep exhaustion lines beneath her eyes, even after a day of rest. There would come a time when he asked too much of her.

Fingers curled about his arm, and he grinned at Alexia, her lashes batting demurely. He still hadn't told her of Charles's disappearance, but as soon as he could spare Ethel, he would send her to find him. Would Alexia look upon him so dearly knowing he withheld that information?

Lester cleared his throat.

Kiren pulled himself out of the mental space and slid a hastily scrawled map across the table, a sketch of the hive directly from Bellezza's mind. It showed three circles, like a target with connecting hallways. "When Miles accesses their thoughts to discover where precisely my pendant is being held, they will know his thoughts as well—including our presence, and possibly our plan. We have to move quickly, in and out, no room for error."

"Which is why you have us." Ethel nodded.

Lester winked. "Like lightnin', they'll wonder what knocked."

Alexia's head tilted toward Miles, her cheeks stretched in her widest grin. Kiren knew how desperately she had missed him, and seeing her so happy, it added a measure of sunshine to his own joy.

"We will unite in a single sharing, before he opens himself to them," Kiren said. "I will serve as a distraction to draw them off. Lester, you will be in charge of finding an exit for Nelly...if we can locate her. Ethel, you will disable all obstacles in his way, keeping to the mist unless it becomes necessary to physically surface. It will be your responsibility to seize the pendant, if it can be done. Should you see failure is certain, you are to abort the plan and remove all operatives." Kiren's hand slammed the table. "I will have no casualties on this rescue. Is that understood?"

They all nodded, Lester grinning.

"Ethel, call Mae in. Let us finish our preparations."

"Sir." She curtsied shallowly and exited.

"I do not like it." Alexia's low comment in his ear made Kiren scowl. "Can this plan only be enacted on the moonless night?"

He lifted her hand to his lips. "It is the only time the Soulless will be connected into one cognizant whole, the only time we can infiltrate their vast knowledge by accessing a single mind. If we are to discern where the medallion is being kept, we will have to sweep their consciousness."

"Yes, I am aware, but I simply wish you would allow me to accompany you—so that should anything go wrong—"

He caught her cheek, tilting his head. "Ethel will be present."

"Yes, but I could be as well."

He groaned. She knew his reasons for keeping her away. "Love."

Her nose flared. "You wish me to stay here on the pretense of protecting the innocents, but I see through your excuses."

He was losing this battle. "Mae needs your help."

"And that is precisely it! I have seen what she can do." She spoke through clenched teeth. "Mae is sufficient."

He cupped her other cheek and used his firmest tone. "Dearest, you *are* needed here."

She scowled and pulled free as Mae stepped into the room. Alexia said, "You will excuse me, I have lost my stomach for this conversation."

He watched her go and Miles averted his gaze, lips twisted to the side. The boy perceived far too much for comfort, even on scorched earth.

Forty-Eight

Emissary

Alexia sat, fuming as the sun set. She flicked an ant off her skirt and glared at the horizon. Her gifts were beyond Kiren's, beyond Ethel's, beyond all their gifts, and he would not allow her to help? Why did he insist on treating her like a child? She was an adult in every sense of the word, and simply because he was her fiancé, he believed he could order her to inactivity.

The crunch of grass pulled her about. Miles stood at the inn's exit, head tilted, translucent eyes fixed on her. She turned back to the view.

He glided into her periphery and took a seat next to her on the ground. She watched him out of the corner of her eye, waiting for him to speak. He leaned on his knees, chin tilted upward as though contemplating the clouds. The call of birds echoed across the landscape.

She glanced at him. He met her gaze and smirked.

Alexia crossed her arms. "Have you come to talk me into his plan?"

He shrugged and went back to watching the sky.

"I am not going to concede—no matter who he sends to convince me."

"If it brings you any solace, I don't approve."

"You do not?"

His head shook. "We should use every talent. Even yours."

She huffed. "Thank you, Miles, but commiserating with me is not going to decrease my resistance or resentment."

He grinned. "But it might make you smile."

She couldn't help herself. She smirked.

He rocked onto his feet and pushed up, brushing his knees. "My work here is done."

Three days Kiren locked himself in a small room, discussing every possible outcome with his cohorts. Alexia burned her hours practicing or helping Mae with chores about the inn, of which there seemed to be a never-ending supply.

How the woman had spared time to help her boggled Alexia's mind. Edward arrived with vagabond Passionate whose entire lives had been uprooted or destroyed by Soulless invasions. So many of them. Miles appeared and disappeared, as though this much company frightened him—or he was on errand for Kiren. She heard whispers of Bellezza between him and Kiren. As the refugees poured in, she spent her days administering to their relief, Kiren at her side some of the time.

John and Sarah stayed hidden below and Alexia brought them food, occasionally lingering to talk. Sarah seemed happy, a hand always rubbing absently across the bulge at her midsection. Kiren knew only that her sister had been present when they first arrived here. Alexia had shaded the knowledge in her mind, and she worked hard to keep the secret of her sister's continued presence. It was easier on scorched earth. They shared only what was open between them, and she despised the necessary distance it created.

A week before the new moon, Alexia stood on the inn stoop, holding in her bleeding heart. Having her other half torn away again, and so soon—she didn't know if she could survive it! His time had been dedicated to healing, plotting, and scrambling together enough food for all the hungry mouths. Their stolen moments together had been bliss. She ached for more of them—for the period of life when he might wake her with a kiss every day.

"This will be the last time," she whispered to herself as Kiren mounted his steed and turned back. He lifted his fingers to his mouth in a kiss and fluttered them her direction. She placed a hand over her heart and smiled just for him, still angry he wouldn't bring her along, but understanding his need as well. He bit down, nodded, and kicked his stallion.

"Come back to me soon," she begged quietly.

Forty-Nine

Inside

Kiren took hands with Miles and Ethel, completing the circle with Lester stationed across from him. Tree branches blocked out the stars, sealing them in an eerie gloom. The entrance to the Soulless hive lay only over the next rise, an ominous dark hole in the ground he could already feel sucking the warmth out of the air. They'd waited half an hour after sunset in order that the hive be as empty as possible.

He squeezed Miles's hand, the signal to begin. He dove down, into their shared thoughts, and waited. Ethel's presence hung in the blankness of their mental void. He greeted her as a haze of quick thoughts drew his notice to Lester's consciousness, and finally the timid waver of Miles.

Ready? The boy's mental question rippled through all of them.

They nodded in unison.

Miles tensed. A tiny hole opened in their linked circle, sucking all warmth down through it, like water rushing over a cliff, crashing into an abyss far below. Kiren hugged his spot, holding fast to the emptiness. The gap widened. The pull increased, an icy gale ripping at him. He reached out to the others, keeping a firm hold on them, and gave each a reassuring nod. As one, they pushed off and dove.

Images hurled past. Here one of the Soulless stood in the night, gazing listlessly at the sky. There another stalked in the darkness, drawn by the succulent call of Passionate blood. One had its nails deep into someone's spine, the pulse of life-restoring marrow screaming to him: *Fill the emptiness. Satiate the hunger. Here is a feast!*

Kiren slammed his heels back down on the ground. *Miles!*

The boy nodded at him. Kiren didn't have to use his eyes—he could see through Ethel, fighting the heave of her stomach, through Lester, battling the need to pull his hands free, through the lad himself, calm in the heart of a whirlwind storm.

Deeper, Miles said.

They all gripped tighter, plunging further. The hunger grew. It turned from a mild irritation to world-consuming ache, strangling all but the need to consume. Kiren wanted to turn on his companions, to sheer their flesh from the bones and suckle this starvation on their life-granting marrow. He bit down. Tension laced into his brain, sparking a headache. The feel of fleshy pain tore him out of his hypnosis. Miles watched him with blank eyes. Ethel and Lester twitched, caught in the thralls of battle.

Deeper, Kiren agreed.

They submerged further and slammed into a solid barrier. It hovered, a giant metallic-looking bubble. The world, laced in sparking veins of suffering, had never been so dark. Kiren pressed forward on the heart of the Soulless's shared thoughts, the surface solid at first, slowly giving under his press. His fingers dipped inside. White electricity shot through him. The bubble inhaled suddenly, wrenching him forward.

A distant scream sounded.

He was inside, at their core, and he could see everything. Lifetimes, people, pain, loss, animalistic sacrifice...

Focus.

He pictured the medallion in his mind, the dull metal, the family crest of Kir.

The distractions drew away like a gathered breath, then exploded over him. One of the Soulless carried it in a handkerchief. He offered it to another, more ancient creature. The elder touched it, and his blackened finger bones shriveled to dust. He shrieked and ordered it away. It was taken down a long hall, through the curve of several tunnels, and settled in a small cavern with no light. A heavy iron door closed, and the bearer backed away, frustrated his prize had been quarantined, but they had what they wanted. Freedom was theirs—this night and always.

Kiren gasped and pulled his hands free. His three companions stood by his side, all watching him.

Miles's head turned. "I have never been able to enter the origin."

Kiren smiled at him, but a heaviness hung in his gut. He turned to Lester and Ethel, forcing his legs to remain steady. "Go."

They snapped out of their stupor. Lester disappeared. Ethel dispersed into mist. Kiren leaned a hand on a tree, bracing himself up, and trying to expel the weight from his lungs.

Miles stiffened. "They know we are here."

Kiren nodded, shivering. "We should move."

Fifty

Delivered

Sarah's scream rattled the rafters. Alexia woke on the floor in Mae's room, the place she'd taken up in consideration of the families now crowding every inch of floor.

Glancing out the window, she recalled: the moonless night started this evening.

Sarah!

She stumbled down the cellar stairs, fumbling blindly until she found the ladder. Rungs flew by, and she shoved her way through the door into the subterranean dwelling.

Her aunt lay on a mattress, knees drawn up, clutching her lower abdomen. Brilliant redness coated the sheet beneath her, her eyes squeezed shut.

Alexia froze.

John knelt beside Sarah, hair disheveled, whispering assurances, but the color had fled from his face. He glanced at her, eyes wide and begging for help.

So much blood... She hadn't seen that much since the night Kiren was shot and nearly bled out. If he were here, he could fix this. But she? She had no gift to battle so much blood loss.

She could ride after him.

But no. He was executing his plan to rescue the pendant.

John's mouth moved in slow motion, but only a low-pitched rumble registered. She blinked, confused. Her hands were clutched in tight fists at her sides, power coursing through her. The air tasted bitter, her clothing too stiff. Had she slowed time—even on scorched earth?

She gasped and time whipped into its natural course.

"—Mae. We need Mae." John's nostrils flared, his usual cool a puddle of panic.

Alexia nodded and leapt back up the ladder. Clumsy clatters carried down from above. She reached the top as a silhouette leaned forward, one hand blindly extended. Alexia took Mae's hand.

Another shriek burst forth.

"She is bleeding," Alexia sobbed.

"It is too soon," Mae said.

Alexia placed the innkeeper's hands on the ladder, making sure the woman had a strong hold before descending. She followed.

The pool of blood around Sarah was larger. Alexia clutched at her chest, taking quick, short breaths as she approached her sister. John held Sarah's hand, chest rising and falling rapidly as he focused on Mae while she examined the blood-stained bed and screaming woman.

"How long has she been like this?" Mae questioned.

John's head shook. "She complained of pains only an hour ago. I could not have known—"

"It is too soon." Mae leaned toward Sarah.

Sarah sucked in a breath. "Can you"—pant—"stop it?"

Mae's cheeks lifted, her eyes squeezing at the corners. "Breathe slowly."

Sarah nodded, sweat dripping down her brow. Her mouth formed a circle and she blew out. Mae stepped into the needed role, coaching the panicked woman, and John finally backed away. He escaped to the tunnel Alexia occupied and closed the door on the scene.

"She is going to die," he whispered. "She has known all along, and I would not listen."

"Be still, John. This is not over. Sarah is much stronger than you think."

He growled. "I know her strength—better than most, but no one can live through severe blood loss. Not like that." He covered his mouth. "What am I going to do without her?"

Alexia placed a hand on his arm. "You are going to be strong, for her."

He met her eyes, his naught but a glistening of light in the darkness. He caught Alexia's shoulders. "You can stop all this, prevent the Soulless from ever becoming!"

She shook her head. "No, John. I cannot."

"How do you know if you have never tried?"

"My mother said—"

"Bollocks."

Her face burned at the vulgar word.

John shoved her away, rounding the little cavity. "It is one big fat lie, because everyone fears what you can actually do. You can stop this suffering, Alexia." He halted abruptly, head swinging toward the closed door. He shoved through it and slammed Alexia back into darkness.

She stood stiffly. Muffled protest echoed through, and then he thrust Mae out, shutting them into near-blackness again. Mae's quickened breathing echoed in the tunnel.

"What is he doing?" Alexia asked.

"Taking his fate in his hands."

"What do you mean?" Alexia turned on her. Scraping noises met her ears, Mae retreating back up the ladder. "You cannot go!" she called after the inn matron. "You are needed!"

The scuffling halted. "If Sarah or the child dies, John will no longer be welcome here. He knows the terms."

"But—"

"I cannot help someone who wishes not to be helped." Mae resumed her ascent.

Alexia stood a long time in the darkness, listening to Sarah moan, scream, and at last, silence. The sudden light blinded her. John tromped out of the room, his coat clutched in one hand, a still, wrapped bundle in the other—so tiny it would have fit easily in Alexia's palm.

She covered her mouth.

John spared a glare on her, looped his coat over his shoulders and ascended.

Sarah lay pale and unmoving in the blood-mottled bed. She had curled up on one side, her arms ringed protectively over her head. Was she dead?

Her body shook. Alexia loosed a breath she'd been holding and stepped nearer. She stopped. She didn't know what to say to her sister. How could anyone possibly make this right? What had she wanted when they'd lost Mother, or the night she found out she was a bastard child? Certainly it was not Sarah's presence, but her sister had been there, holding her while she digested the horror.

She climbed onto the bed next to Sarah, ignoring the stains, and wrapped her arms around her sister. Sarah's sob shook them both, but Alexia kept her silent tears to herself, hugging her sister in the only way she knew to express her love.

Fifty-One

Cornered

Kiren pulled on his reins. Miles's beast skidded to a halt beside him. He nodded at the boy, welcoming him into his thoughts. *Have we lost them?*

Miles scanned the dark horizon, his hollow cheeks pinched from heavy breathing. He met Kiren's stare, the word clear in his pupils. *No.*

Kiren snapped the tethers and kicked his stallion. His riding companion fell into stride, leaning over his animal's neck. Kiren shouted over the roaring hooves. "Did Lester and Ethel retrieve the pendant?"

Miles grimaced. "I think they did. There is so much noise!"

If he held still, Kiren almost thought he could hear them, the buzz of a thousand voices clamoring.

"They are driving us away from the inn." Miles's teeth clenched, eyes mere slits.

"We should split up."

The boy's brow crinkled. Kiren groaned—hating that he should even suggest it. The Soulless sensed Miles the same way he felt them—ever since he'd shielded Alexia from their detection and opened his own mind to their touch. Though Edward had argued with Kiren for years that he should stay far, far away from the lad, he couldn't bring himself to do it. The boy had needed him. Still needed him. More than that, he needed the boy. Miles was his family.

"Ambush, ahead." Miles jerked his horse off the road and into a field of wheat.

Dirt churned up beneath the animals' feet, throwing stalks into the air. Miles yanked his steed to a halt.

Kiren slowed and circled back around. "What is it?"

The boy's pupils nearly consumed his eyes. "We're surrounded."

Kiren's fingers bit into the leather of his saddle. Ice seeped into his veins. "Then we make a hole. Where are they the thinnest?"

Miles's head shook. He grabbed the back of his neck, elbow rolling up over the top of his head, eyes squeezed shut, skin crypt white.

Kiren's blood ran cold. Had he fallen into their trap by trusting the lad?

He scanned the landscape, wheat fluttering like the ghostly fingers of a white sea. In the distance two skeletal willows stood, young and choked for nutrients.

Kiren lifted his face to the sky in desperate prayer.

He only had one chance at this, and despite what everyone told him—even himself at the moment, he still believed in Miles. "Can you evade them? Make yourself invisible to them, like before."

Miles head whipped up. "You have a plan?"

"Miles."

He nodded, brows quirked, frown weighed by guilt. "But what about you?"

Kiren palmed his reins. "It is best you not know my course of action. Now go." He slapped the boy's horse on the rump. It whinnied and shot forward. Kiren watched the dust cloud distance, taking slow, even breaths and stilling the dread in his breast. He would *not* draw them to him by panicking.

He turned his mount and aimed for the only break on the horizon, the young trees. Movement swung his head toward the road where a ribbon of blackness swooped toward him. He dropped from his horse's back and ran, bent over, head down, obscured by stalks. His beast shrieked and thundered away.

Kiren sprinted faster, glancing up. The little hollow loomed just ahead. Wind whipped in his ears, the rich scent of grain masking his own perspiration. Hisses whispered through the frosted breeze, nearing.

Searing heat raked across his back. He whirled and slammed a fist into the creature's jaw. It flew off to the side.

He kept moving and reached back to examine the flesh, still intact, but his jacket was shorn. Midnight writhed toward him from all directions. His heart sank.

Reaching down, he found a dead tree branch and hefted it. If they wanted to take him, they were going to see a fight like they'd never known!

He turned at the crunch of stalks, swinging the branch upward. It rammed into a creature's chin and threw it backward into a mass of blackness. Creatures toppled like wooden dolls.

Kiren lumbered past them, toward the pitiful copse of trees. Twenty feet more.

The enemy circled in, cutting him off. He bit down. His muscles tightened. His knuckles popped.

He swung!

Two bodies thudded to the ground. Weight slammed into the back of his legs. His knees crunched into the earth. Pain shot up his legs. He couldn't move, weighed down by multiple enemies. He flailed around, swinging blindly. The wood connected again and again, but he couldn't free his legs. The branch was yanked out of his grasp, raking a trail of splinters across his palm.

Bodies crashed down.

Blackness consumed the world.

He couldn't breathe. Desperately, he tore at the creatures scraping through his clothes. This was it. They had won.

Alexia.

He shivered and pictured her face in his mind, her soft lips, her compassionate, evergreen eyes, the wonder of her fingers gliding across his skin, and the warmth of her soul intertwined with his own.

No, they would not capture him. Not tonight.

He grabbed hold of the nearest assailant, begged a silent prayer of forgiveness, and sucked the creature's life into himself. Sickly energy trickled into his skin. The limb beneath his fingers withered and narrowed.

A shriek pierced his ears.

A chorus of wails echoed.

He shoved upward off the ground, launching the startled creatures backward and hurdled a dead log. His knees screamed in agony. The damage was deep, and he didn't have to look down to know how much healing would be required.

Kiren banged into the nearest trunk, no wider than his leg. This was an insane idea. There was no way he could make it work, not in time.

He wheeled around, unarmed and exposed. Five black bodies billowed toward him from different angles.

No choice. He had to make it work. He grabbed the feeble trunk and pressed his free palm into the other one. He closed his eyes and focused. Bark thickened beneath his skin. He commanded the roots to dig, following them with his mind, deep into the earth, burrowing around stones in their way and lacing together in an intricate network of lattice. They dipped into that gulf of groundwater, hidden far below the surface.

Up, he commanded. *Help me.*

The roots gulped water, drawing it in along with needed minerals. Energy suctioned out from his center, wringing him like a rag on a press as that power flowed into the plants. Kiren gasped.

Branches burst through the ground at his feet, shaking the earth. Limbs shot out of the weeds, tripping his enemies. Roots launched upward, impaling the fallen creatures.

He let go and dropped to one knee, clutching at his heart. Wood beveled around him, cocooning him behind copious thin bars, like a wild prison, but too thin a barrier to protect him from the oncoming tide.

The breeze died against his cheek. A chill raced over his skin. His eyes snapped to the black figures hedging in a circle. Clicks echoed off the half-formed trees. Outside his protective circle, crimson pupils burned into him.

Not yet. You will not take me yet!

He shoved both hands into the earth and thrust his strength outward. Branches burst out of the ground around him. They groaned and stretched, thickening.

The Soulless screamed and rushed forward.

Wood filtered up from the earth, green and new, bloating and pressing together. The Soulless disappeared. Branches groaned as they locked into place, blacking out the night. They wrapped across the sky. He turned his head up, taking in the last of the stars as limbs wound together and widened, sealing him into darkness.

He collapsed.

Fifty-Two

Tidings

Alexia set the tray of food down next to Sarah. Her sister had not moved, not since the birth. The distraught woman stared blankly into the corner of the room, quilt shifting only when she breathed. John sat just as silently across the room, staring at his hands, still dirty from the little grave he'd dug last night, just beyond scorched earth. He hadn't expressed it, but Alexia sensed he'd hoped stepping over the brink would somehow save the child. The weight on both of them was breaking her heart.

She turned for the ladder.

John cleared his throat. "Do you wish to learn what has become of your fiancé?"

She stopped. Every nerve snapped to awareness. There was only one way John could know what happened to Kiren—if the Soulless had apprehended him...unless he was attempting to deceive her. But why would he do that? She was here, vulnerable in his presence.

"You can have no news of him, John."

He chuckled bitterly.

She whipped around. Her airways constricted, blackness dancing before her eyes. It couldn't be true! Surely they hadn't caught Kiren or she would know. Wouldn't she? She took quick, shallow breaths, slowing her heartbeat, and pried the nails from her palms one at a time. "What do you know?"

"He was on the road, headed north." John climbed out of his seat and stepped toward her. "He was in the company of a young man called Miles shortly before he was hunted down and surrounded."

Her vision danced. She reached for the wall and stumbled. John's warm hands latched around her arms and braced her up.

She locked her knees. Surely the Soulless didn't wish him dead or they would have murdered him when they took the medallion—but they might make him one of them. "Is he..." She couldn't finish. Her body was shaking.

John wrapped his arms around her shoulders, tucking her up against him. She inhaled chestnut, and could think of nothing but that Kiren was in danger, or—dare she think it—*gone?*

Father didn't believe in an afterlife. She had often questioned its existence herself—until stepping out of time and meeting her mother. But Kiren believed. He believed enough for both of them.

He was not gone!

She looked up and realized her entire body was trembling, that she'd crinkled John's coat with her white-knuckled grasp. Tears spilled over her cheeks. "What more do you know, John?"

His brows crushed together, tears pooling in his eyes. "He was entombed."

Her head shook "How?"

"To escape them, he interred himself in a crypt of wood." He pulled his handkerchief free and offered it to her.

"Then he might have survived."

"No."

"You do not know for certain."

"Alexia." His crimson eyes bored into hers. "He was my best friend."

Fifty-Three

Clinging

Was. Was my best friend. Alexia stumbled out the kitchen door and into the yard, a ring of wild blossoms hedging her in. Their little heads bowed in the pink light of sunset with the heaviness of her heart.

A tear rolled down her cheek. What could she do? Reverse time, stop him from ever leaving—an entire week? Just the thought made her dizzy. Would such a jump kill her? And then how would she convince him to abandon the medallion?

Golden light trailed across a sky of clouds, fading into red and finally violet—the violet of loss. She pulled in a shaky breath and stepped over the line.

Silence touched her ears. Where she expected to find his warm presence in her heart, there hung a black stillness. Her legs shook and weakened, knees smacking into the dirt. Her lungs wouldn't work. The thump of her heart slowed, as if shriveling.

The whisper of movement pulled her head around. Miles stood against the setting sun, his skin paler than normal, a traveling hat clasped in his hands. His near-translucent eyes met hers, glassy. They widened.

Her vision narrowed, hazing around the edges. Colors faded.

Miles rushed toward her.

The thump of her heart dulled, echoing through her ears.

Hands grabbed her.

The world dipped into blackness.

Alexia gasped, sucking in air. Her eyes shot wide, strength pulsing back into her limbs. Miles knelt over her, staring and panting.

The cast of violet light painted his skin ashen, and she wondered if he was feeling well. He'd always been a good friend to her.

"No dying today, Alexia," he whispered. "You are not allowed to die."

She blinked up at him, memory rushing back over her. Her stomach heaved dryly as her insides hollowed out. This could only mean one thing, one terrible thing. "Tell me it is not true," she barely managed. "Tell me he is safe. Tell me he is well."

His bottom lip trembled. Tears pooled in his eyes. He crushed her in his arms, his cloak reeking of smoke and perspiration as his shoulders shook.

Her brain worked like sludge. It wouldn't grasp what she already knew. "Miles, tell me he is not dead!"

The word hung in the air. An empty omen. A dark void. A nothingness that would consume her.

"Show me," she whispered, clutching his shirt. "Show me he survived."

Miles pulled back, tears streaming down his grayed skin. His jaw clenched. Long fingers landed on her cheek and she met his troubled eyes, wide with pain.

She did not want to see this.

She had to see this.

She had to know.

Alexia nodded.

Hunger pulsed through her. The man's heart was strangely silent as they tore at the cocooning trunks. Already she knew it was impossible to reach him.

Then kill him.

The command rang clear through all of their minds. As one they turned to the east and bowed their heads. A few individual wills twitched against the order, their protests no more than blips in the collective consciousness. They all understood the Passionate leader would torment and destroy their kind until he was disposed of. Tonight that war would end.

In unison they gathered dry reeds and lay them at the base of the mutant tree. Many heavy hearts weighed on her. Were they capable of tears, a few would have shed them, but that power had long since faded, along with their humanity.

Solemnly, almost reverently one of them knelt with flint and steel, shooting sparks at the dry foliage. It caught. Tendrils of smoke rose.

Flames appeared. They grew until the entire mass of wood was consumed, black clouds billowing up into the sky.

All night it burned.

The air stung her lungs, charred flakes littering the trampled wheat like snow in a demented world where light was darkness—the place her soul had been banished. Alexia closed her eyes, squeezing everything down into the pit of her stomach. She opened them and slid off her horse.

No, not her. Miles.

He thudded to the ground, scraping ash into a clenched fist. The tree tomb was nothing but cinder.

The field dampened into black, twilight-heavy clouds, Miles fingers warm against her cheek.

She breathed in, chest aching from the weight.

Kiren was gone. He was really and truly gone. The few precious moments they had shared, her memories, these were all that remained of him.

The world disappeared behind her tears. Her fist flailed forward, connecting with something solid. The agony rattling through her bones couldn't break the numbness, the emptiness consuming her soul.

Fingers wrapped around her trembling fists, pulling them away from the warm surface they'd struck, rubbing along the aching flesh she no longer wanted to possess.

She blinked through her tears, her soul tearing like the weft of fine velvet. Arms squeezed around her. She shook as a wail leaked from her lacerated core. The sun had melted into blackness, beaten into a pit of deformed coal that would never warm again. Her world, the vibrancy of flowers that dotted her mental landscape, shriveled instantly and disintegrated to dust.

Screams pierced her ears. Her lungs ached. Her mouth was open, pain ripping at her vocal chords.

There would never be another sunrise. She would not dive into the infinite sea of Kiren's eyes again and drown beneath the waves. She would not know the caress of his touch nor the aching compassion that bled through his every word.

"No!" She slammed her fists into Miles, one after another, and he let her. She wailed and crumbled in his embrace. She gasped, and gasped again, unable to draw enough air. Panic rocketed through her.

She sucked inward, but no air entered.

She tried once more.

Nothing.

"Breathe, Alexia. Please." The words were distant, like an echo down a tunnel.

She tried. Her airways seized.

It wasn't working. She couldn't breathe!

Alexia sucked again. Her throat had swollen shut as though filled with clay!

She really was going to die. Their war had come to an end. The Soulless had won, and Kiren? Her dear, wonderful Kiren had paid the ultimate price. Did an afterlife await for her, or did something else happen to the Maiden of Time? Would she be locked in some strange purgatory waiting for an heir in the absence of time who would never arise?

Lips crushed down over hers.

Chill rolled into her. Icy air. Her skin cooled. Frozen light bloomed through her being like an empty glass, filling from an endless, iced-lemonade pitcher. She welcomed the cold, soaking in its wintry vitality.

His mouth pulled away. "Please."

Her lips parted and air filled her lungs. Fingers stroked through her hair and cupped her cheek.

She focused on Miles, startled and amazed by the way his gray eyes trembled, the violet sky staining them with an unusual hue.

They were almost beautiful.

Her skin tingled where his fingers pressed it, the icy prickles that woke her into a crisp dawn.

Ice to sunshine. But she craved the warmth of summer! She jerked away from him.

Beautiful? What was wrong with her?

He'd kissed her.

How dare he kiss her!

"You were dying." He reached out to her, but his hand fell short, eyes turned down as if ashamed.

She shivered. Of course he was only doing what was necessary to keep her alive, but what did it mean? Why couldn't she look at him without her heart hiccupping?

She touched her lips. Was bonding after a loved one's death possible? Was that how he'd saved her? By initiating the first hopes of a new bond?

She didn't want to think about that, didn't want a new bond.

Miles clasped his hands in his lap. "He is the only one who ever treated me like a whole person, the only one besides..." He glanced up at her and back down, russet hair tumbling across his brow and hiding his eyes.

Tears blinded her. Of course. Miles had lost his father figure and truest friend. Who else had completely understood, trusted and loved him? She was not the only one suffering.

She reached out, hesitated, and placed a hand on his shoulder.

Miles's gaze lifted to hers. "I cannot lose you too. Please."

She shook her head, biting back a sob.

His Adam's apple bobbed. "Please do not leave me."

She closed her eyes, forcing her heart to slow. Her own sorrow she could face, but Miles'? He had known so much suffering already—losing his parents to the Soulless, being forced to abandon his home because of her... She would not see him suffer more.

"No." She shook her head.

"You promise?"

Alexia blew out a long breath. "You are not going to lose him, Miles. And neither am I. I do not care the cost."

Fifty-Four

Powerless

Alexia buckled Slayer onto her hip. Even broken, it would prove valuable as a last resort.

Chatter from the great room pulled her out of Mae's chamber. Ethel stood in the room, the cloth wrapped medallion lifted in one fist. Mournful faces crowded the mist maiden, uttering their subdued congratulations, although it would make little difference.

She was too late.

A shiver of hope streaked down Alexia's spine. What if she could take the necklace with her through time?

Dana climbed to her feet as Alexia arrived in the absence of time. Dana lifted her chin regally. "You have decided."

"Can I save him?" Alexia asked.

Her mother's hands clasped before her, eyes dropping as she gave a single nod. "There will be consequences, and only you will recall the reality that is no more."

"It is a sacrifice that must be made."

Dana smiled sadly. "Remember that when faced with the penalties."

Alexia bowed her head in gratitude.

Ethel placed the wrapped pendant in Alexia's hand. "It can only be wielded by the Master's bloodline."

"Thank you, Ethel." She tucked it into a secret pocket in her skirt, and prayed it would remain with her through a jump.

"Alexia?" Miles touched her arm. She nodded at him. It was time. She followed him out the back of the building and down the steps. He caught her in a hug. "Save him."

"I will."

Energy surged up from her toes, firing through her muscles like bursting stars as she stepped over the boundary. She reached into the past, feeling for two days back. Her mental fingers clasped around a moment, like seizing a single grain of wheat in a flood of granules. She hoped that was right.

Alexia pulled it toward her.

Blackness engulfed her—tar. She forced her eyes open and couldn't breathe. It was as though she'd stepped away from reality, and reality was the only place air existed. Her muscles contracted. The world around her reared in blurry lines. She was going to die!

Be calm, she told herself. *Welcome the change.*

She placed a palm over her chest and focused on the slowed beating of her heart, her fingers gripping the hilt at her hip. She stilled. Her fears washed away in a rainbow ray of hope. She would save Kiren, and no amount of time, no travel, no obstacle would keep her from doing it. She inhaled. Her airways expanded. Cool night air rushed in.

She dropped to her knees, limbs trembling. A tear slipped free, a silent prayer of gratitude she still lived, that she hadn't destroyed herself by jumping too far. She was not alone in this. He was out there somewhere, alive.

Kiren, she whispered mentally, searching deeper. His sunlight surrounded her heart, his assuring life essence.

Alexia rose. Her legs shook, every muscle weak as though she'd been running for an hour. She froze.

Clouds obscured the navy sky.

It was night. The moonless night.

She'd meant to arrive at least half a day sooner. Was she already too late?

Sarah's scream echoed into the night. Alexia paused and turned back toward the inn, but her sister would be well. She had so little time!

Alexia ran for the barn and threw the door open, Slayer smacking her thigh as she moved. She searched her pocket, heart leaping when her fingers curled around the linen wrapped charm. At least it had arrived with her.

She halted in the doorway. She didn't know how to saddle a horse—and it wouldn't matter. Kiren and Miles had the only two. Cursing herself for the oversight, she pulled back her skirts and ran.

Rocks bit into the soles of her shoes, but she sprinted on.

Her muscles burned from the effort. Alexia didn't stop.

The road passed beneath her feet, and she clutched Slayer in a fist to keep it from bruising her leg.

The inn disappeared behind her. The landscape slowly changed into rolling hills.

Her lungs burned. A cramp seized her side, but she kept going.

How much time had passed—an hour, two? Was she already too late? Sweat trickled down her back and plastered the curls about her face. She ignored them.

She knew the spot when it appeared, the wide open field. No smoke blackened the sky, and she thanked the Lord. Wheat stalks tickled at her elbows as she waded through them, pollens suffusing the air with richness. Clouds shrouded the heavens, the field silent except for the whisper of wind across the grain and her labored rasping. Two meager willows stretched above the stalks, spiny wood hard for her to imagine becoming the crater that had occupied the space.

Strange.

Like the weight in her pocket. She slipped the linen-wrapped pendant out of her skirt, peeling the covering back. Cold metal gleamed up at her, somewhere between a pentagram and triangle, with a Z whose bottom lip curled back like the swirl of a seashell. A short line crossed its center, the arms of a headless character. Small rune-like impressions circled the central shape, a continuous ring of indecipherable script. She swirled her hand above the face, its heavy chain slipping free and dangling over the sides of her palm, separated only by the cloth.

A distant rumble pulled her around. Dust billowed up.

She caught her breath.

His silvery stallion streaked into view, escorted by the brown Miles always rode. Alexia could have cried for relief. She stood on her toes and waved.

They sped past.

She let out an indignant grunt.

Kiren pulled to a stop. He turned. Even across the distance, his gaze sent lightning zipping through her soul as though she'd dived into a glacial pool the first day of spring.

He spoke to Miles whose head shook. Kiren slapped the brown's flank and sent Miles charging away. He bent over his own beast and galloped straight for her. She bit back the tears, so thankful for his beating heart she could burst into a ray of sunlight.

He leapt from the animal and came to a halt only a step away from her, confusion crunching his brows down.

Her heart thundered. Here he stood, the man she never thought she'd see again, and he was whole. He was hers!

She threw her arms around him and kissed his neck.

Kiren lifted her away, shaking her shoulders. "What are you doing here?"

She scowled. Couldn't he at least allow her an instant of relief? "I do not think you appreciate what I have been through." She swiped wet hair away from her face. Over his shoulder, blackness swooped toward them, a continuous stripe of death. She hefted his necklace, the links clinking.

Kiren's eyes widened. He lifted it over his head, pausing. "How did you...?"

She crossed her arms.

191

He smirked, shaking his head at his own question. He dropped the chain around his neck, eyes closing like a boy who had found his way home after days of being lost. She'd only once seen such relief in the pucker of his lips—the night he'd discovered her in Ethel's cottage after months of searching.

His brow quirked.

"What is wrong?" She touched his cheek.

"I..." His head shook. "Nothing."

A chorus of hisses hit her ears. Kiren slid a protective arm around her, twirling to take in the ring of dark cloaks. They were completely surrounded.

Kiren frowned down at her. She was squeezing him, her fingers cutting into his ribs. She loosened her grip.

The wind died.

Kiren pressed her tighter.

She peeked around him, gripping Slayer. A line of dark shrouds fenced them in, each at arms' length from one another. Brilliant red eyes speared into her. Her heart raced.

"They cannot hurt us," she reminded herself. He had his medallion and all was right again.

Kiren slid the pendant free in one graceful movement. It glimmered, dull metal, a molten angry thing. He sucked in a breath and lifted the charm.

She shaded her eyes, ready for the brilliant light to take away their enemies. His muscles stiffened against her. They trembled. He lifted the pendant higher, his back as hard as stone.

She glanced up. What was he waiting for?

He panted. Sweat glistened down his neck, seeping into his collar.

"Kiren?" she whispered.

He dropped the pendant and gripped her fingers. Words shot through her mind in his voice: *It's not working.*

She gasped.

Screams pierced her ears, hungry wails. Clawed fingers lifted as the entire ring surged forward.

Fifty-Five

Obliterate

NO!

Everything stopped.

Alexia looked about the circle of blazing red pupils and sucked in the stagnant air. It smarted against her tongue. Death. She tasted the death.

She glanced up at Kiren, his jaw set, shoulders bent slightly forward, bracing for the onslaught. His eyes blazed with defiance.

He was the very essence of everything contrary to the Soulless: life, light, strength.

She lifted a hand to his cheek and traced the stone-like skin. She would not let them take him.

Not now.

Not ever.

No matter the cost.

Releasing the moments slowly, she tore Slayer out of her belt, slipping free from Kiren's grasp.

The circle closed in slow motion. She twisted the weapon, as long as her forearm, pointing the jagged blade at the nearest enemy.

Her heart sped, palms sweaty.

The creatures' cloaks floated on the suspended air, almost translucent. She squinted closer. Particles darkened the space around them, but no cloth moved like that. What were they wrapped in?

Skinless bones reached for her face.

The heart. She had to aim for the heart.

But how? Between the ribs? From below? What if she missed?

Her hand trembled as she lifted the blade. It halted at the wraith's chest cavity. With a shove, it cut in from below, splitting the skin like butter.

She gagged.

Up she thrust, horrified but unable to look away as the weapon slid in, one excruciating inch after another. She could stop this. She could pull away now before it was too late, before she'd taken a life.

Everything inside her faded to ash.

No. This had to be done.

The weapon disappeared up to its hilt and jolted to a stop.

It was done.

The creature swiped at her. She ducked, pulling the blade free. The blackness wrapping the demon's arm grazed her face, liquid ice: darkness embodied. The emptiness stole her breath.

She leapt back.

Murk oozed from the wraith's wound.

Her insides turned to slush.

Gray slush.

The creature's eyes pierced hers as it dropped to the ground, squeezed in confusion; innocent questions harbored in them.

Why? How?

Her stomach roiled.

Tears burned at Alexia's eyes. She blinked them away and faced the next victim.

The world blanked into one black mass after another. She thrust, pulled the weapon free, and thrust again.

Bodies tumbled before her. How many, she didn't know. They just kept coming. She wiped tears away between stabbing, pulling back only to find another target, and stopping time completely when one of them grew too close. Kiren remained behind her as she whirled, dispatching each of the mindless attackers.

The minutes weighed on her. Her neck ached from the forming headache. How long had she been at it? It felt like hours, but she didn't stop. One after another after another...

Stab.

Pull free.

Don't think.

Next.

Her brain was an anvil.

She didn't stop.

Her arms didn't want to work anymore.

She didn't stop.

Her vision fogged.

Stab.

Pull free.

Next.

Alexia collapsed to her knees, landing in a pile of limp bodies. No more darkness streaked toward her. It bled across the ground in dizzying circles.

She released time. Kiren caught her before she toppled over on her side, weapon slipping from her fingers. His eyes stretched wide, mouth open.

Alexia ran her hand over his cheek and gave him a weak smile. They would not hurt him, not ever again.

No matter what.

Fifty-Six

Fear

So many. So many dead.

Kiren lifted Alexia against his shoulder to keep her from seeing and clenched his teeth. Blood clung to the strands of her hair and dotted her clothing.

Blood.

On her hands.

No matter what he did, he could never wash it off.

This was going to crush her. His angel.

His angel of death.

He would never escape the vision of her standing over a heap of corpses, the blur of motion as her broken weapon gleamed, the deadly precision and determination in her eye. He could only imagine how she would struggle to reconcile.

Kiren turned his gaze up, away from the bodies. He did not want to recognize friends from ages past, for it was enough that she'd saved him—saved them both. He would not burden her with his depression.

He rose, taking her with him. Her arms wrapped feebly around his shoulders, her face pressed into his neck. She shook.

"Shh," he encouraged. *He* was supposed to protect *her*, to shield her from this sort of heartache. He had failed.

Her sadness pierced into him like the fabric of her heart had been shredded and set free on the waves of a torrid sea. She was drifting apart, and no matter how he held her, he couldn't keep her whole.

Carefully, he stepped over the prostrate bodies.

And why hadn't the necklace worked?

It didn't sit right. The weight was off. It was empty. No power. No connection. Only emptiness.

A counterfeit?

Or was the counterfeit somehow himself? Was it possible that entering the Soulless consciousness had altered him?

Lucian would know. They needed to get back to the inn, to the heart of the Passionate, to safety. But there was no safety. Not from this. Not anymore.

Fifty-Seven

Torment

The steady rhythm of the horse's hooves vibrated through Alexia until they resonated in her head, a constant drumming to exasperate her growing headache. Each shock sent pain lancing up her neck, and she just wanted it to end. Kiren held her firm, anchoring her. Her heart should be fluttering out of control, her entire soul warmed by his presence, but a dark cloud hung over her.

They were dead, all of them. There must have been fifty.

Fifty like John.

Or Sarah.

She could barely breathe around the knowledge of what she'd done.

But she had saved Kiren.

Was his life worth so many of theirs?

Of course it was! How many Passionate had he saved? How many more would he save?

After an hour of riding, he pulled into the quiet of someone's barn and slid from the beast. Starlight spilled through gaps in the wood, dappling the ground in patches of silver. He took her elbow and aided her down. She landed and stumbled. He caught her and she stood chest to chest, face to face, his breath curling over her lips.

Alexia couldn't look at him. She knew what she would see: disappointment, disgust, guilt. Part of her wanted him to kiss her, to tell her he was not repulsed by her actions, although she knew he must be. She wanted him—no needed him!

But she didn't deserve him.

Alexia turned away and dropped into the straw.

He stood over her, not moving. Once or twice his breath hitched like he might speak, but what would he say? Reprimand her for so blatant an abuse of her power? Thank her for saving his life while his tone thrummed with accusation?

Slayer thudded in the straw next to her. She scooted away from it, wishing he'd left it behind.

Kiren cleared his throat, clearly waiting for something. Her fingers bit into her legs. She visually traced pieces of straw, unable to summon the power to lift her head. She curled in on herself, locking her arms around her legs. He would never be able to look on her the same way, but he lived. Her mother had warned there would be a price. Well, she'd paid it. Would there be any coming back from this?

Kiren exited the barn, leaving her alone.

The knotted rafters reminded her of Father's stables, though she'd rarely been out to them. Her nanny had often warned about the unbecoming things which came of noble young women consorting with men in such places.

Her nanny who was dead at the hands of the Soulless.

She brushed a hand over the straw. Tears trickled down her cheeks. She had lived such a simple life then. Perhaps Kiren had been right to insist she stay safely within the human world. At least then he would have still had use of his pendant.

Alexia shuddered.

He returned, a bucket sloshing at this side. He knelt before her, pulled the handkerchief from his jacket, and began washing the filth from her neck and hair. She still couldn't meet his gaze.

The water chilled her, but his fingers grazed her skin, leaving a simmering trail of desire. He set the cloth aside and caressed her chin.

She blinked up at him.

"There you are." The words were tender, his lips curving gently.

She bit down on the insides of her lips. Kiren slid closer, cupping her face. Her heart sped. His breath warmed her lips.

He was going to kiss her, to kiss the lips of a woman who had knowingly and intentionally killed and killed again. He didn't deserve anything so tainted!

Uncontrollable tears burst through.

"Alexia." He wrapped her in his arms and kissed the top of her head. His lips traveled to her brow, warming the skin. He kissed her cheeks, her nose, and finally her mouth.

She wept and kissed him back, yanking him closer, needing more of him. He kissed her more fiercely. She grabbed his waistcoat, pulling him over her as she laid back. He leaned in, his breath swirling across her bare neck, fingers caressing her sides.

Everything else disappeared while she was buried in him. He could heal this, heal anything, save her from herself. She didn't want to think about anything but him.

She groaned hungrily and rolled over top of him. Night light streaked across his face, whitening his eyelashes. His stare cut her to the very center: so hungry, so vulnerable, like the crimson pupils of the creatures she'd slain.

She fumbled off him, heart stuttering.

He sat up, brows squeezed together. "What is wrong?"

She slowed her breathing, closing her eyes. She couldn't do it, couldn't be with him knowing what she'd become for his sake.

Warm fingers brushed a curl of hair behind her ear. "Love?"

She turned away. "Am I a horrible person?"

"Why would you think that?"

She met his eyes, unable to stave the tears. "Only this morning I believed you lost to me, forever."

He stroked her jaw. "And was I truly lost to you?"

She hesitated and nodded, more tears escaping. He pulled her against his chest, brushing her curls. "You dreamed it?"

Alexia shook her head. "I jumped through time, Kiren. I came to stop them from killing you."

His fingers froze.

She pressed a hand against his chest, searching for the rhythm that gave her a valid reason for drawing air. "And I did. I stopped them. All of them." She blinked up at him. "Is it wrong that I should value your life above so many others?"

Kiren brushed the hair back from her face. "It should have been me."

She shivered and he wrapped himself more closely about her. What was he saying? That he should have been the one to die?

He groaned. "I should have stopped them."

"Would it be any less horrid?" She choked on the last word. "Are we so much better that we deserve to live and they deserve to suffer?"

"Love, they are set free."

"Who am I, Kiren? I am not God. I am not the one who should decide it is their time!" The last word struck her. Time. Wasn't that her gift? *Was* she intended then to decide such things—the beginning and ending of things? Why else did she have this gift? And what kind of merciful God would place so great a burden upon her?

He nuzzled her ear. "I believe these creatures are allowed to suffer, and I believe their merciful release is acceptable."

"Then why does it feel like murder?" She faced him.

Light glistened across his pupils, but they were turned thoughtfully down.

She clutched his coat. "How have you survived it all these years? *Setting them free?* Tell me the secret, Kiren. I need to know!"

He pried her fingers from digging into his skin, lashes lifting. "There is no secret."

She swallowed in horror.

"I do what I do for the right reasons, to preserve a nation that would otherwise cease to exist." He stood back. "Perhaps I am wrong. Perhaps we should have faded from existence long ago."

She couldn't believe that was the right answer.

"Or perhaps God puts people in places at specific times because he knows how they will act." His eyes drifted shut. "Perhaps he places his trust in us to act with the information or power with which we've been entrusted."

She rose and pulled him close, wishing she could comfort him. How could she marvel at her own actions and not recognize the guilt he bore for so many difficult moments? Her hand landed over the bulge of his necklace. Had it failed to function because she pulled it away from proper time? Had she damned them all by bringing it with her? "Why do you think it did not work?" she asked quietly.

He tugged the links from beneath his collar and lifted it into the light. A scowl curled the corners of his mouth down. He squinted closer. "That is not right." He stepped to the barn door and shoved it open, scrubbing his fingers across the pendant's surface. "This rune, here. It should curl on the end."

"It is a fake?" She could barely believe it.

His jaw muscles flexed. "It seems perhaps the Soulless are more cunning than we had anticipated."

Hisses carried through the night air.

Kiren retrieved the horse.

Fifty-Eight

Fate

Charles shivered, despite his layers. His estate home was chilly with no servants to light the fires, and it felt haunted now in his weapon gallery. He latched a rapier across his hip and stowed his powder horn carefully in his satchel.

After Bellezza's disappearance a week and a half ago, he'd spent three days waiting for her return, the damnable imp, then made his way home. He now believed her interview had led to more trouble than she'd anticipated. Not that he cared. About her.

And yet he worried. Why had he remained in the house if not to receive the child?

"Bewitched," he grumbled.

Still, he had come to believe her words, that a society of Collectors existed and that he had the power to infiltrate and dismantle them, something he anticipated with a surprising mix of excitement and dread.

Movement caught the corner of his eye. He tensed. He slid his hands around the pistols lodged in his belt. Shadows shifted. He hooked fingers around the triggers.

The cold weighed around him, silent and still, like death.

He whirled, aiming.

A shadowy shroud stood in the doorway. Crimson eyes glowed at the heart of shifting blackness, as though all the light immediately around the being had been sucked out of the world.

He fired.

Sparks exploded out the back of one weapon. The ball launched into the creature and it rent, crackling into a haze.

Charles hastily reloaded the pistol, seized his shotgun, and latched another one over his back. Hefting his satchel over one shoulder, he sprinted out the door.

It had been a mistake to come back here. They didn't want *him* per say, but they wanted his carcass for leverage against his daughter and her terribly important fiancé.

A creature launched out of the darkness. He fired.

Three more shots and he'd be down to his rapier and the dagger hidden in his boot. His footfalls echoed ominously as he thundered down the back stairs and out the door.

Heavy clouds obscured the stars, blocking even hope from view. Veering into the stable, he snatched a saddle and rope, and returned to the night.

A shriek. He shot around. A wraith glided across the yard, arms outstretched. He lifted his shotgun.

Boom!

Gunpowder perfumed the night. A horse whinnied and stamping hooves drew him. Charles hurdled the pasture fence.

Two skittish animals butted at the gate, their eyes wide.

"Steady now." He looped the rope around the larger steed's neck and tied it down to the fence while saddling it, watching for the enemy. Mounting quickly, he kicked off into the night. It was time to seek out the Passionate the only place he knew, the place this whole mess began.

Fifty-Nine

To the Inn

Kiren held the horse steady. The Soulless weren't far behind, and he was lucky they'd been able to evade them thus far.

The grinding of Alexia's teeth was driving him mad, her pain echoing acutely through him. She had pushed herself too hard. He'd done what he could while galloping away from the enemy, begging her body to heal and gifting her the necessary dose of his strength. Still, there was so much he couldn't heal.

Like what she'd done.

The memory of her tears tore at his heart. More so, the break in her voice after they'd outrun the Soulless, as she'd related her past two days—how she'd clung to him and begged him never to leave her. It killed him, being the reason for her weeping—and the worst part: her guilt.

Perhaps it would be better if he had died. Maybe that was what the fates intended, and if that were so, did he defy the natural order by continuing on? Was it possible the alteration in his medallion was a result of how they'd twisted reality?

No. It was a counterfeit.

He clenched the reins. A coldness weighted his chest, almost as though part of him was missing, the part that knew it should have ceased upon the earth.

For Alexia's sake he needed to be here. He understood that.

Loose curls curtained her neck, her pastel lips pulled back as she hissed in a breath. He would do anything to keep her from suffering.

But she was so strong. So much stronger than himself. To dispatch that horde of creatures, one by one, even knowing she would forever regret it...

Starlight glazed the broken blade latched across the front of the saddle. He hadn't seen the weapon before, or at least he didn't think he had. To his knowledge there was only one blade in existence that could end the Soulless, and it belonged to his greatest mistake of all time, one he hoped Alexia would never have to face.

He placed a hand over her stomach. She twisted, eyebrows lifting.

"I think it is time I married you." He kissed her cheek.

204

"You would still marry me? Even after—"

"I should have married you the instant you were restored to my care."

She shivered.

"But I wanted you to have a real marriage, not some forced counterfeit." He smoothed the hair from her brow, hating what he was about to confess. "I can see that may never happen."

She touched his cheek, her brows squeezed inward.

He exhaled. "We are stronger together than we are apart. I need your strength." And she needed his, more than he dared to admit.

"If you will still have me, I do not care the manner of our union. It is more important that we are together."

He nodded. She had always been too practical, too self-sacrificing. That she now must give up the one thing every young girl craved, it pinched a hole in his heart and filled his eyes with tears. "I love you, Alexia."

"Forever." Her fingers slipped between his.

Sixty

Deeper

Alexia was so relieved to step back over the dulling line of scorched earth. Ethel met them on the inn stoop, followed by Lester and a contemplative Miles. Others spilled out, fugitives of this battle, curious bystanders. Everyone watched her, and Alexia didn't like it. Did they know what she'd done?

Of course they did. With the grime coating her dress…

She stopped shy of Miles and turned to Kiren who dragged his feet up the stairs. Lester grabbed his shoulder and exchanged an inquisitive look. Kiren gave a weak smile. His companion patted his arm and escaped to stable Kiren's stallion.

"I have need of Lucian," Kiren called, and the crowd parted to reveal a man with black hair, narrow eyes, and a flatter nose than most. He wore a simple robe like a traveling monk.

A smile furrowed Lucian's one cheek. "I knew you would seek me."

"Of course you did." Aside to Alexia he whispered, "He has the gift of foresight." He nodded again at the monk. "Then you know what it is I desire?"

Lucian gave a slight bow from the hips.

"Let it be done," Kiren muttered. "Now." He offered a hand to Alexia and she took it.

He could not possibly mean for them to be joined this instant—having just walked in the door, her dress stained in gore! But the granite of his eyes and squaring of his jaw said just that.

They descended the steps and crossed over the barrier, leaving behind scorched earth.

The monk wove two silver ropes about their wrists, joining them. The rope glittered, warming her wrist like a wreath of light.

"What is joined this day let none put asunder." A new language rumbled up, not Latin, yet something ancient and lyrical, a tongue that resonated with her very soul. She couldn't isolate a single word, but she understood the collective meaning:

206

We begin alone. In the eternities we are separate, individual. Here only can the bond be made, and here, under the vigilance of heaven, two are bound for a lifetime or so long as both shall live, with the hope of eternal love and eternal companionship.

Lucian turned to Kiren. "Will you cherish this woman with all your heart, to love and keep her until death claims one or both of you?"

"From the beginning until the end of time." His low voice shook with emotion. "Yes."

"Alexia Dumont, do you receive this man and his vows, through weakness and folly, through heartache and joy, and return your own pledge until death claims one or both of you?"

She nodded. "Forever."

A shimmery warmth washed over her, as though sunbeams had been sprinkled on them all. The hairs on her arms stood up. Kiren squeezed her hand, drawing her notice to the gooseflesh of his wrist.

Luminescence spilled off his skin, matched by the glow of her own. The particles merged, pulsing brighter, creating a dome of radiance over them.

Lucian resumed. "By the power of my station, I proclaim you husband and wife. Be constant to one another. Grow together, not apart, and shape the world in your wake."

Kiren brushed a thumb across her fingers and she met his stare.

"This day begins the rest of forever," the monk said.

Kiren's brow quirked. Alexia blushed, and grinned at their looped wrists.

"May joy be showered upon you. May you live until the Kingdom be restored, until the golden age when our cares are laid to rest." Lucian placed a hand on Kiren's shoulder, voice lowering. "I leave it to you to seal the binding."

He turned his back to them and Kiren smirked. He tugged Alexia closer and lowered his lips toward hers. She closed her eyes. The tender press of his mouth promised a lifetime of sweetness, a lifetime of commitment, an eternity of love. He pulled back slowly, cheeks dimpling.

Tugging at the ends of two silver strands, he nodded for her to take the other ends. She did and he laced his through hers, sewing them more permanently together.

"It is our tradition," he whispered, "that the new bride and groom are to be bound until they are truly one."

She flushed.

Ethel departed, leaving them in the quiet trees. Kiren led Alexia into the grove, the trickle of water brightened by the first hint of sunrise. Blossoms perked as they passed, as if rejuvenated by their shared light. Butterflies flitted from bloom to bloom.

Alexia didn't like that they'd left Slayer behind, but she also didn't want it with her. Not here.

Kiren set the spare clothing they'd brought down on a large, flat stone, the very place he'd sat her several months ago to reveal truths about himself and his role among the Passionate.

She glanced back at the tree bed as he tugged her to the water's edge.

This was real. It was finally happening. She was married! Surely there was a hitch. Something would go wrong. Some unforeseen tragedy or emergency would rear its monstrous self.

"Are we safe here?" she whispered.

Kiren met her stare. His eyes were a glittering spring, a lost Atlantis, her own eternal ocean. "No one will disturb us."

The solidity of his words convinced her.

Carefully, he unfastened the ties of her ruined dress.

She trembled under his touch, too aware of the heat in his fingers, or the way his pulse thundered in time with hers. His lips caressed her shoulder as he bared it, his breath hot on her skin.

Heat burst all around her, within and without, sheer sunshine firing free from her depths. He guided her through the blaze, mingling their joined light in a fury so potent even the stars would tremble for jealousy. She consumed him. Took all he offered and returned her entire flaming soul. Every movement, every thought, every touch belonged to them both. The doors of his crystal palace flew wide and their combined luminescence beamed from all seven towers.

The sun clung to the apex of the sky as Alexia roused on the feather mattress. Kiren's arms cradled her, his chest pressed to her back, but as intimate as his hold was, it paled to the way he was touching her soul. They were twined for eternity.

Like the rope that had bound their wrists.

She grinned. His arms tightened around her, and she could feel his happiness leaking through their connection. He was a boy again, not a care in the world. How long had it been since he'd been so free?

She rolled to face him, and his lips were moving, eyes closed.

"What are you doing?" she asked.

He cracked one eye open. "Praying."

She kept quiet until his mouth stilled. "What were you praying about?"

"Thanking the Lord for you."

Her cheeks heated. "I thank Him for you as well."

He sighed and turned onto his back, hands braced behind his head.

She blinked at the trail of clothing strewn across the grove and stifled a giggle. "We are an awful pair. You would think a monster stamped through this place!"

He tugged her onto her back and leaned up over her, his smile bursting. "I believe one may have." His eyes widened. "A hungry monster."

She gave an exaggerated gasp and placed a hand on her chest. "Did he get his fill?"

He laughed and kissed her. "Never."

Alexia giggled and slid her fingers through his hair. "May I tell you a secret?"

He braced on his fist, eyes glittering with amusement.

"I really, truly, desperately like the monster who made this mess." She leaned up to whisper in his ear and a shiver shook across his skin. "But do not tell him. It will inflate his pride until no person can stand his presence."

He attacked, tickling her until both their sides ached from laughter. He collapsed next to her and the press of his skin to hers lit an invisible fire, an energy that grew and encompassed them both in its protective aura. She couldn't fathom how she'd existed without it.

"Why am I not sleepy?" she asked. For all their play, she should be exhausted, unable to rise for hours, and yet energy bubbled at the surface.

He nudged the hair away from her neck with his nose. "You will experience many of my appetites, and I shall experience yours."

She pulled him back and met his gaze. "You are saying I do not crave slumber because you do not?"

His smirk was vulnerable and boyish. His eyes glimmered, filled with rakish mischief as his fingers glided across her cheek. "I may never sleep again."

Heat pulsed outward, filling her world, her universe.

Kiren's fingers curled over her jaw. "You will rarely hunger as you have, rarely need the sleep that has been so precious to you, and I shall crave both more often than I am accustomed."

Alexia swallowed.

He chuckled and kissed both her overly-warm cheeks. "I adore you, Alexia."

"The sensation is mutual."

"You adore you too?"

She swiped his hair into his face, laughing.

"You should." He blinked up at her and brushed the ginger locks away. "You are utterly adorable."

She tucked into him, resting her chin on his chest, listening to his steady breathing and tracing circles across his skin. She loved being here with him, but the storm was coming. When and if they retrieved the necklace, their peace would only ever be short lived. If she could continue to chase away these phantoms at the back of her mind, they might have a chance at happiness.

And she was not the only one with phantoms. She'd run across the shaded places in his mind, and now that she was less distracted, she wished to know what hid behind each of the curtains. Would he allow her?

"When will it be over, Kiren?" She couldn't keep the longing from her voice. "I want to stay like this, to be with you always."

A cloud of sadness dropped over them both. "Soon, love."

She gasped, startled by the emptiness behind his word. "You just lied to me."

His face pinked, his mouth working but no words escaped.

Amazing! Finally, she was on equal footing with him. She rolled on top of him. "You are going to have a hard time with this new development, are you not?"

He cleared his throat. "I suppose I shall have to alter my ways."

"Good." She rested her cheek on his chest. "But do not answer my inquiry. I wish only for this moment."

They arrived at the inn well after dark, and she had not experienced nearly enough of Kiren, but for the moment, it was all the time they could spare. Stepping back over the line of scorched earth was like having a down coat torn away. Alexia shivered at the sudden chill.

Kiren's fingers slipped between hers, clinging like he needed her strength the way she craved his.

Mae sat in her rocking chair, knitting. Her head tilted as they stepped through the doorway. Children's footfalls and playful calls shook the rafters, a mother's chastisement chasing after them while the murmur of bass voices built an undercurrent of buzz.

Stomping echoed through the kitchen. Alexia whirled and Kiren caught her shoulders, twisting with her.

John burst through the doorway like a rabid bear. His teeth grated as his glare fixed on Alexia, an unresponsive body dangling in his arms. Raven hair sagged over his arm.

Sixty-One

Sarah

Alexia's heart clenched.

The noise of the inn faded into an empty chasm. The only occupants were her faltering heart and the absence of thought.

John set her sister down.

Alexia jolted forward, but Kiren's fingers cut into her shoulders.

John's chest heaved, his eyes promising murder. "You did this to her." He pointed with a hooked finger, his frame trembling.

Sarah's skin was the color of chalk, her eyes blank.

Ice crinkled through Alexia's veins. She fought for a voice, discovering none. *Me?*

"You told her how to..." He covered his mouth, threw his fist down and rounded away. People scattered out of his path.

Metal protruded from Sarah's chest, the jagged edge of a broken blade, the once-pastel frock stained brown with her sister's blood.

Alexia's hands dropped limply to her sides. Sarah's upturned palms were sliced from inserting the metal.

Two nights ago. Sarah gave birth two nights ago to a dead child...

Alexia's knees gave out. She slid to the floor. Because she'd gone to save Kiren, she hadn't been there to comfort Sarah. John was right. Sarah was dead because of her.

Alexia's chest collapsed. Sobs tore through her.

She'd done this.

Kiren's arms wrapped around her. Even the warmth of his presence could not combat the hailstorm gusting through her chest.

Everything was falling apart. Her whole world—it was wrong, in ruin! Her sister couldn't be dead! Kiren could not be powerless! She had saved them both once, was that not enough?

She wished it was her instead, that she could escape or cease to exist—like her sister. The inn disappeared, Kiren's touch, all gone.

To the absence of time.

A soft palm cupped her cheek. She blinked up into olive eyes and raven tresses. *Sarah*, her heart gasped. The sorrow shook free like snow from pine boughs. Her joy burst through in luminous daylight—transforming the emptiness around her into Father's garden, her favorite memory of a picnic with her sister.

But the cheekbones were too low, the skin a shade too dark. This wasn't Sarah—only someone who greatly resembled her best friend.

Light faded back into the nothingness of a place without time. Alexia wept, drowning in the folds of her skirt like a bitter sea. She remained, folded in the depths, gasping for breath while raging emotion broke her soul in pieces. Even when she'd believed her sister lost, even when she believed Sarah damned forever by the Soulless taint, even while she doubted her motives, Sarah had still been alive. Now they were forever parted. Her dearest relation had been banished to a crueler fate than any person deserved: bereft of child, betrayed by love, devoid of life.

Alexia surfaced eventually, a hand gently rubbing circles over her back.

"One sacrificed to save another."

Alexia grabbed her mother's bodice. "You knew this would happen! You knew she would die if I saved Kiren. You knew I would have to—" She stared at her hands, washed clean but still covered in blood.

Dana's eyes lowered, her voice soft. "I did not know, Alexia, but I guessed. You made a difficult decision. Would you undo it?"

She hugged herself, shivering from an impossible cold. "How much worse can it be?"

Her mother's brows scrunched down over her closed eyes. "You could lose them both."

Alexia's insides collapsed. "It is not a gift we possess. It is a curse."

Dana took hold of her arm and gave it a squeeze.

"I wish I could undo it all." Alexia covered her face. "I wish I could stop the Soulless from ever existing. I hate this all so much!"

She wept again.

Somewhere in the bleakness she decided. Since his medallion was first taken, she'd known it was her fault—and her duty to return it. If only she'd heeded that intuition sooner! Kiren would have been present to heal Sarah. They would have been married, bonded before any of this awfulness occurred. Now it seemed fate had forced her hand, placed her between two impossible choices so she would wake to her impending duty and make things right.

"Proceed with caution," Dana whispered.

Alexia nodded and withdrew from the absence of time.

Sixty-Two

Enemy at the Gates

A scream carried through the back door, rending the night.

Kiren's hand flew to his neck, searching for the chain.

Their enemies were come, as expected. The Passionate were here, and there was a high concentration of negative emotion.

His fingers curled over the lifeless metal, and his breath hitched. Loss spilled through him anew: the loss of his family, of his father's trust, of his family relic.

He hurried to the door, leaving Alexia behind.

A lookout raced into the protective ring of the inn. Ragged capes glided out from the darkness, tromping Mae's carefully planted crop.

He called over his shoulder, "Mae!"

Hissing screams tore the air.

The blind woman walked calmly through the bustle and panic. She descended the steps and paused at the perimeter, fists clenched, her head down, daring them to come closer.

If she waited a second longer, it would be too late—they'd be on neutral ground and free to drag the Passionate from the premises.

"Mae, go!" he called.

Her shoulders tensed. He knew how this killed her, how she hated and craved it, but she also recognized the necessity. She stepped over the breach.

He whirled and nearly ran into Alexia. Tears clung to her face, but her mouth was a tight line, determination in her glare.

Kiren lifted her chin. "You stay inside, do you understand me?"

Her eyes rose to his, guilt and pain locked in her evergreens. He cupped her cheek and kissed her brow. "You have done enough."

Her eyes trembled, glistening with new tears.

"Stay inside." Kiren pulled away, snatching a broom from the closet as he went.

If he knew anything, he knew how these creatures thought. They would lay siege, attacking from the back to keep Mae occupied while a detachment forced their way through the front, but why hadn't they heard from the other lookout?

"To arms!" he called and sped back through the great room, where a number of terrified people huddled. He threw the front door open.

Two sets of crimson eyes turned up at him. He shoved the broom into the first one's chest, throwing it off the front stoop, and he whirled on the other, knocking it over. Both creatures tumbled down the steps. He jumped down, beating them away from the inn and through the safety line, following them off scorched earth. They hissed and shrieked.

Movement caught his periphery. He whirled.

A bare hand reached for his exposed skin. He stumbled sideways and tripped.

Dead, white fingers followed, their exposed tips like miniature moons reaching to snuff out the life he'd known and replace it with a nightmare.

Sixty-Three

Soldiers

BOOM!

A flash burst out of the night.

Kiren landed on his shoulder, clutching his ears. The bony hand reaching for him splintered apart at the center, the creature thrown to the ground.

A horse roared closer. Kiren shoved up onto an elbow. The beast whinnied and reared, hooves crunching down over the accursed attacker. A sturdy form slipped off the animal, rifle clutched at his side.

Kiren grappled to his feet. "Charles?"

"Are they as hungry for you tonight as they have been for me?"

He couldn't close his mouth to answer. The nobleman tossed his horse's reins aside and posted himself at Kiren's side, head swiveling as he eyed the darkness. "There are more coming."

Hisses raked the wind. An icy chill dropped over them.

The floods arrived. Lester delivered Alexia's sword to Kiren and they fended off the hordes. Charles held his own with a rapier, and others filled the perimeter. The Soulless could not turn anyone on scorched earth, but in these overwhelming numbers they could certainly overpower and drag the Passionate to their doom. Kiren prayed Alexia was safe and that Mae was successfully defending the back side of the inn. Only another hour and dawn would banish their enemies to the shadows.

The clatter of hooves yanked Kiren's chin up.

Edward sped through the horde of enemies on horseback, pulling to a halt and sliding free of the animal at Kiren's side.

Oh no.

"Report," Kiren called, swinging his saber.

"I let her go when they attacked."

Kiren bit down, slashing with too much vigor. Black smog exploded around them. "Had Bellezza recovered enough to travel by mist?"

Edward's head shook. "The gold is still inside her. I begged her to ride with me for our collective strength, but she ran. There was too much chaos."

A group rushed them. Kiren and Edward attacked in unison, cutting through the throng. It thinned to sickening smoke.

"Do you know if she escaped?" Kiren asked.

"I tried to follow her..."

Blackness blotted out their vision, death filling the air like a constant hum of hornets.

They came in waves. Kiren missed their hearts more often that he hit them, so unaccustomed to using a blade. He cut through the mass and obtained a twenty second reprieve, only to be assaulted by the very creatures he'd just sliced down. They danced back and forth over the perimeter, beating the enemy back only to lose ground again.

A scream burst through the ranks.

A girl. Kiren whirled and fought his way forward. Miles appeared at his side, eyes wide, a dagger clasped in one hand. They battled their way through the horde, working in unison. The mass cleared.

Golden hair streaked loosely in the starlight, frayed and ragged. Bellezza's skirts were muddied and they swished as she whirled with a small ax. Her chest heaved as she sliced through the Soulless.

Kiren paused. She had come to them after all, finally given in to reason?

The girl rounded, her teeth clenched. Her eyes squeezed, oozing toxins, her nose crinkling with rage. "You did this to me!" she shrieked. Lifting her ax, she charged.

Kiren was frozen in shock.

Miles stepped between them, his dagger clanging against her ax. He shoved her back and took a stance.

Tears rolled down Bellezza's cheeks. "I cannot mist!" Her grip tightened on her weapon. "I cannot heal!"

Kiren's saber drooped. Had he truly destroyed her? Never had they forced one of the Passionate to ingest gold, but he'd believed it would pass through her system eventually. It had been more than a week. It should have exited her body by now.

She growled and sprang at him again. Miles threw her off, and writhing black bodies flooded in.

Kiren cut through them, determined to find the girl again, to set things aright. He chopped through the mass, searching for the end of the wave.

Black haze littered the air as Bellezza's scream carried above the skirmish. Kiren forced his way through.

Whoosh! Metal flashed toward his neck.

He ducked.

The girl recoiled with her weapon and lunged at him. He stumbled backward. Miles jumped out of the blackness, smacking Bellezza in the shoulder and knocking them both to the ground.

Creatures circled in. Kiren rushed forward. He swung, blinded by the number of them.

The clash of metal rang in his ears, Miles's grunts and Bellezza's shrieks launching the hair on the back of his neck upward.

"Bellezza, stop!" he called. They did not have time to battle one another! He plunged his weapon through the writhing blackness and retreated toward the skirmish.

Miles's panting pulled him through the ebony fog. Golden tresses whirled as the girl danced back, raking her ax free from the boy's dagger.

Miles jabbed.

The girl gasped. Her back stiffened, still as stone. Kiren circled.

Bellezza's eyes were wide, her lips open in shock, the dagger protruding from her chest. She tottered.

Kiren caught her as ice raked through the air, the wind gone. Piercing red eyes rushed from the darkness. He set her down and turned on their foe.

The minutes stretched as his weapon whirled, every second counting against him, against her life. Forcing the tide back, he returned to the girl.

Miles stood over Bellezza, his dagger still lodged in her chest, her body motionless.

Kiren couldn't believe what he was seeing.

He was too late.

But she was so strong. Maybe if—

He dropped to her side, but her chest wasn't moving, her eyes glazed over. She was empty.

Miles eyes shot wide. "Watch ou—"

Simmering fingers wrapped around Kiren's throat. He grabbed the bone, tearing at it and searching for his necklace on instinct. The waste of a counterfeit. He cursed silently, the wall of midnight blocking him from Miles and the dead girl.

Bony claws caught his limbs and yanked. His arm tweaked, saber lost. Burning hands lifted him off the ground, slicing into his legs, his side, his shoulders. If they dragged him off scorched earth he would become one of them. He couldn't let that happen!

Fire tore into him.

He lurched. Searing nails pierced his flesh through his clothes, multiple lacerations. He couldn't breathe. The darkness around him suddenly felt very far away, as if he were viewing it through a window.

He screamed.

Sixty-Four

Rally

The warming sky spun above Kiren. This was happening. This was really happening. A moment longer, and they would succeed in pulling him beyond the perimeter. They would have what they wanted: his essence. Alexia would be left alone, bonded to a man who craved her flesh. Dark hunger was the only happiness she could hope for, an emptiness that should have been heaven.

Never.

She had destroyed her innocence for him, killed for him. He could not fail her. Never again.

Kiren reached into his core and pulled. Light burst around him. It beamed off his skin, cutting through the blackness.

Gasps rang.

Sixty-Five

Piercing

The howl was unlike anything she'd heard. Alexia's blood turned to ice. The scream shook her frame and tore at her lungs as if it originated from her own body, but it was not her.

She shoved out the inn door and stopped on the stoop.

Light trickled across the land.

She scoured the ground for shrouds, but other than a periodic fallen corpse, they were gone. Passionate dropped to their knees or laughed for relief, patting one another on the back.

They had done it!

She shoved her way through allies, needing to discover her husband was safe. She could feel him, weakly, like the cord that bound them had been stretched into a thread and coiled about the yard.

People huddled together, their joy lost on her as she squirmed through them and almost tripped over Miles. He knelt on the ground, staring at the dagger lodged in a small body.

Golden ringlets spilled across the dirt, frayed and loose, the child's royal velvet gown mucked and ragged.

"Bellezza..." she whispered. The girl didn't respond, her body still. "Miles?"

His shoulders drooped, head bowed.

"She is not..." Alexia covered her mouth. The girl could not be dead. She was one of those eternal creatures, the kind that would torment them long beyond this wretched battle.

No, Bellezza was merely injured. She needed help.

Kiren could heal this.

Miles's gaze again dropped to the unmoving girl. "She attacked him. I stopped her."

Miles had done this? Her heart throbbed for him, broken and weighed down by her own numerous murders.

She dropped on the ground beside him and wrapped her arms around his shoulder. "Oh, Miles..."

His eyes closed and he reached out, sliding his palm over the dagger handle. He pulled it free of Bellezza's form. Instead of blood, white mist oozed out of the injury, releasing into the sky. The particles deflated her form, ribs and shoulders sinking in. Her body disintegrated, like an exhaled breath until nothing remained.

Gone. Just like that, the girl was gone.

"Miles, where is my husband? Why couldn't he stop this?"

He didn't move, his knuckles white around the dagger hilt.

"Miles?" She wanted to shake him.

His head lifted, gaze drifting to the horizon.

She followed it. White brilliance beamed in the distance near the boundary line, a dome of unearthly light, not the foggy yellow rays of sunrise. It diminished, pulsating inward as the glow died. A red haze gleamed over the edge of the horizon, silhouetting the man who knelt on the ground, head bowed, shoulders back.

Kiren.

She rushed forward.

Kiren toppled. Lester appeared at his side, catching him. She stepped over three prostrate bodies, pools of darkness against the road, silenced Soulless. She dropped to the runner's side.

"He's alive, if that be what yer fearin'," Lester said.

Kiren's eyes fluttered. He grunted. Words garbled in his throat.

Alexia wrapped her fingers around his and awareness burst through her. Warmth crept into her skin, a cloud-like consciousness that trickled up into her mind: *You should not be out here.*

She scowled. "Says the man who cannot even lift his head."

The corner of his mouth twitched. She leaned close and pressed her lips to his ear. "You have given me of your energies before, I wonder whether it is possible for me to lend you strength."

A crystalline nexus appeared in her mind, an orb that lodged within her own breast.

Kiren grunted. A dark cloud billowed up in her thoughts. She pushed it back, focusing on the sphere he'd revealed deep within herself. She pressed it toward his consciousness. Zaps of light coursed through her veins, reaching for his skin.

Kiren's hand jerked, but he was too weak to pull away. She gripped harder. She was a kettle, tilting and spilling into a nearly empty glass.

Kiren's fingers tore free.

She lifted her head and met his ocean sky. Her entire body wanted to collapse and sleep for a week, but he was well.

"Never do that," he whispered.

She crossed her arms, her voice shaking. "Promise me I will never find you as I did just now, and we are agreed."

He frowned.

220

Lester chuckled. "She's a spitfire, that one."

Alexia leaned into Kiren, stealing a moment to gather her strength. "How did you do that—without the necklace?"

Kiren slid an arm around her. "It was not the medallion that enabled me to act. It was something within, but I have never been able to unleash it on my own. Or perhaps I have never tried."

"Because you always possessed the weapon."

He nodded. "A weapon we must retrieve." His gaze turned to Lester. "They will come and come again until it is within our possession. I am not strong enough to keep them away, and clearly Mae's threat is no longer enough."

"Agreed," Lester said, turning back toward the inn. "But we've far too many needin' protection."

"I will go." Kiren righted himself and climbed to his feet. "Apparently I can defend myself."

"At what cost?" Alexia rose. "Had they come back you would have been easy to finish. You cannot go alone."

His brows scrunched together. "I would risk no one else."

"Good." She dismissed Lester with a nod and faced Kiren. "We are agreed."

"Alexia, no—"

"You saw what I did."

His face paled.

She hated his reaction—hated that she could feel his horror through their bond. He had known many of the creatures she'd sent on, and his pain was palpable.

Yes, she was a murderer. Whether he was horrified by her actions or not, he had to recognize her power, and she would never allow anyone to hurt him.

Kiren's jaw muscles clenched. "Let us be off then."

Kiren had barely spoken the entire journey, and Alexia was frustrated that he remained so quiet, but—with the regular twitching of his brows—she discerned a battle must be raging inside. Whatever he was thinking, it came at her in waves—the reluctance, then a deep-set determination, followed by mental agony. Perhaps he was equally torn over the loss of Bellezza, or perhaps he was still seeking an excuse to send her away to safety.

Alexia didn't want safety. She wanted him.

The clouds cooled from orange to purple, drowning the trees in shadow. The dusty trail was rutted from multiple footprints, greenery setting off the bleak tributary.

Kiren stopped and grabbed her hand, pulling her quickly into the trees. Silence filled the wood.

Eerie silence.

A chill crept up the back of her neck.

Shadows flitted by through the fading greenery, at least a score of creatures slipping into the night. Alexia pressed closer to Kiren, seeking his warmth. His arm rounded her.

The silhouettes disappeared and crickets hummed in the darkness. A breeze washed against her cheek and Alexia resumed breathing.

They hurried into the shadows, nearing the hatch to the underground. With a wary look, Kiren slipped in ahead of her. She followed, relieved as he reclaimed his grip on her hand.

Earth and fungi mingled in her nose. The darkness was as deep as tar. Kiren tugged her forward and she scuffed her feet along a pebbly surface, worried about stumbling into a rock or wall.

Heat latched around her ankle.

She squeaked.

The grip tightened, searing fingers around her thin stocking. She grabbed the instant five seconds back and jumped.

The veil of reality shifted before her and Alexia pulled Kiren to a halt.

His voice echoed through her mind. *What is it?*

She opened her memory to him. His fingers wrapped around her shoulder and the cave exploded into a fracture of senses. His senses. A distant drip echoed off the walls, dulled against the cavern floor where bodies must muffle it. Decay curled in the back of her throat and she gagged. The vaguest light touched a dozen corpses strewn across the narrow stretch of hall, still in the blackness.

She slowed her heart and moved forward, stepping gingerly between the prostrate forms.

A dim glow appeared from around a bend. Light pooled in grooves that beveled the walls, like they'd been excavated one fingernail scrape at a time. Heavy doors lined the hall, laden with iron brackets, locked into place by metal bolts. Kiren slowed as they passed, his senses bleeding through their connection: the echo of heartbeats on the other side, the warmth of Passionate energies.

Prisoners? Alexia wondered.

Kiren's grip tightened on her, his jaw clenching.

They hurried down the hall. From what Bellezza had told them, the hive consisted of three circular tunnels, each connected by small inlets. If they were right, whatever was most precious to the Soulless—the medallion—would be kept at the heart.

They came around the bend and froze. An open door gaped before them, cloaked creatures standing just inside. Hisses refracted off the prison, jeers that formed words she couldn't quite understand.

Alexia readied to jump them back, but Kiren tugged her forward, his shoulders stiff.

Oil lamps leaked sickly shadows across a tiny chamber, illuminating a thin, black-haired man crouched against the far wall. Grime stained his clothing, and exhaustion weighed his shoulders.

Regin. Kiren pulled her closer and his memories seeped into her: *The man stood between Kiren and an army of Soulless, putting the creatures to sleep with a single touch.*

Edward had told her stories of this man. Dull manacles encircled his wrists, cruel irons that suppressed Passionate gifts. Keys glinted at his jailor's hip, mocking their prisoner with the hope of freedom, yet no means by which to reach it. It was cruel, and Alexia would not see her husband's friend suffer more.

She seized the seconds, slowing time. She grabbed the keys and dragged their brick weight across the stale chamber to the prisoner's side. She tested keys until one slid into the lock and freed both his wrists, slipping the keys into his pocket. She returned and took Kiren's hand, then let time go.

Fatigue washed through her.

The manacles dropped from Regin's bony wrists. His mouth twisted one direction, then the other as the Soulless stood over him, frozen. He glanced between the jailors and his eyes lit. A grin broadened the hollow planes of his cheeks. He leapt to his feet and smashed a palm into each of the Soulless creature's brows. They dropped to the floor.

"'Bout time ye got yer lazy hide here." Regin stepped around the fallen forms, his Irish brogue fascinating Alexia.

"When you could infiltrate the whole hive and put them to sleep? Why would I bother?" Kiren winked.

"Aye, why would ye bother? That's what we have her for." Regin bowed to Alexia. "Much obliged." He patted his pocket and keys jangled.

"Who else is here?" Kiren asked.

"Nelly, Bran, and Cecil are the only ones I know of. I hear the screams though. There are others."

Nelly. Alexia swallowed hard. The poor cook!

Her husband's good humor faded. "There will be a fight on the way out. Creatures litter the exit."

"Oh, I got a good fight in me to be had." Regin saluted. "Get to it then. Ye have business, I assume, and I've got a dungeon to clear." He moved to the next cell and threw the door wide as Kiren pulled Alexia away.

They sped into the unknown, silence so heavy that every breath felt like a scream. They made it to the second circle when a whisper of cloth froze her. She stopped. Two creatures breezed around the corner and paused.

She closed her eyes. *Ten seconds back, make a turn in the tunnel and circle back around.* She seized the moment and jumped.

Kiren halted when she teetered. "Dearest?"

She dragged Kiren around the corner as the two beings shuffled by. He turned a questioning eye on her. She pulled him along, leaping to safety with every encounter. She jumped back more and more frequently as they neared the inner circle and Kiren gifted her with doses of energy as she wearied. Still,

Alexia could feel the weight of exertion in her tired muscles, the way her vision occasionally swam, the increasing ache at the back of her skull.

They rounded the corner and came face to face with one of the Soulless. She gasped and reached back thirty seconds, but before she could grasp the moment, Kiren grabbed hold of the creature. Its mouth flew open. Sickly energy trickled into Kiren's skin. The limb beneath his fingers withered and narrowed as its life bled into him. The creature dropped to the floor.

Alexia turned on her husband.

"I can give life, and I can take it," he admitted softly, not meeting her gaze.

"It cannot be dead?"

His head shook. "Weakened." He tugged her onward and added softly, "May God forgive me."

The inner circle.

They skidded to a halt at the ring of the sanctum, lamplight glistening off slow ripples of a pond that occupied the middle of the chasm, reflecting lines of radiance from lamps across two doorways, one on either side of the water. Kiren aimed for the nearest one, energy rippling through his fingers, the sense that his medallion was near. He threw the door open.

Sixty-Six

From the Shadows

A robed being stood in the corner. Another prisoner? Alexia waited for red eyes to appear, but only darkness filled its hood.

Kiren held perfectly still. "Identify yourself."

"Welcome to my home," the woman spat.

Brazen alto smacked Alexia with an undercurrent of rage. Kiren trembled as though he'd been speared by an arrow to the heart. Chills flashed down her arms, but it wasn't her own reaction, rather Kiren's horror. Who was this?

"Deiliey," he whispered. "Let me see you." His voice trembled with longing.

Alexia squeezed his fingers, needing him to explain this, but he wouldn't meet her gaze. He was mesmerized. She needed him to look at her, just to look at her. Why couldn't he tear his eyes away from the shrouded woman?

Slender hands slid from beneath the cloak, her skin ivory smooth. The curve of her nails was like almonds, their edges chipped and dirty. She lifted her hood away.

Short hair grazed her jaw, unevenly hacked off and white where it reflected lamplight, but dark at its roots. Pale skin turned upward, a pointed chin, a thin nose and high cheekbones. Lashes lifted, a wave of luminescence skittering across them.

Jade eyes cut into Kiren.

He extended his fingers, reaching for her—as though in a trance. His eyes were wide, his breathing shallow and quick. Yearning burst through their connection, a desperation that left Alexia leaning toward the woman. How did she have so strong a hold over him?

Deiliey's jaw tightened. "Do not look at me that way. I do not want your pity!"

"This is not pity." His Adams apple bobbed, a rush of emotion exploding behind his words. "This is love."

Alexia let go of him, her breath catching.

Sixty-Seven

The Other Love

Bitter guilt and soothing relief pooled in Kiren's mouth like curdled milk. The lamplight flickered odd shadows across the folds of Deiliey's cloak, beveled with dark rivets, mysterious and lengthy, like her disappearance. How long had he believed, hoped, and yet feared she was dead?

Alexia pulled away from him. He distantly registered the movement, but Deiliey stood before him. Deiliey! He ached to wipe the uncertainty from her gaze, to ease the tremble in her cheek. Time had not been good to her, robbing her face of its roundness and stealing the kindness from the lines of her mouth. He wished he could have protected her, that he could turn the clock back and start again.

Deiliey backed away a step, her eyes squeezing. Her shoulders rolled back.

And there it was in her stare, the smoothing of all expression—blankness, apathy. She didn't care. His emotions had failed to reach her once again. His toes bit into his boots, the muscles in his back and legs taut.

"It is time, Kiren."

He flinched. He didn't know which hurt worse, the way she spat his name, or the dread of her insinuation. It couldn't be time. Not yet. There were still things undone, events that must take place.

Alexia covered her mouth.

"You are wrong," Kiren grated through clenched teeth.

Deiliey's eyes crinkled at the corners. "Have you ever known me to be wrong?"

"Yes."

Her fists balled. He dove into her gaze and reached for her thoughts. *The Vatican hall reared up in her memory. She cringed, wearing nothing but her revealing chemise, her womanly shape exposed. Bishops and priests stood, their jaws dangling as they worked to fathom how this woman had fooled them all for decades, her stolen robes drooping from Kiren's hand. She couldn't breathe. They would kill her—worse—for this betrayal. He had taken everything from her! His brow furrowed.* I am sorry, *he had mouthed, but she didn't believe him.*

Deiliey blinked. "You left me for dead."

Alexia gasped. Kiren half turned her direction, speaking to them both, "I allowed you to escape."

Deiliey's lip twitched upward. "Shall I return that favor? Is your life worth so much more than mine?"

"Corona—"

"Tell me!" she shouted, grabbing his suit coat, her face inches from his. A hint of apple blossoms rolled over him, almost masked by the earthy fibers of her covering.

Kiren closed his eyes. He wanted to confess how deeply he regretted his actions every day, how much he loved and feared her, how thoroughly he realized he had failed her. But the truth—after he had banished her for the good of the Passionate—would make no difference in how she hated him.

Her breath raged hot across his cheek.

"I am sorry," he whispered. The hollowness of his words filled his ears—like the gaping emptiness within her that he could never fill.

Sixty-Eight

Corona Deiliey

A hand clamped down over Alexia's shoulder. Searing fingers bit into her. Hisses clacked about her.

Blackness swooped in. Fiends crooned, ivory nails gleaming murderously down.

"No!" Deiliey's cry echoed through the cavern.

The creatures screamed in unison, falling back like dominos. One plunked into the black water outside the door, another crumpled against the wall, a third tumbled to the floor. Alexia uncovered her head.

The woman stormed toward her, burlap robes swooshing around her feet. Short, dark hair fell across her cheeks, pale skin ghostly, crimson eyes a bonfire in her ethereal complexion.

Crimson? They had been green but a moment ago.

Kiren lay on the floor across from her, clasping his temples, eyes squeezed tight.

Alexia gasped and pressed backward. The woman halted over her, glaring at the fallen creatures. They groveled and slunk away, disappearing into the shadows.

Who was Deiliey? The queen of the Soulless? And more importantly, if she was so powerful, why had she not harmed Alexia? Wasn't she Kiren's past lover? How could he have lied to her all this time?

No decaying stench wafted from the woman, rather a pleasant spring pollen mixed with dirt. Her face and hands were smooth and perfect, no exposed bones. Deiliey reached down and caught Alexia's arm, tugging her forward.

Alexia stumbled. Her rescuer dragged her across the cavern and Alexia wanted to resist, but she already planned to jump back in time and prevent Kiren from being harmed. Curiosity kept her moving.

Deiliey snapped and one of the Soulless grabbed Alexia's other arm and shoved her into the adjacent room. In the center stood a stone pedestal, like a lonely, gray finger. Dull links glimmered atop it, leading to a diamond-like wedge of metal.

There it sat, a simple pewter face that called their world to war.

Deiliey pushed the door closed. They occupied darkness alone, except for a faint light that emanated off the necklace.

The woman's eyes pierced Alexia's. They were all that existed, those vibrant, ruby circles, rings of eternity, lucid promises of joy and pain. They didn't hunger, but promised to feed her hunger. They didn't ache, but promised to soothe her suffering. They were everything she could ever want, the promise of forever, the hope of a million lifetimes all wrapped into one.

"Welcome, Alexia Dumont, to the inner sanctum of the accursed."

Alexia couldn't think beyond the promise in those wide eyes: the hue of violent roses at full bloom, the blush of ripe strawberries, the color of life.

"You will not fight us."

Of course she wouldn't. Why would she do such a silly thing while everything she could desire was within arm's reach?

Or was it?

She frowned, certain something was missing, but what? Or whom?

Those eyes crushed down over her, like a barrel of burning coals, erasing all but the fire. It seared into her brain—flaming fingers that slithered, gripped, and tore.

She screamed, eyes flying shut.

Blackness.

Stone pressed against her cheek.

"Very well done, Alexia."

She lifted her head. The woman sat next to her, fingers curling and uncurling like she wanted to reach out. Why? To further torment her? To prove her superiority? To prove once and for all that Alexia didn't deserve Kiren?

"You were able to resist my control." Her tormentor's pastel lips curled upward. "It is true. You are the one."

Had the woman been attempting to seize possession of her mind—invading as Kiren, Miles, or Edward, but grabbing the reins rather than gleaning or planting information? Deiliey's eyes no longer burned red, rather they were dark in the pulsing light of the medallion.

Alexia sucked in a breath. "You control minds?"

Hopeful eyes lifted to hers. "Those too weak to resist." She picked at the hem of her sleeve. "There is one, only one who can withstand me."

Chills seeped into Alexia's skin. Had Kiren been controlled by this woman? And for how long? She gasped. That must be why he feared Deiliey, and perhaps also why he loved her. Her heart ached. Had her husband been taken against his will?

Deiliey shifted. "I apologize if I frightened you. It is difficult to keep them under control all the time. Locking them on the other side of the door helps."

The Soulless. Then she did command them. When they had come for Alexia—the night Miles sacrificed himself, the night Kiren fought them off, the night she truly began to use her gift—their eyes had beckoned her, just as this woman's had a moment ago. Miles had said they were coming for her, not to consume her, but because of her gift.

Alexia pushed up into a sitting position, her head spinning. Kiren's necklace lay across from them, pulsing with a golden glow.

"I am Deiliey," the woman's head bobbed demurely. "Corona Deiliey."

Alexia squirmed, uncomfortable with her companion's expectant stare. Were they to be friends, despite the hold this woman had taken on Kiren? "You are clearly not Soulless. Why are you here?"

The lines deepened around Deiliey's nose. "I am the subject of unfavorable circumstances, but that story can wait for another time." She brushed a hand through the luminescence cast by the medallion, finger shadows cutting across the walls. "Let us say, I am here by choice to preserve my existence, but no, I am not one of the Soulless."

"Your eyes..."

The woman scooted forward. Her skin was rough and her mouth turned downward naturally, as though she'd long ago forgotten how to smile. "My gift is to possess the minds closest to me. By that means I am able to preserve my own existence here, but it has proven..." Her gaze shifted away. "...precarious on more than one occasion."

Alexia bit down. Like when she'd possessed Kiren's mind and it nearly resulted in her death—as had been insinuated? "You attempted to possess my mind."

"To protect you from them." Deiliey lifted her hands in a gesture of surrender.

"To confirm your uncertainties about me," Alexia shot back. She was not going to play this woman's game, and she had to know why Corona wanted her. "What is it you think I am?"

The woman leaned forward, her breath quickening. "You are the one who can save us."

Alexia glared. "From destroying one another?"

Deiliey reached out, as though to touch her, but stopped short. Alexia burned the woman's fingers with her stare, hating her like no other. Corona's hands came together in supplication. "You can go back. You can stop the destruction of the Passionate."

Leaning as far away as she could, Alexia scowled. So this was her intention—manipulating Kiren and controlling him in order to force her obedience. "I cannot. It is beyond my ability."

"It was," Deiliey lifted a hand over the throbbing metal, "but no longer." Her mouth worked, overly excited, nothing spilling out, then starting in a rush. "The pendant, it gathers power from the life about it, as though siphoning light off every source in existence, only a little so as not to do harm. It strengthens the bearer beyond any natural capacity, even beyond understanding."

So it could strengthen the bearer, but what did that matter? "Only one person can use it."

Deiliey shook her head. "No, only his bloodline can utilize it, but you will one day bear his child." The woman's eyes gleamed. "With his heir growing inside you, you will be able to use his pendant. You can go back. You can intervene and stop our people from being destroyed."

"Then why have you taken the medallion?"

"I could not come to you. You had to come to me." The smile faded. "Do not allow him to prevent you from fulfilling your destiny like he did to me."

Alexia blinked.

Deiliey tugged at her sleeve. "He is so afraid of what's to come he will allow our people to grovel, to suffer, and to succumb to fate." Her voice softened. "Love makes us do strange things."

Alexia's throat tightened as her mind whirled into a realm she didn't want to consider. Love. How did this woman know so much about her husband, and more especially, what had he meant about loving her? Was he manipulated by her, or had he naturally cared for her? He had been so sincere in his proclamation.

Alexia slipped into her memories, reliving the many times Kiren had pushed her away, the fear constantly in his eyes, the sadness that always possessed him. There was another woman, despite his insistence otherwise.

She knew one thing for certain. She did not trust Deiliey.

The woman rose, brushing debris from her skirt.

"It is truly possible?" Alexia scoured the woman's face for the slightest tick, any hint that she lied. "I can go back?"

"It is not only possible, it is inevitable."

"And how can you be so certain?"

Deiliey licked her lips. "Because you are my mother."

Sixty-Nine

Mother

The world circled her head like a falling leaf.

Mother.

And then an avalanche of snow.

Mother.

Her veins turned to ice, a glacier palace crushing down on her chest.

Mother.

Alexia sucked in air and blinked twice. "You are saying..."

Shadows amplified Deiliey's grin. "You will return to the past, and there I shall be born. I have waited long to meet you."

Mental fuzz buzzed through her ears. Mae's words returned: *I have waited a long time for you, Alexia.* Had they also met in the past, or did the innkeeper mean something else entirely? Did Kiren know about this? Had he been withholding this truth from her?

She shook her head clear. "To meet me? Why did we not know one another in the past?"

Deiliey's brows scrunched down. "Some say you died. Others insist you merely disappeared, but in five hundred years, this is the first I have heard of you."

Spider-shivers crawled over Alexia's skin. "And how can you be certain I am the one who gave...will give birth to you?"

Deiliey sat back. "Kiren told me."

Alexia blinked, shocked. That Deiliey knew his name... "He is—?"

"My father." A tremor traveled down the woman's cheek.

This grew stranger and stranger by the moment. Alexia studied the woman, her straight nose and high cheekbones, like Kiren's. But her eyebrows were thinner, her mouth the same shape as Alexia's, and her eyes were more pointed at the inner corner—something Alexia had always liked about her own. She was, without question, Kiren's relation, but could she be mistaken about Alexia? Was there any way this might be his lost sister?

Alexia cleared her throat. "If you are my daughter, why do you not possess my gift?"

Deiliey frowned. "It appears I inherited something of my father's line. He is, after all, from a lineage of dominant royals."

Alexia had to admit there was a similarity in gifts—Kiren's ability to read people's thoughts as compared to this woman's power to control thoughts. "We chose the name of *Deiliey* for you?"

"Corona." Her voice softened. "To remind me of my heritage, though I much prefer Deiliey."

Corona. Crown. A child born into a royal family.

Alexia rubbed her arm. "Where did Deiliey come from?"

"The man who should have been my father, the one who taught me everything."

Alexia blinked. "Kiren was not there to raise you?"

Deiliey's head shook.

She swallowed. She didn't want a future without him, a place in time before his existence. If what Deiliey said was true, she would not survive long there anyway.

But the choice was hers. She didn't have to go back. She may not even be able to go back.

The door burst inward.

Seventy

Reconcile

Two Soulless carried Kiren into the chamber, dragging his feet. His chest heaved, his head dangling. They dropped him before Alexia and closed the door behind them.

She brushed the hair out of his face, the coppery scent of blood stinging her nose, mixed with his sweet oak. Kiren's fingers brushed against hers, twitching as he groaned. A shiver of heat rolled up her arms. It lifted the weight of despair that had been crushing her and warmed her cheeks with the awareness of his closeness.

Kiren jerked upright. He sucked in a breath and leaned his forehead against hers. He grunted, fingertips curling between hers.

"Has she hurt you?" she whispered.

"Has she hurt you?"

She bit down. Not in the conventional sense of the word, but she had so many strange ideas to consider, and such a deep and abiding sorrow lodged in her throat. She glanced at the woman in the shadows, the waiting pendant, and forced the words through their connection: *Have you always known I would go back?*

His forehead dropped to her shoulder.

"Kiren?"

His head shook, but the depression seeping through their clasped hands said otherwise.

She blinked into the darkness. "You should have told me."

Kiren groaned. "And taint what little time we had together?"

"Have together," she corrected and squeezed his hand. *Deiliey told me who she is.*

"I was afraid of that," he muttered.

Her chest squeezed. Then it was true. Their child had been alone, waiting to meet both her parents in the future, parents who couldn't possibly fill the gap in her life or compensate for the cruelty of being abandoned in another time.

And for all Alexia knew, she would die in that past. "Why did you say nothing? Why did you let me believe it was impossible?"

He caught her face between his hands. "Because I am not ready to lose you." His lips found hers in the darkness, an apology in their tender press.

What of Deiliey? she whispered mentally.

She hates me, and she is right to. He pulled in an uneven breath. *She led the Breeders. She always believed in her cause, breeding our kind to try and create the most powerful elementals.*

"Why would she—?"

He shrugged. *My theory is, in hopes of finding you.*

The hint of a lie hovered in his words, a half-truth. "Kiren."

He grunted, gaze flashing to their watching daughter. *I do not know her full motives, but she was crazed for power.* His eyes returned. *Imagine if the most powerful Passionate were under her control. What could anyone do to oppose her?*

She squeezed his fingers. "Tell me what happened."

Deiliey gained too much power. Her experiments... His palm grazed across her cheek and images flashed through her brain: A woman being force-fed blood, another sliced open right after death so her fertile organs might be implanted in someone else, a man in chains raving incoherently about being bonded to multiple women while blood seeped from his wrists in a suicide attempt. *I had to stop her.*

Alexia shivered. *And she hates you because of it.* She nestled up against his chest, working hard to keep from watching the atrocity across from them. *Is she mad? I mean truly, deeply touched in the head?*

She is driven. Kiren's arms curled around her. *Her presence here explains why Passionate have been disappearing, taken by the Soulless. It seems she has begun to rebuild her army by force, and perhaps she has even begun her experiments again.*

Alexia shifted up onto her knees, coming nose to nose with him. "Then you *always* knew I would go back?"

He shook. "We decide our own destiny. I intended to stay away from you and prevent it from happening, but I could not."

Tears gathered in her eyes. He loved the Passionate enough to sacrifice his own happiness for them. *Oh, Kiren, how could our daughter become this?*

"She may not have to," he whispered.

He was right. Alexia had a decision to make. If she remained in this timeline, the Deiliey who now existed might never come to be. She would grow up with both her parents, a happy, loved child, and perhaps her determination might be turned to aid the Passionate.

But Alexia might die in childbirth. That was probably the reason for her disappearance in the past, and if she died in childbirth, Kiren would follow her into the afterlife. Who then would be left to check their child? Who would stop her from inflicting cruelty and unspeakable tortures on her brothers and sisters? Was this a lesser of evils?

Furthermore, if she could go back, she might prevent others from suffering: Sarah from dying, John from becoming Soulless, Kiren from losing his parents...

"What if I could change things?"

Quiet.

"Kiren?"

He tugged her to her feet, arms rounding her waist as she threatened to topple. *Shall we away, my love?*

Blue had never known such definition, such depth as it did in his eyes. She would go with him anywhere. This was where she belonged.

He surged forward the same instant Deiliey leapt for the necklace.

Seventy-One

Mind Tricks

Kiren's finger caught one link before the cool metal jerked forward. He held tight. Deiliey had the pendant's face, the amplifier. He growled.

The possessive eyes of his daughter glared at him through the gloom. He tore the metal from her grasp, jerking her forward, links clinking together as they swung at his side.

The woman stumbled to a halt. "You must send her away or you will kill us all!"

He lifted the chain over his head. "I believe that is the fate we were assigned from the beginning."

She hissed and lunged at Alexia.

He threw an arm between them and nails pierced into his flesh. He swept her away from his wife, slamming her back into the wall, fingers clutched about her neck. Deiliey tore at his hand, legs kicking.

Power surged through him from the necklace, a familiar warmth he had been missing. He felt three feet taller, energy pulsing through his skin, threatening to burst it for the magnitude. The charm had not been emptied in some time, and a lesser man would have succumbed to the blast, exploding like an overstuffed sausage.

Trickles of power escaped through his connection with Alexia.

Her eyes widened in shock. *What is this? Why have I never felt it before?*

He held the overwhelming flow in and turned on Deiliey. "It is best to know when you have lost a battle."

She glared.

The ground beneath them trembled. Little rocks clattered and vibrated across the uneven floor. Brackets cracked. He whirled about, ready to face a new foe, but the doorway was clear, the iron door lying useless against the wall.

Nelly.

Something must have happened and the cook was using her gift—but if she brought down the caves...

He sprinted through the door, pulling Alexia after him. The ground shuddered again, shaking boulders into the underground lake, throwing gleaming spatters of water at them like razors.

Deiliey ducked around them and shot through the quaking tunnels.

He silenced his inner workings, ignoring the pounding of his own heart and focused outward. Locating the tremor in the ground, he searched for the direction it amplified, the way it shook the walls harder—such a fine difference in the frequency of grinding stone it was almost imperceptible.

He took off toward the source. Alexia's feet scuttled beside him, her breath rasping in his ears.

Fissures ripped through the walls, widening cracks. He pushed himself faster.

A low moan curdled beneath the crash of falling stone, the cry of the earth reaching to obey its master.

"Nelly!" he shouted. "Stop!"

His voice was drowned out by the cannonade of rubble. Thick dust billowed around them. Stones crashed down from the roof.

Alexia shrieked.

Kiren threw himself over her.

Shards bit into his arms and back. The world disappeared in a storm of dust and stone.

Seventy-Two

Rubbish

Weight crushed down over Alexia, Kiren's weight. The tang of blood hung thick in her nose, along with dust and a hint of oak.

She blinked her eyes open.

Darkness.

She closed them and heaved upward. His weight shifted, rolling and toppling next to her.

Dull light emanated from the pendant exposed on his chest, a bubble of light that surrounded them both. She shivered where it touched her, its raw power saturating the air. Loose stones trembled atop the arch of radiance, energy holding the rubble back as if the slightest disturbance might bring it down.

She gasped.

Kiren's leg was pinned under the stones that locked them into a pinched berth. Blood pooled down his trapped limb and etched random streaks across his clothing—multiple lacerations.

Injuries he'd sustained while shielding her.

She covered her mouth and held back a sob. She brushed a hand over his bloodied and still brow. A weak exhalation feathered across her palm.

"Kiren?" she whispered.

His chest lifted shallowly, eyes closed and unmoving. She placed a hand next to him on the ground, into something wet. Dark liquid stained her palm. The pool spread below him, murky in the light. Lifting his shoulder, she bit back against her lurching stomach. A stone had penetrated several inches into his back. She'd freed it by moving him, leaving a gaping hole right next to his spine.

Her fingers shook. She forced herself to breathe, promising herself all would be well.

He could heal this.

It was what he did.

He would heal.

She just had to wait.

Alexia held him. "You are going to be well."

No response.

"Please!"

Rocks shifted above her, dropping down an inch, the barrier failing. She cringed.

Pressing an ear to his chest, her heart stilled. His barely beat.

Once.

Twice.

Three times.

Silence.

"Kiren, no!"

But this didn't have to be the way it ended. She could go back. She could fix this. Couldn't she?

She lifted her shaking hands, searching for the sands of time, but they blurred in her mind. Thoughts muddled together in a blinding haze. Her arms collapsed. She wrapped them around him but couldn't move them further. They wouldn't heed her command—it was like tugging at a bell rope that had been severed.

Something was happening. She couldn't draw enough air. Her throat was closing off. Blackness blistered in the corners of her vision.

Her heart stuttered.

This was it—the moment when the bond would claim them both.

She wasn't ready to die!

Closing her eyes, she thought of her short existence, of all the hopes yet unfulfilled, of the child who would die with her. Perhaps that would be best.

No! She wouldn't let that happen.

Alexia tensed and leapt out of time.

Seventy-Three

Fates

Sucking in air, Alexia marveled at how powerfully her heart slammed against her ribcage, how her still trembling limbs responded to her requests. The scent of decay and dust had been replaced by nothing, a complete absence of smell.

A soft light pulled her around. Dana sat calmly examining her nails, raven locks loose about her youthful face and a snow-white gown. It set off the woman's pastel cheeks.

"I made it," Alexia realized.

Dana nodded. "And welcome back."

Alexia brushed her own face to verify its solidity. "I was dying."

Her mother laughed.

Laughed? Alexia wanted to slap the woman. How dare she laugh in the face of such utter tragedy!

A smile pulled at Dana's cheek. "I almost died several times. It is a part of our existence, and if you wish to live through your experiences, you must steel your stomach against the concept. It will slow you down."

Alexia blinked at her.

"You can jump from here." The woman rose to her feet.

Again, Alexia blinked. She could jump through the timeline from the absence of time?

"It is how we cheat." Dana tapped the side of her head. "Here, you are not set upon by the limitations of your physical body—but you will feel it on the other side. The repercussions are more severe."

Did she wish to know how severe?

She shook her head. It didn't matter.

Dana lifted a hand to her cheek. "Knowledge is freeing, is it not?" A sadness trembled in her eyes. "I am afraid we shall not have much more time together for me to impart what I know."

Alexia swallowed. "Why would we not...?"

Dana gripped her shoulder. "Deiliey was right."

"About what?" She mentally surged back through the discussion she'd had with Corona Deiliey, latching onto the idea of going back, way back, to stop the Soulless from becoming. A tear streaked down Alexia's cheek. "How can I leave him?"

Her mother's nose scrunched. "That, you will have to decide for yourself. I was speaking of your ability to use his necklace."

Alexia placed a hand over her abdomen. "Do I already carry his child?"

Unnervingly green eyes met hers. "I do not know." Dana lifted both hands. "A warning: What's done is done. You can only alter your own actions, not those of others, but if you do decide to go, we shall not meet again."

Alexia scowled at her. "You are speaking of the earthquake or my future child?"

"Escape the caves and jump back when you are ready." Dana nodded and paused. "I wish you would not, but if you do go back, he will find a way to survive. My father is a master like no other."

"I will miss you."

Dana smiled. "Save your husband, Alexia."

Seventy-Four

Alternate Paths

Alexia seized the moment before the quake and pulled herself toward it, like latching onto rising dough and dragging herself across the room as it stretched, hoping it wouldn't tear before she reached her destination.

Blackness clipped at her vision. A growl echoed off stone. Rot assaulted her nose.

Deiliey zipped past Alexia, aimed for the exit. Alexia dropped to one knee, the world twirling in snatches of white and black.

Kiren called her name. Warm hands cupped her cheeks, the heat of his breath caressing her skin.

She blinked the weariness away. There was no time to be incapacitated. No time!

She grabbed his arms. "We must leave. Now!"

His mouth dropped open, but he nodded.

The ground beneath them trembled. Gravel vibrated across the floor.

"Nelly..." he whispered.

Alexia grabbed his face. "Take me to safety, please."

A war battled in his eyes, contradicting waves that fought for dominance.

"Die if you must," Deiliey called, and slipped out the door ahead of them.

They rushed into the gloomy halls as another tremor shook through their feet. Kiren paused. Alexia pulled him onward.

Stones crashed behind them. Fissures shot up the walls. Dust rained down. Lamps sputtered. They sprinted through the blackened halls, dragging their fingers along the unevenly ridged walls for guidance.

Light gleamed ahead, not the radiance of lamps, but daylight. Alexia ached to feel it on her skin.

Rock tumbled about their feet. A crevasse split the ground, widening with every second. She stepped wrong, slipped on the broadening ridge and crashed into Kiren. He threw one arm around her, sure footed.

The ceiling above them shifted like the boiling of water.

She shrieked.

The ground before them ruptured, like jagged teeth in a stretching mouth, opening to swallow them whole.

Kiren lifted her off her feet, leaping across the broadening gap. He threw her forward and she skidded over the brink of the far ledge. He smacked into the fissure wall, fingers scraping for purchase. She grabbed his arm.

Booms carried down the collapsing corridor, the billowing cloud of gray rushing after them, a grinning smoke of death.

His eyes met hers. They were too late.

Seventy-Five

Power

Alexia's brain shrieked.

A trickle of heat seeped through Kiren's grip, a golden power that waited to be seized. She inhaled it and pulled with all her strength.

Her brain lit up like a bonfire.

The approaching cloud slowed. Rock groans dulled to a low-pitched buzz. The air about her stilled.

She turned to Kiren. Ripe lot of good freezing time would do her but make him more impossible to move!

He gasped.

She blinked back into his eyes, startled. His mouth hung open, Adam's apple bobbing.

How was this possible? She could not drag others out of time, could she?

Her gaze landed on the pendant, the glow, its power tingling through her arm from his. Was it possible to share power and use her gifts for him? Whatever the case, she wasn't going to waste this chance. The muscles at the back of her neck began to knot like a fisherman's net.

Kiren stepped onto a falling boulder like a stair, rising higher. She backed away, as he cleared the ridge, keeping her grip on his arm.

"By all that's holy, my clothes feel like stone." He clutched his throat. "And why is it so hard to breathe?"

"The joys of my world." She laughed.

Pain burst from behind her eyes, a migraine worthy of a giant. She toppled. Debris rained down, the roar of collapsing stone deafening.

Kiren looped an arm around her waist and shot forward, shoving her to safety.

Sunlight blinded her.

Boom!

The day disappeared behind slate-colored fog. Alexia landed hard on her side, wind knocked out of her, stunned by eerie silence. She tried to draw air. Her muscles refused to work.

Again.

No air.

She rolled over, and her lungs flexed. Dust flooded into her nostrils and throat, catching between her teeth. Choking, she clambered to her elbows and knees and coughed. Her limbs shook. She collapsed and covered her mouth, drawing in clearer air.

Gritty earth passed below her fingers. Where was Kiren?

She crawled toward the cave entrance on bruises, biting the side of her mouth against the stab of sharp stones.

"K—" She coughed. "Kiren!"

Her fingers grazed something soft and warm. She reached back and found knuckles. Searching the rubble, she uncovered an arm. She brushed the wreckage away. Alexia followed his arm to his shoulder, neck, and face. His head was turned to the side, breath stirring the dust, one of his lips sliced.

The cloud of dust began to settle, thinning as sunlight filtered down over them.

Debris had turned his hair gray and dirt layered his skin, but he was alive! She threw her arms around him, cradling his head to her chest.

Tears slipped down her cheeks and streaked over his dirty brow. He was alive! She was alive! They'd done it.

He moaned. Dust shook free. One of his legs disappeared at the knee, trapped beneath two crossed boulders.

"Shh, now," she whispered. "Stay still. I will find help."

A shadow fell over them. Alexia tensed, ready for battle, and turned to the silhouette. Raven hair glimmered in the sun, dust thinning to reveal the concerned face of Regin, the *sleeper*.

He frowned at them and cupped his hands to his mouth. "Over here. I need help!"

Shrill voices mixed with gravelly ones and the crunch of feet. He stumbled away.

Kiren's eyes fluttered open, the purest sea, sprinkled with white ripples of brilliance, shimmers of sunlight that filled her heart with purpose.

"Hello," she whispered.

He coughed, hacked, and groaned.

She pressed a kiss to his brow, tasting dirt, and brushed the hair back from his face, knocking grime loose. Alexia cradled his head, unable to contain her smile. "You look horrid, and yet you are the most wonderful thing I have ever seen."

"Horrid," he wheezed, coughing out a puff of dust. "You say the sweetest things to a man who has been grazed by death."

"You should grow accustomed to it. From what my mother says, it is our lot in life, those of us who travel through time."

His cheek dimpled, stretching his scar. "We did, did we not? Together."

She nodded and lifted his hand to her lips.

He reached up and looped his finger through a ringlet, pulling it forward. Black and white strands of her hair curled together. He slid a thumb over them, wiping at the coil, but the lock did not change color.

She met his gaze, shocked. He smiled. "I think I like this."

Shuffling feet kicked up more dust. Alexia twisted.

The sleeper returned carrying a thick tree branch. Several others appeared behind him, a couple children, captives from the Soulless prison. Regin shoved one end of the branch beneath the stone crushing Kiren's leg and braced the lever across another rock.

Three others joined him. "Don'a touch me now," he warned and took his place. "Wee bit o' trouble we'd have haulin' yer sorry hides away if ye all plunk off to slumber."

The others chuckled and positioned themselves.

"With me now, lads!"

They all heaved and the stone rocked aside.

Gashes cut across Kiren's leg, his trousers speckled with blood, but no bone protruded.

"Can you move it?" she asked.

He lifted his chin toward the sky, eyes closed. "Not yet."

She kissed his dirty cheek and he slid a hand into her hair, trapping her there.

He pulled her closer and pressed a tight kiss to her mouth. "Never leave me again."

She looked away, guilt prickling across her skin. She understood what he meant, that he believed he'd lost her when Deiliey attacked, but she couldn't tell him she was debating their daughter's words—not after so close a scrape with death. She traced his torn lip. "I love you."

"Always and forever." Energy prickled at her skin from his fingertips.

Regin cleared his throat. "Hey now, stop makin' the little ones squeamish." He wrapped a skinny hand about her sleeve and hauled her up. Two others hefted Kiren up—the teenage girl and a bone-thin man. Kiren steadied with a limp.

Behind him, the world had collapsed inward like an empty bowl.

Alexia gasped. The depression was large enough to encompass her father's entire estate grounds. She covered her mouth. How many souls had been trapped beneath the debris? And did they still live—buried in stone?

Her fists tightened. "What has become of the Soulless?"

Silence filled the air.

She whirled on Kiren. "You said, '*Nelly.*'"

"God rest her soul," Regin muttered.

Kiren's head bowed. "We must go." He pointed to the setting sun. "If any of them were outside the compound, they will be returning."

Seventy-Six

Reunited

Charles tensed when the group emerged from the trees, several children of different ages and a few ragged adults, all covered in dust. He counted fifteen heads.

His grip tightened over his sword handle. He'd searched the inn for Alexia after the conflict and came across Ethel who had the good humor to explain that his daughter was now married, and she'd been dragged off to face the Soulless. He'd left that very hour.

Alexia stepped out from the woods, supporting the weight of her limping husband.

Her husband.

Charles ground his teeth. The miscreant should have waited to marry her proper, with her father present. He should have been there.

But none of that mattered. They had survived!

He slipped off his horse at her side, throwing his arms around her. "Thank God you are safe. When I heard the collapse, I thought you were all dead!"

Her husband laughed. "You, of all people, should know how difficult I can be to kill."

"And by virtue, her?" He held his daughter away as heat rose to his cheeks, remembering those early weeks after Dana's death, after his child had been dropped in Rosalind's arms and his entire world destroyed. Loading his rifle, he'd excused himself to go hunting. And hunt he had—twice firing shots which must have grazed the man who would become his son-in-law.

Alexia straightened her husband's collar, and he slipped his fingers through hers. Charles's fists tightened. He reminded himself he had consented to their marriage, even if he'd been cheated out of the actual ceremony.

"So long as I live," his son-in-law vowed, "she shall."

Charles inhaled through his teeth. How many years had he known this man, and yet he had not aged a day. If what he offered Alexia was timelessness, a world without age, without end, it was more than Charles could ever hope to give her.

And yet...

He frowned, studying her. Powder clung to her clothing and skin, but something about her hair... He scowled. A patch of white swirled through the curls very near her face, a sign of premature aging.

He lifted the strands.

Alexia pulled them out of his grasp. "It is nothing, Father."

He bit down, nodded, and followed them down the woodland path.

Seventy-Seven

Nelly's Gift

Kiren could not hope to travel on his leg. He rode, most of the time, holding one of the Passionate children who'd been prisoner, and Alexia led the horse. They made slow progress with the exhausted little ones and camped in the open, taking turns to watch. He slept deep and true, deeper than he had in ages. Come morning, he had only a strong limp and a couple bruises. Alexia stared in wonder, rubbing a finger along his no-longer split lip.

The children rode, and Kiren staggered along with Alexia for support.

"You said the Soulless could not be killed but by your necklace or my sword." She clutched his arm about her shoulder. "What has happened to them? Are they gone?"

He rested his cheek against her curls. "Buried, yes, but not dead."

"They may as well be. I cannot imagine them digging out from under that rubble."

"But in time, they shall."

The sound of her swallow tickled his ears.

"And Nelly?" she asked.

He nuzzled her brow tenderly, inhaled her pomegranate sunshine, and sighed. "Her parents both died at her birth—you see—Nelly is very rare. She is what we call a *true elemental*, one who connects with the very earth and can command it at will."

Alexia blinked up at him, her white lock catching the light.

Kiren slipped the ringlet behind her ear. "When one of these rarely gifted Passionate are born, their talent manifests. There is no safe haven for those closest to them, and indeed the babe cannot control the violence."

Her mouth dropped open. "She killed her parents?"

He grimaced. "When I met the old girl, she was but a child—a very gifted child."

Alexia tensed. He groaned, realizing he'd just affirmed his longevity to her. Not much he could do about that now. Did she understand how lonely those decades had been without her?

"Nelly had moved from one home to another, always shuffled off elsewhere, until someone recognized her dangerous gift—one of the Passionate—and decided she should be the tool for undermining our peace."

Alexia squeezed his arm. "They used her as a weapon?"

"Intended to." He smiled sadly. "They did not obtain their goal as the poor dear was apprehended by the Soulless because of her extreme emotions."

Again her jaw hung. "Nelly was taken by the Soulless?"

"Almost. What they did do effectively was break up this little rebellion, and as I was in pursuit of the other Passionate the Soulless had in their sights, I happened upon the scene."

"You saved her."

He cleared his throat, tugging a hand through his hair. "She had been made to use her gift often and in the benefit of her enslavers, frequently to her utter exhaustion. They used anything she cared about against her, which, for Nelly, is pretty much every living thing, especially animals. At the time I carried her away, she had lost all trust, all confidence and tenderness. She lived only in fear, only to punish or be punished. It took decades to win her love."

Alexia slid her fingers through his. "I can hardly imagine anyone hating you."

"And yet it happens." He kissed the top of her head. "I promised Nelly she never need use her gift again, and I have held to that." Wrapping his arms tightly about her, he whispered into her ear. "She thought to save us all from the Soulless in her selfless act, and we must not forget."

Seventy-Eight

Going Back

The inn was a welcomed sight, the grounds quiet as when Alexia had first seen them, not the chaos of their recent battle. She breathed easier. She wasn't certain she could have faced the war-zone without crumbling. But it was too quiet.

She aided Kiren through the door as the others made their way inside.

Regin whistled. "Mae, darlin', ain't you still the lassie o' the lee."

She waved the sleeper off and hurried forward to the children.

"Where is everyone?" Alexia asked.

"Ethel brought word this morning," Mae said. "They have returned to their homes, or to rebuild."

"They, but not us?" Alexia turned to Kiren.

Happiness drained from his eyes. He seized her fingers, studying them individually. He met her gaze briefly, then returned to her hand, twisting her wedding band as he whispered, "One day I will be enabled to return home, and you will go with me."

"To the kingdom that is lost?"

He bit his lips from the inside and glanced around. He nodded her toward the stairs.

They entered her old room on the second floor, and she settled him on the bed. He lay back and slid one arm beneath his head. "The kingdom may be lost, but it will always be my responsibility to restore it."

She sat next to him and clasped his hand in both hers. "And what will that mean for us?"

Shifting onto an elbow, he faced her, his earnest eyes probing hers. "Will you leave with me, Alexia? When that day comes, will you be my queen?"

She slid her fingers through his and averted her gaze, smiling. The decision still lay before her: this dangerous life with her husband, a future king, or going to the aid of thousands to stop the Soulless from becoming. And if she hadn't succeeded before, what were her chances of doing so this time? Was there a good choice?

He leaned back, apparently satisfied with her physical response and closed his eyes.

"I love you, Kiren," she said.

Kiren slept. Alexia slipped away, down through the kitchen and into the secret basement. She carried with her a lamp, one that warmed the tiny chamber her aunt had occupied. She sat on the bed, thinking of Sarah, how she had yearned to save her. Perhaps it was better that Sarah was not here, one less thing to hold her back.

If the Soulless never existed, Sarah would never have become one of them. Nor would John. And Miles—what kind of wonderful life would he have, living with his parents rather than running from them?

And Nelly—the kindly cook who cared for poor, estranged Miles, her loud jokes and straight forward manner. Alexia's heart cried for the loss of so dear a friend, for Nelly's last gift to them. But perhaps Nelly need not be lost after all?

She rubbed a hand over her abdomen. What of her daughter and Kiren? Would leaving destroy either?

A noise in the hall pulled her around.

Mae shuffled into the room, feeling her way forward. "Never did like coming down here."

Alexia scooted over, making room for her on the bed.

The woman joined her, head tilted. "It still smells like them."

Alexia hadn't realized, but it did. Sarah's perfume clung to the sheets, almost drowning out the slight hint of decay.

Mae's hand landed over top hers. "I did everything in my power to save her."

"I know you did." Alexia held in the sob that wanted to escape.

"If we'd had the medallion, she would have survived."

"But we did not." Alexia closed her eyes. This was what her mother meant—that some people's fates were sealed, and that she could not save everyone. But perhaps she could. "And what became of John?"

Mae's lips cut a tight line. "Gone. He buried Sarah and departed."

Alexia's fists clenched. "I tried to change it, Mae. I went back and tried, but it was not enough."

A kindly hand patted her shoulder. "You did not go back far enough."

"How far back should I have gone?" She turned to study the woman, wondering precisely how long Mae had been waiting to see her.

Mae's lips twitched upward, pulling down just as quickly. "It was over five hundred years ago when the Soulless came to be."

"Is that when we first met?"

The lines across Mae's brow deepened. "It is."

The breeze in her ears died. Her muscles froze. Stillness settled over the world as she worked to rectify those words.

Alexia rose to her feet. "You are saying I can prevent it, all of it?"

Mae's mouth twisted and she stood. "I am saying you did go back, and you made a difference."

Her throat was suddenly too dry. "But if I failed before..."

The woman straightened the sheets they'd ruffled. "You did not fail, Alexia. Not to me nor any of the others who depended on you. You are needed." She glanced back over her shoulder. "You are powerful beyond your own understanding."

Alexia touched her belly absently. The miracle that would allow her to go may already be in place, and yet how would she provide for a child in another time? What did she know of the thirteenth century after all? And how could she leave Kiren?

"I can tell you everything you need to know," Mae whispered.

"But my husband..."

The woman stepped around her, clasping her shoulders. "You must do this for him. For us all."

Seventy-Nine

Separation

The first golden rays of sunset touched the horizon and danced across the clouds, painting them orange. Kiren nodded for Miles to join him on the outdoor bench, his nearly mended leg propped up.

The lad halted next to him, rubbing the back of his neck. "You should send me away."

Kiren tried to meet the boy's gaze, but Miles shifted.

"Is there something you wish to tell me?" Kiren asked.

The youth's nostrils flared. He paced down the porch and back, tearing both hands through his flimsy hair. Kiren turned his gaze back to the setting sun, giving his protégé all the space he needed. This request was certainly due to Miles's guilt about what happened with Bellezza. He had never taken a life. Kiren had always been so careful, keeping Miles away from the heart of the conflict.

Miles groaned. "I just, I can't be near you. I can't. I'm sorry."

Miles fired off across the yard.

Kiren jerked after him, but halted. The boy's guilt must be tied to the fact he'd acted to save Kiren, and every moment together would only add to his pain until he reconciled the act. Miles would reach that state, eventually.

Kiren had to trust the boy and let him go.

Eighty

History

Alexia took three months. She rested and watched over her husband, enjoying every second, always weighed by her secret sadness. Everyone made a full recovery and departed except for Regin who flirted ceaselessly with Mae, her laughter frequently echoing through the inn.

Alexia too prepared to leave. She and Mae conferred every day at length, training in linguistics and necessary survival skills such as building a fire, identifying wholesome herbs and plants, cooking, and techniques for building a temporary shelter in the open. She was ready. Despite her unease, she had the assurance she would have one friend on the other side, one who may not know her yet, but whom she could trust.

Kiren watched her through all these efforts—when not called upon by his duties. His silent gaze was filled with sorrow which he attempted to cover by smiling.

It was when he gasped and pressed his ear to her stomach that she knew. She was with child. The time had come. He waited on her, filling her every whim, his sorrow stinted by the wondrous miracle of life and an eagerness to serve her.

She said her goodbyes without a word and finally executed the last part of her plan by asking Kiren to take her back to the woodland haven. He was hesitant but agreed.

They arrived at noon. Leaves littered the earth-grown bed, flowers wilted and dead, a chilly breeze cutting between the trees.

Kiren wrapped his arms around her, warming her against the season.

She turned to him. "I need you to do something for me."

"Anything."

She swallowed. This would not be easy. "I need you to let me go."

His face froze, mouth barely open, brows low and slightly quirked together. He leaned back, diving into her eyes. She allowed him to see everything, her struggle for the last many weeks, the resolve to leave, and her hopes for a brighter future.

"Not yet," he wheezed.

She swallowed a lump that felt impossible to move. "Kiren, I have to go."

He stilled. His widening waves cut across her, their desperate undertow dragging her forward. "Alexia—"

"I have thought this through at length, and I must at least try. You will be able to stop Deiliey because...because my death will not result in yours."

His shoulders drooped. He reached for her chin but his hand fell limply to his side.

She slipped closer.

A tear spilled down his face, his cheeks twitching with emotion. "I told you I was the most selfish creature. I do not want to let you go."

His tears loosed her own in a cascading torrent. "I do not want to leave you!"

Catching her face between his hands, he smoothed the hair back and leaned in. His breath curled across her lips. "You are my better in every way."

"Then you understand?"

He sucked in a breath between clenched teeth. "My head understands. My heart will not." He kissed her, hard, the world exploding inside her mind. She saw him struggling through the decades, searching for a glimpse of her, lonely and frustrated by failure after failure. It broke something inside of her, and she was no longer certain she could do it.

Kiren pulled back. "I will not stand in your way."

She searched for new resolve. "Perhaps if—"

He pressed a finger to her lips. "You are right, Alexia. You must go."

"I have to take your pendant." Tears blinded her.

He nodded. "I have the false one. No one will ever know."

"I will know!" Her sob broke free and he kissed her, walking her backwards. The back of her knees hit the mattress. She sat and he leaned over her, laying her back. She slid a hand across the chain about his neck, turning an imploring look up at him.

He grunted and lifted it free with one hand, looping it about her neck. She surrendered herself to him, savoring every touch, every shiver of pleasure, every texture and taste, knowing these would be her last.

At last he held her, his nose nestled into her hair, his breath warming her neck. "I wish I could protect you through this. I hate that you will be forced to bear our child without me. I should be there to..."

She squeezed his arm.

"Mae will not be who she is now. You must remember that, but she needs you."

She pulled his arm tighter around her.

"You will not see many whom you recognize, but be patient with those you do. Recall that they have five hundred years to become who they are now."

Alexia rolled to face him.

257

He wouldn't meet her stare. "And there may not be Soulless in that time, but there are dangers. You are capable to face them, but you must be wise in whom you trust. I..." His chest rose with a shaky breath. His arms tightened around her, lips finding her ear. "You must watch the sky. It is said the night the Soulless were born, a pillar of light shone. And this land, hold to this land. Where the inn now stands, that is where they were spawned—where life was scorched from the earth never to regenerate."

She nodded. She could do that.

"Promise me," he rasped, "no matter what happens, promise me you will return."

Tears erupted. Although she yearned to give him the comfort he needed, she could not.

He wiped away the tears and kissed away the sadness. An hour disappeared within the protective ring of his arms, and it was not enough. She wanted another. And another.

Alexia waited until his breathing evened out, then slipped from his grasp and off the bed, careful not to look at him. If she hesitated now, she would never go.

Wiping new tears from her eyes, she wrapped trembling fingers around the metal charm. Energy buzzed up her arm, a stampeding herd of wild horses, almost knocking her off her feet. She steadied herself on the bedframe.

Opening herself to the sunburst of power, she inhaled. Every cell of her body filled to bursting, saturated with a strength no person should ever possess. She could erupt into flight and leave the jealous earth behind her, borne on the wings of this unexplained force. That, or explode into flame and light the entire earth with her radiance.

But those were not her gifts.

She reached into time, and the line stretched further than it ever had, like a rope suspended in space that faded into the distance. She pulled it toward her, hand over hand, thumbing over the days, weeks, years, hauling herself into a new century, then another. A glow appeared on the horizon, one that neared with every tug. It was an instant—she knew instinctively—that had changed history forever. It drew her with curiosity, with excitement, as if her very body resonated with the same frequency. Fascination buoyed her spirit.

It was where she belonged.

The moment shimmered before her, just below her fingertips, casting its warmth between her hands, shedding long shadows across her face and dress. It begged her to reach inside and become one with her destiny. Every instinct called to seize the instant.

She hesitated. Glancing back the way she'd come, she gazed through the mounting darkness to Kiren, upright now, his chest heaving, his blue eyes drowning her in their desperation. Her throat closed off, soft tears welling in her eyes and rolling down her cheeks.

He was all she wanted. All she'd ever wanted.

Still, she couldn't bring herself to stay. That future was not one she could embrace, not yet. Her path lay in the past. Hers was a duty no other could complete.

His mouth moved, words swallowed in the void between them. *I will find you.*

She didn't know if it was possible, if she'd ever see him again, but she hoped. Like the sunrise beneath her fingers, she hoped to one day find her way back to this moment.

"No matter when I am," she vowed, "I will always be yours."

She seized the light.

Epilogue

Miles halted in the road and lifted his head as a chilly breeze trickled across his cheek. He straightened and squared his shoulders, listening to the insubstantial whispers wrapping around him.

One path in exchange for another.

He dreaded that he'd chosen an irredeemable road.

The draft curled over his skin again, launching goose bumps down his arms. He lifted his voice, "Do not make me regret helping you."

A wicked giggle burst out of oblivion.

TIMELESS

Book 3 in The Maiden of Time Trilogy

One

Five-Hundred Years Back, Five Months Forward

The ground exploded next to Alexia's foot. She stumbled backward, her broken-sword-turned-dagger clasped tightly in one fist as she scanned the horizon through raining debris. Men writhed across the beach in rawhide jerkins or white tunics bearing red crosses, the chaos of clashing metal like the roar of hungry lions.

Lions. The symbol woven into the enemy's armlets and stamped upon their wooden shields—an emblem that marked them as King Edward's elite killing force.

Lovely. Now the enemy had a catapult. Not that their sheer numbers weren't bad enough. On a ship beyond the war-torn beachfront stood the wooden monster that had launched a boulder and scarred the earth next to her.

A jolt in her womb brought her hand up, the babe within pounding to break out and join in the battle. Soon. Very soon her child would enter the world, and her chance to save the Passionate would end. "You will have your time, little one."

Alexia's mere nineteen years were far too few to be with child and centuries away from her husband and home, far too few for her to be in the midst of a war. She clutched the pendant dangling around her neck, heavy metal too dull to hold any monetary value, and focused on the power stored within, pulling at its strength. Golden energy trickled into her fingers, like being filled with sunlight. The world around her slowed.

Weapons crept toward their intended targets, and battle cries thrummed, a rumbling bass.

Five months ago she'd discovered this raggedy band of talented people like herself, the Passionate. Unlike the powerful sub-society of Passionate she'd left behind, these were vagabonds and nomads, a struggling force who gathered others like themselves and fled to safety. They were more suited to living in holes and caves than behind four walls. Many had been rescued from noblemen who enslaved them and used their talents for gain, which brought about the current conflict: too many of the rich had lost their precious prisoners. They begged King Edward to send the Knights Templar—his witch hunters—after their slaves.

Alexia stepped through the slowed conflict, her burlap skirts pulling against her swollen womb like chainmail made for a giant. Dirty faces twisted about her.

Always dirty.

Her own hands were covered in grime, the nails corroded black. What she wouldn't give for a bath in Father's estate!

But Father's estate had not been built yet, and it would not be for another several hundred years. The best she could hope for was a warm rain or chilly river. At least to staunch the smell.

A white haze curled off to her left—one of the Passionate who could transport people across the globe in an instant through mist. Velia. She wrapped herself around a child and would fade to nothing in a heartbeat. The woman had been frantically clearing their band out, carrying them one by one to safety—an effort that would cost her days of sickness and exhaustion.

Alexia was the diversion, along with others who could fight back. She and this battered band had evaded the king's forces for so long, but somehow they'd been tracked to this remote island.

She dragged past another distraction—Amos. Pitch spilled from his fingers, creating a cocoon of midnight that blinded the enemy. Chocolate-hued hair hung to his shoulders, copper skin glowing in the gloom.

With his ability to summon darkness, he had hidden Alexia and their band many times over the months they'd been allies. He was the leader of the Passionate, and a powerful one at that. It was strange working with him. She drew a hand across her neck, remembering how he had slit her throat in the future, how Kiren had saved her with his healing gift.

Kiren.

She bit down and pressed forward.

One battle at a time.

Alexia reached the water. She had done this only once before, and despite her sweating palms, she stepped onto the near-still swells. Water seeped around her foot like thick clay. The glassy waves reflected her countenance—which she would be able to see if not for her oversized paunch. The waves led to an ocean far deeper than she could breech, and she had never learned to swim.

She hurried forward several yards. A rope ladder dangled from the side of the ship, solid as stone in her grasp.

Kingsmen surged around the catapult in slow motion, loading it with another large boulder as she topped the deck. This was more than Edward's force. These men had been sent by the allied kings and Church to destroy the abominations, but their secret agenda was to capture all Passionate.

Killing for no real reason.

Alexia took a deep breath of crypt-like air, the heaviness that settled in improper time. Now to draw the men away from the catapult so she could dispose of it. She dropped Kiren's pendant, releasing the captive minutes.

Time leapt back into sequence.

Four soldiers jumped and shrieked at her sudden appearance. Swords flashed in the late afternoon rays, bloodied by the sinking sun.

The men rushed her, and she slowed time once more, stepping past them. Next to the machine of death, she eyed the thick ropes and splintering frame. If only she had the gift of fire.

And then she noticed the wheels. Mounted at the cusp of the ship, all the catapult needed was a good shove. She sliced the securing ropes with a single swipe of her dagger. The added pressure once time resumed would do the rest.

Alexia backed up several steps and charged, releasing time a little more with each step. The momentum of her time-inhibited dash added force. She slammed into the catapult with her shoulder. The wood groaned. Wheels squeaked. The machine grated forward.

She doubled over, her body protesting the movement with an intense tightening as she lost her grip on time. Her child should not make an appearance yet. Not for another eight weeks. She needed to be careful.

Men shouted behind her, turning, befuddled. Their swords shook. She faced them full on, challenging the lot.

Hiss.

She stopped time completely and whirled.

An arrow hung, mid-flight, only inches from her chest.

She huffed. *How incredibly unkind.*

Alexia stepped away from the deadly tip and squinted through the sprawling limbs on the beach.

There.

A bow dipped as the frozen archer reached for another arrow from the quiver at his back.

She took hold of Kiren's pendant. Warmth flooded into her fingers, filling her with strength, and she crossed the water once more. This was war. Death was expected, but to target the only woman in sight? And one with child? She halted before him, slipped her dagger beneath the bowstring and released time. It snapped.

The man jolted backward and landed on his rump.

She crossed her arms and spoke in old English. The words sounded odd to her, a language she'd practiced with Mae in the future, preparing for this time. Even after months of using them they felt clumsy, but the meaning was what mattered: "Were you aiming for me?"

Crash!

The catapult broke the water and launched a wave over the side of the ship, sweeping three soldiers overboard into dagger-like splinters.

Would it knock one or two of them unconscious? Would they drown? What if one was speared through? She groaned. No more. She would not be the cause of anymore death.

Alexia gathered her strength and reached back through time, into the past five seconds, bracing for the toll it would take. Blackness flashed before her as the world reset. She held time still and stood several seconds, allowing her body to ease into this moment. She did not like going back in time. It was dangerous. Traveling more than a couple moments could alter reality forever, but she had done it when necessary.

The catapult dangled over the edge of the ship, ready to break the glassy swells.

Alexia grabbed the three men. She released the seconds to a slow draw and pulled her enemies to safety. A weight hung at the back of her brain, the exhaustion from manipulating time. Satisfied the wave wouldn't take the men to their death, she let go of time.

The catapult splashed down.

The soldiers stood dazed, water lapping at their feet. One gasped and lifted his sword. Her weapon's hilt felt natural in her grasp, ready to respond to the threat, but the world shifted in her mind.

She faced a horde of Soulless, their eyes crimson, talons extended to tear the flesh, their hunger insatiable. They had come to take what mattered most to her: Her love. Her soul.

She blinked the vision free as the blade flashed toward her throat.

Alexia ducked. The sword sheared off a strand of curled dark hair. She fell back. *Kill him*, her inner voice shrieked. *He would do the same to you and all your kind. Protect them by eliminating one more threat.*

It was true. He would come again and again because he believed his cause was just, or because the king's pay supported his family. His hunger was no different than the Soulless.

But she couldn't take a life.

Never again.

She was here to undo all the mistakes of her past, the future, to stop those murders from ever happening and save her dearest sister, Sarah, from succumbing to the worst of fates.

Alexia yanked time to a halt, the air thickening around her. Her clothing dragged at her limbs.

6

The babe lurched within. She was pushing too hard and the child was warning her. The last thing she needed was to begin labor in the midst of war…and forfeit her life. What she really wanted was Kiren—his peaceful alternatives and confidence. His compassion and steadiness. His ability to read others and guide them toward the best solution. But she had none of those, only her ability to stop the minutes or alter time.

She faced the soldier's threatening weapon, seized his arm, and released time. He jumped.

"There is another way," Alexia said.

Soldiers charged. A tunnel of darkness roared up around them, sealing them into an onyx haze that emanated from the shore. Alexia shoved her attacker into the gloom. Amos stepped through the waves, waist deep, both arms lifted her direction, holding the soldiers within a midnight cloud.

"We are all cleared out!" he shouted and turned his head toward a white silhouette on the shore. Long hair floated translucently behind the mist child, as if she were half in and half out of reality, ready to instantly appear on some foreign continent.

"All?" Alexia called back, waving to him.

Amos motioned her forward. "You are one mighty distraction." He pointed to her baby girth. "But you are wasting precious time and energy."

A soldier stumbled out of the darkness and over the edge of the ship.

"Final retreat!" Amos shouted.

"Take him first," Alexia called to the child of the mist. The Passionate needed their leader safe.

Velia burst into nothingness and faded.

War cries broke through the midnight pitch. Alexia hefted her dagger, the one that had slain numerous Soulless, the one that had stained her soul. But those creatures did not exist here. Only men whose souls were debatably tainted as darkly.

Metal flashed toward her.

She lifted her weapon.

Steel clanged. Her muscles shook under her enemy's blade. She shoved his weapon away, the brush of chilling mist the only evidence that her friend was being swept away to safety. And then the world blanched into whiteness, and she was hurling through nothingness, reminding herself not to breathe.

Get the book now! http://crystal-collier.com/buy

Acknowledgements

It's awe inspiring to see my second book in print, and my first thanks goes out to you, the reader. Thank you for giving me a reason to share my stories with the world. Thank you for demanding a sequel after reading Moonless and all your enthusiasm.

Huge thanks goes out to my editor, Bethany, at A Little Red Inc., for her fantastic guidance and incredible eye.

To my fabulous critique partners, thank you Rachel Hert and Misha Gericke.

My amazing sister, Cindy, thank you for being my second reader and talking me through the rough patches. Mom, for encouraging me even when I wanted to sleep rather than write, thank you.

All my blogging pals, thank you TONZ for helping me spread the world and being your fabulous selves. You rock!

Incredible thanks goes out to my rockin' Daydreamers Anonymous, WS4U friends, and Write On Build On writers. Your daily support and encouragement has been a life saver!

My amazing kids, I thank you for your patience when you lost Mom to the computer. And lastly, to my amazing husband, thank you for being my creative partner, my best friend, my heart. You are the bestest!

About the Author:

Crystal Collier is a young adult author who pens dark fantasy, historical, and romance hybrids. She can be found practicing her brother-induced ninja skills while teaching children or madly typing about fantastic and impossible creatures. She has lived from coast to coast and now calls Florida home with her creative husband, three littles, and "friend" (a.k.a. the zombie locked in her closet). Secretly, she dreams of world domination and a bottomless supply of cheese.

You can find her on her blog, follow her on Twitter, or visit her on Facebook. Subscribe to her newsletter to receive freebies and learn about exciting new developments.

http://crystalcollier.blogspot.com

www.ingramcontent.com/pod-product-compliance
Lightning Source LLC
Chambersburg PA
CBHW070323260626
47160CB00003B/928